Alouette

For your library

Motivate + Encourage.

Santa Barbara Secrets
A
"J" Team Novel

For

Sexual and Domestic Assault Survivors:
May you thrive through motivation,
encouragement, support & enjoy your
life free of fear.

Jonathan.

Jonathan McCormick
Copyright 2019

Santa Barbara Secrets portrays women struggling with violence. The characters share their successes, failures, overcoming fears and apprehensions through emotionally griping dialogue and defensive tactics.

The agents' physical and emotional responses to antagonists draw the reader to the protagonists' techniques and style used to overcome adversity. Jessica, Rebecca and Elisabeth encourage readers to leave abusive situations, to change their environment and to accomplish their goals and dreams.

Jackson and Jason exemplify supportive colleagues, comfortable with their sexuality and masculinity, both male traits appreciated by many women.

Santa Barbara Secrets is the third in the "J" Team Series which began with *Wyoming Secrets* and the development of the Team to interdict the radical conservative Christians for a Better America. It was followed by *30,000 Secrets* where the "J" Team tracks down the CFBA leaders and fouling their attempt to eliminate hundreds of Democratic politicians on a flight from Minneapolis to LAX.

In *Santa Barbara Secrets*, Dr. Penelope Barker sells her veterinarian business and Rebecca retires from the Secret Service. They move to The Ranch, a Spanish style house in the Santa Barbara Hills, which Rebecca had purchased as an investment a decade previously. The Ranch boasts fifty-two-hundred square feet, two-stories, five bedrooms, five baths, a family room and a one-thousand square foot guest house next to an Olympic size swimming pool, garages for four cars, and landscape done and maintained by her neighbor, retired Beverly Hills landscaper, Alejandro. The basement houses a professional, fully automatic pistol range with almost inaudible extraction fans.

They develop R&P Investigations with Rebecca training Pen in firearms/defensive tactics. Their first case is a collaboration with the Santa Barbara Police Dept. and the Secret Service. Their task is to determine how American currency from Los Angeles makes its way to the Caribbean and back to the US in the form of political donations, one of the major recipients being the Christians for a Better America.

Marc Stucki, former President Bakus' executive chef, is invited by Rebecca, Penelope and a group of investors to open "Marc Stucki's" in a former train station a block from the beach with Penelope and Rebecca providing the interior design of the restaurant and Marc's three-bedroom, two bath condo.

Supervising Secret Service Agent Jessica Fukishura is deployed to Santa Barbara undercover as an attorney and quickly becomes entangled with a prominent lawyer who has connections with Colombian drug cartels. She works with R&P Investigations and local authorities to determine the depth and breadth of the Southern California cocaine business.

Secret Service Agents Jason Spencer, Elisabeth Peltowski and Jackson Pennington, having been released by the LAPD from completing their investigation of the downing of the Mahalo Airlines plane off the coast of LAX, join Rebecca and Penelope at the ranch to aid in the investigation.

The agents and R&P collaborate on the investigations, developing parties at the ranch, enjoying Santa Barbara's finest cuisine while integrating their expertise with LAPD detectives.

Praise

For

The "J" Team Series

"What a treat for me to receive your book! ... Thank you so much for sending it and remembering me ... Made my heart feel very good. I had no idea you were as 'dangerous' as you are ... Heh!"
Dr. Barrie Bennett University of Toronto

5.0 out of 5 stars *Wyoming Secrets*, March 4, 2012 by Colleen

This review is from: *Wyoming Secrets A "J" Team Novel*: "J" Team Series (Paperback)

"The beginning of the book was like a Robert Ludlum book, but once the characters are introduced, it gets very intense. I could not put the book down, and disappointed that the next book wasn't sitting waiting for me to read. I would highly recommend this book to readers."
University of Alaska

"Former University of Alaska Student Publishes First Novel. Some of you may remember Jonathan McCormick, who took graduate courses in Diagnostic and Prescriptive Teaching while working in Hoonah before transferring to the University of Portland. He has just published his first novel: *Wyoming Secrets: A "J" Team Novel*, which was released on Amazon.com recently, available in paperback and Kindle version.

Take a look on Amazon to read the synopsis, and check out his author website at jonathanmccormick.com on Facebook and Twitter @lazeejjs.

"If you like to read, try this book, a very good read and hard to put down." Curtis Leithead corrections Officer

"Congratulations on the publication of "Wyoming Secrets…" I trust you are at work on the next book." Sue Grafton

"The University of Washington Libraries each day (sees) more than 25,000 people visit our facilities on the three campuses while another 100,000 access our resources via the Web.

It is my privilege to express our appreciation for your contribution of *Wyoming Secrets.*" University of Washington Libraries.

"I hope by now your Jessica has found a literary agent worthy of her exploits. Be well! Write on!" Harley Jane Kozak.

"The author was my former high school English teacher and a few years later was my instructor in a self-defense program. He certainly knows the subject matter which is evident by the rich detail in this story. Only someone with his training and experience could add the necessary realism to this kind of story. I look forward to the next instalment of these characters and their exploits." Kris Patterson

"Thank you for your generous and thoughtful donation of carnations, cake and forty copies of *Wyoming Secrets* for our clients on Valentine's Day. Your generosity makes a positive difference to the health and well-being of our family clients."
Chris Pettman, Executive Director, Cariboo Family Enrichment Centre

"In *30,000 Secrets,* a genre novel by Jonathan McCormick, we are presented with a taut and captivating thriller that travels the lengths of the world and the depths of the human heart as it works to clear the convoluted plot.

The title for the novel seems to this reader to be a key to expectations, signaling a sense of mysteries and hesitancies, of the importance of what is said and what is unsaid. The overall design of the book is professional. It features an interior layout that is clean and clear with text design on each page that is readable and crisp. Also, the cover image for the book has the gloss of a political thriller but with perhaps too much of the wedged title elements interposed.

The characters here are fully realized, vivid and alive, and often do surprising things – or do / say things that are very human, which can be rare. I especially like Jessica. In short, she is a well-developed character, fully realized on the page with a plausible sensibility in an increasingly tragic and complex world. The chapters are nicely paced, with enough meat to make them satisfy, but not so ponderous as to make it difficult to keep track of the narrative as it develops.

In fiction, so much of the pacing comes from the deployment of the chapters, how they build the suspense or momentum of the narrative arc, and in this case, things move along in a compelling manner."

Writers' Digest

Prologue

It was a murky, moonless night, 150 nautical miles off the Costa Rican coast, with waves churning to three meters, as an easterly storm gained velocity to batter the Central American coast. Fishing and tourist vessels had sought protection hours ago when the weather warning systems sounded alarms.

But not all boats wanted shelter or wished to navigate the tropical eastern Pacific before the storm hit, some were maneuvering with total disregard of the surface turmoil.

Lurking 300 meters below the choppy surface was a two-person, Germanischer Lloyd Mini Submarine, identical to those seen on various television documentaries, with fixed pontoon tanks on each side and a raised glass bubble conning tower, currently unlighted, save for the few control switches and buttons, providing an eerie perspective of the stealth, low-profile vessel.

The unnamed device was undetectable from the surface by the naked eye, or by sonar from coast guard cutters, neither of which were currently relevant given the current weather conditions.

The use of sonar was disallowed by International Marine Law within 200 nautical miles from any coast line to protect marine life, primarily dolphins and whales. With the protection of the raging surface storm and the absence of visual or sonar contact from law enforcement, the Mini maintained a steady, undetected, northerly course between Cocos Island and the mainland, at thirty nautical miles an hour, with its multi-million-dollar cargo connected by a tow-line, 300 meters to the rear.

Cocos Island National Park, owned by the Eastern Tropical Pacific Marine Corridor, a marine conservation network, is known locally as Isla del Coco as well as, Isla del Tesoro or Treasure Island. It is a world-class diving destination, home to numerous endangered species such as the Scalloped Hammerhead shark, Silky Shark and the Galapagos Shark, drawing enthusiasts to a unique marine ecosystem.

The mini-sub's captain had to ensure his course didn't vary from the coastal protection or veer into the Isla del Coco's coral reefs as he maintained a northerly route.

Behind the mini was a Columbian drug cartel's latest transportation vehicle, carrying an impressive pay-load of five-thousand kilograms of cocaine, street value of approximately four-hundred and twenty million dollars US, in Los Angeles. Uncut.

The twenty-meter/sixty-five-foot submarine was the proud development of Adrian Achterberg, the son of a WW Two German Boatwright who gained fame within the Nazi regime for his U Boat designs. Adrian had learned the trade quickly under his father's tutelage, acquiring his own notoriety within the boat industry for his steel fabrication brilliance.

Never considering himself a Columbian, regardless of his Medellin birthplace, Achterberg harbored considerable resentment against western powers for what he felt was an unfair treatment of his father, who fled Nazi Germany on the tail of the

Nuremberg Trials, fearing reprisal for his role in the development of the deadly submarines which killed hundreds of allied sailors, destroyed millions in cargo and a wealth in lost vessels.

When the cartel approached Achterberg at his shipyard with the request to design and build a twenty-meter submarine capable of carrying a thirty-metric-ton payload and four crew members, capable of thirty-knots submerged and an air supply for ten days, he asked few questions, taking delight in the opportunity to retaliate against the Canadians and Americans whom he blamed for his father's decades of anguish, while reaping several million dollars for his efforts.

His creation was pure marine brilliance and so eclectic in appearance few would have made a connection between the sub and its use in any nefarious activities. It didn't have a coning tower of a traditional submarine, nor did it have any of the outer fittings usually associated with subs. The surface was smooth, almost glass-like to the eye and touch. The exterior was coated with phononic crystal, an acoustically tuned material off which sonar waves bounce, or more accurately, bend off the hull to loop back around to the vessel's surface again and again, never returning to the source of the sonic pulse, thereby creating the impression the ping did not meet a solid object, such as contacting a submarine. The cargo space was generously spread throughout to provide adequate balance, particularly during submersion and surfacing. Propulsion was created with lithium batteries, designed by a British Columbia firm, which were less than half the size of conventional power supplies and rechargeable from a diesel engine, so quiet that it was undetectable with coast guard hydrophones. The hybrid system was designed jointly by Ontario and Nova Scotia firms destined for commercial, law-abiding vessels.

Achterberg borrowed NASA and International Space Station technology to design a system to recycle crew urine, sweat and breath to create a water source and the electrolysis of water to generate oxygen, the power for the process provided by the lithium batteries. In the case of an air supply failure, the sub would rise just below the surface and extend a tubular air intake, just long enough to absorb a twelve-hour air supply. Back-up emergency air supply with autonomous breathing devices was available for each crew member, along with a vessel escape hatch from which they could surface while scuttling the vessel and cargo in case of a total system failure. The sub lacked radar to detect patrolling ships and planes, so their reconnaissance was strictly visual, necessitating as short a surface time as possible.

The cargo sub relied completely on the Germanischer Lloyd for protection from Canadian and American Navy interdiction. The cartel lost millions from a recent joint operation involving the Canadian HMCS Saskatoon and the US Coast Guard Hamilton off the coast of Central America. The drug financiers were committed to eliminating the catastrophic losses.

Finding competent seamen willing to stay submerged for ten days wasn't as complicated as the cartel had anticipated. As politician Michael Myers of the Philadelphia House of Representatives was noted as saying in 1943, "Money talks and bullshit walks," and the drug kings had little difficulty finding unscrupulous, retired U.S. Navy submariners willing to take the job for a few million each, half deposited in a Caribbean bank before they sailed and the other half when they dropped their cargo. Considering one shipment from this vessel would bring a street value of five-hundred million, a few million crew costs was irrelevant.

Loading and launching the Chica de Oro, Golden Girl, was as unobtrusive as one could imagine amidst the turmoil surrounding the Columbia peace accord, which ended one of the world's longest running armed conflicts.

The half-century war which killed 220,000 people, disrupted six million lives and consumed ten billion dollars of American involvement, saw ten thousand guerrillas demobilize, come in from the jungle and transition to civilian life.

The massive social change created a party atmosphere throughout the country with friends and family of the freedom fighters jubilant with celebration, creating a cloak under which Achterberg supervised the loading and launching of the Chica de Oro.

Night and day were obscured as the mini-sub led the way north with its multi-million-dollar cargo trailing behind, destined to capture the souls and minds of substance abusers in North America. If this operation was as successful as the cartel anticipated, the next run would enter the Canadian market, utilizing the west coast's many fjords and uninhabited coast lines.

Chapter ONE

Rebecca woke leisurely, without a start, without her usual trepidation, or reaching for her firearm, something she hadn't experience during most of her adult life. She turned her head slightly and noticed Penelope almost completely enveloped by the light cream duvet with spring birds and flowers, which thwarted the fifty-five-degree mountain night temperature which slipped quietly into their bedroom through a slightly open security window.

Rebecca inhaled deeply, propped her head up with one hand as she gazed at Pen. She was almost overcome by Penelope's scent as she sighed and gently, with a slight whisper of motion, swung her legs out of the queen size bed and traipsed lightly across the master bedroom's avocado Italian tile to the bathroom, oblivious to her nakedness.

Gently closing the door, she used the facilities, then donned one of her full length, cobalt blue bathrobes she had acquired from Nordstrom at the Grove in Los Angeles years ago. She had purchased two, only because she loved the style and color, never thinking she would be sharing the second one with the person who had changed her life so dramatically.

She shuffled over to the ten-foot fuchsia and cream patterned Italian marble counter in her matching cobalt blue fuzzy slippers and looked at herself under the bank of six bone tear-drop lights above the mirror, fluffed her short 'do, then, drawing closer to the mirror, she thought, *I think I look about five years younger. No, wait, make that ten years,* she corrected herself, allowing her face to break into a huge grin. Noticing the uncontrolled expression of happiness, she laughed outload, something she had never done, ever...then did a little self-expression dance of pure joy.

She reopened the bathroom door, saw that Penelope was still asleep, gently closed the door partially, then exited the bathroom by the opposite entry and made her way to the kitchen.

Her walk down the short hallway was just a murmur as her slippers graced the oak hardwood floor into the open concept kitchen, past the Miele Stainless Steel, Double Door, Built-in Fridge, stopping in front of the double-wide country sink and white framed bay window. Stretching over the sink, she extended her upper body to see if there was any morning frost in the garden. None. *Good,* she thought, as she glanced upward toward Big Pine Mountain just as the morning sun's sliver made its way over the 6,820-foot peak.

Rebecca had owned the house for many years, having obtained it on the advice of Alane Auberée of Birdcage Investments, her financial advisor for the past decade. Auberée put her into Warren Bates' Berkshire Hathaway Investments immediately upon taking her as a client, investing her entire monthly salary in Hathaway. He invested six thousand dollars for six shares on the date of Berkshire's initial public offering, and that amount every month since. The stock split fifty to one later.

Auberée knew Rebecca worked for the federal government, but not that she was undercover and had zero expenses not covered by the secret service. Her portfolio grew over the years, to which she liked to refer, an obscene fortune, or more specifically, over six million.

When the California housing market collapsed, Auberée took a loan out on Rebecca's portfolio, which produced an interest that was a fraction of what she was earning on her investments. His astute planning allowed her to avoid qualifying for a mortgage, a move that would have revealed too much of her covert activities. The spectacular Mediterranean estate with a dual gated entrance and four car-garage was previously owned by a hedge fund manager who found himself heavily in debt with two mortgages on the estate when the market disaster hit. The two banks foreclosed and with zero buyer initiative it sat empty for several years. Auberée purchased the property in Rebecca's name and she signed the documents in StoneHead while working undercover against the Citizens for a Better America. Jessica, although unable to practice law in any state, having never taken a bar exam, could act as a notary and certified Rebecca's signature.

Early in her career, Rebecca knew she didn't want a White House or protection detail and acknowledged that working out of embassies would force her to leave the service out of boredom, which was why she jumped at the opportunity for permanent undercover.

It didn't take much effort on her part to become a minimalist; renting furnished apartments for several months, then leaving without a trace. But she did miss horses, the aroma of their hair, the essence of their bodies as she groomed, curried and saddled for a few hour's ride into the back hills...somewhere. She couldn't return to Montana for her R&R since every sheriff's deputy within the state's boundaries, and a few outside of them, knew her on sight, which would invite too many questions.

It was while sequestered to the FBI in Flagstaff, Arizona, beating the desert for Al Qaeda trainers, that she stumbled on an infomercial while doing a surveillance gig at the Hacienda de Cerveza in Winslow, Arizona. Having tailed two suspects from the Hopi Reservation into Winslow, she followed them into the bar, ordered a Bud Longneck and surreptitiously watched the two males meet up with two others, who were obviously First Nations by their physical characteristics, but only slightly in contrast to the Al Qaeda with their long-braided hair, sun weathered complexions, sinuous, gnarly hands and arms. She had feigned interest in a broadcast of the Northern Arizona University Women's Lacrosse Lumberjacks and took a slight joy in watching the University of Berkeley, Jessica's alma mater, sweep the Flagstaff team embarrassingly while mentally recording the suspects behavior and body language. It was during a game commercial that she was drawn to a tourist ad for Santa Barbara with its breathtaking beaches, green mountain trails and clean air that she decided to give it a visit during her next R & R.

That initial holiday grabbed at her heart and soul and it was shortly thereafter that she met Auberée and began a profitable relationship.

"The secret of success is learning how to use pain and pleasure instead of having pain and pleasure use you. If you do that, you're in control of your life. If you don't, life controls you."

Anthony Robbins *Awaken the Giant Within*

Chapter TWO

Rebecca made her way over to the Cuisinart Grind and Brew coffee maker at the end of the L counter beside the stove. She took out the water reservoir and walked back to the sink to fill it. As the water was running, she glanced back at the coffee maker, looked at the faucet, then the fridge where she kept the coffee, back to the coffee maker and said, out loud, "What the hell is the coffee maker doing way over there? Shit, I have been in isolation too long, I don't know how to coordinate a fuckin' kitchen. Take out five suspects, yes, but a simple kitchen? Shit." Shaking her head at her ignorance, she smiled to herself that the new Rebecca could make time for the simple pleasures of a home.

Elementary the kitchen may be, but uninviting it was not. Amber toned oak paneled cabinets above and below the sink, wrapped around the L shaped kitchen, meeting a Stainless-Steel Miele built-in convection oven with a matching microwave above. The countertop was quartz with swirls of cream and copper tones and matching backsplash. The theme was repeated for the six by eight-foot island, which hosted a six-burner gas stove top with a wine refrigerator hidden behind one of the eight amber storage cabinets.

She put the filled reservoir on the counter, returned to the Cuisinart, unplugged it, carried it over to the sink and plugged it in beside the refrigerator. Reaching into the fridge she pulled out a canister of Café y Pasteles' coffee beans from the coffee house on State Street, grabbed a filter from the cupboard by the sink, poured the beans into the grinder and got the black going.

That minor chore out of the way and the machine properly located, she opened the double-doored fridge again and brought out a package of Pasteles cinnamon buns, which Alejandro had purchased for her the day before. This was the incredible downtown coffeehouse and bakery to which he had introduced her the day they met, the day she thought her neighbor was going to have a coronary seeing her weapon.

Alejandro was a retired gardener who made his small fortune over a forty-year span of applying his landscape design to hundreds of Beverly Hills' elaborate properties. Rebecca and he met while she was riding the trails behind her property and he was grooming his perennial gardens. Rebecca was taken aback at first when she saw Alejandro's shocked expression as she dismounted to say hello, and he caught sight of her semi-automatic in a shoulder holster. It must have been her charm as she held the reins with one hand and extended the other to shake hands, explaining that she was his new neighbor, worked in Washington, but got here as often as she could.

Alejandro was a weathered, bronze skinned Latino with short cropped black curly hair, greying at the temples and above his ears, creating a very distinguished aura. At about five-foot, ten inches, he was stocky and muscular from his years of manual labor, and probably a lot of gym time post retirement. His square headed facial structure complimented his physique with a Grecian shaped nose, broad at the base and flattened across the front as though it had received repeated blows.

It had to be her smile, demeanor, and probably a little sex appeal, because he didn't ask any questions but rather invited her in for coffee and sweets.

During that first coffee and pastry meeting, Alejandro commented about her property, being diplomatic, trying not to offend, but needing to convince Rebecca that seeing the neglect daily was depressing. When she discovered his background, she asked for his input, an opportunity at which he jumped.

That first meeting seemed years ago but was just within the last five years that Alejandro took custody of her gardens.

Filling their coffee cups and grabbing another delicacy that one morning, they walked down to Rebecca's house and she saw, through Alejandro's eyes, the reality of what had been ignored.

After one particularly lengthy absence when she was scouring the Arizona desert for Al Qaeda operatives who were instructing America's First Nations on the finer points of bomb making, she arrived at her house that looked abandoned. The winter storms had been cruel, to the once beautiful landscape she tried so hard to maintain.

Observing the beauty of Alejandro's place made her property even more distressed. Alejandro had experienced this customer reaction many times and quickly turned her depression into hope by saying, "Would you like your property to sing to you?"

And sing it now does. Rebecca had given him carte blanche with a promise to settle-up either over the phone with a credit card or in cash during her next hiatus. Alejandro responded with an infectious smile and said, "Rebecca, a woman with your dynamic personality, stature and shoulder holster has to be trust worthy," then bent over laughing at his own unsubstantiated character analysis. Rebecca joined in the laughter and hugged him, wondering if a day would come when she could be honest with this very kind man.

It was several months after their initial meeting with Alejandro's offering to revitalize her property when Rebecca could escape her StoneHead responsibilities and spend a long weekend at her retreat. She had texted Alejandro from the Santa Barbara Airport to let him know she was grabbing a rental and was on her way…fifteen minutes. As she approached the entrance and clicked the gate control, she entered a natural wonderland of fragrances and eye-catching landscape which enhanced the Mediterranean taupe stucco, two-story house with red tile roof.

Closing the gate with a click, she parked and walked slowly through the newly created elegance. Rounding a corner of the house, she spotted Alejandro, the landscape virtuoso, sitting in a fawn tone wicker chair, savoring a glass of chilled Rising Oaks Chardonnay from a local winery. As she approached, she found a lightness in her step and a tug at her heart she hadn't experienced since her teenage rodeo days. She saw that he sat at a glass coffee table with brushed green wrought iron legs which held plates of appetizers and between he and another chair was a matching wrought iron stand holding an iced cooler with two more Rising Oaks.

Rebecca was smiling as she tried to take in as much as she could, turning her head constantly seeing the amazing beauty. She considered the transformation overwhelming as she gave Alejandro a hug, thanking him profusely. He responded by saying, "It has been my pleasure Rebecca. I haven't had this much fun since leaving the business and it is I who am thanking you for this opportunity to bring joy back into my life. Sit, please. Chat. Tell me what you saw when you opened the gates. And please enjoy this lovely tart chardonnay with a hint of citrus."

He poured a glass for her, refilled his and offered the plate of appetizers. He had prepared zesty strips of chicken and bits of onion atop jalapeño halves wrapped in bacon and grilled. Small serving dishes contained a blue cheese dip as well as a spicy guacamole. Rebecca took two, dipped each in the blue cheese, placed them on a plate, grabbed a napkin and sat back with a very audible sigh saying, "I am blown away Alejandro. I knew you would transform this place, but you have gone far and beyond what I could have ever expected or thought I wanted. Here is to you my friend," as she reached out and they clinked glasses.

They finished the jalapenos, refilled their wine glasses as Alejandro rose and offered her a tour. "These appetizers are delicious Alejandro and the tartness of the chardonnay is a perfect pairing. Thank you for doing this," she offered as she grabbed the wine bottle and followed him as they wended their way through her property, Alejandro sharing the execution of his vision.

Alejandro had removed all the dead foliage and created a breathtaking and bucolic setting that greeted her as she entered the remote-controlled wrought iron gate area. On one side of the driveway were massive sandstone boulders interspersed with drought tolerant plants. His choices created a soul lifting fragrance with Hummingbird Mint, Red Penstemon, Russian Sage, Yarrow and Coneflowers. The other side of the driveway embraced an immaculate lawn of a drought resistant grass, a mixture of Sheep, Chewings, Hard and Creeping Fescue blended with Perennial Ryegrass. As they walked from the driveway to the front of the house, Alejandro spread his arms, introducing a flower and shrub bed of cinder-block, four high, with a mammoth Sky-High Juniper as the center piece and repeated the entry flower choices. On the other side of the curving walk leading to a portico, he had designed yet another garden, this one being at grass level with a circumference of ivy and two large Russian Sage bushes centering the creation.

He had repeated the theme throughout the property enhancing the pool and hot tub area by adding California and Western Sycamores, Eldarica Pines and Eastern Red Cedars for shade. All were evergreen, creating an almost maintenance-free landscape.

They spent the better part of an hour meandering through the new gardens with Alejandro providing a running commentary of his reasoning behind every choice and how little maintenance was required. They ended up back at the table and chairs and sat once more while Rebecca prepared herself to settle with Alejandro. She had brought a considerable amount of cash but seeing what he had created wondered if she was going to be embarrassed, having to owe him the balance until she could get to the bank the next day.

"Words don't seem enough Alejandro for what you have done here. The beauty and your creative genius have blown me away. I will be forever in your debt. May I pay you now?"

"You are most welcome, but please remember always that you gave me more joy than I have experienced in a very long time. So, it is I who am thankful too," he concluded as he produced an itemized list of everything he used and gracefully passed it to Rebecca.

Accepting the several sheets nervously, she sat her glass down and perused the papers quickly then said, "This can't be accurate Alejandro. The total must be far more than what you have listed here. The mature trees alone must be worth hundreds of dollars each. Do you have your labor and landscaping architect fee on a separate sheet?"

"No. There isn't another sheet because there was no charge for joy. My heart soared doing this renovation which cannot have a price," he replied with a friendly smile.

"Oh, Alejandro, I appreciate your enjoying your gift to me, but we are talking about thousands here just in materials."

"This is so. But I am a man with many business contacts and my name and reputation seemed to extend beyond the Beverly Hills city limits. The suppliers refused to take retail so all of this," he spread both arms to claim the remodel, "is a gift from my fellow gardeners. Enjoy."

"Thank you very much my friend," she said and rose to give him a hug. As he sat down again, she extended an envelope containing thousands over his invoice.

Alejandro opened the package and said, "Oh, Rebecca, this is far too much money for this job. I cannot accept your generosity."

"Alejandro, I expected the job to cost at least that much and was prepared to be embarrassed by coming up short and having to owe you so please, accept it as a gift to your favorite charity, knowing it is your creativity and kindness that generated the donation."

"A charitable donation. I can do that. I will graciously accept your generosity and give the extra to a local group which helps sexual assault survivors. Thank you very much, they will find this largess very beneficial," he concluded with a nod.

Rebecca would learn months later that Alejandro's daughter had suffered at the hands of a sexual assailant and received little if any justice from the California judicial system. After he was caught, it was discovered that he had a long history of sexual assaults as well as violent small store robberies where he had beaten his victims. He had been convicted numerous times and should have been serving a lengthy sentence but was released with little time served due to over-crowding in the state's correctional system.

As Alejandro was preparing to leave and gathering up the dishes, he said, "Beverly Hills is alive and thriving with my landscaping and years of maintenance. Each client signed a contract that I had exclusive rights to maintain my work. I would like to do that for you. Maintain this beautiful setting year-round without charge. The only cost to you will be allowing me to be your friend and meeting periodically over a glass of wine and plates of appetizers. Deal?" extending his hand to seal the bargain.

Rebecca had very little experience accepting generosities, but her instincts told her that this was a once in a lifetime opportunity to connect on a very organic level with another human being, so she didn't hesitate, grabbed his extended hand and replied, "You have a deal Alejandro," then sealed it with a hug.

Feeling very happy and satisfied that he had brought joy to another, Alejandro walked slowly back to his home, taking a short-cut through the back of Rebecca's property, turning once to wave to his smiling neighbor, who returned it magnanimously.

Little did Rebecca know that it would not be long after this initial friendship that she would be returning with her life partner, retired from the secret service and starting the next chapter in her life as a distinguished private investigator.

Chapter THREE

Rebecca pulled herself from her revere as the Cuisinart signaled, 'Ready to Go'. She pulled two large white mugs from the cupboard, filled them with black, placed each on a serving tray of distressed pallet wood with a slight raised edge and a black cabinet handle on each side. To that she added the warm cinnamon buns which had been heating in the convection oven, included a ceramic butter dish, knives, forks and napkins and headed to the bedroom.

Holding the tray with one hand, she quietly opened the bedroom door and stepped into a short anti-way, closed the door and softly made her way to the nightstand, placed the tray, then crawled up on the bed and snuggled with a still sleeping Penelope.

Pen was a cocoon sleeper with her head buried under the covers. She claims she is not hiding but exhibiting a habit learned at university to shut out residency noises. Rebecca was tired of waiting to enjoy her company so she, unselfishly told herself, slowly removed the covers from Pen's head only to find she was wide-awake staring at Rebecca.

Rebecca was so taken aback that her upper body flipped back in shock, then relaxed in laughter as Pen pulled the covers all the way down to reveal her nakedness, offering Rebecca a seductive view. Without hesitating, Rebecca quickly removed her bathrobe, flipped off her slippers and descended upon Penelope, cupping her face in two hands and kissing her passionately. Pen's dancing tongue sent shivers through Rebecca, passing through her mouth, neck, to her now hard nipples and down to her moist groin. She kissed and licked her way slowly down Pen's body, over her equally hard nipples, past her flat stomach while caressing her inner thighs with one hand and cupping her breasts alternately with the other. Pen's fragrance, the softness of her skin and velvety pubic hair had become an addiction to Rebecca, finding herself drawn to her labia.

She turned her body slightly gaining access to Pen's vulva as Pen shifted imperceptibly, accommodating Rebecca's probing, then swung her partner's leg, grabbed both cheeks and pulled Rebecca's groin to her waiting tongue. No words were spoken as they brought pleasure to each other through their sixty-nine-position. As is often the case with developing relationships, it was not long before the probing and swirling tongue gained each a violent orgasm accompanied by loud groans of pleasure and body vibrations.

Penelope was the first to unwind, to bring her head next to Rebecca's and continue the previous kiss, running her hands through Rebecca's hair, down her neck, around her shoulders and breasts. Rebecca tossed her head back and held Pen's lips to her breasts as she experienced two orgasms within seconds of each other.

Spent, Rebecca collapsed on the bed with her arms spread out, face flushed and looked up at Pen saying with a mischievous grin, "I suspect the warm cinnamon buns and black will be anticlimactic now," her laugh deep, guttural and sexual.

Penelope, not to be undone in humor or wit replied, "Not at all. I am sure the buns are just as sweet as yours," as she bent down and kissed Rebecca again, then jumped up, ran to the bathroom, used the facilities, dawned the Cobalt Blue bathrobe laid out for her, and scurried back to join Rebecca at the seating area next to the gas fireplace. Rebecca had placed the coffee and buns on a round, solid oak, three-legged coffee table and was sitting in one of the cream and cranberry patterned chince occasional chairs sipping her black.

Penelope sashayed across the carpet saying, "And good morning to you too," as she reached Rebecca, bent, kissed her, grabbed her mug, a roll and sat in the matching chair.

After several bites and half a cup of now lukewarm coffee, she said, "I was too tired, and it was too dark last night to see what your place looks like. Did I imagine you opening huge iron gates remotely then drive up to your house or did you really do that?"

Rebecca laughed and replied, "Yes, I did that. Kinda cool really. I love doing it. Makes me feel like a baroness with my own estate."

"I think I am going to be blown away with your home, or is it really an estate? How big is this place anyway?"

"We can go on a tour when we are done here but quick answers, it is fifty-two-hundred square feet, two-story, five bedrooms, five baths, family room and a one-thousand square foot pool and guest house next to the Olympic size swimming pool, garages for four cars, and the landscape was done and is maintained by my amazing friend and neighbor, retired Beverly Hills landscaper, Alejandro. The basement houses a professional, fully automatic pistol range with almost inaudible extraction fans," Rebecca offered, only to see Penelope's mouth open in amazement.

"Before you ask the obvious, no, I didn't inherit money. I bought it from a bank which had foreclosed on a hedge fund manager and it had sat empty for two years. They were only too happy to sell it for far below market value and my financial advisor, to whom I will introduce you in the next day or so, borrowed from my portfolio so I don't have a mortgage and the taxes are paid from the portfolio income. Alejandro doesn't charge for his maintenance, so my costs are minimal, just the pool guy, whom I have never met, utilities and the security system which includes neighborhood roving responders and monitoring."

Penelope sat in awe, with her mug hanging down the arm of the chair as though the wind had been sucked out of her. Momentarily she regained her composure and said, "If you were telling this story at Cassandras, I would have raised my eyebrows and wondered if you had too many Longnecks. This is truly amazing Rebecca. I am very happy for you. And now, after all these years you can enjoy it full time."

"We can enjoy it together Pen. This is what I was so excited about back in StoneHead, being able to share what I long considered just an investment. When Alejandro remodeled the gardens to what you see today, I thought, maybe, just maybe I would meet someone, someday and have a chance at life beyond chasing bad guys, living out of a suitcase, never knowing why I was unsuccessful with male relationships. And, here we are, the two of us, together in this magical place."

"I am speechless Rebecca. How can I participate in the investment and maintenance when you have already done it all?"

"We can figure those details as we go. We have each other, and I believe our companionship, affection and emotional support grows daily. Sure, we will have our differences. We have been single for so long we are set in our ways, but for me, I feel as though I have been released, that what I had before, what I thought I enjoyed, was like shackles on my soul.

"When we met, I knew immediately there was something between us, but my work prevented me from acknowledging the feelings until that long weekend in Denver. That was when I knew I had to leave the service and be honest with you. Once I did that, with Jessica's help, the shackles flew off, releasing my heart and soul, allowing me to feel and express for the first time in my adult life."

Holding back her tears, Penelope responded, "I had those feeling too. Do you remember when you helped me suture the colts? You handed me the instruments and I felt electricity race through my body and knew there was something there." Wiping her tears away, she expressed a nervous chuckle and added, "Little did I know I was falling for a bad-ass federal agent who ended up kicking the shit out of, how many guys now?"

Rebecca put her mug down, jumped up emotionally and gave Pen a massive hug, burying her now teared face in Penelope's neck.

Breaking the embrace, Rebecca stood back with her hands grasping Pen by the shoulders and said,

"Maybe we could join a martial arts academy and take on guys as a team," laughing, sniffing and using her robe sleeve to wipe away her tears.

Their conversation referred to Rebecca being undercover in StoneHead as a horse trainer, unofficially working for a Montana deputy sheriff who operated a training business and authenticated her cover story.

Penelope met Rebecca while Pen was treating two colts at the facility where Rebecca was working. They socialized considerably in and around StoneHead, particularly on Friday nights at Casandra's line-dancing bar with other friends and it was during a three-day shopping trip in Denver, where they acknowledged and accepted their relationship.

Penelope broke the spell, grabbed Rebecca around the waist with one hand, her mug with the other and offered, "How about that tour?" she asked as she pulled Rebecca to her and started for the kitchen.

"There's a Greek legend—no, it's in something Plato wrote—about how true lovers are really two halves of the same person. It says that people wander around searching for their other half, and when they find him or her, they are finally whole and perfect."

Nancy Garden *Annie on My Mind*

Chapter FOUR

Their first stop on the tour was the kitchen where Rebecca refilled their mugs. While she was trying to highlight the room's working parts, Penelope was wide-eyed, turning her head back and forth, taking in the trappings of her new home. "A basic kitchen with a few extras, like this very cool wine fridge," Rebecca noted, bending down and opening one of the island cabinets, revealing at least twenty bottles of various vineyard's whites. Continuing, she added, "We can crack some of these later if you like."

"I'd love that. Maybe we can make some appetizers too. Hey, how about inviting Alejandro over. I am dying to meet him. By the way, I love that bay window," she ducked down, bent over and looked out and up at the mountain imposing on the landscape.

"Sounds good to me too. Before we leave the kitchen, behind us is kind of a breakfast area and out the doors behind that is one of the patios with a wrought iron table for six with a glass top. There is another patio outside the living room. I am not sure what the builders had in mind when they designed the house, maybe separate parties or something similar.

"Anyway, let's go through the kitchen here," she offered as she walked into the formal dining area complete with a heavy classic country oblong light oak, twenty-eight-foot table for twenty-five with an end to end table runner complete with several dried flower arrangements and six brass candle holders with candles matching the arrangement's colors. "I have never entertained here but maybe it is something we can do together as we make friends. Let's go around the corner." And as they did, they were met by a huge living room complete with a red-brick, floor to vaulted ceiling, eight-foot by eight-foot, gas fireplace with a curved hearth which rose half-way to the ceiling with an inset in the brick displaying an oil painting of one of the early Santa Barbara Missions.

There were two seating arrangements; one facing the fireplace, creating a half-circle with a dark-green, floral patterned sectional accompanied by accent pillows, while at the other end of the room, by the French doors leading to the other patio, there was a similar setting incorporating a semi-circle sectional with a round glass coffee table, replicating the patio sets with wrought iron feet, these being a rubbed light grey.

Rebecca continued, "Opening both sets of French doors allows for a breeze. We have mosquitoes and other annoying fliers, hence the screens, but generally we aren't bothered too much, thanks to the constant breeze. Let's go out this way," she gestured with one hand, heading through another doorway, "and into the foyer."

The entry-way was massive. Penelope craned her neck and estimated the height had to be at least thirty-feet, rising to the roof peak, the foyer and stairs cutting off part of the second floor, creating a cubicle affect.

"We came down to the kitchen via the back stairs, but these are great for easy access from the front door, although I always enter through the garage. Much more convenient I find. Through here," she gestured again like a Hearst Castle guide, "we are behind the kitchen and this leads to the family room, oh, and another patio with French doors. You know most of the second floor from this morning, but what you may not have seen is the additional two bedrooms with baths and a view of either the ocean or the pool. Speaking of which, let's tour that. Oh, I almost forgot, the exterior has flood lights hidden within the arches and curves. The lighting is timed to coordinate with daylight, coming on at dusk and staying on at a varied schedule with all of them coming on if any of the motion sensors are activated. I learned a lot from my colleagues Jason Spencer and Jessica when they were upgrading the Western White House. This house has ground sensors placed strategically around the perimeter with a CCTV system monitored from both the master bedroom and office. The monitoring is automatically recorded on a hard-drive. I'll show you all that later and give you the codes, but for now let's get to the pool," she said gleefully, jogging over to one of the French doors, pulling it open for Penelope and the two scurried behind the house.

As they were walking along the sandstone walkway, Rebecca added, "the music you hear in the house is from a main control system in the office with satellite radio. Each of the rooms has two speakers spaced strategically to provide stereo with an on/off and volume knob by the light switch. The only rooms without speakers are the garages and bathrooms. Oh, and there is a separate system in the pool house."

Rounding the corner, Rebecca stopped and spread her arms and said, "Voila! Here it is. Olympic size, with sandstone deck and straight ahead is the one-thousand square-foot pool house, complete with its own kitchen, bedroom, vaulted ceiling living room and gas fireplace. We can try out our Denver bathing suits! What do you say?"

Gazing in amazement, Penelope ignored Rebecca's swim suit invitation and replied, "I am still in shock Rebecca. This place is surreal. Surely you don't clean it yourself."

Rebecca laughed and replied, "No, Alejandro recommended a Santa Barbara company which came two days before I arrived and did the entire house, but now we will have to make more concrete arrangements. What do you think? Once a week? Two weeks? The furnace air circulating system really keeps the dust down."

"I don't know. How about trying it every two weeks and see how that works?"

"Sounds good. Let's put a rain-check on the swim till later and how about we shower, get dressed and head to town for brunch and I will introduce you to Alane Auberée of Birdcage Investments, the guy who made all this possible. You are going to love him personally and his investment success will blow you away."

"Okay. Let's go! Speaking of all of this," she added, sweeping her left arm in an arc, "How did you come up with the decorating ideas with every bedroom a different theme, the bathrooms, kitchen and all of it. The window dressings?"

"That is part of this crazy, cool thing. I didn't do any of it, nor did I pay for it. When I saw the place, it hadn't been lived in or cared for in two years as I mentioned. Everything was layered in dust. The beds were unmade, and things thrown about in every room as though the family had just up and left. Which is what Alane said they had done. The realtor explained somewhat of the financial predicament of the owners. Having over extended himself he had bankrupted the family. After filing, he was fortunate in getting a job in New York, so they walked away from the house with a suitcase each and never looked back.

"Alane recommended purchasing even if I never wanted to live here, and by the terrible state it was in, it seemed unlikely. But and here is the big but, Alane took it upon himself to hire a crew to refurbish the interior and they cleaned absolutely everything, inside, outside, sheets, duvets. You name it, they cleaned it. A few months afterwards, I was visiting and called Alane to set up an appointment to review my investments and he advised me not to book a hotel but to come straight to his office. I thought that a little strange, had no idea what he had in mind, but did as he wished. I took a taxi to his office and after greetings and without another word, he drove here. As we approached the main gate, he stopped, handed me the gate clicker and said, 'Welcome home.'

"We drove in and although the gardens looked neglected, the house was immaculate. Giving me the keys, he said, 'The surprise is my housewarming gift,' then added, 'Now I need a cocktail.' And that is how this all developed," she said with a swooping of both hands.

"Alane sounds like a pretty fantastic guy. I am anxious to meet him. Very French I presume."

"Very," replied Rebecca, "and one of the sweetest people you will ever meet. Very gay too, I might add."

"It will be interesting to know I have something in common with him from the get-go," she offered, laughing at her own humor. "Does he know about us?"

"No, not yet. This will be the first time I have met with him in recent months, but I will bet he will comment the moment he sees us together."

Penelope smiled, leaned against Rebecca's shoulder and linked arms. As they walked back to the main house, arm in arm, Rebecca explained her wealth, how Alane had made her obscenely wealthy with income continuingly outpacing her expenses by a vast margin, how Jessica had negotiated an accelerated retirement package which included full health benefits and a cost of living clause that kicked in immediately rather than when she reached sixty-two, which she says is a long way in the future.

Walking up the second story stairs, Rebecca shared three of Alane's impressive Warren Buffett quotes:

"It's better to hang out with people better than you. Pick out associates whose behavior is better than yours and you'll drift in that direction."

"Do not save what is left after spending; instead spend what is left after saving."

"The most important investment you can make is in yourself."

Warren Buffett

Chapter FIVE

Brian Sawyer had conducted a drug operation in Alberta's southern interior for over a decade. He began his successful career innocuously, thinking he would supplement his unemployment benefits until he was able to regain his high-income oil field job. Low oil prices persisted and showed no sign of rising above thirty-dollars a barrel, leaving Sawyer in a predicament of exhausting his unemployment benefits, unable to afford his expensive Edmonton apartment and having to return his tricked-out pick-up to the dealership and be without a ride.

His lifeline arrived in the form of Stan, a fellow party-goer who had an ear for a financial opportunity, and listening to Sawyer's melt-down, opened the door to expand his business. A few days of back-ground checking, and Stan offered Sawyer his economic salvation.

His operation began as a meager, outside grow-op for high-quality cannabis which he shipped via concealed containers welded to Canadian Pacific railcars' undercarriages while the train waited to cross from Alberta into Idaho. But the demand increased beyond his seasonal production capabilities and he was forced to create a temperature controlled underground bunker where he could increase his production a hundred-fold, only pausing during Alberta's severe temperatures of November through March. *

He was highly paid for his efforts, cash being left at different drop sites around Edmonton and Calgary, amassing a fortune in the long running operation.

Sawyer was in the process of shutting down the operation for the winter when he received a text from Stan with instructions to meet a Manitoba courier at the end of the forestry road which led to the main highway near his grow-op. He was then to place the package they delivered into a container on the CP rail car, destroy the facility, leave no trace, then disappear...forever.

He met the van and the three passengers, spoke to none, tied the package to his quad rack, ignored the gut-wrenching spasms generated in his torso when he saw the automatic rifles in the van's cargo area and left immediately for the rail staging area. He was unaware that while he was completing his tasks and preparing to leave for Idaho, RCMP Constable Richard Drought was engaging the delivery drivers in a firefight, killing two and capturing the third.

It would be years later that he discovered the package was radio-active material the far-right religious domestic terrorist group, Christians for a Better America, used to take down a commercial flight to LAX and that the proceeds of his operation had been a substantial cash flow for the CFBA.

*The railcars which transported Sawyers drugs into Idaho were owned by parent company Berkshire Hathaway, creating a satirical relationship...Rebecca Simpson's retirement fortune was heavily invested in Berkshire Hathaway and she would be sequestered to the Secret Service as an independent investigator to participate in taking Sawyer down.

After depositing the canister and sealing the lead-lined rail-car container, he sprinted back to his compound to dismantle the operation and prepare to drop out of sight. The process had been planned well in advance from the inception of the operation with numerous fail-safe systems incorporated into the vastly successful grow-op.

He had few personal possessions except for the ancient fifteen-foot trailer and beaten up truck, neither of which were registered in his name. After the last crop was shipped to Idaho, he hadn't replanted, so the underground cavern was empty except for the grow lights, air filter and hydroponic systems. They would remain, as would the diesel generator, hidden in the adjacent cave, the entrance of which was concealed by years of brush growth.

Disabling the generator, wiping down every surface with bleach, padlocking the steel door to the grow-op, he hitched his trailer to the pick-up and headed out via an alternate route, skirting the forestry road and connecting with Highway Three several kilometers east.

Once on the main highway, he headed for the border, stopping momentarily at the first rest stop to wipe down the trailer of his prints, puncture a tire and abandon it. He thought of torching it but figured the blaze would bring immediate scrutiny. With the flat tire, the rig would sit there for several days before a curious local or Mountie enquired. By then he would be lapping margaritas in his Costa Rica home established years previously, complete with a safe holding sufficient local currency to last a lifetime.

The last leg of his departure, once he crossed the border unfettered, was to gas his Piper Seminole, grab a coffee from the small airport's self-serve dispensary and take off for Limón, Costa Rica, a trip he had made dozens of times with four fuel stops. The pick-up was left in the airport parking lot with Idaho plates stolen from a truck stop just south of the border. After arriving in Limón, he sold the plane, loaded his beater 2000 Chevy Tracker he kept in long-term parking, and headed south, an exciting hour's drive.

Brian had spent all his adult winters in Alberta. When it became obvious that he couldn't run his operation year-round, he decided to enjoy the fruits of his labor away from snow and ice. His choice was based on the country's security, lack of an aggressive drug trade, vis-à-vis Mexico or other Central American countries, a viable economy and welcoming locals.

His first trip to Costa Rica was to find a secure location to enjoy the weather, culture and to get locals to accept him as a retired oil-field worker. It took some time to find a community with zero expat Canadians, Americans or Brits, but once he found the ocean-side village of Manzanillo, he spent months mingling with the locals, learning the language and blending in. Slipping into the economic and social sphere of the community created a somewhat simple process to make deposits into several local banks which, over several years, produced an acceptable house down payment.

He wanted to be a neighbor, not a wealthy foreigner, to conform and be as inconspicuous as possible, so after the house purchase was finalized, he hired locals to do extensive but inexpensive renovations to create a modest, but secure structure.

His quaint fishing village was home to howler monkeys, lizards, sloths and a wealth of tropical birds which, along with reggae music, the turquoise ocean hosting manatees, barracuda, tuna marlin and dolphins, became his serenity. He was often seen swimming, snorkeling, spear fishing and nurturing friendships with hard-working villagers who were delighted to help him create a permanent home in Manzanillo.

His renovations began with the demolition of a five-foot brick wall which surrounded the modest beach-front house. Sawyer was convinced the wall's removal signaled the community that he was not a Norteamericano, people who visit or relocate to Costa Rica and behave with an arrogance of superiority, looking down at the simple village life.

The house would be described by some as reflecting the seventies in décor, a style he found depressing, so he embarked on a renovation, the spirit's origin emulating from some unknown talent. He began with the kitchen, but rather than removing the mahogany cabinets, he had them stripped, painted a canary yellow, then did the walls in a lemon yellow creating an appealing contrast. The sink back-splash was patterned and when painted a cadet blue, blended spectacularly with the two yellow shades.

The floors were a heavy, flat tile which hadn't been washed or the grout cleaned for some time. The locals teamed up to produce a cleaning solution they had been using for generations, a mixture of baking soda and lemon juice, the latter of which was available in abundance. Scrubbing, often on hands and knees by a team of ten men and Sawyer, revealed a lime green flooring which blended perfectly with his wall color choices.

He carried the color scheme throughout the rest of the fourteen-hundred square foot, two-baths, two-bedroom beach house, including the vaulted, five paddle fanned ceilings.

A week's labor. The house was transformed, and he celebrated with a beach cook-out catered by Mariscos Punta Manzanillo, *Mariscos* being seafood, *Punta* meaning the tip and of course Manzanillo the community's name. The owner's sons were on Brian's renovation team and a deal was struck with dad to create a Fiesta en la playa Mexicana, Mexican beach party.

The entire village was invited, and it was said days and months later that the modest renovations and beach party sealed his future as a local.

S.B.S

Little did Sawyer know that his idyllic lifestyle was about to be interrupted with covert inquiries about his past.

RCMP Corporal Karen Winthrop and Toronto Police Service detective Tom Hortonn had been sequestered from their respective agencies to CSIS, Canadian Security and Intelligence Service, Canada's spy agency, by senior intelligence officer, David Kopas.

Winthrop and Hortonn entered the investigation of stolen cesium, a national security threat, from a Manitoba mine. The radio-active substance made its way on to an American flight which crash landed in the Pacific off the coast of Los Angeles. They began their task by interrogating the lone survivor of the delivery van tasked with dropping the cesium off to a drug dealer in southern Alberta.

The theft was carried out professionally with three bandits attacking the courier van a few kilometers from the mine. Responding RCMP officers obtained a vehicle description from the company drivers and that vehicle was picked up by surveillance cameras on Highway One as the vehicle headed west. Constable Rick Drought's police car's ALPR, Automated License Plate Recognition software, recognized the vehicle as he was patrolling in south western Alberta.

Drought allowed the van to pass then doubled back, blocked the forestry road into which they entered and engaged all three in a firefight with his Colt 8 automatic carbine, killing two of the three suspects without any injury to himself.

Unfortunately, the cesium had already been delivered to the drug dealer who had transferred it to a waiting Canadian Pacific rail-car heading south into the US.

It was Drought's surviving suspect from which Winthrop and Hortonn obtained vital information that led to the discovery of the ill-fated plane with the radio-active cesium aboard.

Chapter SIX

After the tour, Rebecca and Penelope dressed for their meeting with Birdcage Investments. Rebecca wore her Galla Ted Baker cropped pants with a floral pattern made from a soft, black, cotton-blend and her black double-breasted jacket, black camisole and Urmi lace black T-shirt. For shoes, she chose a pair of Sole Society Freyaa' wedges in a nomad suede.

Pen chose her Mikado Osaka pants in a dark orange with a muted yellow and orange pattern, a persimmon scoop-neck tank and orange mesh pullover sweater. She paired the outfit with an ankle boot by Blondo with topstitched suede, hidden zipper and stacked heel.

Their intent was to look professional and yet sexy, which they pulled off with a flare, as they noted to each other standing in front of the full-length bedroom mirror. Grinning broadly, they high-fived each other, bumped hips, then strolled downstairs, arm in arm to the garage.

Getting into the rental, Rebecca commented that somewhere on their agenda during the next few days must be a couple of used SUVs, noting she was done with pick-ups, completing her transformation from country girl to urban country.

Penelope turned slightly with raised eyebrows and a quizzical look, but keeping her thoughts to herself...for now, knowing they couldn't be without a pick-up if they were going to have horses and ranch requirements.

The short drive out of the hills took them on to State Street and a direct route to The Toast, a quirky, hippie, upscale restaurant on Anacapa, a block from the beach. Parking was abundant mid-week and they pulled up in front and exited as though they were long-time residents, not newbies.

Rebecca opened The Toast's door and noted immediately that the interior didn't whisk one back to the counterculture of the early '60's as one might expect approaching the multi-colored store-front, but met diners with a soft elegance of muted pastels, framed photos of various Santa Barbara landscapes adorning three walls, complementing a twelve-foot chalkboard with daily specials presented with unique cursive.

Self-absorbed in her environment she was pulled from her revere as Pen put her arm around her waist, giving her a hug. Rebecca returned the affection then stepped aside to allow Penelope to precede her, wondering if Pen would spot Alane without an introduction.

Rebecca was not surprised when Penelope walked immediately to a forty's something man, who was already standing as she approached.

Alane was wearing a multi-colored shirt with bold colored geometric shapes. The slim-fitting top with its Milanese collar and double-buttoned simple cuffs, paired perfectly with his knee length Tommy Bahama starboard green shorts and black tasseled loafers, sans socks. He broke into a welcoming smile as Penelope approached.

With Rebecca at her heels, Pen extended her hand and said, "Monsieur Alan Auberee, c'est un plaisir de vous rencontrer. Je suis Penelope Barker, votre nouveau client et cette belle femme derrière moi, est, comme vous le savez, Rebecca Simpson, anciennement du service secret des États-Unis. fais-tu le monsieur? "

("Mr. Alan Auberee, it is a pleasure to meet you. I am Penelope Barker, your new client and this beautiful woman behind me, is, as you know, Rebecca Simpson, formerly of the Secret Service of the United States. How do you do sir?")

The smartly attired gentleman didn't miss a beat. Extending his hand to accept Penelope's, he bent at the waist, kissed the back of her hand and replied, "Madame Barker, ou devrais-je dire, docteur Barker, j'ai le plaisir de rencontrer enfin la belle amie et partenaire de mon amie et client de longue date, Rebecca Simpson. J'attends avec impatience de nombreuses années d'enrichissement financier et d'amitié. S'il vous plaît, asseyez-vous et permettez-moi de vous traiter de belles dames à une expérience culinaire uniquement disponible dans Santa Barbara sans précédent."

("Ms. Barker, or may I say, Dr. Barker, it is my pleasure to finally meet the beautiful friend and partner of my long-time friend and client, Rebecca Simpson. I look forward to many financially fulfilling and friendship years. Please, sit and allow me to treat you beautiful ladies to a dining experience only available in unprecedented Santa Barbara.")

Alane swiftly and deftly moved his hand from Penelope's, wrapped it around her waist and pulling her to him, gave her a quick brush on each cheek, stepped aside, pulled out two chairs, bent at the waist, giving the women a graceful sweeping of his arm, gesturing for them to sit.

Rebecca had been treated identically for many years and smiled at Alane's manners and elegance as she accepted his invitation to sit...but only after she gave him a hug.

Chapter SEVEN

Originally named Punta de la Limpia Concepcion by Spanish explorer, Sebastian Vizcaino in 1602, Point Conception juts out abruptly from the California coast as the topography shifts from a northerly direction to a westerly variation, then cuts back and continues north.

A ninety-minute drive north of Santa Barbara, California, the point is home to an old Coast Guard lighthouse, complete with a red roof, sea green lantern room and living quarters, all of which had been maintained for years for its historic value, but after being shut down and without public access, the interior had been allowed to decay.

Although some adventurous hikers have made their way to the lighthouse, the area is cut off by Vandenberg Air Force Base to the north and the surrounding area by a private ranch's grazing rights.

Since the Coast Guard automated the light in 1973, if the few hikers were to walk carefully from the lighthouse to the southern edge of the cliff and peer to their left, they would observe a massive gouge in the sandstone formation, eroded by years of wind and waves. It couldn't be described as a fiord given its short length from sea to beach, but it was of sufficient length and depth for a vessel with a minimum draft to navigate at high tide through the narrow opening, anchor and perform any number of activities, then leave at the next high tide, undetected.

The Hermanos de Wall Street, Brothers of Wall Street, was one of the largest biker gangs in the state, albeit unknown to most. Organized during the tumultuous seventies by greedy San Francisco lawyers, disbarred for their manipulation of their customers' portfolios, they struck back at society with highly organized and profitable operations which created a wealth far beyond their law school dreams and more than they could ever steal from clients.

Their biking was as recreational now as it had ever been. Their criminal status didn't motivate them to ride with outlaw bikers or patronize the former's bars. They had their own drinking establishments. Private of course, and only open when they would be riding through. A phone-call a couple of days before their arrival would set in motion a lavish lunch, sans alcohol, and their enjoyment of partying with their fellow Hermanos de Wall Streeter members. Conversations could be open, honest and unobserved/recorded as their security team scanned the facilities, then had all personnel leave.

The Bar, if one wanted to be so crude as to call it that, was more in keeping with a high-end San Francisco or Vancouver hotel lounge, where sushi and seafood towers compliment handcrafted cocktails. Each of their lounges was unique with classy English-style décor, complete with tapestries and mahogany furniture.

Hermanos de Wall Street was cult-like in its furtiveness, fashioning itself after the Bilderberg Group, a secret financial society originating with the Dutch Royal Family to control world finances. Bilderberg is reported to have been influential in the careers of

Canada's Steven Harper, who visited the group one year prior to his election as prime minister, Germany's Angela Merkel, who did likewise also a year before her election and Bill Clinton who sought their input two years before his first US presidential term. Ben Bernanke, American Federal Reserve Chairman for many years, is suspected as being advised by Bilderberg.

Henry Kissinger, who wrote *World Order* in 2014, and was foreign affairs advisor for president Nixon, made a speech to Bilderberg in Evan, France in 1992, "Today Americans would be outraged if U.N. troops entered Los Angeles to restore order; tomorrow they will be grateful. This is especially true if they were told there was an outside threat from beyond, whether real or promulgated, that threatened our very existence. It is then that all peoples of the world will plead with world leaders to deliver them from this evil. The one thing every man fears is the unknown. When presented with this scenario, individual rights will be willingly relinquished for the guarantee of their well-being granted to them by their world government." Control, diversion and secrecy, all were used in the 2016 American federal election and were the building blocks of the lucrative North American west coast drug trade.

The connection between the two groups is somewhat like the 'Three Shell Game' which challenges the participant to guess under which shell lies the pea. Manipulate truth, make it disappear and reappear as a new reality, or a lie altogether, then reorganize that lie into a truth and watch the public buy into it, either emotionally as in an election or physically as smuggling drugs through many ports via a variety of transportation systems, always keeping law enforcement deploying resources and never able to slow the flow.

Bilderberg met in Chentilly, Virginia, June 2017 with 131 participants from 21 countries, including Portugal, Turkey, America, Canada, France, Italy, Switzerland, Belgium, Germany, Austria and Sweden.

Bilderberg's current steering committee comprises many heads of state from the above countries and their leading capitalists such as:

Altman, Roger C. USA, Founder and Senior Chairman, Evercore

Barroso, José M. Durão Portugal, Chairman, Goldman Sachs International

Hammand, P.K. Canada, Chair of Hammand & Associates

Elkann, John Italy, Chairman, Fiat Chrysler Automobiles

Enders, Thomas Germany, CEO, Airbus SE

Gutierrez, Mariana USA, CEO of Gutierrez & Associates

Sabia, Michael Canada, CEO, Caisse de dépôt et placement du Québec

Sikorski, Radoslaw Poland, Senior Fellow, Harvard University

Hammand and Gutierrez are well known by the one-percent social sphere for their fund-raising capabilities, both amassing millions for various political candidates in Canada and America through $5,000 a-plate-dinners. They are founding members of Hermanos de Wall Street, the only non-disbarred attorneys in the organization.

Their forensic accountants were experts at risk management and manipulating accounts and funds. They took the millions raised at various political functions, deposited them into a legitimate American business account, then sent that same money around the world electronically through various virtual, private networks, which are securely encrypted, guaranteeing anonymity. They falsely report the millions raised, infuse the drug funds, contribute a portion to political parties and invest the remainder. Any government agency attempts to follow the transfers would be bogged down in the encryption and the funds bouncing from one country to another, landing in an obscure account, totally undetectable.

In addition to the political funds' investments, once a month, the group sends an associate from Los Angeles or Vancouver, British Columbia, in a private jet, with cash from drug revenue on the pretense of a reward for the most billable hours. The employee enjoys a week on the islands at the firm's luxury condo, not knowing that the Lear jet landed in a foreign country with millions hidden within the plane's opulent interior.

The pilots and crew are treated similarly on another part of the island, leaving the plane unattended, albeit within the confines of the hanger, to be visited covertly by a messenger who retrieves the cash, then deposited it in the off-shore account...no questions asked.

The attorneys owned various businesses in to which part of the drug currency was filtered. One in particular was a California highway maintenance company, a firm with multi-million-dollar fluid contracts. Fluid in the sense that many contracts activated their cost override clauses, adding hundreds of thousands to an already bloated project.

The company CEO was a trusted lieutenant, as was the banker, who accepted the millions monthly to filter.

California, as many other states, are riddled with independent banks, many with local boards of directors with little or no financial acumen, the lack of which created a corporate atmosphere ripe for manipulation.

However, these banks are still regulated by the state of California and must submit to an annual audit by state bank examiners. This oversight was not an issue with Hermanos since they had numerous lieutenants throughout the examiner's office and could control the outcome of any one of its banks.

The complexity of Hermanos' financial empire was controlled and shaped by a team of Santa Barbara accountants, all of whom had generated loyalty to the attorneys through years of dedication, expertise and personal fortunes.

The Hermanos de Wall Street all live comfortably, not lavishly, but serenely. None live in multi-million-dollar homes or have outlandish vacation getaways, albeit several villas in Vanuatu, a South Pacific country seventeen-hundred-kilometers east of Australia without an extradition treaty with the United States or Canada.

The Melanesian topography consists of eighty islands, stretching thirteen-hundred kilometers and attracts scuba diving vacationers who pride themselves on exploring the coral reefs, underwater caverns and various WWII era shipwrecks, such as the SS President Coolidge troopship. It is Vanuatu to which Hammand and Gutierrez plan to disappear when they reach the young age of fifty, to retire in luxury, untouchable by any government.

All had invested conservatively with the modest income they received from their respective firms. All have healthy post-secondary education funds for their children and contribute generously to various charities. The only caveat to their financial transparency was their business finances. The complexity would require a forensic accountant to uncover the laundered drug money and the hidden off-shore monthly direct deposits.

They lived well and were honest, well respected members of their communities, with no overt connection to the drug trade.

ॐ♭ॐ

The Chica de Oro continued to navigate its submerged, northerly route, undetected and unfettered with its cargo destined to alter the minds and souls of North Americans, controlling their lives, propelling many to oblivion.

Chapter EIGHT

RCMP Corporal Karen Winthrop and Toronto
Police Service's Sgt. Tom Hortonn were given a few
weeks leave after their involvement in the international
terrorism case of the stolen cesium masterminded by a
US Senator.

Cesium is a radioactive mineral mined in
Manitoba. It was stolen, inserted into a casket carrying a
deceased Idaho man and loaded on to a Mahalo Airlines
727 flight from Minneapolis to Los Angeles. When the
cesium was exposed to air, it interfered with the plane's
electronics and navigational system, causing the 727 to
crash in the Pacific off the California coast.

Winthrop and Hortonn traced the cesium to a
drug operation in southern Alberta but were unable to
apprehend the thieves before they had a deadly
encounter with an RCMP Member. A surviving suspect
was interrogated in an Edmonton RCMP detachment by
a CSIS, Canadian Security Intelligent Service agent,
David Kopas. Accepting the agent's offer for an
extended Canadian prison sentence rather than being
extradited to the US, the suspect revealed how he and his
partners were hired by a stranger in a Denver bar to steal
the cesium and deliver it to a person at the end of a
forestry road in southern Alberta.

Denver police detectives joined the investigation
through a unique American intelligence sharing software
system, coined CHAP. Not an acronym, but named for
its developer, Cheryl Chapman, a former Navy SEAL
who ran their covert operations out of a secret location in
southern Texas with several all-female units. Chapman

was sequestered by US President Bakus to develop an intelligence sharing system which all local, state, and national law enforcement agencies use to coordinate potential terrorist threats.

Karen had previously been a Sky Marshall, flying various routes with Air Canada, primarily to and from Toronto, Vancouver, British Columbia, Miami and Los Angeles. It was during one of her flights that she met Secret Service Agent Jessica Fukishura who was heading from Washington, DC to Toronto to visit her parents before she began her assignment of training a team of agents to update security at President Bakus' western White House in StoneHead, Wyoming.

"Met" is probably a misnomer. Fukishura was armed. She advised the crew, who, per protocol, notified Winthrop. Sheriff Karen arrived moments later and interrogated Fukishura, given that foreign law enforcers were prohibited from being armed in Canada. Winthrop quickly learned that Fukishura was Canadian with a concealed weapons permit signed by a Canadian Senator, an old friend of her parents; dad Glen a tenured professor at the University of Toronto and her Mom, Shelia, an executive assistant for a federal member of Parliament.

The two agents hit it off and spent time training at the Toronto Police Academy, shopping at Holt Renfrew and dining at the Calgary Steak House in Toronto.

The women hadn't been together since Fukishura left for Wyoming and Winthrop was sequestered to CSIS. Karen was anxious for a couple of down days at home in Toronto, so she could get some much-needed rest, have some quality time with Tom, contact Jessica and hook-up for drinks and dinner.

The morning after arriving at her condo, she breakfasted on yogurt, fresh fruit, raisin toast and eggs benedict she had ordered on her app, and coffee which she had brewed herself. She was musing over the past weeks' investigation, wondering if Canada and the US would ever rid themselves of domestic terrorists. They had been successful in eliminating the key component, the US Senator, senior lieutenants in Idaho and Wyoming, several bomb designers and the CFBA member who detonated the explosion which leveled a Marina del Rey convention center, but hundreds of members of Christians for a Better America had disappeared underground, only to reappear in another city, with new identifications, to rekindle their terrorist network.

Finding her rhetorical thinking exhausting, she tossed her breakfast dishes in the trash then she used her smartphone to find Jessica's parents' phone number, Jessica having asked her not to call until she left StoneHead. She took her phone, coffee and, still in her Cozy Chic Plum Barefoot Dreams robe she had snagged during a Nordstrom shopping spree with Jessica, sat beside her fortieth-floor window overlooking Lake Ontario and called Shelia.

Chapter NINE

Supervising Secret Service agent Jessica Fukishura was physically and emotionally spent post investigation. She and her team were only at the ranch a few weeks when they discovered the right-wing terrorist organization was operating in StoneHead under the supervision of a church and its aldermen. A hurriedly arranged assault on their farm complex outside of town revealed a massive stash of explosives. Further investigation exposed a similar stash in the mountains above Orofino, Idaho, both managed by CFBA members. It wasn't until Fukishura asked for the help of local law enforcement that they were able to track down a killer on a Nez Perce Reservation in Idaho and a drug supply line from Alberta.

The Secret Service bureaucratic wheels being what they are, it would be days, if not weeks, before new assignments were forthcoming fro m the "J" Team, so Jessica had Elisabeth, Jackson and Jason help with the aftermath at the Marina del Rey outside of Los Angeles, putting together the criminal puzzle; interviewing witnesses, assisting with the LAPD and FBI forensic teams examining the garage where the Suburbans were modified and loaded with explosives.

The agents had no difficulty accepting the extended assignment given they were no longer lead investigators and were enjoying their hotel accommodations at the marina and frequent dinners at the Firewalker Pub at the Marina owned and operated by a retired SEAL, Tobias Armishaw.

Armishaw's relationship with the agents began innocuously with an attempt by the Christians for a Better America shaking him down for weekly contributions to their cause.

Their mistake.

He introduced them to a forty-five, moved them to a back room while a staffer called the FBI. When the federal agents arrived, the CFBA personnel's hands were plastic cuffed behind their backs and their mouths were taped.

Armishaw was a profiler's dream. In his mid-fifties, Tobias is close to six feet and about two-hundred pounds, a barrel chest, piercing green eyes, square jaw and sports a close-cropped grey hair. He doesn't display the typical belly of other men his age...his slim waist and fifteen-inch biceps reflecting hours in the gym.

A little research would have signaled to the CFBA goons that this was one business to avoid, but their arrogance overrode common sense. Had they put forth a little bit of effort, they would have found that Armishaw was a retired, thirty-year veteran of the Navy SEALs, having been on active duty around the world for twenty years, then an instructor for another ten, retiring as a Commander with a reputation as having a no bullshit personality and an attitude of kicking ass first and introducing himself second.

What their research would not have revealed was the fact that Armishaw carried a .45 custom Kimber in a small of his back holster. Armishaw practiced daily...after his morning workout on Venice Beach and before he came to the Firewalker. It is also doubtful that any patron or local would have revealed the pub's nom de plume, so to speak. Customers were all encompassing; you were, or you were not.

Although the SEAL moto of, *The Only Easy Day was Yesterday,* was etched in brass with a polished mahogany background over the bar, Armishaw wanted the pub's name to reflect what he and hundreds of other warriors had endured, *Walking on Fire* for America. The orthodox drinkers knew the history, knew that Armishaw loved the Navy, still does.

He had a romance with the lifestyle, the bravado camaraderie, living on base unfettered by civilians or their lifestyle. He was unprepared when mandatory retirement stuck its ugly head into his life. But he received a reprieve, at least momentarily, of a year to find something to do in retirement. The Navy honored his devotion to duty, his heroism, numerous Purple Hearts, battle ribbons and allowed him to be duty free, maintain his housing and all that encompassed his lifestyle for the year.

He had amassed a small fortune after thirty years of limited expenses and investing his salary; $90K a year at retirement. He did his due diligence and after about seven months found the Marina del Rey pub which had been allowed to fall into disarray with limited clientele. With the help of a retired Marine, now a prosperous realtor, he made the retiring owner an offer which was immediately scooped up. The next five months he drew upon his many contacts, both current and retired, to completely renovate the building and recreate a combination of an enlisted mess hall and officers' club.

It was a renovator's dream and the Navy's designated watering hole once it opened.

It didn't take much of an explanation to a San Diego interior designer for the plan to come together. The interior was massive with seating for one hundred and fifty comfortably. The finished product was a bar which stretched from just inside the door to the end of the room with the ubiquitous brass stools topped with dark brown leather seats. The bar was three recycled bars professionally joined, sanded, dark stained, shellacked and adorned with various polished brass ships fittings. The entire wall behind the massive bar was a beveled mirror with various chandeliers spreading the length, twinkling in its reflection.

The back wall of the Firewalker itself was polished mahogany with brass plaques honoring the fallen Frogmen from World War Two and every Navy SEAL since the Warrior unit's inception. Each honoree was highlighted with an individual subdued ceiling light, so subtle that you had to peer into the ceiling to see the light source. The Wall was a spectacular memory of the hundreds who gave the ultimate for their country, and there was never a patron who did not spend many quiet moments reflecting on their presence.

There were the usual Sports Bar high definition television screens dispersed throughout the Firewalker and one in each of the upstairs restrooms, accessed via a curved staircase. The establishment was unique in many ways, principally in that there was no sound coming from any television. The best way to describe the audio ambiance was to call it respectful. Firewalker played a little country, a little old-time rock and roll and jazz -

and considered itself eclectic, which blended with the atmosphere. Neither music, nor television was the center of a patron's thoughts. Diners could sit and chat, reflect on their individual experiences, honor those they knew had died and enjoy a quiet, meaningful dining adventure.

The Firewalker didn't need a formal announcement and didn't place ads in the local papers or on television. The Naval Base's commanding officer took the liberty of announcing the grand opening with a caveat; each day was devoted to a base command and with over five thousand personnel, Opening Day, took several weeks.

Firewalker reached the hearts of every Navy man and woman, regardless of their command, as well as thousands of locals who overwhelmingly were Navy supporters. Armishaw was a survivor and knew it was with the grace of God that he was not killed many times over.

He knew it was his duty to give back, to provide for those families who gave the ultimate for their country, for the Navy and for the SEALs.

Shortly after the overwhelming success of Firewalker, he met with two retired SEALs, one an accountant and the other a tax attorney. These men designed a charitable foundation with fifty thousand of Armishaw's seed money and another five hundred thousand from the SEALs.

The foundation's board was comprised of current and retired SEALs, widows of SEALs as well as several siblings of those lost in action. The board met once a month to approve requests for financial assistance, not only to Navy personnel and their families but to hundreds of children and others in need of a leg up. They paid for many university scholarships, fulfilled the dreams of children suffering from debilitating and terminal diseases and enriched the lives of thousands yearly.

Armishaw was the reason the Firewalker didn't know a slow day. With ten percent of the daily receipts going to the foundation, patrons were constantly overpaying their bill, some by as much as a hundred dollars, giving the server instructions, "Give it to the kids."

Elisabeth, Jackson and Jason had celebrated post investigation at the Firewalker with Tobias and scores of military staff. The agents, no longer under cover, Armishaw delighted in introducing them to his customers and when the trio contributed several thousand dollars to the Swabby Bucket, thinking they had bucketed the currency on the sly, the observant crowed went ballistic with applause and appreciation.

Dining at the Firewalker most evenings, they had become regulars after several weeks of no new assignments.

Chapter TEN

Jessica had been ordered back to Washington by supervisor Sorento to debrief in person, finalize the paper work regarding the massive investigation, collaborate with Cheryl Chapman, her CHAP system and attempt to piece together a probe into how the cesium was smuggled into the country totally undetected, the location of the perpetrator or perpetrators and whether there were further threats against the president from CFBA.

She was on a business flight from Denver to Washington, having been choppered from StoneHead Ranch with her limited luggage, when her personal cell chimed its soft Piano Guys' Cello Song ringtone.

Feeling quite awkward with her personal phone activated for the first time in months, she fumbled to get it out of her camel Kristen Blacke, single-breasted walking coat laying over the table next to the window. Unlocking the screen with her security code, she didn't take the time to note the caller ID, knowing there were few who had her number and none with whom she didn't want to speak.

"Jessica here."

"What happened to 'Yo'?"

"Karen?"

"It is," she replied with a laugh. "What's with the new greeting?"

Jessica laughed slightly, vaguely acknowledging that she previously answered the phone with an attitude that was criticized by her boss during her last assignment, with him commenting that her phone etiquette, or lack-there-of might reflect why she has professional interaction issues. "I had an epiphany of sorts, generated by a slap down by my boss regarding my professional attitude. I took his advice, learned to play nice with my colleagues and it worked. With collaboration of numerous law enforcement agencies, we accomplished more than I could have ever done on my own. And we caught most of the bad guys.

Laughing with delight, Jessica replied, "You caught me with perfect timing. I finished a few days ago and am on a flight to Washington, for debriefing and a few days off. Where are you?"

Karen sighed a fake exasperation, replying, "Well, *my* assignment wasn't classified," she bantered with a little snort, "and I just got back to Toronto after spending days and days with the yummy Tom Hortonn in Whistler." She knew her remark was completely unprofessional, but felt comfortable with Jessica as a friend, not as a colleague, so she continued with the charade.

"OMG, you and Tom, Whistler. I am envious. Is he there with you now?"

"Sadly no. I had to pull out my green boyfriend last night, so I could get some sleep," she laughed, referring to her trusted electric dildo.

"Karen, you are bad! But hey, if you have some time off, why not drop down here, stay with me and we can have some down time together. Are you up for some shopping?"

"Am I? I saw amazing outfits in Whistler, but had zero time to browse, not because of Tom, but work. So, yeah, I'm on my way. I'll check some flights and maybe I can get bumped on the first flight out of Pearson. Just could happen there is a business class seat for Sheriff Winthrop," she quipped, knowing the airlines went out of their way to give her the royal treatment, given their gratitude for the number of in-flight incidents she had intercepted, one with Jessica when they met.

"Fabulous! Text me when you land, and I will give you my address and you can cab it there."

"Sounds good. See you tomorrow. Very exciting Jessica. I am glad I called your Mom and she gave me your number. I hope that was okay?"

"Certainly. I have had the phone off for months, which is why I didn't give it before. But for now, I am going to recline in Air Canada's business class, sip my Burrowing Owl Chardonnay, nibble my appies and get some sleep. See you tomorrow sheriff."

"See you Canuck."

Jessica had chosen a pair of Cady Trapunto Tie-Waist White Trousers with a wide leg, paired with a black Graydon Silk Blouse with ruffle collar and cuffs. She matched the outfit with a pair of Kristin Cavallari Kane Booties in clay suede. The outfit was the perfect choice for comfort on a flight.

Air Canada's 747 Dreamliner's business pod was a welcoming respite from weeks of tension, and she relished in the plush leather recliner as she sipped her chardonnay.

The flight was only five hours, give or take, depending on either a tail-wind or head-wind, but regardless, Air Canada had a meal for her. She was going over her notes in her mind, preparing for her meeting when the flight attendant arrived.

Served on white-bone china with sterling silver flatware was a Niçoise salad: fingerling potatoes, hard-boiled egg, green beans, fennel, corn, grape tomatoes, Kalamata olives and garlic aioli. The entree was flamed cod, Catalan red pepper coulis, chickpeas, fava beans, red quinoa and a vegetable medley.

Thanking the steward profusely, she relaxed by pushing her body back into the curved seat, took another sip of her chardonnay and enjoyed her meal.

Chapter ELEVEN

Introductions and pleasantries aside, Alane introduced Rebecca and Penelope to The Toast's menu, which had been designed for patrons' eclectic tastes, what Alane would later explain, had its origins in Topanga Canyon in the Santa Monica Mountains. Topanga has been a hippy haven for generations, with the rise of various businesses, creating an environment to sooth the soul, while inspiring creativity.

Susan Morgan describes the area in her piece for *W Magazine.* "Topanga's artistic roots date back at least as far as the McCarthy era, when Will Geer, a blacklisted actor and trained botanist, fled Hollywood and bought a parcel of canyon land. With his family, he established a large, working garden and an open-air theater, where Arlo Guthrie, Pete Seeger, and Ramblin' Jack Elliott performed. In the '70s, when Geer gained new fame on the hit TV show *The Waltons* as Grandpa and his children had grown up to be actors, the family created Theatricum Botanicum, now a venerable woodland venue for performances and workshops."

Open from seven-thirty until three daily, The Toast offered breakfast and lunch specials, but by far their greatest attraction was their signature potatoes; roasted baby reds tossed with the chef's guarded secret herbs and served with every dish. Alane pointed out a few specialties: *The Everything Omelet*; sun dried tomatoes, spinach, mushrooms, banana peppers, red onion, black beans, cumin and Swiss cheese, and *Green Eggs & Ham*; two scrambled eggs with pesto and Swiss cheese, grilled smoked ham and a slice of multi-grain toast. Admiring the eclectic offerings, the item they all chose based on his recommendation; *Cayenne in the Rain*; two scrambled eggs, signature reds, sautéed red onions, sundried tomatoes, spinach, melted cheddar, feta, dill sauce, cayenne pepper and salsa served with a slice of multi-grain toast.

Having given their order to their server Christie, a five-six, petite woman of indeterminable age, shoulder length, naturally blonde do, wearing black Bermuda shorts, a white peasant blouse and taupe Berk sandals, Rebecca and Penelope explained to Alane, as best they could, their relationship and their decision to move to Santa Barbara.

Rubbing his hands together in delight, Alane asked, "Sounds marvelous and you two are an obvious delight as a couple. Rebecca, you could retire permanently and live quite comfortably off your investment income, but I doubt that lifestyle would suit you. Penelope, I don't know your financial situation. What are your investment objectives and business plans?"

Rebecca and Pen bent over the table and leaned into Alane and said simultaneously, "R&P Investigations," then leaned back and waited for Alane's reaction.

It was instantaneous as he clapped his hands together again and almost shrieked, "Oh, my god, oh, my god," I cannot believe how incredibly fortuitous this is girls. I have numerous business associates who are constantly in need of a highly ethical investigator to scrutinize various business opportunities. Santa Barbara is a very small community, albeit almost one-hundred-thousand relatively wealthy residents, who thrive on knowing everyone's business, both personal and business. I will send more business your way than you may want," he took a deep breath and continued, "and speaking of that, a word of advice, these people are filthy rich so make sure your fees are very high and reflect your extensive investigative abilities as well as your desire to not work a forty-hour week."

"Thanks for the vote of confidence Alane and the support. We never dreamed of being able to start off so quickly. I am applying for my state investigator's license this afternoon as well as a firearm carry permit, both of which I have been told will be primarily a paper process and Penelope will be apprenticed to me enabling her to bypass the post-secondary education in police science or related fields. Having a doctorate certainly will pave the way as well," she concluded as she reached across and gave Penelope's hand a squeeze.

Pen returned the affection and continued the conversation, "Alane, Rebecca is going to train me in martial arts and firearms' fineness. I am not sure how the latter differs from conventional firearms training, but I am looking forward to both, maybe fineness is something kinky," she winked at Rebecca and snorted her characteristic guffaw.

"But on a more serious note Alane, Rebecca explained her investment portfolio and said that you could take my inheritance from my grandma and the capital from selling my business and create a sound program. This is the figure I have in mind for investment," she concluded by writing a number on her napkin, including a desired monthly income, folding it and sliding it across to Alane.

Alane smiled, reached across the table, retrieved the napkin and slowly opened it. Being totally uninhibited, as was his nature, he put the napkin in front of his face, raised his eyebrows and responded with, "Oh my Penelope, I can help you tremendously.

"How well versed are you in the stock/bond market, mutual funds and real estate?"

"I'd say beginner to intermediate level, if there is such a classification. I am not concerned about the security or safety of my principal Alane, given your track record with Rebecca. The inheritance was from my grandma who supported me all through school and encouraged me to live my life on my own terms, so we are sort of investing for her too. Does that make sense?" Receiving a nod from Alane, she continued.

"I've seen what you have been doing for Rebecca all these years and I know that your reputation is considered solid throughout the industry. So, what do you have in mind, as I know you have been giving it considerable thought."

Alane segued smoothly from social interaction to investment broker and replied, "We are looking at long term here and I suggest that you follow a pattern developed by Warren Buffet, spreading your capital discreetly throughout a series of blue chips stocks, real estate, insurance holdings and manufacturing. Let me put a program together for you in the next day or so, I'll ring you and we can get together over appetizers and chardonnay. How does that sound?"

"Delightful Alane," she responded, making a wide gesture with her arms. "I look forward to the information and getting together." She glanced at Rebecca, who nodded in return.

"How about our place around 4 on Thursday and we can do dinner too? Oh, and Rebecca, how about we invite Alejandro for dinner and Alane, how about a couple of your friends as well?"

Alane looked at Rebecca, then Penelope and back to Rebecca again and said, "You two make a delicious couple. Life is going to be so much more fulfilling and fun with you in my life. Certainly, that time and date work perfectly for me and I know just the friends to invite," he concluded, "But may I offer a caveat? Please allow me to provide dinner. My mind is swimming with absolutely delicious West Coast cuisine ideas that I know you and your guests will think are divine. I will have all the ingredients delivered and prepare the dishes myself. May I?"

The women looked at each other, smiled with Rebecca squeezing Penelope's hand and answered in unison, "Absolutely Alane," Rebecca clarified with, "We would be delighted to have you share your culinary expertise, but we have to supply the wine and I know Alejandro will want to do appetizers."

Alane smiled, raising his coffee mug to toast his two new besties he replied, "Deal."

"Now before we conclude this delightful brunch, I must ask about your working conditions. I don't mean to be nosy, although I do tend to have that reputation, but I presume you are not going to have clients trapes up the mountain to your fabulous ranch. The reason I ask is, if you need office space here in town, I have a well-lighted expansive area next to my office that would only need decorating and you are ready for business. What do you think?"

Penelope and Rebecca exchanged glances with Pen giving Rebecca a nod which said, you take this one since you know the area.

Rebecca accepted the unspoken communication and replied, "I recall that space Alane, and it would be perfect. We wouldn't want it decorated as an office but a living room. Do you know someone who can make that happen?"

Her mischievous grin wasn't missed by Alane who responded by standing up, taking a bow, smiling and saying, "I am at your service mademoiselles. I can have my furniture contacts email you photos of various arrangements. I will give you her phone number and you can discuss style etc., maybe an area rug, a wall fireplace and knickknacks. We can talk about rent later, but I will tell you now that whatever figure we choose is being donated to charity. How will that work for you?"

"Perfectly Alane. You have been so charming and helpful, we feel we are part of the community already, and we aren't even licensed yet," replied Penelope with a wave of her hand as though anointing the community and laughing at her own magnanimous gesture.

"You are part of the community already for what you bring to us, to me, and I know everyone you meet is going to be a lifelong friend," Alane offered with a bow and a hand gesture, stepping aside, sliding his chair back to the table and walking around to do likewise for his guests.

As they were leaving The Toast, he hugged both women, kissed each on the cheek and said, "I am beyond excited about your house warming party next Thursday and will begin planning the moment I get back to the office. For now, au revoir my beauties," held the door for them, and almost sprinted up the street to his financial den.

Rebecca and Penelope exchanged smiles, linked arms and walked back to their vehicle to head to the police department for Rebecca to file for a firearm's carry permit and her private investigator license.

Warren Buffett's investment rules.

Rule One. Never lose money.
Rule Two. Remember rule one.

S.B.S

Brian Sawyer had operated his successful drug operation in southern Alberta for so long and with such success he was positive he had anticipated every aspect of its eventual termination. Stan had informed him from the onset that it would have a limited life and that calculating the end could mean the difference between a life of luxury or ten years in prison.

Brian was methodical in cleaning the bunker grow room, wiping down every possible surface with bleach. His adherence included the generator, gas cans, extension wires, used grow pots and even the outhouse.

Near the end of the several-day disorder, he was exhausted, and believing he had completed the termination process, sat in his dilapidated trailer one last evening, watched the Alberta sun set over the Crowsnest Mountain Range with the last of his Molson's Canadian, daydreaming of the next phase of his life, free of financial worries. He didn't notice that his burner cell wasn't in his back pocket.

ᔑᗷᔓ

"What interested you as a child? When you were 6, 10, 12 years old was there something that you loved to do? Maybe that could be your passion. If not, try more things, passions are grown out of interests. Find more things that interest you and try them."

Daniel Bourke on Warren Buffett

"I tap dance to work. It isn't work, it's play." Warren Buffett

Chapter TWELVE

The RCMP forensics technicians from the Edmonton detachment scoured the marijuana bunker. Drought and his colleagues discovered the cave after his shoot-out with the cesium thieves near the main highway and the forestry road. The team gathered every object; several partial bars of lead, metal cutting blades, a tape measure, several black markers and a T square-the outdoor privy-a job none relished but agreed it needed to be done, even items at the bottom of the pit-discarded bottles and cans from the primitive recycling pit. Items were marked according to their location, photographed and bagged. They took tire tread impressions from where Brian parked his travel trailer, hoping to match them if they found the home on wheels.

And they did.

While the forensics team were analyzing the material from the grow operation, members hunted for the trailer on every connecting trail and forestry road. Their discovery was hailed as an early break in the case. Not only did they find the trailer parked in a highway pull-out not far from the drug operation, but they discovered Brian's abandoned quad and the trail he used from the operation to the Canadian Pacific Rail line.

From the latter, they found an area by the tracks that had been scuffed, the bedding rocks disturbed as though someone had been working by the tracks. They bagged and photographed what appeared to be metal shavings, stripped metal screws, several nuts and bolts and a couple of black markers.

The quad and travel trailer were transported back to the Edmonton forensics lab under heavy RCMP police escort to maintain the chain of evidence and be examined by analysts. RCMP euphoria hit a new high when the scientists discovered latent fingerprints on the underside of a propane tank handle. The bracket was old and rusty, and officers speculated that the suspect used gloves whenever handling the tanks but may have had difficulty loosening the bracket and took one glove off to manipulate the small wing-nut. All four fingers provided clear prints which were removed for computer analysis. They found other prints on the quad battery cover under the seat and index prints on two of the black markers.

The prints were immediately processed by the Canadian Police Information Centre, CPIC and CHAP, the world-wide system designed by the American SEAL, Captain Cheryl Chapman. Already discussed

Their first hit was with CPIC on a Brian Sawyer who was in the national system when he was finger printed for security clearance by the Alberta Oil industry. Further checking found Sawyer had left the industry several years previously after being laid off when production fell with the drop in international oil prices. Officers could find no further employment, but they did uncover a photo of him in his early twenties, computer enhanced it to cover the unemployment time and circulated it immediately to the Alberta Rural Crime Watch Association whose thousands of members are ranchers, agricultural and fuel merchants, grocery store managers and ordinary citizens who act as eyes and ears of the RCMP.

RCW merchants spent hours perusing old digital video - Albertans don't throw anything out - looking for Sawyer in their place of business during the last number of years.

Simultaneously, officers sent Sawyer's prints and photo to Canadian and American Border Agents. Both agencies scanned Sawyer's photo into their systems, which was then analyzed by their security software. Border agents knew the investigation's background as they too were tied into CHAP, so the RCMP request received top priority.

The Edmonton detachment hosted a state-of-the-art operations room which enabled detectives to utilize massive wall mounted screens interlaced with digital video software perfected by various Fortune 500 companies for interoffice training and conferencing. The twenty-plus seasoned detectives conferred simultaneously with CSIS agents in Ottawa, American and Canadian Border agents and Staff Sgt. McDonald, CST. Drought and the entry team.

The RCMP investigators came and went from the conference room throughout their shifts, leaving for a spell to check on other investigations, then return when their video conferencing app signaled the arrival of new information.

It was during one of these lulls that investigators were recalled. American Border Agents had found Sawyer being processed at the southern Alberta border crossing. While their senior officers were conferring with Edmonton and CSIS, they took the liberty of bringing the Secret Service into the conversation with supervisor Sorrento joining the discussion. In addition, they notified the Idaho State Police which dispatched officers to the various communities immediately south of the border to look for the pick-up identified in Sawyer's crossing video.

The investigative pace was moving quickly and within an hour, Idaho officers found the truck parked in Bonners Ferry, thirty minutes south of the border, in Heavy Wreckers compound.

Troopers were told that the truck had been left at the Boundary County Airport passed the maximum long-term parking and management lacked any valid contact information. The vehicle being old and without value, it was towed and stored by Heavy Wreckers which would eventually sell it at auction.

Troopers impounded the vehicle, sealed the doors with forensic tape and, time being of the essence, commissioned Heavy Wreckers to transport it immediately to the closest State Police lab in Coeur d' Alene.

Boundary Airport was where Colton Moore, the nineteen-year old Barefoot Bandit stole a Cessna 182 Turbo airplane, flew it over the Cascade Mountains and crashed in Granite Falls, Washington. Walking away from the destruction, he continued his theft across America, fleeing to the Bahamas where he was eventually arrested and extradited to Seattle.

In discussing Sawyer with airport managers, they hoped to have similar success in tracking him as their colleagues had with Moore. They were disappointed.

Managers brought up Sawyer's flight plan data which indicated a flight to Seattle but that was never confirmed. Backtracking, they determined that his aircraft, which he had flown in and out of Boundary for years, had sufficient fuel for several hundred miles before requiring refueling. Troopers speculated that Sawyer could have landed in any number of isolated airports throughout the US undetected and disappeared.

Registration data for Sawyer's plane was sent immediately to the State Trooper's headquarters which logged it into CHAP.

"Three things cannot be long hidden: the sun, the moon, and the truth."

Buddha

Chapter THIRTEEN

Penelope and Rebecca walked down the street arm in arm and often head to head, laughing and sharing their good fortunate to have both a new friend and what appeared to be, a successful financier to guide them to financial security, allowing them to pursue their philanthropic goals.

Once in the car, Penelope drove them to the police station while Rebecca shared her idea of helping teenage girls. "Pen, one of my life goals is to give back to girls. I was very fortunate to have two parents who provided me with love, a nice home, an education and motivation to excel as an adult. Many girls don't have that. What do you think of starting something here in Santa Barbara?"

Without turning her head, Penelope replied, "I totally agree Rebecca. I come from a similar background with folks who supported even my wildest and craziest dreams and actions and I remember girls from high school and a few from university who were on their own. Many floundered and a lot failed. What do you have in mind?"

"Several things actually. The first one is self-defense. I didn't learn it until I was a deputy sheriff and then that was tame compared to what I learned with the Secret Service. I want girls to develop a mind-set that will enable them not to hesitate to strike out at a threat. So, I want to teach that. Then I was thinking about asking several of the women counselors from the local sexual assault survivor's group to give seminars on what girls can expect as they enter womanhood, how to navigate life on their terms, not society's. What do you think so far? Too heavy maybe, particularly the last one?"

Pen turned her head briefly as she approached a stop light, then back again and said, "Not at all. I love the self-defense lessons. Maybe that could be where I learn it as well and if you think I need to crank it up a notch from what you teach the girls, we can do that at the ranch. The counselors though, I would recommend we leave the agenda to them and not prompt one way or another. We want this to be perpetual and not draw attention from the media. With the #MeToo and #Times Up agendas, I can see a certain journalist element seeking an angle."

"You are probably right. I get myself so psyched up about this issue, I tend to lose focus. We are going to make a good team. You can keep me on track," she replied, reaching over and brushing the hair from Penelope's right ear and caressing her neck.

"You better stop that, or we won't make it to the cop shop at all."

Rebecca let her arm grace Pen's shoulder, then sat back smiling and continued the conversation. "What about having several cosmetologists give lessons on skin care and make-up, also a hair stylist to provide tips on quality hair care, give away a ton of products, things like that.

"I will wager that Alane has connections with Hollywood and make-up artists and we can get one of the Westwood department stores to donate the products. No, on second thought, I want to pay for everything. Oh, and I like what you just said, this will be ongoing, with say twenty girls at a time, with parent or guardian permission," she was getting excited and her voice was rising, so she took a breath and continued, "I also want to make arrangements with several of the shops in town, if they are interested in taking the girls to Nordstrom at Paseo Nuevo for clothes. There, I think I have it all out. What do you think?"

"I am with you on everything but to really be a part of this I need to participate financially. Are you okay with that?" again, straight faced, not taking her eyes off the road.

"Are you sure? This was my idea and I don't want you to feel that you are getting roped into anything. Sorry for the pun, force of habit," she concluded with a smile, referring to her rodeo days.

Penelope couldn't see her face as she was pulling into the police station lot and held her comment until she had parked, then turned to Rebecca to see her massive grin and said, "You con artist. You were going to let me pay half all the time, weren't you?"

"Of course," she laughed, but it must be our ideas, not just mine. What are your thoughts?"

They sat while the car idled, Penelope thinking. Finally, she responded, "I really think teens, both boys and girls, need career counseling at an early age and they are not getting it in junior high or high school. What if we had professional career placement personnel work with them, asking pertinent questions and coming back in a week or two with career options, education needed etc. Not school counselors. I feel they are already over-burdened with helping kids emotionally to ask them to stretch themselves further. I also think that these kids need to see that college or university is open to them financially. I'm not sure how we can work that but between the two of us and some creative financial planning we can come up with a way. How would that blend with your concept?"

Rebecca undid her seatbelt, reached across the console, grasped Pen's face between her hands and gently kissed her lips, then her nose and said, "Perfectly. We have a plan. How about we get these permits and get this lifestyle moving?"

Penelope smiled, kissed her back, undid her seatbelt and exited the car, rounding the front to join Rebecca as they made their way into the police station.

The stark white building, with its red tile roof was what one would expect in a city of Spanish architecture dating back to the sixteen-hundreds. Explorer Sebastian Vizcaino and later Gaspar de Portola with Franciscan priest Junipero Serra heralded in the Spanish New World hacienda style. Its exterior palette blended with the multitude of accompanying buildings, capturing the Mediterranean flavor and heritage with its numerous rotundas and massive, arched, entry way and front door.

The duo made their way under the arch, through the front door and were met by stately twenty-foot ceilings and more curved archways leading to hallways and offices. The interior was a combination of stucco and brick walls and six by six wooden beams, with those in the ceiling being colossal and at least twelve by twelve.

What they found interesting immediately, and in contrast to the majority of police departments Rebecca had been to, was the lack of bullet-proof glass across the Information area. Instead, it was adorned with a highly polished ornate wooden front and counter top.

Rebecca introduced themselves to the civilian staffer and asked to speak with the duty sergeant, handing over her portfolio of documents.

The employee excused herself and was replaced by another as Rebecca and Penelope stepped aside to allow another person to enquire.

By anyone's count, it couldn't have been two minutes before a woman appeared out of the long, arched hallway. Stunning in a J. Crew bright persimmon, fitted blazer with ample room under the arms for her holster. It appeared to be of a lightly stretching material that would give with her movement as would her vibrant, multi-patch, Conceited print, buttery-stretch, leggings. She paired the outfit with a stunning Vince Camuto, Feteena Bootie in a French taupe swede. The open-toed, three & one-half-inch block heel accented the stacked, slim leather straps and side zipper. She walked up to them and said, "Agent Simpson and Dr. Barker, I am Detective Elise Pelfini. Welcome to Santa Barbara. The chief is inviting you to join him and me back in his office and we can discuss how to expedite your applications and, I must warn you, the chief is a former Secret Service agent and very affable," she said with a smile as she led the way back down the corridor.

Entering a modest office decorated in a masculine fashion, was the extension of the Spanish influence of the exterior and vestibule. A six by four walnut desk appeared in the far back facing a corner window, which looked out on a flowered courtyard. A visitor might have expected the dark paneled walls to embrace heavy Mediterranean furniture, but what lay before them was a seating arrangement of two, eight-foot couches in an off-white linen with yellow California wildflowers, facing each other across a contemporary four by eight-foot glass coffee table adorned with bronze, ornate wrought iron legs. Four matching end tables with tall, LED lighted, bronze reading lamps with off-white pastoral shades accompanied each couch. At each end of the seating area were two matching occasional chairs. A large Persian rug, patterned in red Hibiscus with oatmeal background, tied the color scheme together as it lay between the seating area and the desk.

Rising from a couch was a man in his mid-fifties, with a somewhat military posture carrying around one-hundred and eighty pounds on a slim frame. His shoulders were not broad but tapered to a narrow waist and flat stomach. His face was square with medium length red hair, turning slightly gray at the temples, ever so slightly noticeable. His dark complexion and red hair created a perplexing analysis: Irish and Latino heritage? His two button, caramel suit with narrow lapels, was well cut for his shape and complimented his skin tone.

"Good morning Agent Simpson and Dr. Barker, I'm Rodrigo O'Connor, please join me for a tasa de café and some delicious pastries from Pasteleria de Ricardo right down the street," he offered with an arm gesture to the couch.

Well, there answers my question about his heritage, thought Rebecca, as she smiled to herself, picturing O'Connor's parents as stunning exemplifications of their combined heritage.

The duo walked over to the couch, shook hands with O'Connor and sat on the opposite sofa while Pelfini joined the chief facing them.

"Welcome to Santa Barbara and to our humble law enforcement oficina. I must say Agent Simpson your reputation honorably precedes you. Although I was in treasury for twenty, your notoriety in the service is legend."

"Thank you, Chief O'Connor, I appreciate the compliment. But it is Rebecca and although I have lived in Santa Barbara on my furloughs, I never took the opportunity to observe our police department, otherwise we would have met some time ago."

"Rebecca it is then, and I am Rodrigo. I see from your applications that you have incorporated in the business name of R&P Investigations. Might I ask what you anticipate your investigative specialty to involve?" he offered, pouring four cups of very black coffee into large, off-white, ornate mugs, then passing the plate of pastries, first to his guests, then Pelfini and finally taking one himself.

All four tasted the pastry, took several sips of coffee, then it was Penelope who picked up the conversation. Wiping her mouth with a cloth napkin, she said with a grin, "Our business will not entail divorce cases. We will deal primarily with business and investor investigations, vetting for both prospective buyers and sellers. It is unlikely we will be involved in any criminal cases, but we certainly wouldn't close the door on the possibility at some point later on."

"I am glad you mentioned criminal cases Dr. Barker and I hope you will not rule out involving yourselves in that genre. With Rebecca's impeccable investigative track record and yours for detail and complexity, I have a suspicion our department could use your services."

"Thank you, Rodrigo for the warm invitation, and it is Penelope please. We would like to share an idea with you both and get your reaction to ensure we are on the right track. Rebecca?"

"Thanks Penelope. Rodrigo and Elise, during the ten plus years I have been a Santa Barbara resident I have seen an alarming growth in the homeless population, particularly among teenage girls. We are sure you see it frequently, that a street person makes them vulnerable to sexual assault, reduces or eliminates any life goals and puts them on a downward spin. We know the city is doing as much as it can to help, particularly with the homeless who are living in their vehicles, with the free night parking in city lots, but these kids don't drive and often don't want to go to social services for fear of being put into the system.

"We are going to organize a committee to create a weekly program at one of the community centers that will offer free self-defense classes, counseling by women from our sexual assault survival centers, hair, make-up and clothing seminars from professionals, career counseling from executive recruiters, as well as lunch and transportation if need be.

We aren't seeking your endorsement, although that would be appreciated. What we would like is the department's participation on the committee with a couple of your officers who could teach defensive tactics. It would help delivering the message as well as enable your officers to connect with them in a more neutral environment.

"We won't be seeking city financial support or their involvement in any other manner. If you would rather observe at arm's length, that is okay too. We wanted to share the idea with you both, get your feedback and any suggestions you may have."

"I have taught self-defense for some time, all to women and teens and I want in," smiled Elise as she sat forward on the couch, emphasizing her enthusiasm, "and I know Chief O'Connor will approve. I might be able to help with a cosmetologist and make-up artist too. Let me ask around."

"That is tremendous Elise. We didn't know your background but were hoping you would participate. What we are concerned about from the get-go is media coverage. We are not saying we want to keep the activity a secret, but we want to keep a low profile and certainly not allow the media into the community center," replied Rebecca.

O'Connor was sitting far back on the couch, sipping the last of his coffee, listening intently when he slid forward, placed his mug on the coffee table and offered, "I can cover that angle. I will ask a select few of my officers to volunteer their services to cover the doors, but it would go over more smoothly if they received an honorarium. How do you plan to finance this?"

Penelope chimed in with her response, "We have private citizens, philanthropists actually, (the women wanted to keep their financial involvement quiet for now), who have offered to cover all costs. We know them personally and can vouch for their integrity and motivation. We hope you can trust us on that aspect."

Rodrigo laughed and said, "Hell, if we can't trust a Secret Service Agent and a woman who has devoted her life to the care of animals, who can we trust?" Refilling his mug, he continued, "Seriously, that won't be an issue and we can work out the details later.

"But back to the homeless issue just so you get the big picture. Santa Barbara has had a homeless population for as far back as anyone can remember. We are an attraction for any number of reasons; the weather, beaches and some say it is because we do too much to ease their situation. The recent count showed about three-hundred less than the twenty-five-hundred a few years ago. Folks tend to be very mobile, as you can imagine, so the numbers could be way off.

"Last year the city granted 1.2 million to various agencies to provide shelter, supportive services, rental subsidies and similar assistance programs and they are hoping to do more this year. Critics claim that helping to get them off the streets is what is drawing more and more to the area. Some cities, such as Vancouver, have purchased former department stores, other cities, former motels and remodeled them into studio apartments with complete health services. We could do something like that here, the medical services being covered by Medi-Cal and California Coverage. I think it just takes creative thinking and your idea falls into that category. This concept being somewhat unorthodox will need some backing from not necessarily local or state government representatives but a few of those who can influence them. I wouldn't be surprised if you get several pro-homeless counselors to bend your ear down the road.

"I hope that clarifies our situation. How else may we help?"

Pen and Rebecca exchanged glances, nodded to each other and Penelope replied, "We appreciate the clarification Chief and I promise not to piss people off before we get their support," she grinned and looked at Rebecca, acknowledging her former comment about them being a good team. She continued, "We are having a dinner party at the ranch this Thursday for some friends and neighbors, sort of a welcome for ourselves to Santa Barbara and we'd love to have you two join us and whomever you want to bring, if doing so isn't against department policy."

"Rodrigo looked at Elise and said, "I can't speak for Detective Pelfini, but it is not against policy. Our social life is our business. I will be there and bring my plus one. I hope you are ready to receive an ear full of the east-side home owners, if any of them are invited," he laughed, then continued, "What time?"

"6ish or whenever you get off duty," responded Rebecca, "and thanks for the heads-up. I suspect we will have a diverse crowd," she said clapping her hands together and laughing, keeping Alane's participation to herself for the moment.

"Count me in. I know James will want to attend. Oh, and by the way, he is kind of a computer guru and would enjoy participating, setting up an organizing software system. if you are amenable to his input. What can we bring?" chimed Elise.

Rebecca acknowledged Elise with, "Terrific. It should be a good time. And yes, we would love to have James help us out. Neither of us are that computer literate to develop something complex.

"Do either of you know Alane Auberée of Birdcage Investments? He and I have been friends for what seems forever. He has taken on the task of preparing the dinner and will be bringing some of his friends, so really, all we must do is show up. My neighbor, Alejandro, I know will want to provide all the appetizers and Penelope and I will make sure there is plenty of wine. So, we are good? We will see you on Thursday?" She was curious as to how they knew her residence but considered that a Pandora's Box she wasn't prepared to open...just yet.

"I don't know either gentleman, but I am looking forward to the pleasure. We will see you on Thursday. But before you head out, let me get those permits for you. We will fingerprint, take your photos here and provide you with a temporary permit. The plastic will be mailed from Sacramento. Penelope, I will approve yours subject to Rebecca's supervision as you noted on the application. Rebecca, yours is straight forward and I will sign the private investigator's license right now. Sacramento will have a fit but that is their concern. The law gives me the power to approve the license and that is what is happening. I am delighted to have you two as permanent residents and even more so as members of our law enforcement community...by extension," he added, heading to his desk and drawing up a document on his screen, printing two copies and signing both.

ॐ.β.ॐ

Once Sawyer's airplane identification information appeared in CHAP, the data flashed across one of the massive screens in the Edmonton RCMP investigation room. The screen showed all the pertinent information regarding the new registration in Houston, Texas: name, address, and phone number. Investigators immediately contacted the commanding officer at the HPD, had him draw up CHAP with the officer quickly dispatching detectives to the owner's home to bring him in to their office for questioning.

ॐ.β.ॐ

Secret Service supervisor Sorento was musing over a report from his counterpart in Treasury regarding an undercover agent in the Caribbean. She had been there as a teller for several years and had observed large quantities of cash arriving regularly. Her local informant told her about an American plane that arrives at the local airport regularly, passes customs seemingly effortlessly, then disgorges one female passenger and two crew members. The agent recorded the serial numbers of numerous bills and emailed the information from her encrypted phone to Treasury headquarters in Washington.

Tracing the serial numbers, agents tracked the currency to California's west coast but couldn't pinpoint the exact location. That information was shared with CHAP, a copy of which Sorento was now reading and trying to determine why he was included in the distribution of this information. *What is the connection between possible money laundering, which is the purview of the Treasury Department, and protecting the president?* he thought to himself.

S.B.S

Back in their car, Rebecca turned to Penelope before she started the engine and said, "Before we go any further, let's find out with whom we are dealing here. That was a complete surprise to me and probably to you too. Secret Service? Treasury? I don't believe in coincidences. I want to know if this guy is really retired or was forced out and little ole Santa Barbara hired itself a doofus.

"I am going to text Jessica and get the low-down on O'Connor. Would you check out Pelfini? She said she had taught self-defense and before we develop a working relationship with her and the girls, we need to know. We're not in any hurry, we can do this and be satisfied, then go get us some cars." she added with a grin.

Chapter FOURTEEN

California's coastal weather, just north of Santa Monica, was wrapped in a low fog with a light drizzle, obliterating all visibility within a few meters of any vessel foolish enough to navigate the treacherous waters. The Scottish Moors-like environment kept all inside as midnight approached.

Two kilometers from shore, the Germanischer Lloyd maximized its speed for five-hundred meters, then the pilot pulled the lever disengaging the Chica de Oro, allowing it to progress to shore under its own momentum, then the mini turned west where it remained just below the surface with its mini-periscope barely breaking the water surface, as it monitored the next phase of its supervision.

As the Golden Girl approached Point Conception, the captain raised its periscope to follow the blinking light from the bluff above the landing beach. Ready for the delivery was a Hermanos de Wall Street five-ton cab-over truck, parked with a flexible conveyor belt running from the top of the bluff to the beach, powered by the truck's electrical unit. Extending from the front of the truck, under the vehicle's carriage, was a cable which snaked its way down the sandy bluff to the water's edge.

As the Hermanos de Wall Street lieutenant watched expectantly from the beach, armed with an H&K submachine gun with suppressor and retractable buttstock slung across his chest with a tactical sling, the Golden Girl's nose blasted out of the pounding surf, its metallic silver monstrous shape broke through the crashing surf and assaulted the beach with such force, the waiting crew ran for protection behind boulders.

Within seconds, the sub came to an abrupt stop, a loading crew member grabbed the cable end and snapped it into the U ring on the sub's nose to prevent the undertow from pulling the giant backwards. Momentarily, the sub crew members emerged one by one, each armed with an Israeli IWI X95, better known as a Micro-Tavor, a nine-millimeter weapon with a folding stock, sound suppressor, tactical sling and a thirty-two-round magazine which they had stolen from the Columbian military.

The Hermanos de Wall Street lieutenant walked through the surf to the sub's nose, closing the gap for a more accurate shooting distance if needed and to hear the code phrase over the roar of the surf.

"How are the Dodgers playing? Didn't they just win a game?" was the question from the retired American sub commander.

The lieutenant replied, "Pretty well. They beat the Angels 3-2 on Sunday."

It was either going to be correct or the sub commander was ordered to kill everyone on the beach.

It was correct.

The commander turned slightly to the crew member behind him, keeping an eye on the beach crew with his weapon trained on them and within moments the first bricks appeared, and the unloading began.

No one spoke, many because they were intimidated by the presence of the automatic weapons, others because they were professionals and knew banter was wasted energy and a one-way ticket to prison.

From the sub to the chain line, to the conveyor belt, the cocaine made its way to the top of the bluff where it systematically was loaded into the truck. Five-thousand kilograms of cocaine cling-wrapped in ten, one kilo bricks, equated to five hundred, ten kilo packages with a street value of eighty-five dollars a gram before it is cut for distribution to street dealers. Five-thousand kilos is five-hundred-thousand grams, times eight-five dollars equates to a pay load of four-hundred and twenty-five million dollars before being cut for street distribution.

Although the cost of a gram of cocaine at its source may be the price of an American hamburger at $3.50 per gram, transportation overhead increases the cost the further from Columbia it is purchased. This shipment is a massive profit for Hermanos de Wall Street.

The Cinca de Oro unloaded without incident, the beach crew disconnected the retaining cable, the Golden Girl's crew disappeared into the silver nose and within minutes it stealthily backed into the surf and sunk beneath the surface. While the Hermanos de Wall Street crew hauled the collapsible conveyor belt to the bluff, rewound the cable, secured the vehicle and corkscrewed its way through the dense fog up to the main road, the mini-sub located the GPS end of the towing rope which was just below the water's surface, being buoyed by an air-filled coupling, manipulated the connection. The submersed flotilla then began its return journey to its Columbian base where it would be hidden from the military drug squads, both Columbian and American, until the buyer confirmed an unfettered delivery and distribution, at which time the Golden Girl would make a return trip.

Some dealers use powdered sugar, boric acid, mannitol, known as a diuretic, as well as any number of similar products, including fentanyl, the combination of which has proven to be a killer of addicts. What the street dealers did with their product was of little concern to the Hermanos de Wall Street organization. Their primary emphasis was the secrecy and accuracy of delivery. Since the winery was owned by a member, there was minimal chance of an investigative trail. The individual dealers were also business men and women whose policies and procedures ruled out any flashbacks from their street sellers, those who contact users.

None of the participants were aware their actions had been monitored from the beach and that unexpected visitors would arrive momentarily.

ℑₒℬℑ

Jessica had just exited the passenger tube and was heading for the taxi stand when her encrypted phone vibrated. She slid into the nearest women's restroom, entered a stall and opened her phone. Appearing on the screen was a text from Sorento, *Tomorrow. As early as you can. Here. Acknowledge.*

Without any thought, she immediately tapped in her code, hit send and returned the unit to her inside pocket. Exiting the stall and the restroom, she continued her way to the taxi kiosk thinking to herself, *well so much for a few days off. I will have to let Karen know.*

This is going to be the absolute shits for her to travel here and have me stuck in the White House.

S.B.S

The millions in cash that was supposed to be exchanged in the winery warehouse would be hand delivered to the Hermanos de Wall Street's comptroller, counted in front of him, verified, then deposited in a safe until it was ready to be transported to the Caribbean. He would then send an encrypted email to all members, certifying the amount and the time schedule for its transfer to the Caribbean. The comptroller held a unique position within the organization. In the hierarchy, he was just below the founding members who trusted him explicitly. He had worked for the Secretary of the Treasury for two decades when Marianna Gutierrez made him an offer he couldn't refuse; a new identity, control of millions and early retirement with a lifestyle he could only dream about as a treasury agent.

Only this time, Comptroller Harrison would not be making a delivery.

Chapter FIFTEEN

Jessica took a cab to her flat and once in the driveway, she immediately checked on her Gecko, undistinguishable beyond dusty grey but the shape still perceivable as a Volkswagen Beatle. She tried unsuccessfully to blow some of the dust off and open the door, changed her mind and decided to get the feather duster from her flat and tackle the problem later. She refused to go to the White House in a cab…the Gecko was her signature. Well, that, her clothes and her attitude. *I wonder if anyone will notice a change*, she thought, referring to the latter, not the former. She stood by the main door and phoned her landlady, the only other tenant in the building.

"Hello. Talk to me. Nobody calls me on this thing. Why don't you call me on the real phone?"

"Mrs. Esposito, it's Jessica. I don't have the new door code. I am at the front door. Might I bother you to let me in?"

"Jessica. Oh, my God Jessica, it has been so long. Yes, yes, I will be right down."

Momentarily a sixties something woman came barging out the door and flung herself into Jessica, giving her hugs and kisses. "Jessica, I have been so worried about you. I read in the papers about that terrible crash and all those nasty people. Then the election and that man in the White House. I hope you don't have to work for him. You aren't going to have to protect him are you Jessica? He is a nasty, nasty, man," she finally came up for air then continued. "Oh, my, I am talking too much. Come, come, dear, let me open the door for you and get you a cup of tea."

As Mrs. Esposito keyed the pad and opened the door, Jessica entered with her carry-on, held the door for her landlady, closed it and keyed her flat's door. Turning to her neighbor, she apologized and said, "Mrs. Esposito. I am beat and must be at work first thing in the morning. How about we pass on the tea and you come in for a glass of wine?"

Clapping her hands together exhibiting a broad smile she replied, "That is even better dear. But first let me get some olives, garlic taralli and prosciutto. I will be right back."

As she hurried across the hall, Jessica entered her flat, disengaged the alarm, then stopped immediately and smiled, the kind of deep, heart moving facial expression brought on by the actions of another, something someone has done for you, unexpected, unasked for and special.

Her flat was clean with fresh flowers on the coffee and dining room tables. She dropped her bag, removed her jacket and hung it in the closet just as a knock came to the door. Opening it quickly, she stepped back to allow Mrs. Esposito to enter, arms carrying a massive tray of Italian goodies. She moved quickly to the kitchen, placed all the items on the counter. Jessica closed and locked the door, slipped into the living room and grabbed two bottles of her favorite Maine winery, Cantina unica della Maine, Unique Cellar of Maine; their delicious Madre di ferro, Iron Mother, a rich Cabernet Sauvignon with a touch of Merlot to give it a western Bordeaux taste.

Entering the kitchen, she opened a drawer and retrieved a cork-screw. While she was releasing the wine, Mrs. Esposito was fixing plates of appetizers and turned to Jessica saying, "I am so happy to have you back in one-piece Jessica," she crinkled her face a little and did a shoulder shake and added, "I just love that shoulder holster and your gun. I read so much about women who believe nothing will happen to them and I always yell at the television people, 'You should be like Jessica and have a mind-set, and a gun.'"

Jessica couldn't help but laugh at this charming and lovely lady who had been her neighbor for so many years she had forgotten the number and always took her advice regarding personal safety, albeit not carrying a firearm…yet.

When she arrived in D.C., she had snagged this spacious two-bedroom, two-bath flat here at Sedgwick House, a quaint historical mansion transformed into two spacious, modern flats, ten minutes from the White House. She'd enjoyed decorating in a quiet manner with furnishings from West Elm Furniture in DC. They weren't as expensive as she had anticipated so she was able to spend a little extra on the window trimmings and bathroom accessories. It was her hideaway from the hectic Washington pace where she could hold up for days, reading and pigging out on Giovani's pizza, one of her favorite local eateries.

Her flat looked more masculine than most women would enjoy but she liked to soak in the leather's fragrance, the red hue walls, and the paintings of east coast landscapes. She contrasted this with silk and frills in the bedroom and master bath. She kept the guest bath, bedroom and office neutral, offering herself and guests an enjoyable balance.

Jessica poured the wine, then carried both to the living room, placed them on the coffee table, and turned on soft jazz background music just as Mrs. Esposito arrived with the appetizers.

They sat, clinked glasses and Jessica thanked her profusely for the clean flat, to which her land lady replied, "You are most welcome dear. Think nothing of it. You asked me to keep an eye on your place and this was my way of doing so, and keeping an emotional connection to you, sending prayers for your safety."

They chatted for quite some time, Mrs. Esposito filling Jessica in on Washington's news, the White House, her children and grandchildren and Jessica reciprocating as much as she could, primarily highlighting her personal interactions with staff and particularly Chef Marc Stucki and his exquisite cuisine.

The sun had long set when Mrs. Esposito glanced out the window, then her watch and said, "Oh my, time has run away from us. I must get going and let you get some rest," as she got up and picked up the empty plates and wine bottles. "I have had such a lovely time Jessica catching up, I didn't realize we had consumed both bottles of your lovely Iron Mother Bordeaux." Placing the plates in the dishwasher, she turned to take the wine glasses from Jessica, gave her a hug and as she headed for the door, stopped and gave Jessica one last hug and said, "Welcome back again dear. I am terribly happy you are okay and back home."

Jessica hugged her back, thanked her again for her thoughtfulness, opened the door and watched her enter her flat across the hall, closed the door, set the alarm and wandered into her bedroom where she set her alarm for five, stripped completely, placing her semi-automatic on the nightstand, climbed into bed and was asleep almost before she had completely snuggled under the covers.

ŠŌŠ

Fukishura rose at her regular time, an alarm almost being superfluous she had risen at this hour for so many years. She completed her bathroom routine, donned her M n M's colorful sweat pants, T, fanny pack with her Sig, runners and was out the door in fifteen.

Forty-five minutes later, she was in and out of the shower, then stood naked in her walk-in closet, relishing in the beautiful wardrobe she had been unable to enjoy during her Wyoming deployment. Her eye immediately caught Armani's three-button jacket & classic two-button pant. She loved the jacket as it was generously cut to cover her Sig but still slimming. Grabbing the outfits off the hangers, she paired them with black riding boots by Marc Jacobs.

Dressed, she did a mirror 360, spinning on her raised right toe as was her habit in checking her surroundings. Satisfied with her look, she shrugged in to her shoulder holster, removed the Sig from the fanny-pack, pulled the slide slightly to view the chambered round and slid the firearm in to the holster.

Glancing at her watch, she realized she didn't have any food in the house. Laughing at her own forgetfulness, she headed for the door, planning to take advantage of Sorento's generous supply of baked goods and his New Mexican coffee.

Her hand was on the doorknob when she realized she had forgotten the feather duster. Slapping her palm against her forehead, she spun around, quickly walked into the kitchen and grabbed the duster. Back at the door, she keyed the security pad, opened the door, looked left and right, closed the door, checked that it was locked, then bounded down the stairs.

Standing as far back as possible, she gave The Bug a quick windshield and driver's door a dusting, fobbed entry, then headed for her favorite car wash near the city center. The Square was the only facility open early and without a line, she drove right to the unmanned payment kiosk, swiped her credit card, drove ahead, placed The Bug in park and took a few minutes during the process to contemplate her meeting with Sorento. *What could be so important that he wanted me in the very morning I got back from StoneHead. Not even a couple of days off. Kinda shitty,* she thought.

The five-minute experience was completed with a loud clanging sound accompanied by the exit door open and flashing lights and *Thank You For Your Business. Please Exit,* in bright neon above the door. Startled from her revere, she put the vehicle in drive and headed for whatever lay ahead.

꒯.ℬ꒯

Edmonton's RCMP detachment's investigators received information back from Texas regarding the airplane they believed Brian Sawyer flew out of Idaho.

The new owners were a couple who had been vacationing in Limón, Costa Rica and bought the Cessna 182 Turbo for thousands less than they could ever find in Texas. Paying in American cash, they had little difficulty with the paper-work and flew it home within a couple of days purchase.

When that information appeared on the big screen from CHAP, the members gave each other high-fives and placed a call to David Kopas of CSIS.

Chapter SIXTEEN

Penelope and Rebecca found their vehicle shopping an experience they wouldn't want to have to repeat. Neither had purchased a car for ages; Penelope had her work one-ton Dodge dually, acquired through her practice and Rebecca had never bought a vehicle…ever. Not unless she counted the beater she had in college and teaching. She had given it away when she joined the Secret Service.

The first two dealers they visited, the salesmen hit on them. It pissed the women off so much, they told the guy to go fuck himself, got in their rental and peeled off the lot.

Chastising themselves for not thinking of Alane, they made a quick call to his office and he stifled a laugh, congratulated them on meeting Santa Barbara's low-life businessmen, then regained his composure, gave them the name and number of a dealer without a car lot or office.

Having had the phone on speaker, Rebecca looked at Penelope, raised her eyebrow, wrote the number down, thanked Alane, closed the app, then said, "What do you think? Is this weird or what?"

"Totally, but then that is Alane, from what I can glean from our first meeting. I think his contact will be an auto broker. Let's give him a call and see what's what."

They made the call. It was answered on the third ring; not too soon and not more than four rings. Busy but responsible. They put the phone on speaker and chatted with Kenneth of Westwood Classic Automobile

Brokerage. Rebecca opened with Alane's recommendation, listened to Kenneth's accolades of his friend and moved quickly into what type, year and price range of vehicles they were seeking.

The women had discussed the issue at length and originally thought they would get one SUV and a smaller economy car but the more they thought about it, neither wanted to drive a car so they opted for two late model mid-size Jeeps, preferably one yellow and the other cobalt blue.

Kenneth laughed a friendly tone and said he would be delighted to find their choice vehicles. He obtained their phone number and promised to get back to them within two days.

After ending the call, Penelope said, "Very weird. I have never heard of a vehicle broker before, but then I have never lived in Southern California."

"Me neither," replied Rebecca. "How about that swim plus we need to come up with the guest list for the dinner party."

"Sounds good to me. Let's do it." and with that they headed back to the ranch to figure out the rest of their day and how they wanted to configure their business model, while enjoying a little of California's boasted sunshine and pool time.

SBS

Jessica had just exited the car wash and was heading to the White House a few blocks away when her personal cell chimed. Hitting the hands-free on the dashboard, she answered, "Good morning, Jessica here."

"I don't know Jessica, if I can get used to this new phone etiquette," she laughed, then added, "I just landed and am getting a taxi. If I can get your address, I can be there shortly."

"You are hearing the new me, Ms. Congeniality," she replied, acknowledging Karen's voice immediately, then realized her error and added, "Aw, crap Karen. I'm sorry. I forgot to call you. I got called into the White House last night and am on my way there now. How about you tell the driver to drop you off at the White House front gate and I will have a pass waiting for you and meet you at the first security kiosk. I will introduce you to my boss and you can try some of his awesome New Mexico coffee. How about it?"

Forgetting the Ms. Congeniality quip, Karen said, "Sure, I'm for it. This might be exciting. I have never been to the White House. I'm on my way."

"Okay. See you in a bit, and I am sorry I didn't call Karen," Jessica replied and hit the off button on the dash before Karen could reply and just as she was pulling into the White House driveway.

Chapter SEVENTEEN

Secret Service Agents Jason Spencer, Elisabeth Peltowski and Jackson Pennington were becoming anxious and bored with their holding pattern assignment.

Being assigned to the LAPD Anti-Terrorism Squad was understandable while Fukishura wrapped up the CFBA investigation and the "J" Team was reassigned, but they didn't know how long they could hold out without saying something to their law enforcement colleagues they would regret.

They had been spoiled, career wise, for they had just their immediate colleagues with whom to coordinate, not hundreds. It seemed that everyone from the squad's captain, down through the ranks couldn't decide or move without obtaining approval from someone else.

They had been in Los Angeles for so long, they were starting to feel like residents, or in Jason's case, a returning native. He was visiting his mom frequently, more so during this time than in the past five years. She was delighted but wondered if he was in trouble with his boss and not allowed to return to the "J" Team. Jason thought it was sweet that his mom was concerned for his career, never realizing how much she thought of him during his absences.

Jackson and Elisabeth continued to live in the Marina del Rey hotel out of a suitcase, although all three agents had made numerous clothing and accessory purchases during their temporary assignment and didn't consider themselves fashionably deprived.

The gym, the beach, various cultural events and a government per diem that allowed them to leave their salaries untouched, kept their boredom at arm's length and yet anxious to return to the "J" Team for their adrenaline fix.

The debris from the vehicles' explosions had long since been cleared, forensics had found evidence in the Suburbans, but it was minimal given they already knew the vehicles were detonated by a drone. The rubble from the destroyed convention center had been cleared and rebuilding had begun.

Joe Sarkowski, the CFBA drone operator and organizational key-pin was dead after jumping off his hotel balcony immediately after releasing the flying detonator. Tracking his movements wasn't difficult and in doing so they found a complete dossier which the "J" Team had compiled during the early investigation of CFBA in StoneHead, Wyoming.

Sarkowski's spouse Martha and her brother, Harold Richards, were in FBI custody in Minneapolis, having been tracked there by a Secret Service drone operated from the western White House outside of StoneHead. The "J" Team had tracked Sarkowski and Richards since before they hit the CFBA's farm compound outside of StoneHead.

Marrington and Shepherd, the two CFBA controllers of the mountain top compound east of Orofino, Idaho where Jackson had found the barn of explosives, were also in custody, for the second time. This arrest, the government didn't violate their constitutional rights and they were being held without bail until trial. They were arrested with a van of explosives on their way to Los Angeles. The women and children of the compound, having not been implemented in the plot, were not being prosecuted, but without CFBA financial support, were struggling.

Neither the Sarkowskis, Richards, Marrington, Shepherd, nor Senator Khawaja Ashean, of Denver, Colorado, code name, Intrepid, were talking, all having acquired legal representation by a Washington law firm.

Jenewein, the pilot and killer of the graduate student, was in the wind. Denver PD had an arrest warrant out but held little hope of finding him. Every graduate student proved to be oblivious to the big picture regarding their research on explosives and were not detained.

The Department of Environmental Studies was cancelled while the school evaluated the years of research to determine if they were vulnerable for prosecution considering the professor was under arrest.

While a bevy of attorneys worked feverishly to justify their million-dollar retainer, the rest of the country was appalled that the domestic terrorists, those born and educated in America, would stooped to such action to justify their political beliefs.

Many Americans and overseas supporters felt it unfortunate that the U.S. Constitution's Sixth Amendment of the right to counsel and the attorney's Canons of Professional Ethics states, "A lawyer's representation of a client...does not constitute an endorsement of the client's political, economic, social or moral views..." had such an influence on the case.

Terrorism charges and the threat to society were

sufficient for a federal judge to hold all suspects
indefinitely during pre-trial motions and trial
preparations.

enelope and Rebecca stopped off at Gibson's
Market on their way back to the ranch and picked up
pool snacks and groceries for the week. Neither having a
clue as what to purchase, they just put yummy things in
the shopping cart and had a blast doing so. They were
unhurried, laughed at some of the weird sounding names
of jarred epicurean delights, reading the labels and
choosing to pass. Local crab cakes and spicy Thai soup
were recommended by a staffer for their lunch, so they
bought several containers of each as well as ingredients
for appetizers. They found Gibson's to be a progressive
store with small kiosks centered in the wide aisles of
dairy and produce with recipes for appetizers and
entrées.

They chose fingerling potatoes with avocado and
smoked salmon caught off the Santa Barbara coast and
smoked locally. They took a copy of the recipe and were
confident they could razzle Alejandro with their
expertise…well, maybe after a couple of glasses of
chardonnay.

They hadn't ever prepared a meal together and
each had only a rudiment knowledge of the basics when
cooking for themselves, but they liked egg whites, sprout
bread and spicy salsa, so they loaded up on those and
figured they could work out the details as they went

along. For the next few days and particularly this afternoon, they were prepared.

They headed back to the ranch to take advantage of the late afternoon sun, a swim, then invite Alejandro over for appetizers, chardonnay and his input for the party.

S.B.S

Jessica had just made it into the protection detail offices and sent a message to the front gate approving Karen's admittance, when she was told there was a call for her from the front gate.

Karen had arrived by cab as planned, paid and dismissed the driver and after checking with the guard detail, stood at the gate with her carry-on, looking like Anne of Green Gables and her carpetbag when Jessica walked up to the gate, smiling and gesturing her to approach.

Karen went through the security check of her person and bag, was relieved of her Smith & Wesson and Spyderco knife, presented her credentials, then proceeded with Jessica into the White House and finally to the protection detail offices.

Sorento was occupied behind his desk when they knocked at his open door. He was perusing the Treasury data and the latest information on CHAP from the continued CFBA investigation. He was now seeing the relationships in the multi-facet enquiry. The millions passing through the Caribbean were unequivocally from

Southern California and he had to put the pieces of the puzzle together. The question was how and with whom.

"Girl logic urges you to demand respect, but it also reminds you that the path to achieving it can be riddled with name calling, doubt and struggle. No one wants to be feared and hated." Iliza Shlesinger *Girl Logic*

Chapter EIGHTEEN

The knocking jerked Sorento from his concentration. He turned automatically and, expecting a staffer request, maintained a pensive expression until his brain did a quick shift to connect with what his eyes were seeing, and immediately jumped up and said with a smile and warm welcome, "If it isn't our glorious and illustrious Agent Fukishura," he bowed and gave a sweep of his right arm across his chest.

He took the few steps from his desk to the door and extended his hand offering, "Welcome back Jessica!" Not noticing the woman behind Fukishura, he continued, "May I express an appreciation from myself, the Service and the president for an outstanding job. That was an incredible accomplishment by the "J" Team."

"Thank you, sir. It was truly a team effort but one that is far from over. And speaking of that, may I introduce Staff Sgt. Karen Winthrop of the RCMP, currently with Canada's CSIS," she said as she stepped aside, allowing Winthrop to pass.

Karen reached out to shake and said, "It is a pleasure Mr. Sorento. I appreciate the opportunity."

Sorento smiled but was taken aback by the presence of the Canadian. He wondered what Fukishura was doing bringing a friend to a tactical meeting but kept his query to himself and extended his hand, just as he heard a faint hum rising from Winthrop's jacket. Karen withdrew her hand, reached for her phone, apologizing, saying she had to take the call, then stepped outside of the office.

Sorento raised his eyebrows to Jessica who mouthed, *I'm sorry*, with a slight shoulder shrug just as Karen stepped back into the room extending her smartphone on speaker saying, "David, I am here in the White House with Mr. Sorento, head of the protection detail and supervisor Jessica Fukishura. Mr. Sorento, this is David Kopas of the CSIS, my boss."

Sorento seemed more confused, but quickly regained his composure, noticed that the agent used an encrypted phone, acknowledged Kopas, closed his office door and, using his characteristic sweeping arm gesture, invited both agents to have a seat.

Karen and Jessica quickly brought Sorento and Kopas current on what brought the two agents to the White House together, creating a smile from Sorento, mentally acknowledging how much these cops were alike, then asked David to call back on a secure White House line.

After closing the call, Karen returned her phone to the inside pocket of her coral frock coat with lapel collar, long sleeves and front welt pockets which fastened in front with one covered button. She paired the coat with matching ankle length, high waisted pants and olive suede Sole Society Paislee bootie with an accent strap and chunky 2-inch heel.

Sorento had just poured mugs of New Mexico's Pinon coffee when his office phone buzzed. He returned the pot, picked up the phone, waited a moment while the connection was made, routed through the government encryption system, then answered, "Hi David. Thanks for calling back. I am putting you on speaker."

"I am completely in the dark here," started Jessica. "What has happened in the few hours since I left StoneHead?"

"David, do you want to start, and we can chime in as we go?" offered Sorento.

"Okay. Here is what we have so far. Unless the Service was following the case, you wouldn't have a reason to be checking CHAP, but since the cesium was stolen from a Canadian mine and one of our members did the take down of the thieves, we have.

"Let me give you a quick run-down. We found prints on a quad believed to have been used to transport the cesium from the van to a waiting rail car. We know that it arrived in Idaho and was then transported in a coffin to the Minneapolis airport and loaded on a flight to LAX. The rest you know.

"The prints belong to a Brian Sawyer who we believe to have operated an extensive drug operation in an underground bunker, transporting his product via the same rail cars into Idaho.

"When he fled, he did so by crossing the border into Idaho, then flying his personal plane to Costa Rica which we know because we found the plane.

"As you all know, although the joint task force was able to cripple the CFBA, it is not dead, just regrouping. We believe Sawyer's grow operation funded the CFBA and he may have simply switched from Alberta to Costa Rica. If that is the case, then we believe the president remains in danger since the regrouping will not take long and another target will be in motion. If they had succeeded in killing all aboard the Mahalo Airlines flight, the balance of power in Washington would have changed instantly.

"I'll come up for air now. What do you three have?"

Sorento nodded to Winthrop who began, "As you know sir, I just got in to Pearson the other day after having interrogated the surviving cesium thief, obtained the information which the Denver PD used to capture Intrepid. Beyond that, what you have shared is new. Mr. Sorento, your thoughts?"

While Karen was speaking, Sorento had drawn CHAP up on his wall screen, entered his three separate codes and as the investigative data appeared, handed the remote to Jessica as he rejoined the conversation.

"This is fascinating David," nodding to Jessica and Karen, "I just received a file from Treasury regarding currency they traced from the Caribbean. You can read the details on CHAP, but the long and short of it is Treasury believes the money comes from Southern California and is drug related. They had all of it tested and millions have traces of cocaine. The samples they took match perfectly with what the LAPD drug squads have confiscated on the streets.

I brought Jessica back for her "J" Team to spearhead a west-coast enquiry into the origin of this money. With Senator Khawaja Aadhean being a key figure behind CFBA, the FBI is investigating his campaign finances. Political high-rolling supporters donate via check and cash as we know. I'm kind of thinking out loud here, but the FBI suspects his campaigns were funded by the CFBA. We have proof CFBA is financed with drugs out of Alberta, what if they are also backed by the LA drug trade?"

"Excellent hypothesis sir," offered Jessica. Sorento knew her comment was a compliment and not snide or supercilious. The old Jessica, maybe, but he had noticed a softening of her personality, more collegial and less confrontational. He smiled as she continued, "After we took down the two CFBA leaders in the Idaho compound, everything pointed to a well-financed operation with its organizational tentacles spread across the country and possibly elsewhere. Certainly Canada, and there could be a European connection we have yet to make. It is quite conceivable that they are tied to cocaine as well, either in California or Arizona."

Before anyone else could speak, Sorento jumped in with, "Okay, I'm going on this. Let me know what you think. What if I asked the FBI to check out the largest political donors in the last election, that is on record with each candidate. They won't take the politicians' word and they can verify it with Internal Revenue.

The problem the Bureau will have is the donation loop-holes. The rules say a corporation can donate up to $100,00 to a committee. That corporation can be controlled by one person and be a paper unit. That one person can have any number of shell, or paper corporations. Now this might be in our investigative favor because if the Bureau's IT personnel can cross reference donors, we will have some names and locations with which to work. I believe they can do this.

"Let me get Cheryl Chapman in on this conversation," he concluded, and made a quick interoffice call to get the connection.

While everyone waited to hear from Chapman, Kopas spoke, "Karen, I want you and Tom to get down to Costa Rica, check out the plane sale and track down Sawyer. We don't want him arrested just yet, we need to see if he is actively involved in drug smuggling there.

"Costa Rica is active in bringing cocaine from Columbia. Just last year you recall the head of the Costa Rica Public Force, Fuerza Publica, was arrested for trafficking almost two-hundred and fifty kilos of the stuff and recently eight-hundred kilos were found stashed near the Liberia airport. Sawyer could be involved and if so, may lead us to the supply line through Central America.

"I want you and Tom to go as a vacationing couple, use your own money etc. so there isn't a connection to us. Keep me posted and I will in turn, share with Jessica."

Chapman joined the conversation with, "Good morning all. Who do we have this morning?"

"Good morning Commander. Sorento and Fukishura with the Secret Service, Karen Winthrop and David Kopas with Canada's CSIS. Let me bring you current on our conversation and you can chime in."

When Sorento had concluded with his summary, Chapman said, "The Costa Rican law enforcement isn't on CHAP so Winthrop and Hortonn will be going into a somewhat blind situation, just so they know up front. I wouldn't trust encryption in that part of the world and encourage you both to take detailed notes, either written or taped and transcribe to CHAP upon your return to Canada. Fukishura, your team can benefit from CHAP more if you can get Santa Barbara law enforcement to join the system. Right now, LAPD is quite adept with the program as are the Highway Patrol and the California Bureau of Investigation.

"You have all these departments connected which will make your job a great deal easier. What I understand from your previous discussion, this may be a multi-pronged investigation; political money laundering, terrorism financing and drug smuggling. Sorento, will your office take the lead, or will it be a joint task force with Treasury?"

"Thanks Cheryl, this is a joint operation between the Secret Service, the RCMP and CSIS. We will input the FBI's contribution into the investigation, but it will be the three agencies. Keep it small, fluid and progressive. I will be point here from the White House.

"We may find the Russians involved along the way, but so far, we have no information to that effect and the rumors may be all political, but the FBI is frantically seeking a connection between them and the last presidential election. We must be prepared for the eventuality of the FBI becoming more involved, but thanks to you Cheryl, they will have access to all our investigation, leaving all agencies free from butting heads as we have in the past."

Anticipating the conversation was winding down and not wanting to go back to work yet, Jessica quickly said, "Before we get on with this sir, may Karen and I have a couple of days off to just hang out, maybe, say four?"

Sorento laughed, having planned to give her the time off she deserved but chuckled to himself, that although her demeanor had changed to a more collegial one, her assertiveness hadn't left her. He replied with a straight face, trying hard not to smile, "I don't know Jessica. This is a complicated and time sensitive investigation. What do you think David, are you okay with a few days off?"

Everyone could hear Kopas laughing as he replied, "I am sure our agency can spare Karen for a few days, how about we arrange for the first of the week? I will bring Hortonn up to speed and those two can meet in Toronto, plan their Costa Rica offense and fly out of Pearson Tuesday. Will that work for everyone?"

Sorento could no longer hold his mirth and laughingly said, "I can live with that. Jessica, Karen, you two good with David's suggestion?

Karen and Jessica stood simultaneously and said, "Sounds good," as they headed to the door. Jessica turned her head as she opened the door and said, "I will contact the "J" Team in Los Angeles and have them meet me on Monday."

"I almost forgot Jessica, as you know Rebecca and Penelope are actively involved in Santa Barbara with R&P Investigations, give her a ring and see if she can help us."

"Will do sir," Jessica replied as the two women headed out of the office.

With that, the meeting was adjourned, Chapman and Kopas hung up and Sorento poured himself another coffee and went back to the mound of paperwork on his desk.

JBJ

    As Jessica and Karen made their way through the White House maze of hallways, Jessica stopped, stood off to the side and sent a text to Rebecca inviting R&P into the investigation.

    Once the encryption system confirmed the text was sent and received, the two continued their way through the White House to head to Jessica's for the evening.

Chapter TWENTY

Penelope and Rebecca had transformed the fingerling potatoes into halves, microwaved, removed the pulp, mixed it with butter, salt, pepper, avocado and smoked salmon, put the mixture in the potato boats, topped with a light cheddar, then broiled them lightly in the oven. They warmed the spicy Thai soup and had iron blue ceramic soup mugs for serving.

Alejandro had accepted their invitation and was expected around 4ish, which gave them an hour by the pool. They removed several bottles of a local chardonnay into an ice bucket and took everything out by the pool, then headed upstairs to change, making sure they took cover-ups back to the pool to ensure Alejandro didn't have heart failure seeing them both in bikinis.

They took the stuffed potatoes with them to the pool house and put them in the oven on warm, placing the pot of soup on the stove on a warm setting. The bucket of chardonnay went poolside with three plastic long-stem wine glasses.

They took a swim, each doing a couple of laps and were drying off when Rebecca's phone chimed. Putting it on speaker, trying not to drop water on the screen, they heard Kenneth's greeting that they were now the proud owners of two Honda CRV SUVs, American made in Ohio, and would they be available to receive them this afternoon.

Rebecca looked at Penelope with raised eyebrows and received two thumbs up from Pen, so she replied in the affirmative and closed the call.

During the remainder of the hour before Alejandro arrived, they checked on the food to ensure it was keeping warm, were in and out of the pool, swimming a few laps, not for a work-out but just having fun, something they'd never done before.

Sitting in their Kensington Teak Love Seat with cobalt blue square cushions by Cabana Coast out of Toronto, they shared their respective research into the Santa Barbara Police Department staffers with whom they hoped to work closely.

Tall glasses of chardonnay on their laps, they each scrolled their smartphones for their data with Penelope offering the opening remarks, "Elise Pelfini in fact, knows self-defense and has taught it successfully to women. I viewed several of her teaching videos online. The personality she demonstrated the other day, coupled with her skills should harmonize well with our plans for the girls."

"I found similar good news. O'Connor is retired Treasury. He took his twenty-five at age fifty and won the chief's job out of thirty applicants, all who had many years of running smaller operations, so his time with Treasury had to have been significant. I couldn't get into his personnel files legally and I wasn't about to hack of course. I think we can be confident he is bona fide.

Alejandro was walking around the pool, approaching Pen and Rebecca when they all heard several horn blasts from the driveway. The women quickly jumped up, put their drinks down, rushed toward Alejandro, each giving him a hug. Smiling copiously, he returned their warm welcome, placed his plate of appetizers on the round black marble gas fireplace sitting next to three matching cobalt blue Kensington occasional chairs and all three headed out quickly to see the new cars.

Kenneth and a colleague were leaning against two bright Honda CRV SUVs, one a Molten Lava Pearl, or muted metallic red and the other Obsidian Blue Pearl, or a metallic cobalt blue, Rebecca's favorite color.

The men offered the keys to the new owners, opened the doors then gave a brief overview of the vehicles' features; all-wheel drive, a 1.5 L turbocharged engine, Android compatible stereo system, forward collision and lane departure warning system, hands free tail-gate, leather seats and steering wheel, electric seats and a large navigational dash screen.

Sitting in the leather seats, which still had the fragrance of a new vehicle even though there were several thousand miles on each, the women ran their hands over the material, played with all the dials, adjusted the driver's seat, then quickly exited their new rides when it dawned on them that they were standing in front of two strange men in bathing suit coverups.

Rebecca felt a tinge of embarrassment but quickly recovered to say, "Thank you Kenneth for your quick discovery," but she was at a loss as what else to say. She felt awkward never having purchased a vehicle previously and didn't have a clue as to how to do it properly. She was prepared to pay without looking at an invoice.

Kenneth seemed to sense her concern as he reached into his inside jacket pocket, retrieved two invoices, handing one to each of his buyers.

As Penelope and Rebecca scanned the paperwork, Kenneth offered, "I appreciate Alane's referral and hope that I have fulfilled his confidence in my services, and you are happy with my selections."

The invoices were extremely simple, offering only the bare necessities of vehicle identification and the delivered cost. Thinking that discussing the price would be considered poor taste and noting that the cost was far below what they had seen on the lots in town, Penelope replied, "Most certainly Kenneth and we appreciate how quickly you were able to find them. I know I speak for Rebecca as well, we will love them. Would you prefer a check or an e-Transfer?"

"I am delighted you are happy with the vehicles and if I can be of any further service, please do not hesitate to ask. You can either mail a check or e-Transfer at your convenience. There is full insurance coverage until the end of the month through my company, a full tank of gas and the navigational system paid for the rest of the year."

Rebecca and Pen looked at each other in astonishment, wondering silently why anyone would purchase a vehicle any other way. Rebecca replied with, "Thank you very much Kenneth. Your kindness, expertise and generosity are incomparable."

Rebecca gave him the keys to her rental, the rental agreement, then each shook his hand and thanked him profusely as they waved the men goodbye.

Once they had exited the wrought-iron gates, they ran to their respective cars and did a few circle eights in the wide driveway then stopped and waved Alejandro over to the first vehicle. After he belted up, they sped around the compound and parked in front of the four-car garage, exited their prizes, beeped them locked and strutted with Alejandro back to the pool, all three arm-in-arm.

Back at pool-side, Alejandro presented a plate of taquitos, small rolled-up tortillas filled with spicy ground beef and cotija, a Mexican white cheese. Often deep-fried, Alejandro chose to bake them, thereby lowering the caloric count and eliminating the accompanying oily taste of deep frying.

He served them with sour cream and guacamole as Penelope poured each a tall glass of chilled chardonnay while Rebecca retrieved their soup and appetizers from the pool house kitchen.

For the rest of the afternoon, the three enjoyed the appetizers, chardonnay and discussed the upcoming party, its significance to R&P Investigations, their relationship with the women's center and setting a lasting tone for their company vis-à-vis the community.

Alejandro was of tremendous help as he knew all the movers and shakers and suggested the following guest list; the mayor, UC Santa Barbara police chief, Rodrigo and Elise, city counselors of which there are five and Alane with his plus four, several of which may be attorneys, Alejandro emphasized.

Alejandro smiled when he saw Rebecca involuntarily cringe at hearing about attorneys, knowing she must have had some unpleasant encounters with defense lawyers.

They anticipated a total of twenty. *Alane will know how to accommodate additions*, Rebecca thought to herself, *I sure don't have a clue.*

As the afternoon waned, they decided to call it a day. Alejandro helped carry the dishes into the main kitchen, loaded the dishwasher, gathered his own dishes, gave each a hug, backed up slightly, gave a bow and offered, "Thank you for a wonderful afternoon. The company and light cuisine was remarkable, the wine delicious and I bid you adieu and adios, thankful I am not driving," he quipped. "I am thoroughly looking forward to your party."

Rebecca and Penelope saw him out the back door, gave him another hug, closed and locked the exit, then headed to bed.

Walking through the kitchen, arm in arm, each leaning on the other, they agreed they were exhausted and maybe a little drunk. They had the foresight to engage the alarm system as they dropped their cover-ups/bathing suits on the floor and crawled into bed, falling asleep almost immediately in each other's arms.

S.B.S

Little did Rebecca and Penelope know that Alejandro not only knew Santa Barbara's movers and shakers, but he was one of them.

He was a client of Birdcage Investments and had built a profitable portfolio during his working years and beyond, to the point of being a philanthropist, giving millions to various local charities and causes.

Alejandro and Alane had met decades previously when the Beverly Hills landscaper was commissioned to develop the estate of Alane's client, who had tired of what the owner considered, British property landscaping. Located in the hills with ocean and mountain views, both had become closed in with vegetation growth.

Alejandro's job was massive requiring an excavator to remove the years of hedges and thick flora. Several months in the planning, development and execution, Alane was present when Alejandro unveiled the creation to the owner. So overcome with emotion of the transformation of his estate, the client used his smartphone to contact his staff and invited Alane and Alejandro to an impromptu luncheon.

The makeover resulted in the ocean being entirely visible from any location on the property, as were the mountains. The imposing hedges had been replaced with flower gardens surpassing those of the Santa Barbara Gardens and Winery.

Alejandro's offer for semi-weekly maintenance was quickly accepted, which lead to extended conversations with Alane and the latter's developing Alejandro's portfolio and his subsequent wealth.

"We are the music-makers,
And we are the dreamers of dreams,
Wandering by lone sea-breakers
And sitting by desolate streams;
World losers and world forsakers,
On whom the pale moon gleams:
Yet we are the movers and shakers
Of the world for ever, it seems."
Ode
By Arthur O'Shaughnessy (1844-1881)

꙾ℬ꙾

When CST Drought and the RCMP forensics team were searching Sawyer's underground grow-operation, they sifted through discarded soil on the work tables and floor. What they found brought joy to the officers who were now sorting once again, but this time through the many retrieved texts between Stan and Brian over the course of several months.

Both men believed, erroneously, that burner phones were untraceable. Testing their theory would have been as simple as deactivating their phone's location and program it not to display its number, then call 9-1-1. The operator would know both their location and number.

That was the technology which the RCMP used to trace texts to Stan and follow his movements. In addition to this equipment, the Force employed their Stingray, or Mobile Device Indentifiers (MDIs). The equipment required a warrant, which, with the evidence they offered a judge, was readily provided.

Stan was followed physically and electronically 24-7.

꙾ℬ꙾

Rebecca and Penelope would wake the next morning with an offer they could not refuse.

Chapter TWENTY-ONE

Elisabeth was analyzing the contents of the warehouse where the CFBA had modified their vehicles and installed explosives. She already knew the material came from the Orofino compound controlled by William Shepherd and Ken Marrington that Jackson had reconnoitered. The two were in custody with little chance of avoiding long prison time. Law enforcement knew also that the explosive components originated in a StoneHead, Wyoming Evangelical church at their rural farm, but to date the federal justice department had been reticent to file charges against the church elders and pastor. Investigators were unable to tie any one individual to the explosive components hidden in their barn and after the FBI SWAT team and Secret Service conducted an assault on the farm to rescue Jackson...without a warrant, the government was legally paralyzed.

During the StoneHead operation, Elisabeth had monitored all participants utilizing equipment she brought with her to Marina del Rey and since the arrests, the NSA took over surveillance of the StoneHead church congregation, elders and pastor, along with numerous persons of interest.

Elisabeth was becoming more and more restless dealing with issues for which she was ill prepared or trained. Surveillance was her sweet-spot, a talent she had performed for the British government's MI6 before being transferred to the "J" Team.

Finding nothing worthwhile in the warehouse material, she rose from her desk, ran both hands through her short 'do and headed to the unit's break room for a caffeine fix, coincidentally meeting Jackson and Jason doing likewise.

"Are you guys losing patience as quickly as I am?" she asked, while pouring a cup of black into a white mug monogrammed with LAPD. She collapsed into the government's idea of an occasional chair; black, short back with busted springs, as Jackson and Jason replied simultaneously, "Yup."

All three were enjoying their Seattle's Best, Post Alley Blend, which Elisabeth had picked up from a marina market, tired of the unit's brand, given that cops were renowned for their poor taste in java, usually settling for burned or scalded brew over something decent.

Almost on cue, as each put their heads back, all their encrypted cells vibrated simultaneously, and each retrieved them, looked at each other and the men pointed to Elisabeth, indicating she was elected to answer. She was used to their shenanigans, touched her phone and said, "Hello."

"Did the boys appoint you the answer person, implying it may be from a disgruntled woman," Jessica quipped offering a little laugh.

"Of course, Elisabeth replied as she motioned to Jackson and Jason to close the break-room door.

"Do you have privacy?"

"Yes. And all three of us are on the line."

"Good morning gentlemen."

"Good morning to you too Jessica, responded Jackson and Jason, one after the other. "What's up?"

"We're back in action, much to your delight I am sure. I am surprised you haven't gone stir crazy there. Here is what we have to date," as she reviewed what had occurred in Sorento's office, providing the necessary details, instructing all three agents to move to Santa Barbara, settle in a comfortable location and for Elisabeth to organize her surveillance equipment, the paradigm of which she would provide later.

Although Jessica had made gains with her interpersonal and management skills, she maintained her propensity for avoiding unnecessary dialog. Once she had given her orders, she added that she would see them in Santa Barbara in a few days and for them to contact Rebecca and go clothes shopping, offering that they all must be tired of living out of a suitcase. Then she disconnected.

Maintaining their concern for secrecy, Jackson mouthed, *Rebecca? Clothes? Nordstrom?* with a huge grin, then rose, emptied and rinsed his coffee cup, turned and high fived his colleagues.

Elisabeth and Jason followed Jackson's lead with their coffee cups and all three exited the break room, dropped by the unit's supervisor's desk to advise him that they had received new orders, and all three almost skipped out of the LAPD headquarters and drove back to Marina del Rey to pack and head to Santa Barbara.

Chapter TWENTY-TWO

Jessica gave Karen a mini-tour of the White House as they made their way outside. Fukishura was specific about showing off her work place, not giving Karen a tourist version. She was sure Karen would have loved to meet the former president, James Bakus, but his successor, not so much, so she didn't invite the subject but rather concentrated on the various historic aspects of the building, giving her a personal touch to the State Dining room, Vermeil, China and Green rooms as well as the kitchen introducing her to all the chefs, sampling the hors d'oeuvres being prepared for a late afternoon meeting and chatting with the housekeeping crew, many of whom had worked for the White House through numerous presidents and all of whom were tight-lipped about the current resident.

The tour complete, Jessica and Karen slowly exited her work place, stopping to chat with security, many of the men somewhat infatuated with an RCMP officer who had Karen's physical features.

The women chuckled often on the way to Jessica's flat about how predictable men are with their cute and shy personalities, which are transformed almost immediately when in the company of an attractive woman.

During the short drive they made their evening plans of quick showers and dress in Washington casual, which was somewhat different than California casual in that Washington tended to be more formal at any time of day. But she had picked up a few hints from her female colleagues over the years as well as having coffee with the White House support staff.

She knew that the best approach was dressing business attire and for that she chose her pink ballet linen, theory dress; sleeveless, with a full skirt and round neck. She paired it with matching Manolo Blahnik, leather point-toe pumps and a Triangle ear jacket from Stella & Dot, which offered ample room for her shoulder holstered Sig.

The agents enjoyed their relaxing time together at Jessica's flat, chatting about everything except work, both intuitively knowing there would be more than enough of that in the weeks to come. They had polished off one bottle of chardonnay and decided to not open another but wait for dinner.

Karen hadn't packed any dressy clothes, so she chose an outfit offered by Jessica; a violet Dara Shift dress from Felicity & Coco via Toronto's Nordstrom. It boasted fluttered, elbow sleeves, a tied front and a jewel neck. She paired the stunning outfit with open toe, ankle strapped taupe sandals.

Excitement riveted them as they called a town-car and headed to famed Michael Marino's Pennsylvania Ave. restaurant, Jessica having called ahead, and giggling from too much chardonnay, used her White House influence to gain a table for two on short notice.

Chapter TWENTY-THREE

Penelope was curled up in her usual sleep position with the covers over her head when Rebecca woke around 4am. Rather than cuddling, which had become their morning routine, followed by exquisite sex, she slipped out from under the duvet, padded naked across the bedroom so as not wake Pen, entered the walk-in closet and chose Lululemon high-rise, Dark Canyon Onyx Blue tights and matching bra. The pattern was a cobalt blue background with a layered coral design. She loved the way the lightweight, buttery-soft, sweat-wicking fabric breathed so she didn't feel confined during her workout.

She made her way to the kitchen, started coffee, placed one of Pasteles' cinnamon buns in the convection oven, placed another on a plate, covered it with a cereal bowl, then sat at the island and penned a quick note to Pen,

"Good morning my love! Coffee and cinnamon bun to start your day. I am in the gym…head to the living room and the door is on the left. Come and join me. No, not that, because I will be hot and sweaty. That's for later." She added a smiley face just as the Cuisinart dinged that her coffee was ready.

Pouring a large mug of black, she took her roll out the French Doors to the covered deck off the kitchen and enjoyed the quiet time, listening to the hills come alive. Checking her text messages, she was flabbergasted to find one requiring the entry of her former Secret

Service access code. Entering the numbers and symbols, she found herself both excited and perplexed, *who is texting me encrypted and for what reason,* she thought.

It took a few seconds for the message to appear on screen. She read it once. Then again. And again, not comprehending the content. Not sure whether she wanted to get back into bed with the White House yet knowing it would be rewarding to work with Jessica and the "J" Team again. She sat the phone aside, regained her composure with plans to discuss the offer with Penelope later.

Fifteen minutes and her blood sugar was normal, she was caffeined and ready to feel the burn.

Back in the kitchen, she placed her plate in the dishwasher, refilled her mug and headed downstairs.

The well-lighted, wide, circular staircase matched that leading to the second floor and was far more elegant than one would think for a basement staircase. But this house was truly like no other.

The hedge-fund manager was earning a low seven figures when he had it custom built and by the lack of wear and tear on the machines and free-weights, she questioned whether they were ever used.

As she walked the short hallway to the gym entrance, she marveled at the designer's success at maximizing the otherwise darkness of a basement: track lighting end to end, floor to ceiling mirrors on one wall and a white pine, two-inch, horizontal tongue and groove paneling on another. The effect with the muted lighting created an uplifting mood, which was counterintuitive.

Smiling to herself, she felt a lightness in her step she had never experienced before. Entering the gym, she admired Alane's decorating sense, a task he took on himself as another gift to his top client.

Flicking on the lights, she stopped in the entry and admired the nine-hundred square foot exercise area with three walls of warm cream and the third a light peach. The floor hosted a light grey, indoor/outdoor carpet under exercise machinery: exercise bicycles, treadmills, stair climbers, rowing machines and a Universal gym. A rack of free weights sat off by themselves, the rubber coated dumbbells with contoured chrome handles, the design often a metonymy by some exercise enthusiasts believing the contemporary equipment incapable of producing sound results. No so for Rebecca, who had embraced free weights for decades, believing that manipulating and controlling the weights increased her core strength, the center of martial arts prowess.

Entering the gym through a glass door, two restrooms were to her immediate left and a thirty-foot by six-foot mirror on the right. Below the mirror on a seven-foot long, four shelve, enclosed ebony bookcase were controls for the stereo system and a sixty-inch flat screen television in the far-right corner, at ceiling height.

Turning to face the room, her vision scanned the mirrored left wall which was duplicated across the back. To her right, were four, six-foot by five-foot shatterproof windows with a sliding glass door of the same material, which lead to a large covered patio with a yellow cedar, circular stairway with matching railing which lead to the pool house.

At the back of the room was another bookcase, this one being wide and open with neatly folded white towels. At the end of, and atop the bookcase and next to the door, was an Elite countertop filled with bottles of water, Gatorade and an assortment of other rehydrating fluids.

Placing a thirty-minute advanced aerobics disc into the player, she took the remote control, laid on the carpet and devoted twenty minutes to stretching and crunches.

Once she was limber and had the kinks out, she started the disc which began immediately with side-steps and arm swings, alternating with hamstring curls and knee raises.

The thirty minutes went by quickly. She was sweating discreetly as she moved to the free weights and began a back and arm routine. Starting with ten-pounds she performed ten receptions of one-arm dumbbell rows, then quickly moved to arm curls using the same weight. Completing three sets of each exercise she went to the universal gym and did a series of seated cable rows, cable curls and press downs.

Repeating the routine three times without rest, she was sweating profusely with an estimated heart rate of one-hundred and ready to call it a day when movement at the door caught her eye. Penelope had entered the gym quietly and was leaning against the wall, one cobalt blue slippered foot against the wall, drinking coffee.

As Rebecca glanced over, Penelope lifted the hem of her matching terrycloth bathrobe to mid-thigh, as she took a sip, and looked seductively over the rim of the mug.

Rebecca was overtaken by the warmth and love, not just the sexual overtones, but the depth of emotion they showed for each other.

Dropping her soaked gym towel, she walked slowly toward Pen, accentuating hip movement, flexing her biceps in a Ms. Universe pose with such flamboyance, Penelope snorted her coffee, wiping he face with her sleeve.

Pen didn't move as Rebecca leaned in, braced herself with her hands against the wall and kissed Pen, absorbing her fragrance cascading energy waves, rippling and cascading from her face to her toes.

"Good morning! You look particularly delicious today. I trust you slept well."

"I did. Man, that chardonnay mellowed me out all night. Then starting the day with coffee and a roll just slides me from one exquisite mood to another.

"How long have you been up?"

"Oh, since about five," she replied, then turned and with a sweeping arm, added, "What do you think of this room? Alane had it decorated before I formally moved in?"

"Utterly amazing. And the former owner was a hedge fund manager? It looked like the room has never been used."

"Yeah, he was. And I suspect you are right about it not being used. When I look at the house as a unit, I wonder if this was built as a monument to his financial accomplishments. We may hear some gossip at the party.

"Let's go down the hall to the shooting range. You will not believe this."

Returning to pick up her towel and coffee cup, she held the door open for Penelope, returned the way she had come, around the staircase and about fifteen-feet to another door, this one metal.

Holding the door open with one hand, Rebecca reached behind Pen as she entered, to flick on a series of overhead, florescent lights which illuminated the eight-foot by thirty-foot preparation area, paneled identically to the hallway. The furthest end held a steel, combination-controlled gun safe, bolted into the concrete floor making it impossible to remove.

Looking further into the sixty-foot deep room, there were six shooting stations with each having its own automatic target track. The entire structure, including the ceiling, was two-layered concrete with blown insulation in between the layers. Visible, over the cement core, were baffles on the walls, ceiling and floor. These absorb stray bullets as well as provide another layer of sound insulation.

The farthest wall was a lead trap for bullets and an exhaust system which pulled air out of the range, into a secure exterior filter. The filter system and the range itself were cleaned monthly by a specialty firm from Los Angeles, hired by the security company responsible for the entire property.

The exhaust system's hum was barely noticeable as Rebecca introduced Penelope to the range by saying, "Is this insane or what? Alane is sure it has never been used. Maybe, as I mentioned about the gym, the previous owner thought he could impress certain clients. I don't know. What I do know is that we lucked out. Do you want to give it a try?"

"You bet," Penelope replied with enthusiasm.

Rebecca smiled, remembering her first time learning from her dad, who taught her the proper use of handguns, rifles and shotguns. It wasn't until she was with the sheriff's department that she was instructed in fully automatic weapons. Although her favorite handgun was never the Sig-Sauer semi-automatic nine-millimeter, she had carried it for so long with the Secret Service, it had become comfortable and her regular carry firearm.

Walking to the end of the preparation room, she said, "I will give you all the combinations today. This lock is simple yet complex. Dialing the combination is straight forward, but like many digital systems, three failures will lock you out and the security company is called through a wireless cell system.

"Kinda cool, really and I hate to think what it must have cost to install. But here," she offered, as the door opened, and she withdrew a Smith and Wesson 632 Stainless, twenty-two revolver with a Packmayr grip and a box of low-velocity ammunition.

Rebecca gave the box to Pen, held the firearm with the other and closed the safe with her hip.

For the next hour, Penelope learned how to hold the revolver by repeatedly putting the firearm in and out of her bathrobe's pocket, up to her face so she could smell the oil and feel the steel against her skin. Rebecca explained that the process may seem unorthodox, but she was determined to have Pen accept firearms as tools, as machines which she could manipulate for her benefit.

Penelope shared that she didn't have any preconceived notions about firearms, so she was open to instruction and emphasized that she trusted Rebecca.

Pen determined that she was right-hand dominant which meant she would shoot with that hand and holster her firearm on that side of her body or in a shoulder holster under her left armpit.

Rebecca had Pen memorize and practice basic rules of the use of firearms; handle the piece as though it were loaded, always point it in a safe direction, keep your finger by the trigger guard until you have aligned your target and are committed to firing and, ensure the surrounding area is safe before firing.

Pen held the small bullets in her hand, rolled them around like marbles, sliding them back and forth from one hand to the other, holding them high in one hand and releasing them like a waterfall, dropping into the other. Rebecca emphasizing that the bullets were inert until struck by a firing pin.

Acquiring a comfortable and controlling grip and learning dry firing or pulling the trigger of the unloaded revolver, developing a natural leg stance and arm extension took time for Pen's fine motor skills to adopt. Rebecca was confident Pen would become weapons ready with regular training and adhering to a mind-set.

Next came opening and closing the cylinder then loading, unloading…repeatedly until she could do it with her eyes closed.

By the time Rebecca inserted a target into the holder and sent it down the lane to ten-feet, Penelope had donned ear protection and was feeling confident, so much so that Rebecca laid the revolver on the shooting platform, turned behind Pen, put her hands on her shoulders, and calmly asked her to take several deep breaths, pick up the twenty-two quietly, line up the sites to the silhouette's body, and pull the trigger... once.

Center mass.

Rebecca whispered, "Again."

Center mass.

Rebecca whispered, "Empty the gun."

Four shots, center mass.

Rebecca, stepped back one pace and watched to see if Penelope released the cylinder, removed the empty shells and placed it on the shooting shelf. She did. Then turned and said with a broad smile, "So, teacher, how did I do?"

Rebecca stepped forward with outstretched arms and enveloped Pen in a hug, then stepped back and replied, "You are a natural Penelope, a real natural."

"I think I might be," she beamed. "The way you have taught me, this feels so natural to have in my hand, not foreign at all. But I realize ten feet is pretty close."

"Close is good. You are not going to need a firearm at a distance greater than twenty-five feet and even ten feet you may decide to use your defensive tactics skills rather than a firearm.

"But let's be real here, the chances of either of us using a firearm during investigating insurance and corporate cases are probably slim to none."

"Do doubt. How are we doing for time? she asked, with a lift in her voice. "Would you demonstrate a heavier caliber handgun at a longer distance?"

Rebecca smiled, knowing Penelope was giving her a chance to show off her skills, something she hadn't done for a long time. Even when she took down the suspect in the barn outside of StoneHead, it was using a knife, not a firearm. Instructing Pen, smelling the acrid bite of the firearm discharge, was a career aphrodisiac, so she replied in the affirmative, went back to the safe, withdrew an identical pistol to what she regularly carried, a box of ammunition and returned to the shooting aisle.

Her stance was what is often called a natural, one each shooter chooses that fits her comfort zone. In addition to having her body bladed slightly with her left foot back slightly, Rebecca kept her left elbow tucked close to her body, a slight bend in her right arm, two hands on the pistol about a foot from her face, sights always lined up.

Penelope was already back several paces from the shooting platform with her ear protection in place when Rebecca, following all the safety procedures she had drummed into Pen, set her ear protection in place, loaded ten bullets into the magazine, inserted it into the Sig, slammed it in place with the heel of her hand, extended the target to thirty-feet and emptied all ten rounds into the center mass of the silhouette, grouped within a two-inch circle.

When the Sig was empty, the slide stayed open. Rebecca laid the firearm on the platform and turned to Pen and said, "Oh, my God, that feels so good, I think I climaxed twice."

Penelope bent over laughing so hard she had to grasp the side of the shooting platform to steady herself.

Recovering from their jocularity, they took the firearms back to the safe where Rebecca pulled out a collapsible table and cleaning equipment and demonstrated the cleaning of the semi-automatic, then instructed Penelope in cleaning the revolver.

Maintenance completed, firearms returned to the safe and secured, they headed up to the kitchen, refilled their mugs and spent time wandering the grounds, often holding hands, sometimes leaning on one another, but always in physical contact.

They settled in the deck chairs by the pool and chatted about the upcoming party, Alane's preparation, the guest list and how they were going to pull it off as their first R&P function.

During a slack in the conversation, they checked their phones for party updates. Rebecca entered her screen lock code then passed it over to Penelope without comment.

Penelope's reaction set the tone for their entire career as investigators. Jumping up and screaming, "Oh, my God, this is unbelievable. Our first contract!" She paced back and forth a little, swinging her arms about, then, getting a grip on her emotions, quickly rounded the table and hugged Rebecca, asking, "When did this arrive?"

"Just this morning. I wanted to wait until after your shooting experience. Pretty cool huh? Of course, we must have the "J" Team stay with us, right?"

"Absolutely. I've only met Jessica, but it will be great to meet the rest of the team. Can you get in touch with them?"

"No, unfortunately. All my contacts were erased when I retired, so I'll text Jessica to accept the job...I wanted to clear it with you first...and make the invitation. Jeez, how are we going to feed everyone," she said joyfully, raising her legs and falling back into her chair.

"How about calling Alane. He will have some suggestions. Oh, and Alejandro probably does too."

"Good idea. We can call them this morning."

They fell back into their chairs, reached for their coffee and clinked a toast to their good fortune and future.

Talked out, caffeined and ready for the day, they headed back to the house to shower and dress. On the way, Penelope asked, "Do you remember the firearm you had strapped to your stomach when we were in Denver? Do you ever carry that now that you are retired?"

Without replying, Rebecca turned slightly, reached into her robe's right-side pocket, pulled out her Seecamp twenty-five caliber pistol, showed it to Pen, grinned, then put her arm through Penelope's and continued walking with Rebecca bring up the topic of kittens and puppies lighting up Pen's already smiling face.

ℑℬℑ

The "J" Team was packed, checked out and having breakfast before hitting the road when Elisabeth's encrypted phone vibrated. Knowing there was only one caller possible, she didn't excuse herself from Jackson and Jason, but withdrew the phone, entered her code and read the text.

"Change of plans boys," she said, giving the phone to Jason. She waited until he had read it and passed it to Jackson before continuing. "I can't say I am surprised Sorento hired R&P, Rebecca may be more in tune with what is happening in the area than the Los Angeles office. And I can't say I am not disappointed with not staying in a hotel again," she quipped with a broad smile.

Jackson added, "Me either. You know, we haven't really talked to her since the review of the Citizens for a Better America raid at the StoneHead Ranch. Retiring to Santa Barbara. Interesting. And with the vet. I hope we are not going to be sleeping on couches."

Jason laughed, adding, "I sure as hell hope not. No, I can't imagine she would invite us as guests without accommodations, but for all four of us?"

"Well, let's get to gettin'. That address should be easy to find with the rental's GPS."

They took the last sip of coffee, each placed twenty dollars on the table and headed for Santa Barbara.

Chapter TWENTY-FOUR

Traffic was light heading back towards the White House and the town-car driver made good time, dropping Jessica and Karen off at Michael Marino's with time to spare for their reservation. Karen paid, and they exited the black Lincoln where they were met immediately by a doorperson dressed in an evening tuxedo who curtsied graciously and opened the door, stepping aside to allow the women to enter.

Karen thanked the doorwoman and quickly slipped a twenty into her palm, then turned to catch up with Jessica who was being ushered into a glass sided elevator. Neither spoke during the brief ride, each marveling at the scenery.

Within seconds the doors opened on the 54th floor to a breathtaking view of Washington with the White House in a starring performance center stage. The maître d', a dashing young male of indeterminable age, greeted them warmly, referring to each guest by name, and guided them to a window table for two, pulled each of their chairs out and ensuring their comfort, stepped aside to herald Michael Marino's sommelier, who appeared with a chilled bottle of Maryland's Liberty Vineyard Chardonnay in a stainless-steel wine bucket with stand, which she placed beside Karen.

Karen accepted the customary taste test, first the cork, then a swirl, nose, sip, swish, swallow, then a quick glance at the sommelier with a nod and a smile.

Jessica's glass was poured next and as their steward departed, they clinked glasses and took a sip with Karen remarking, "Did you arrange this? It is delicious with what I taste as unoaked, rich pineapple and fig."

"Me too. And no, I didn't request this and have never been here before," Jessica added as their server approached with an attractive plate of soft goat cheese, flat, quarter size crackers, cherry tomatoes and sliced cucumber. Bowing handsomely with his right arm behind his back, he placed the plate between them offering, "Ladies, goat cheeses and crackers to pair with your chardonnay. Compliments of Mr. Marino. Enjoy. I will be back shortly with menus."

Jessica and Karen exchanged puzzled looks, as though, *is this protocol?* then buttered the soft cheese on several crackers, reached across the table clicking the items in a toast, followed by several chardonnay swallows.

They were finishing off the appetizers and commenting on the spectacular view when Karen turned quickly to Jessica and remarked, "You made the reservation using your Secret Service status. I bet this treatment is a result."

"It could be I suppose," she replied, thinking about it for a few seconds, then continuing, "but is it okay? I mean, agents could throw their status around and get special treatment anytime and anywhere." Once the words were out of her mouth, she put her hand over it and said, "Oh my God, I just did that. Shit. I feel like such an asshole and hypocrite."

Karen laughed slightly, reached across the table touching Jessica's hand and said, "Don't be. It happens to all of us at one time or another. Flying here, I made my reservation online without any employment reference. Checking in, I was met by an Air Canada staffer who took me to their frequent flyer club where I was given an upgraded ticket for business class. I tried to reject the offer, but the staffer insisted, saying she was told refusal wasn't an option. This is the company for which I provided inflight security for years and I didn't feel comfortable rejecting their generosity. Technically I am no longer with the RCMP, but that would be splitting hairs. I just accepted it graciously, enjoyed a coffee and croissant, then the lovely flight."

"I can see that happening and the awkwardness. I've just never had anything offered before. Ever. Agents are always in the background, invisible and seldom does anyone take notice of us. I guess it is kind of nice. Okay. I will shut up and enjoy."

"Good," insisted Karen adding, "perfect timing because here comes our server with the menus."

Their server slipped discreetly to their table, introducing himself as Devon and said, "I trust you enjoyed the hors d'oeuvres to whet your appetite and are receptive to perusing our entrée offerings?" as he slipped each an attractive albeit limited selection menu, a style both diners had experienced previously in high-end restaurants.

"May I be so bold as to suggest starting with an array of our Narragansett Bay, Rhode Island mussels and Alaskan King crab caught this morning off the Aleutian Islands, arriving a few hours ago as well as Belon, Maine oysters?"

Karen and Jessica exchanged glances, each nodding, with Jessica replying for them in the affirmative, adding, "And for my entrée I would like the

Montana Angus Filet, medium, with the oven roasted vegetable medley and smashed red potatoes."

Without writing her selection down, Devon turned to Karen, waiting.

"That sounds delicious Devon, please make that two and mine medium as well."

"Certainly ladies. I will return with your seafood momentarily. In the meantime, please allow me to refill your wine glasses."

While they waited for their meals, the conversation swung from the view to men and particularly who Jessica had been dating, if anyone and Karen's relationship with Tom.

Jessica explained that her part of the chat was zip as she hadn't seen anyone in months. She shared how Sorento had forced her to work with several other agencies and that, like many behaviors under duress, she found working with men wasn't as distasteful as she previously experienced.

Karen told of her time with Tom in Vancouver and Cheryl Chapman's presentation to the anti-terrorism group, which stunned attendees while uniting them simultaneously, of their weekend in Whistler, the detachment commander greeting them at a restaurant with a firearm and most recently, interrogating a suspect in the theft of the cesium from Manitoba and helping catch those responsible for the bombing of the Mahalo Airline at LAX.

Jessica knew most of what Karen shared, but not about Whistler or the interrogation, so she said, "I hadn't heard about Whistler, but I take it you and Tom were able to spend some quality time together?"

"Oh my God Jessica, it was just like Santa Monica all over again," she said with passion, referring to the days she spent at the Channel Road Inn waiting for the employment dispute with the airline to be settled. She had texted Tom, so he wouldn't question her whereabouts and Tom, in his spontaneous enthusiasm, grabbed the first flight to LAX on another airline and hitched a helicopter ride with a patrolling California Highway Patrol unit to meet her. The chopper dropped him on Santa Monica Beach, much to the dismay of sunbathers and he arrived at the inn before she did and was waiting in her room.

They spent every minute together developing a deep relationship that Karen was hoping to advance in Costa Rica. She continued, "We stayed at the Chateau in Whistler and on the way to dinner at Araxi, we crossed paths with a group of drunks from Vancouver who were doing a weekend bar crawl.

"Even with Tom there, one guy grabbed me as we passed. Unfuckin' believable," she laughed nervously, recalling the anger she felt at the time. "Tom didn't do anything at the moment, for which I thanked him. The offense was against me, not him. Anyway, I broke the guy's arm and when his buddy tried to intervene, I put him in the hospital too. It took only seconds as you know, and when the incident concluded, Tom clapped, took my arm and we went to dinner," she concluded, coming up for air, her adrenaline flowing as she relived the experience, just as Devon arrived with their seafood medley.

They didn't realize how hungry they were, neither having eaten since breakfast, so they were not surprised by their own actions as they devoured the entire presentation quickly, topping off the cuisine experience with several sips of chardonnay.

No sooner had they laid their cocktail forks to the side, when Devon arrived with their entrées.

They thanked their server as he bowed and backed away, then Jessica asked as she began cutting her fillet, "Hell of a way to start a dinner date," she said smiling, taking a bite, then continuing. "So where does the detachment commander come into the story?"

Karen savored a section of roasted rosemary broccoli, wiped her mouth, took a sip of chardonnay and responded, "That is part of the weirdness of the aftermath. Apparently, some folks walking by called 911 and the police arrived. Not surprisingly, the two had records so a Mountie went with them to the hospital.

While the other officers sorted out the details, Tom and I were well into our Araxi experience but, unbeknown to either of us, our server had seen Tom's service firearm as he sat down, and the manager called the police. Then we glanced out the window and saw several bike patrol officers arriving at the front door, and we suspected several more were at the rear. We no sooner noticed this, when a woman entered wearing a stunning pale blue pant suit, spoke with the manager and walked over to our table. She invited herself to join us, sat with one hand on her lap, under an attractive scarf, covering, we found out moments later, a 9mm pistol.

Karen laughed in a nervous way, remembering the embarrassing experience, took another sip of wine and continued, "We sorted it out quickly after we gave her our identifications, but it was somewhat scary with her believing she had two armed diners in a Canadian restaurant."

"Holy crap. I don't think I can top that. As a matter of fact, I know I can't. I have never had an encounter with another law enforcement officer. Now Jackson, he is another matter entirely. Hopefully you will get a chance to meet him and the rest of the "J" Team soon."

"J" Team? That is what you call the four of you? Who coined that title? Mr. Sorento?" she asked with a complimentary lift in her voice.

"No," Jessica responded with a smile. "Me. It was after the warrantless raid on the Christians for a Better America in StoneHead, when the shit hit the fan and we all expected to be transferred to northern Alaska or some other hinterland. Instead, Sorento was very gracious, pissed, but gracious in his evaluation. It turned out, we had uncovered a proverbial hornet's nest which he wanted the "J" Team to solve."

Karen laughed, genuinely and asked, "So, are Tom, Dave and I part of the "J" Team?"

"Could be. My gut tells me there is more to the millions in cash the Secret Service is concerned about."

They continued to chat about their joint investigation, albeit in general terms, while enjoying their meal. Even though they were totally isolated from other diners with tables set well apart, William Shakespeare's, *Discretion is the better part of valor,* came to mind with Jessica thinking an indiscretion would come back to bite her in the ass.

Dinner savored, they accepted Devon's suggestion for Bushnell's Calvados cognac. As he poured the amber liqueur, he asked about their plans were for the rest of the evening. Having none, he suggested they attend the Wizard of Oz, performing at Ford's Theatre.

Devon left, and Karen said, "What do you think? We have tomorrow off. Do you want to give it a go?"

"Sure. I'm game. But they might not have tickets available at this late date. Let me go to their web site and see what they have available."

As Jessica was perusing the Ford's Theatre web site, Devon returned. Karen turned her head expecting him to present the bill, but instead he handed her two tickets, offering, "Mr. Marino has season tickets and wishes you to enjoy the play with his compliments."

Before Karen could reply, Jessica, hearing the conversation, stopped scrolling, put her phone down and said, "Oh Devon. Thank you very much, but we really can't accept this expensive gift. It would be totally inappropriate."

Devon grinned broadly and replied, "Ms. Fukishura and Ms. Winthrop, Mr. Marino expected that reaction and suggests you donate to your favorite charity in the amount of the tickets, attach a copy of the receipt to the tickets and keep on file in case the White House enquires."

And with that closing comment he left, with his customary backward retreat and bow, leaving the women flabbergasted with Jessica shrugging her shoulders, arms spread out and mouthing, *what is this*?

Karen shook her head and mouthed, *I have no idea,* then said, "I don't have a clue to what is happening here Jessica. First, how does he know our names? I can stretch it a bit to accommodate knowing yours, but mine? But then, getting over that, the generosity is beyond belief, the idea of quid pro quo with a charity, I don't see any problem with that, do you?"

Jessica's head continued to move back and forth in astonishment. "No. None. The theatre is sold out for the entire season, so I am good with this and Devon's suggestion of a donation makes perfect sense."

"Let's do it then."

Devon was hovering nearby and noted their positive response and immediately appeared with their check along with a portable debit machine. Karen graciously accepted it, processed the payment with a fifty-percent gratuity, then rose and gave Devon a hug. Jessica did likewise.

Devon was taken aback with a noticeable flushed complexion but managed to reply, "Thank you ladies for allowing Michael Marino and staff to provide you with an enjoyable meal and a memorable evening," then he left.

They walked the two blocks to the historic Ford's Theatre, Jessica sharing some of its history.

The building was first built in 1833 as the First Baptist Church, then leased to John Ford in 1861. After converting it to a music hall, it was destroyed by fire in 1862, reopening the following year as Ford's New Theatre. Abraham Lincoln and his wife attended Our American Cousin April 14, 1865 where he was murdered by a Confederate sympathizer, John Booth.

The government purchased the building a year later and it was unused as a theatre until reopening in

1968 offering theatrical productions, interactive museum exhibits and educational programs.

Karen was enthralled with the education, remembering that Jessica spent seven years at the University of California at Berkeley.

Arriving at the theatre, they found the unassuming exterior belayed its inner beauty. Once inside, the historic presence was overwhelming, with Lincoln era photographs and dedications dominating the entry. From a replica of Lincoln's funeral car to details of the man hunt for Booth, the theatre's past was brought to light before entering the hall itself.

Neither Karen, nor Jessica having been to the theatre previously, were unfamiliar with the seating noted on their tickets. They were pleasantly surprised to trail the usher down the orchestra, center section to Row C, seats 112 and 113, right on the aisle. Three rows from the stage. Once seated, they immediately noticed that being close didn't mean craning their necks to see the action since the beautifully upholstered seats reclined, allowing a perfect, eye-to-stage, straight line of vision.

The red carpeted floor blended smoothly with the light chocolate seats with mahogany arms and upper back trim. The two levels of balcony seats spanned a concaved line when observing from the stage.

Relaxing prior to the opening number, Jessica remarked about how the theatre's intimacy with a six-hundred and sixty-one seating capacity, enhanced their enjoyment since the audience doesn't feel overwhelmed by the presence of the crowd as they would if it were four thousand.

The Wizard is an adaptation of the classic, had won seven Tony Awards in 1975 and was performed live on NBC in 2015. The configuration offers a spectacle of intricate and colorful costumes celebrating African American culture with smoothly performed dance routines by the funky monkeys, munchkins who tickle the funny bone with their bell-shaped costumes and on-stage antics.

Jessica and Karen were thrilled by the voices of the Lion, Tinman and Scarecrow and particularly the play's finale with the Good Witch of the South and her entourage attired in traditional African attire, resounding their rendition of Everybody Rejoice utilizing a drum as the heartbeat of the Winkies.

Having thoroughly enjoyed the musical and the evening in its entirety, the duo made their way through the limited crowd to Tenth Street to hail a cab. Being close to the stage, they were among the last to exit the theatre and found scores of patrons ahead of them for a taxi.

Not wanting to wait, they jay-walked to what appeared to be a popular watering hole, Amber House. Inside, they were not surprised to find a traditional pub atmosphere of dark wood, mirrors and end-to-end bar, yet illuminated with subdued lighting from wall sconces and chandeliers. Greeting them upon entry was not the loud, clashing rock, Caribbean, R&B or funk, but soft jazz. Karen turned to Jessica and said, "Music for old broads like us."

Karen laughed, thinking, *not quite yet...hopefully*. They found two seats by the window with plans to enjoy a drink, allow the crowd to thin, then order a cab from their phone app.

They had just taken their seats when a twenty-something server in black pants, white shirt and Joseph's Coat of Many Colors, literally from Genesis 37 of the Bible, greeted them. The women stared, speechless, not realizing that the jacket was not one chosen by the server or by the owner by chance, but specifically to bring attention to and promote positive, social interaction.

Their server, quite familiar with the reaction, briefly explained the movement, to which the women warmed immediately, chatted lightly, then ordered two Manhattans.

The Manhattans arrived quickly and they reviewed the play, each sharing their favorite segment. Thirty minutes later, they saw that the crowd had dissipated, called a cab, paid the tab with a generous tip and headed to the street.

Turning right once outside, they placed their backs to the brick wall with one foot pulled up behind them, arms folded as they waited and continued their previous conversation.

Jessica had never had someone sneak up on her or create a surprise movement and tonight was no exception. As she engaged in a conversation with Karen, a six-foot three, pale complexioned male, with shoulder length bleached blonde hair, weighing about one-eighty leaned in to her left side, put his right hand on her shoulder and whispered, "Hi gorgeous. I'm Jerry. I'm recruiting lovelies like yourself for a promo party at a loft, two-blocks from here." His hand roamed from her shoulder to her left breast, as he continued, "Free booze and mingle with Washington's hip crowd, sweet cheeks. It's still early, why don't you and your girlfriend join us?"

Karen heard the conversation and was running the next scene through her mind and it was nanoseconds before her thoughts materialized.

Jessica turned slowly, looked at the groper directly, albeit at an upward angle given his height advantage and without saying a word, dropped her left arm, swung it up under his right, wrapping it around his bicep, thereby trapping it, spun on her left toes delivering a violent blow to his groin...twice with her right knee. As his head came down from the natural reaction and he tried to protect himself with his left hand, Jessica grabbed his head with her right hand, pulled it down forcefully and delivered two powerful knee strikes to his head, knocking him out. She aided him to the ground and quietly returned to her waiting position alongside Karen.

The scene was over so quickly and silently that bystanders didn't see or hear the altercation and many probably figured the guy passed out.

Karen glanced at Jessica, smiled and the two bumped fists.

Moments later their taxi arrived. They flagged it down, got in and headed back to Jessica's flat where they shared the remainder of the previously opened chardonnay, retired, happy, satisfied and excited about the upcoming investigation.

J.B.S

Jessica would later reflect on Devon knowing their names and shared her concerns with Karen. With the time restraints of their schedules, their misgivings floated from the immediate to their preparation for the investigation with Devon receding to their peripheral thoughts.

Unknown to either of them, Michael Marino perused each evenings' reservations, noted the Secret Service connection and called his friend, a White House sous-chef, who, after consulting with his boss, the executive chef, enlightened Mr. Marino regarding his law enforcement guests.

Karen and Jessica followed through with their agreement and wrote checks for three-hundred dollars each to their favorite charities before they flew out of Ronald Regan Airport.

J.B.J

Shortly after the women had arrived at Jessica's flat, a passerby stopped at the fallen figure by the Amber House, noticed his broken nose and jaw and called the police. During their questioning at the hospital, it wasn't revealed that the groper had invited an RCMP Sergeant and a Secret Service agent to a party. What was unearthed was an upscale hovel where women were wined, dined and entertained with ketamine, or Special K in their drinks.

Once incapacitated, the women were undressed and photographed in compromising positions with their male hosts, later to be blackmailed into acting as escorts for unscrupulous out-of-country businessmen.

Washington's Metropolitan Police were quick to follow through with their acquired information, raiding the apartment early the next morning, finding sufficient evidence of drugged women, several hundred grams of Special K, as well as gamma hydroxybutyric acid, the photographs and computer records of hundreds of other women under their control.

The groper was sufficiently wise as to describe his injuries as the result of tripping and landing on his face and groin.

℘℘℘

Rebecca and Penelope contacted Alejandro and Alane on a conference call, asking for assistance in locating a caterer who would supply three daily meals and snacks for four adult guests for an extended stay.

Both friends were curious as to the identity of their company but were sufficiently educated in diplomacy to keep their queries personal. Instead, they offered to collaborate and have an answer by the end of the day.

The women ended their participation in the conversation while the men shared ideas and knowledge, culminating in calling Concepción's Catering for a quote.

Alejandro took it upon himself to enlarge the number to six, discussed the query with the owner who promised to call Alejandro back before the end of the day.

Rather than returning R&P's call, the men arrived around 4pm with several bottles of an

Argentinian chardonnay 2014 and Alejandro's peppery jalapeno & Havarti appetizers.

Not surprised by their friends' spontaneous arrival, Pen and Rebecca graciously invited them to the poolside where the four enjoyed the men's offerings while they shared details of Concepción's quote. The caterer would arrive daily at 6 am with a light breakfast of muffins, fruit, yogurt and proteins on alternate days, salad or sandwiches for lunches and semi-elegant dinners. They would create table arrangements and remove the dishes the next morning.

The cost was affordable, and Rebecca was confident Sorento would approve, particularly knowing all agents would be housed in a secure environment, in Santa Barbara's semi-rural residential area, immune from inquisitive tourists' eyes.

The details out of the way, Alane called Concepcións to finalize the arrangements, accepted the email contract to Rebecca's PC, then turned the conversation to satisfying his curiosity.

"Rebecca, my dearest, it is totally none of my business, but my curiosity is burning so I must ask, who are your guests?"

Before she could reply, Alejandro cleared his throat and said, "Me too, curious I mean."

Penelope couldn't stifle her humor and laughed at the closeness the four had developed in a very short time, well, at least the men and her, Rebecca having known both for some time.

"As you know, I retired from the Secret Service but, it seems they cannot get along without me," Rebecca said standing and offering a curtsy, "and they have added Penelope to their list of needs. They hired R&P to aid in an investigation," she exaggerated, "and four agents will be arriving shortly to stay. We figured it must be better here than a hotel and my former boss agrees. Being up here in the hills is definitely more secure than a hotel.

"We might have to get you two White House security clearance," she quipped.

Still hungry after the appetizers, Penelope ordered several large pizzas as they continued the discussion.

Chapter TWENTY-FIVE

Marianna Gutierrez was relaxing in her small, floral backyard sipping her first Sex on the Beach cocktail. She enjoyed this time of the day as the day's sun made its way towards the western horizon and behind her fourteen-foot stucco block wall, affording her the enjoyable heat without the burning rays.

Her feet were propped up on a charcoal, oval, glass-covered, wicker coffee table as she inhaled the fragrance of her nearby gardenia bush and the beauty of several Bellfire Begonia bushes interspersed with two variegated flowering maples.

The beauty her landscaper had created provided an oasis, a refuge from the pressures of the office, court room and the ever presence of the Santa Barbara Police and County Sheriff's officers.

She reached over and placed her drink on the table, rose from the matching wicker recliner and stretched, feeling the Lycra of the denim, long sleeve, front-button jumpsuit with drawstring waist move with her. Wiggling her toes in her Birkenstock open-toe taupe sandals, she felt happy with her body. Not what she had at twenty, but at fifty-three, it was firm, while showing a few age-induced lumps and bumps.

She attributed her good health and body to a combination of her Latina genes, daily exercise in her lower bedroom gym and a steady diet from Concepción's deli, a kitchen with which she fell in love years ago after moving to Santa Barbara from the Bay Area.

Sitting down, she topped her cocktail from the nearby pitcher and leaned back into the luxury of the thick cushion, thankful she had splurged on the velvety black and white striped fabric. Curling up, with one leg under herself, she smiled at her good fortune, nodding to herself thinking, *good fortune, maybe. Damn hard work and subterfuge? Exactly.*

She continued to muse her life; where she started, how she had slipped through the San Francisco law enforcement sting which brought down so many of her fellow law school colleagues.

Although she was equally guilty of taking the easy money from trustful investors, none knew her real identity, and still do not to this day. The identity of Gutierrez lived only in her mind until she recreated herself decades previously and joined the California Bar Association with that name, complete with university credentials and bar exam results, thanks to the technical wizard who had created the financial scheme which had netted her millions, even before the introduction of the drug business.

It was almost ten years to the day when she contacted her disbarred and now released former colleagues and suggested they meet.

The first connection was over a long weekend at a Big Sur campground, where she arrived on her Yamaha Stargate 650 sans sleeping bag or toiletries.

A casual observer wouldn't pick up that this group of university educated, recently released convicts, were co-conspirators, none of whom held a grudge against the sole attendee who didn't serve time.

Gutierrez had created Caribbean bank accounts for each member of the Hermanos de Wall Street with aliases and access codes, both of which she energetically distributed with a hug for each. Their camaraderie was infectious, each knowing that Marianna had followed through with their plan if they were caught. What the police discovered of their financial scam was twenty-five percent of their net worth, the seventy-five being held by Gutierrez and now in their hands.

The cocaine smuggling was her concept, taking months of arranging and negotiating with local distributors, all of whom she had defended in Los Angeles courts. Her brilliance in manipulating the law and the court system in favor of her clients created ongoing hostility from the LAPD and prosecutors, who, unfortunately, had shared their animosity with local law enforcement, attempting to find some means to eliminate her from the legal profession.

The irony in their enthusiasm was that Gutierrez was a community leader in Santa Barbara, highly respected with none of the negative undertones she generated within the Los Angeles law enforcement and prosecutor's offices.

Regardless of her contentious relationship with LAPD and LA Sheriff's officers, the state gave her a concealed weapons permit based on the potential for violence from her clientele. Although the threat was her sworn basis for the permit, she feared none of her clients who revered her for her skill in keeping them out of prison.

Her firearm of choice was a Smith and Wesson Centennial, .38 caliber with a Packmayr grip, giving the piece more stability and shooting comfort. She carried the .38 in a small-of-the-back holster, completely concealed by any one of her stylish jackets. *

She was a member of the National Rifle Association and competed in pistol shoots with the United States Pistol Shooting Association in the open revolver category, going head-to-head with males, many of them police officers in California and surrounding states.

The importing business had expanded to such an extent over the past decade that she could no longer manage it solo and needed the help of her recently released colleagues. It took little convincing for all members to join the business and share the responsibilities.

Donating to political aspirants and parties was the idea of one of the disbarred attorneys. He felt it would be a perfect opportunity to hit back at the system, which as corrupt as it was, had the audacity to chastise him for his unscrupulous dealings. The procedure was as simple as writing checks from the legitimate accounts to which the drug profits in the Caribbean were funneled.

It was the same attorney who had developed a fondness for the Christians for a Better America through Orange County friends. Millions were donated to them without the Hermanos knowing how the money was spent.

With that initial meeting, they developed the current Hermanos de Wall Street management structure, so efficient as to increase their profit margin by twenty percent in the first six months.

Arrangements were made to establish a club-house, three-hours south of San Francisco, where each former convict maintained a home and three hours north of Santa Barbara on Highway One. Secluded. Yet accessible.

Smiling at her ingenuity, Marianna stretched, glanced at the sky and noticed the sun had long ago set below the neighborhood, shivered slightly as the night cold and early fog set in and meandered through the back door, knowing she had one too many beaches and not enough sexes to get groceries.

Once inside her elegant living room with its Tuscany rubbed stucco walls, cream, floral couch and occasional chairs and gas fireplace, she marveled at the center of the three-point nine million home she purchased ten years previously. Admiring her decorative sense, she dropped her gaze to use her app to order curried chicken with coconut rice and peas from Concepción.

The ceilings throughout were vaulted with horizontal distressed oak boards supported matching six by six beams, spaced two-feet apart. The brown tinted Tuscany décor enhanced every room with various furniture pieces and accents to highlight the wall tones.

While she waited for her order, she mixed another pitcher, turned on the gas fireplace, stepped into the adjoining open kitchen with pocket lights over a marble island, and readied a plate and utensils, refusing to eat out of the paper containers from Concepción.

Having about half an hour to wait, she headed up the wide, cream tiled stairs to her office to check her emails.

The master-bedroom was immediately off the landing, facing west and stretched the entire length of the house from the walk-in closet at one end, to the ensuite at the other. The stairway cream tile extended upstairs with off-white, floral cranberry area rugs on either side of the elevated queen bed which provided a panoramic view of the ocean, a ten-minute walk west.

The furniture throughout the house was light, feminine, utilizing pastels; pink, mauve and baby blue chintz on duvets, occasional chairs and couches.

To the right of the landing was a comfortable second bedroom with French doors leading to a ten by ten balcony with six-foot privacy railing, home to a mauve Clematis which weaved its way through the railing and grew so prolifically, the landscaper trimmed monthly.

She turned to her left on the landing entering the third room, a duplicate of the spare bedroom sans bed, complete with French doors, balcony and a pink Clematis.

One end of the office housed her library, from floor to ceiling, twelve-feet on both sides of a gas fireplace with a twelve-inch Italian stone hearth and matching mantle.

A Chippendale office desk sat at an angle facing the French doors. The desk was adorned with multiple drawers on one side and a computer area swinging out in an L-shape to the left, accompanied by an ergonomic chair. The desk was set off by a large, chartreuse, floral area rug paired with several seascape paintings placed asymmetrically on the other two walls.

Marianna sat at her desk, moved the mouse slightly to activate her computer and clicked on her email account. She eliminated several that were obviously spam, marked others to read later, then stopped scrolling and opened one from Alane Auberée. Although he wasn't her financial adviser- hers were too nefarious- she knew him well, having socialized at various fundraisers and similar functions.

Perusing the brief invitation, she leaned back into the chair, putting one leg over the other and thought, *Rebecca Simpson and Dr. Penelope Barker, new residents. I am flattered I suppose, being invited to an Alane event but why haven't I heard of these women before now?*

She did a quick Google search on both and found Barker, a veterinarian in StoneHead, Wyoming who recently sold her practice and retired. *Okay,* she thought, *that makes sense. Santa Barbara is a perfect retirement community, but why nothing on Simpson. Everyone has something on Google, even me, well, at least the legitimate me.*

Oh, my God, did I just answer my own query? If there is nothing on Google, could she be as unscrupulous as I? Well, this is going to be interesting, very interesting, she smiled to herself as she replied in the affirmative then wondered what she would wear.

S.B.S

*Gutierrez's weapon of choice, the Smith and Wesson Centennial, was designed by former CIA operative, Col. Rex Applegate, who was undercover during the Cold War when he was required to draw his firearm, then a S&M revolver with a hammer. The protrusion caught on his pocket lining and the Colonel says he, "Damn near died because of that hammer." Once stateside, he approached S&W designers and the Centennial was created.

Chapter TWENTY-SIX

Elisabeth had little difficulty following the digital map, but their preconceived notion that Rebecca lived in an apartment, condo or similar structure vanished as they climbed through the twisting roads entering the Santa Ynez Mountain foothills.

Jason was riding shotgun, reading the dashboard map and scanning the neighborhood, convinced they had made a wrong turn. Jackson was following in his tricked out pickup. Jason checked the written address from Jessica against the map and said, "The map claims we are in the right area but look at these houses. Either we are lost, or our Rebecca has become a one-percenter."

Before either Elisabeth could reply, the map voice sounded, "Your destination is on the right."

Elisabeth stopped, and they gazed at a sprawling estate, several acres in size, a five-foot sandstone wall running across the front with iron gates at the driveway.

Jason said, "What the hell, let's give it a try. This is California, not Texas, no one is going to shoot us if she doesn't live here."

"We hope," added Elisabeth as she turned into the driveway and crept up to the gate, expecting to see a call box. They were taken aback when the massive structure opened inward without a sound.

Neither of the agents noticed the numerous cameras imbedded in the perimeter wall at the gate or the sensors implanted into the cement driveway. Rebecca and Penelope knew of their arrival and came to meet them in the driveway.

Elisabeth parked, with Jackson sliding in beside her in his modified pickup, the same one which prompted a Washington Sheriff to run the plates, associating the stunning vehicle with drug runners.

Elisabeth was the first out of the car and upon seeing Rebecca, she spread her arms out in dismay and said, "What the hell Rebecca, this is yours? Holy shit!"

By then Jackson and Jason had exited and stood with their arms on their hips in dismay, gawking at the landscaping, the impeccable two-story stucco structure, then finally, shaking their heads, came over and gave Rebecca a hug.

Elisabeth was the first to introduce herself to Penelope with, "Dr. Barker, I am Elisabeth Peltowski. I have heard a great deal about you post StoneHead and it is a pleasure to meet you."

"The pleasure is all mine Elisabeth and please, call me Penelope, the doctor is for dogs and cats," she laughingly added.

The men followed immediately with introducing themselves with hand-shakes, adding compliments regarding the property.

Rebecca interrupted the foursome with, "Please, let's get your luggage and we will show you to your rooms. We will answer all your questions by the pool in a few minutes."

"A pool? Shit Rebecca, did you win the lottery or something? This place is amazing," commented Jackson, as the three removed luggage and equipment from the rental and the pickup bed.

Rebecca was walking her former colleagues to their rooms and Penelope was arranging wine and appetizers when a text from Jessica was announced on Rebecca's phone, advising them that she had arrived and was registered at the Jalama Creek Inn, spreading out their effectiveness. She was undercover, so to speak, as an unemployed attorney in Santa Barbara for job interviews.

Although Jalama Creek was five-hundred dollars a night, she knew Sorento wouldn't consider the cost extravagant given that the hotel was removed from the main stream tourist industry with its foothills location, leaving her less vulnerable. Jessica didn't have any difficulty with the appearance of opulence, ocean views, decadent décor and superb service.

Her text concluded with instructions for Rebecca's fivesome to get their shopping done and meet her at the Santa Barbara police station at 2pm, tomorrow afternoon.

Rebecca relayed the message to everyone, then continued with the room allocations, each with their own accommodation. Elisabeth received the room with the westerly view and ensuite, while the men settled in the other two very large bedrooms, sharing an adjoining bath, which Jason would later say was, "Almost as big as my mom's living and dining rooms combined."

The agents settled in, placing their meager belongings in drawers, closets and bathrooms, the men exchanging comments that they had to figure out how Rebecca scored this house and retirement as they each wanted this lifestyle too. Elisabeth took the time to set up her surveillance equipment which began monitoring immediately.

Changing into shorts and T shirts, they made their way downstairs and into the kitchen just as Penelope had finished. They all grabbed something and followed Pen out the back door and around to the pool, the agents' heads swiveling back and forth, trying to take in as much as they could.

Once everyone was settled around the pool and under the awnings, Rebecca gave her brief history of acquiring the property. She shared her background with the Secret Service and how her career, from day one, had been undercover, never having her own place or vehicle.

Jackson was the first to comment, "You were with the sheriff's department, were you undercover there too?"

"No, I had a furnished single and had the cruiser to take home, so it seems I have been living out of a suitcase for decades. This place was never intended to be my residence, but an investment. When I decided to retire, albeit early by most standards, my friend had it cleaned and my neighbor Alejandro, whom you will meet at a party tomorrow night, did the landscaping."

"Okay, I am getting the idea now," added Jason, "Some dude just up and left this!" He got up, unclipped his holster, set it on the coffee table, took his drink and walked over to the pool, stuck his toe in, set his glass down, took off his shirt and jumped in.

Breaking the surface, he shook his dreads letting out a scream of delight, splashing the water, expressing his joy with a broad grin.

Jackson was up next, duplicating Jason's entrance strategy, followed by the three women, none of whom removed their blouses, but all three jumped into the deep end with all five floating, treading or swimming side to side.

Jackson interrupted the mood with, "So when are we going shopping?"

Jason added, "Did I hear the word 'party'?"

Rebecca had just come up for air from doing the breast stroke when she heard the comment and started to laugh, water rocketing out of her nostrils. Holding on to the side of the pool, she yelled, "Oh my God Jackson, I have never heard you interested in shopping. Penelope, Elisabeth, let's get these two out of here and off to lunch and Nordstrom before Jackson changes his mind. We know Mr. GQ will always go clothes shopping," referring to the dapper Jason, "and, yes, Jason, you are the guest of a party here with Santa Barbara's movers and shakers," she added, watching to see a reaction.

With that levity, and seeing no reaction from either man, all five pulled themselves out of the pool, grabbed their gear and headed back to the house to change and meet at the garage in twenty.

Jason and Jackson were waiting by their rental wearing the only shorts and foot wear they owned plus Tommy Bahama shirts; Jason in a sparkling grape Miami camp silk, short sleeve, untucked and Jackson in an ocean deep stretch-cotton, also untucked.

When the women arrived in exactly twenty minutes with wet hair, sun dresses and sandals the men moved automatically into the back of the SUV as Elisabeth shouted, "Shotgun," and Rebecca slid in beside Jason in the back. Jackson turned to Jason and mouthed, *Shotgun? Women say that too?*

Jason replied by raising and lowering his eyebrows several times, then turning back to the female conversation already in progress.

Jackson turned to Rebecca sitting to his right and asked, "So, R&P, where for lunch?"

"Let me check," she replied as she retrieved her smartphone from her sun dress side pocket and quickly sent a text. "Give this a moment. Elisabeth, would you head for the beach, I'll have a name for you momentarily?"

"Will do."

The men sat in silence, gawking out the windows at the magnitude of the surrounding properties. Moments later Rebecca's phone chimed. She read the text and said, "Onward Elisabeth to the Yacht House, I'm texting the address to Penelope and she can put it into her maps app." Finishing that brief task she texted again, then closed her phone.

It took a few minutes to come out of the hills, hit the 101, then south to Las Positas and straight to the restaurant. Elisabeth parked, and everyone quickly bailed, exhibiting excitement and hunger.

Rebecca was the last through the door as Jason held it open for her. Penelope was in the process of giving the maître d' their table needs when she spotted a familiar beaming face, standing by a large table window set for six, bowing with a familiar arm gesture of welcome.

Penelope let out a sound, almost like a squeal, turned to Rebecca, caught her eye and pointed. Rebecca responded with, "Ladies and gentlemen, we believe our table awaits us," pointing to Alane.

Penelope stepped aside allowing the others to lead to their table and as Rebecca passed her, she smiled saying, "Sneakyyyy."

Rebecca smiled and did a quick curtsy, then headed to the table.

Alane, dressed in a Costa Sera light Havana camp shirt, dandelion Ralph Lauren knee length shorts and taupe, tassel dress shoes, sans socks, smiled broadly as his friends and their guests approached the table.

Before Alane could introduce himself, Rebecca spoke from the back of the group, "Ladies and gentlemen, a little R&P surprise. This well-dressed gentleman is none other than Alane Auberée, our friend and financial advisor. He is also organizing the upcoming party. Alane, may I introduce your new clients, Elisabeth Peltowski, Jason Spencer and Jackson Pennington."

Elisabeth was the first to respond as she took the nearest seat to Alane, "It is a pleasure to meet you Alane. We understand you are responsible, in a round-about way, for our luxurious accommodations."

As the others chose a place and sat, Alane smiled broadly and replied, "The pleasure is all mine Elisabeth and I can assure you that I am simply a financial advisor to pragmatic and progressive investors such as Rebecca. Her foresight to invest at such an early age, and of course with me," he tipped one finger to his forehead, "has enabled her to retire early and, with colleague Penelope Barker, continue her criminal analytical prowess with R&P Investigations."

"Alane, it is I who is forever grateful. I had no idea when you took over my monthly paycheck that twenty plus years later, I would be in this position," Rebecca replied, rising slightly and bowing.

Alane bowed his head gracefully, then changing the subject said, "Thank you Rebecca for the dining invitation and although the invite was yours, lunch is on me. And Elisabeth and gentlemen, before we proceed, all I know about Rebecca's background is that she retired from the federal government, but since you three are friends, and you have law enforcement written across your foreheads, I will not enquire into your purpose in Santa Barbara other than to visit your friend."

Rebecca replied, "That obvious Alane?"

"Yes. As dapper as these gentlemen are with their Tommy Bahama attire, their body language and movement spells law enforcement, as does Elisabeth with her intense scrutinization and awareness. In a good way of course for us honest and law-abiding citizens, but our criminal element may spot you quickly.

"Thank you for your frankness Alane, it certainly relieves all three of us to come up with a cover on the quick as well as aid in our daily deportment. Now, to lunch, what do you recommend?" asked Jackson.

"Excellent Jackson. I suggest we try an array of local wineries. The Yacht House has a fabulous tasting offering from various vineyards, as he glanced away and caught the eye of their server.

Luciana saw Alane's gesture and gracefully approached their table acknowledging Alane with, "Welcome back Mr. Auberé and welcome to your guests," as she turned to recognize the others. "What may I start you off with this afternoon sir?"

"Delightful to have you as our server Luciana," he replied glancing around the table, seeking agreement with his suggestion. Seeing that all were nodding approval, he continued, "We would like to sample today's choices of our local vineyards in each of the grapes. Would that be possible?"

"Certainly Mr. Auberé. Give me a few moments and I will be right back. In the meantime, here is today's menu, drawing your attention to our seafood special?" replied Luciana as she passed each diner a menu, turned and headed to the bar.

Conversation turned immediately to the city with the agents taking turns in asking questions about its history, age, population and cuisine. Rebecca and Alane provided their input, Alane more so than Rebecca given his longevity of residence. His curiosity was rampant, but he managed to contain his enthusiasm regarding the agents' recent deployment and personal history, his common-sense grappling with civilian curiosity.

Rebecca, noting a conversation lag and ignorant of Jessica's disclosure paradigm, turned the discussion to Alane and the upcoming party.

He was ecstatic for the anxiety relief and immediately elaborated on his and Alejandro's plans in general terms, saving the menu as a surprise.

Elisabeth expressed the most fascination with the event, turning to Rebecca, exploring outfit options. Rebecca deferred to Alane with, "Alane, would this engagement be considered California casual, which I interpret as a dress and sandal with a heel, and men, dress shirt, slacks and shoes? Socks optional ala Alane?"

she added with a head tilt, pointing a flirtatious finger toward Alane.

"That is a perfect interpretation Rebecca. I thought you said you were basically fashion ignorant?"

"Actually, I am Alane, Penelope is educating me quickly. We spent a weekend at Nordstrom in Denver not too long ago, so my learning curve has flattened somewhat."

"That explains a great deal and speaking of Nordstrom, you might want to explore ours. I understand there are considerable deals to be made on summer and fall fashions."

Penelope and Rebecca exchanged looks just as Jason said, "Didn't you guys say we were shopping there this afternoon? I for one, am ready for new threads."

Just then Elisabeth noted Luciana along with two colleagues approaching their table with several bottles of wine, a wine cooler on a stand and several plates of Rockfish Ceviche, their house specialty along with crackers and brie to accompany the wine tastings. She welcomed the servers with, "Oh, my, that looks absolutely scrumptious. Thank you so much."

Luciana placed the Ceviche in the table center, the wine cooler beside Alane, uncorked the rosé, and pinot noir while her colleague did the chardonnay, offering a taste to Alane as Luciana explained, "These wines are from our local Sandalwood Winery just north of town in the foothills which was almost lost to the forest fires last summer. You will find their chardonnay is a delightfully light offering with aromas of vanilla, pineapple and nutmeg, while the pinot noir will have a nose of roses, black cherry and currant. The rosé is citrusy and melon with a hint of rhubarb." Both servers completed their pouring, then Luciana finished with, "I will give you a few moments, then return for your entrée order."

Compliments were numerous to the Yacht House and Alane for the delicious wines, as they savored the wine, along with the crackers and cheese while they perused the menu. Within about twenty minutes, Luciana returned for their orders.

Neither Rebecca nor Penelope had eaten seafood lately, so they chose the Cioppino; a spicy tomato broth, mussels, clams, the day's catch, shrimp and scallops. Alane had the Seafood Pasta; scallops, crab, shrimp with penne and spicy cream sauce. The men, although not opting for total carnivore, having had their fill of beef at the Firewalker Pub, went for a modified meat eater with the Pulled Pork Grilled Cheese; slow roasted pork with BBQ sauce, caramelized onions, Shishido peppers, smoked gouda and gruyere cheese on a ciabatta bun with fries.

As their server turned and left, a forties-something male approached their table, stood beside Rebecca, cleared his throat and said, "Rebecca Simpson, the only woman I ever dated just once."

Taken aback by the abrupt interruption in their table discussion, Rebecca stood, as a force of habit, and faced her inquisitor, commenting, "Well, I'll be damned, Jack Barlet, what has it been, twenty years? How are you?"

"I am fine Rebecca. I was traded to the LA Kings a few years ago and am here with my girlfriend for the day, enjoying the sites. What about you?"

"That is good to hear. I hope you are happy with the Kings. I retired from the Secret Service and now my partner and I are private investigators in Santa Barbara."

"Son of a bitch, you, a Secret Service Agent. I never knew?"

"Well, to be truthful Jack, there wasn't much to learn on a first and only date."

"You got me there Rebecca. I just didn't think we clicked," as he glanced at Penelope, an astonishing expression crossing his face as he noted her beauty and her cold stare.

"No we didn't, and you undoubtedly have noted the reason why," as she reached down and graced Penelope's shoulder warmly.

Rebecca turned to her dining friends saying, "Everyone, this is Jack Bartlet who plays hockey for the Los Angeles Kings and one of the men I dated in Washington back in the day." She turned to Jack and continued with, "I guess I can't say dated since we went out but once. Jack, these are my friends," as she went around the table politely introducing everyone.

"Nice to meet you all," Jack replied as he glanced to the restaurant's entrance. "I see my girlfriend waiting for me, so I will head out. Nice meeting you all and Rebecca, I am delighted to see you happy," as he turned and headed toward the front door.

Alane looked back and forth from Rebecca to Penelope as a huge grin embraced his face, but in the true fashion of a gentleman, said nothing.

The conversation returned with Jason asking, "So, question to the party organizers, this is happening, where?"

"At our place. We thought about making it more of a pool party but Alane thought it wise, considering the guest list, to have it indoors and more of an evening function."

Jackson chimed in with, "Might we be so bold as to ask who might be attending?"

Penelope rattled off the names, having memorized them from the brief introduction from Alane previously and added, "You will meet two tomorrow at the meeting with the police chief and his lead detective. The others, I defer to Alane as we haven't met them. Alane."

"The original plan proposed by Rebecca and Penelope was a get to know your neighbor's function. My co-planner is their neighbor Alejandro, then there will be the mayor, several counselors, several attorneys, one being Marianna Gutierrez whom I know, the police chief, Detective Pelfini and the University of California police chief. The list segued into an R&P introduction so to speak.

"It should be fun and hopefully give R&P an introduction to those who might provide them with business."

"I can't remember the last party I attended," said Jason. "Going from LAPD patrol to undercover, then over to North Africa, then to the Secret Service and the last operation, it has to be many years."

"Ditto for me," continued Jackson, "Pretty much the same, although I was invited to a few parties at Northern Michigan University, partying with twenty-year old kids wasn't my idea of fun. Besides, they all thought I was an old guy, sort of a grandpa."

Listening to Jason and Jackson discuss their background, Alane was mesmerized, his face an expression of shock and awe, never thinking the agents would reveal their true identity.

Rebecca, seeing his expression and knowing there wasn't a breach of security, jumped in with, "Well, now we have some background for Alane, Elisabeth, why don't you give him your brief history?"

Elisabeth, looking totally unfazed, said, "Sure. Alane, I was a Junior High school computer teacher before I joined the Secret Service and upon graduation, I was sequestered to the UK to evaluate internet chatter in the European Union and the Middle East with MI6. After several years I was ready for a change and without any preamble, received a transfer to Jessica Fukishura's team, a unit to which all three of us belong. I am a hacker," she concluded with a smile of pride.

Alane was so taken aback by their frank and open dialog, he was speechless and for him, that was unique. His first word was, "Oh," then took a long swallow of his chardonnay, wiped his mouth and continued calmly, more in control. "Thank you for sharing your exciting backgrounds. Rebecca, I presume you were a member of this team?" he said raising his eyebrows.

"I was Alane. Jessica calls us the "J" Team and there is nothing confidential about us. For all intense and purposes, they are here visiting us and although nobody needs to know who they are exactly, it would come out eventually, it always does. As you noted, the three are easily identifiable as law enforcement, so we can keep their entire presence on the down low. I think it will be easier now with you in the loop and they're staying at our place rather than in a hotel."

Penelope beamed at the mention of, *our place*, but remained quiet, as they all turned to see their lunch arriving.

The conversation slowed as they enjoyed their entrées with the occasional comment of the spectacular ocean view.

Lunch concluded, Alane signaled Luciana for the check, paid, leaving her a thirty percent gratuity just as Penelope and Elisabeth rose with Elisabeth saying, "Thank you so much Alane for the lovely lunch. Your generosity is greatly appreciated. We look forward to learning more about you and your financial expertise at the dinner party."

The men reached across the table and shook Alane's hand while Rebecca walked around giving him a hug and a cheek kiss, bringing a slight rose color to his face, then said, "Off to Nordstrom."

"I don't design clothes. I design dreams."
Ralph Lauren

S.B.S

"California Casual: This is a cute way of saying, 'Wear something synonymous with the California life style.' Translated, that means a comfortable, wholesome look that will be great when you're seated around the pool or on a sofa in a private home. Wallerich says: 'The California Casual look never means shorts and sneakers. It means wear something trendy and fun, or something flowy or strapless with a designer sandal.' Men can wear silk blend slacks, and a sport coat with or without a tie."

Ann Conway Los Angeles Times
"Don't be into trends. Don't make fashion own you, but you decide what you are, what you want to express by the way you dress and the way to live."
Gianni Versace

Chapter TWENTY-SEVEN

The day following their pleasant, previous evening, Jessica and Karen enjoyed a run through various Washington parks, Jessica carrying her service pistol in a fanny pack and Karen going without. Not having obtained a license to carry in Washington, DC, Jessica quipped as they left the flat with, "I know you feel naked without it, but I will protect you," giving Karen a little poke as she bolted down the stairs and into the parking lot, laughing at her own humor.

Ms. Esposito heard them returning and met them in the hall, introducing herself to Karen and insisting the two join her for lunch. Karen was delighted to meet Jessica's landlady and immediately accepted the invitation. Once back in Jessica's flat, she asked, "I hope that was okay to accept without asking you. She seems like a nice lady."

"No worries. She is delightful. When I was gone, she cleaned my apartment every week and the day I returned, she brought over wine and appetizers."

They showered, sat on the deck overlooking the building's parking lot with its variety of perennials in full bloom, drinking coffee, dressed in shorts and Ts, then walked to breakfast, Jessica providing a guide's monologue of the upscale area and how she developed the "J" Team, snagging the three agents from their then current assignments.

Breakfast and the tour consumed the morning.

Lunch with Ms. Esposito was both educational, with her sharing the years she had lived in the building and delicious, with the array of Italian sausages, cheeses, spreads and buns. Two hours later, they returned to Jessica's flat and chose to take naps having consumed way too much Pinot Noir and Ms. Esposito's cheese and sausage.

It was after 5 pm when they woke, wondering where the afternoon went. Still groggy, they decided to stay in for the night, order pizza later, drink wine and binge chick flicks from Jessica's Pay for View.

One Mediterranean pizza, two bottles of Pinot and *The Devil wears Prada, The Notebook* and *Dirty Dancing* later, they called it an evening and crashed.

The next morning it was back to business with booked flights to LAX and Toronto, a connecting drive to Santa Barbara for Jessica and for Karen, a direct flight to Toronto with a twenty-four layover, then non-stop to Limón, Costa Rica.

Chapter TWENTY-EIGHT

Karen texted Tom Hortonn from the airport providing him with her flight number and arrival time, writing that she would meet him at his office with Toronto Police Service to discuss the operation. While waiting for her flight, she made reservations for them both, under her name, leaving the next morning from Pearson International Airport outside of Toronto, directly to Limón.

During the interval for the Air Canada staffer to confirm tomorrow's flight, Karen noticed a woman approaching on her right, dressed sharply in the Air Canada uniform; tailored navy-blue pant suit, sky blue blouse with a maroon neck scarf and blue pumps. She appeared to stand about five-foot, seven with short, spiked brown hair with blonde highlights, around her mid-thirties.

"Sheriff Winthrop, Deidre Hall," she said, extending her hand, brandishing a broad smile. "It is a pleasure to have you traveling with us today. I understand this trip is one of pleasure and not work related, therefore it is our delight to upgrade you to first class. It is Air Canada's way of expressing our appreciation for the years of safety you provided our passengers."

Karen felt a little shell shocked in that she received this VIP treatment coming down and figured it was a one-time deal, never expecting the treatment to reoccur. She smiled, accepted Hall's handshake and replied, "This is very kind of you Ms. Hall but totally unnecessary. I was just doing my job and I don't expect such treatment."

"Of course you don't expect it sheriff, which is why we love pampering you so much. We have never had a female sheriff on our flights, ever, and your personality and expertise shocked the airline. I hope you will accept our hospitality in the good spirit in which it is given. We have no other way to express our gratitude."

"I sincerely appreciate your kindness Ms. Hall and thank you, I graciously accept the upgrade," Karen replied, somewhat embarrassed and feeling her cheeks flush.

Karen shook the staffer's hand as she accepted her boarding pass from the other agent. Hall gestured that she would escort Karen to Air Canada's Signature Suite where her VIP treatment would embrace the design of Montreal architect Heekyung Duquette in the comfort of their chocolate brown lounge chairs, sipping a latte and nibbling a croissant. As they walked the concourse, Karen thought, *I wonder if this is going to be a forever thing. Kinda nice. Embarrassing. But nice. Hope it doesn't come back and bite me in the butt.*

The luxury treatment continued on the flight, with Air Canada's Bistro, offering cuisine from Freshii. She enjoyed a Biiblos, a combination of quinoa, spinach, walnuts, chickpeas, feta cheese, dried cranberries, cucumber, carrots, with a drizzle of spicy harissa tahini dressing with pita bread and guacamole. And another latte.

Upon landing, she immediately taxied to Tom's office where she was greeted, once the door was closed, with the warmth and affection she had missed coming home from Edmonton. Although they almost ended up on the black leather couch, they stifled their hormones and made plans for their Costa Rica operation.

Tom had already been briefed by David Kopas and logged into CHAP, so he was well versed with the background and David's instructions.

They discussed their cover; a couple searching for Karen's brother, missing from Alberta, when he was last seen at his job in the oil fields. They had the picture provided by the Edmonton RCMP and their story was that there was a rumor he had moved to Costa Rica. They just wanted to know if the comments were true and that he was okay.

The discussion and memory process took several hours, including her cover as an Air Canada flight attendant, and Tom as a bartender at The Calgary in Toronto. Tom called his former Ottawa University friend, Craig Stevenson, also known as Soul Train for his legendary time as a bartender in Whistler, and now general manager of the iconic eatery. Karen knew her cover was automatically confirmed, given her recent treatment by the airline.

By five o'clock, they were exhausted and called it a day, comfortable with their plan.

Karen's condo was closest to TPS, so they taxied there and ordered from Brown's Social House. They chose Yucatan chicken tacos which were flour tortillas with achiote chicken, queso blanco, or white cheese, avocado, cilantro, salsa and jalapeno crema, while Karen uncorked a bottle of Cave Springs Niagara Peninsula 2016 Riesling, which paired smoothly with the tacos.

They were on their second bottle of the Peninsula Riesling and watching Audrey Hepburn and George Peppard in *Breakfast at Tiffany's* when their dinner arrived.

Neither had eaten since breakfast, or in Karen's case, her Air Canada brunch, and they were famished, devouring the tacos, accompanying fried rice, even the sprigs of parsley, then moved to the balcony.

They shared the last of the Riesling overlooking Lake Ontario and the movies' trendy-behind-the-scenes-morsels: writer Truman Capote wanting Marilyn Monroe to play Holly, Shirley MacLaine turning down the lead role, Steve McQueen destined for the male role and other tantalizing gossip until they realized they were exhausted and had a full day's travel ahead of them.

They dropped their clothes on the bedroom floor, crawled under the covers and snuggled briefly before they were sound asleep.

Jessica landed at LAX, immediately gaining access to an SUV rental and checked in as herself at Santa Barbara's Jalama Creek Inn, an upscale boutique hotel in the foothills. She chatted with the registration clerk, explaining that she was an unemployed attorney seeking a position in criminal law. *May as well get the rumors going accurately,* she thought.

Sorento had provided the necessary paper work supporting a Washington, DC history as a paralegal who experienced a recent divorce, had just passed the California Bar Exams and wanted to relocate on the west coast.

His staff had created a Facebook page and Google presence promoting her cover. Considering that most, if not all employers performed an online query for every applicant, Jessica's only challenge would be the interview.

Jessica's room overlooked the Pacific, albeit from a mile into the hills, while numerous perennials offered a combination of delightful fragrances: White Evening Primroses with their large white flowers, white California Mock Orange and numerous purple Nightshades.

The accommodation was feminine, decorated with off-white walls, floral curtains and duvet cover. The matching occasional chairs flaunted a white frame with tan cushions. The hillside hideaway included a white bricked gas fireplace with white mantle and a Victorian writing desk and chair.

While unpacking, she was interrupted by a knock at the door. Viewing her visitor through the peephole, she acknowledged a staffer with a tray.

Jessica had yet to remove her jacket, but she checked her pistol as a force of habit, then opened the door offering the staffer, a smile and, "Hello, what have we here?"

"Welcome Ms. Fukishura. I am Luca and will be your attendant during your stay. I offer our concierge's honored greetings with this chilled bottle of our local Sauvignon Blanc, which is somewhat tart, compared to our chardonnay. She has paired the wine with this delicious goat cheese, Tuscany herb crackers and fruit selection. May I place these in your room?"

"What a delightful surprise Luca. Thank you and yes, please do," as Jessica stepped out of the way, holding the door for her guest.

Luca placed the tray with the wine in a silver cooling container, then turned and said, "We hope you enjoy your stay. Please do not hesitate to call the front desk for any need we have overlooked." She curtsied briefly, turned and departed, with Jessica thanking her profusely again, then closing and locking the door.

She poured a tall glass of the Sauvignon Blanc, created a plate of appetizers and took both on to the deck overlooking the gardens in the foreground and the Pacific in the west. She swirled the liquid, nosed, then tasted the flavors of lime, green apple and passion fruit. She tasted the Tuscany crackers and soft, smooth goat cheese, followed by a sip of wine, delighted with the zest, as she contemplated tomorrow's meeting with Rodrigo O'Connor and her "J" Team, the formality of which Sorento had previously arranged.

Reviewing Sorento's curriculum, she memorized the details of her Juris Doctor degree from the University of California at Berkley, the years as a paralegal for Weber & Weber while there, her anger and frustration with her cheating husband and the living arrangements in Berkley, California while studying for her bar exams.

Flipping through the pages she smiled, thinking of the intricacy and detail the Secret Service put into the cover. She had a letter of recommendation from Weber & Weber, her California Bar Exam results, the scores of which were lower than what she obtained herself ions ago and a copy of an email from Mr. Weber Sr. to Katrina Barbados, a Santa Barbara defense attorney.

Satisfied she had her background solid, she called Ms. Barbados' office and made an appointment for nine the next morning, then texted Sorento from her encrypted smartphone with an update.

Glancing at her watch and noting the late hour, she changed her mind about freshening up, grabbed her room key-card and went for dinner at the hotel's dining room, on the deck, overlooking the Pacific.

Although the dining room was full, her timing was perfect in obtaining a two-top facing the Pacific. The maître d' greeted her profusely, pulled out the charcoal wicker chair with matching cushion, offered her the folded, cloth napkin, proffered the wine selection, mentioned that the sommelier would arrive momentarily for her wine choice, then took his leave.

Right on his heals a male approached, and Jessica thought to herself, *he should be in high school. Oh, my God, I must be getting old,* then smiled as he said, "Good evening Ms. Fukishura. My name is Tomás, may I offer you an evening cocktail?"

"Good evening to you as well Tomás. Yes please. May I have a Canadian Rock Shot?" fully expecting him to question her choice, suspecting the bartender didn't know the ingredients.

"Certainly Ma'am. We serve Grey Goose vodka and this an excellent choice for a warm evening. The peach schnapps, Jägermeister and cranberry juice will be refreshing," replied Tomás, then departed.

Jessica smiled broadly, wondering where the locals would have heard of the Rock Shot, then chastised herself for ignoring the hotel's sophistication.

Santa Barbara was enjoying another beautiful evening as the sun made its way over the Los Padres National Forest and the Santa Ynez Mountains, destined to say goodnight at the horizon. Jessica basked in the late afternoon sunshine, wanting to remove her jacket but realizing her cover would be blown immediately.

Momentarily Tomás arrived with her Rock Shot and an umbrella. Placing the drink on a white triangle coaster, he gestured to the umbrella with Jessica nodding her approval, thankful for the heat relief.

From the small of his back, Tomás removed and offered a miniature, leather-bound menu, which Jessica accepted graciously. Tomás said, "Ms. Fukishura, we are renown for our seafood, while our Montana beef and lamb are equally outstanding. I will give you a few moments to peruse our unique cuisine and be back shortly for your order."

Mm thought Jessica, *a server who is also a wine and spirits expert. Very nice. Unique.*

After scrutinizing her options, she decided on the abalone with house pasta, rainbow chard and lemon beurre blanc, a delicate French white sauce of emulsified butter, white wine and grey shallots.

Placing the menu down, she took the last swallow of her Rock Shot as Tomás approached with another cocktail. As he removed her glass and placed the fresh drink, he said, "Have you made a selection ma'am?"

"Yes, I have Tomás," she replied, then stated her decision.

"Excellent choice, Ms. Fukishura. I know you will be happy with our chef's preparation and plating," he said, not writing the order but simply spinning on one toe and leaving.

Jessica was taking a sip of her Rock Shot when she observed his maneuver and almost snorted the Canadian up her nose. He was doing what she has done since her first days of Combat Martial Arts training, twirling on one toe to scope her 360 and know her surroundings.

Jessica spent the moments anticipating her meal, gazing out at the Pacific, remembering how much she enjoyed her brief beach encounters at the University of California at Berkeley, always too busy studying to allow herself leisure, which may have been why she was so tightly wrapped when she received her law degree.

Pinching the bridge of her nose to dispel the negativity, she drew her attention back to the peacefulness and beauty. Although she knew that the Channel Islands National Park and Santa Rosa Island were thirty miles away, they were not visible, hidden in off-shore fog, allowing an unobstructed view of the deep, azure waves caressing the sandy shore directly below her, one of the main drawing features of America's Riviera.

She snapped out of her revere with Tomás' arrival bearing her entrée, placing it neatly on her table, then offering her a fresh, white cloth napkin and departing.

Thanking Tomás, she savored the aroma from the exquisite plating while taking a bite of the abalone and chard and thought of her outfit for tomorrow's meeting.

She felt she chose well with the tailored, one-button, wool blend, blush pant suit with slash pockets and medium lapels. Although she would have loved to wear her tangerine shorts and blazer, she knew from experience that a conservative look influenced both male and female judges and won cases. The perfect tailoring allowed sufficient room for her nine and two magazines on the alternate side. Smiling to herself, she thought of the impression her suits created…a larger bust.

She paired the suit with Jimmy Choo's patent leather 'Romy 100' pumps. Although they set her back almost three-hundred dollars, the comfort and fit far outweighed the price, considering she could wear them all day with comfort.

Comfortable with her choice, she moved on to tomorrow's agenda, her presentation and cover story to ensure she had it down pat without notes.

Enjoying the last of her meal, she admired the flaming sun as it passed overhead, joining the darkening horizon with the crystal, flat ocean. As darkness set, she signed the check from Tomás, leaving him a thirty-percent gratuity, gracefully removed herself from the table with Tomás's assistance and returned to her room, comfortable with her day's accomplishments and tomorrow's anticipations.

Setting the hotel's automatic wake-up call for 6 am, she placed her outfit on the clothes voiturier, skipped teeth brushing, crawled under the light-weight Florentine Paisley duvet and fell asleep, confident she would nail tomorrow's interview.

S.B.S

Karen slept in comfort, next to Tom, feeling the tranquility they had at the Channel Road Inn on the Santa Monica coast. Deep in REM sleep…until thoughts of discomfort slowly seeped into her subconscious, dragging her from the emotional warmth, raising her heart rate ever so slightly as she left the cocoon.

Visions of the Whistler attack brought a smile to her otherwise comatose face as her memory adjusted the vision, clarifying the scene of Tom's grin as she kicked the crap out of two guys who attacked them. The scene changed abruptly, and she was being confronted by the Whistler RCMP commander in Araxi. A tension developed in her upper body as she remembered the standoff as demands were made and identifications exchanged.

Deep slumber memories are not always sequential, for her the next vision was being called to Air Canada's First-Class flight to Toronto from Washington, DC to find a passenger wielding a fork at a woman who had his hand in a wrist lock and in the process of taking him to the floor. Smiling again as she rose from the final stage of her REM sleep, Jessica.

Now completely awake, she yawned, glanced at Tom. Out. Then at the clock, blinked several times, then yelled, "Shit."

She jumped out of bed, simultaneously shaking Tom, shouting, "We're late Tom. We are going to miss our flight. Let's go."

Tom was up, out of bed, running naked for the ensuite while Karen headed for the opposite end of the condo for the guest facility.

ॐ.ॐ.ॐ

Brian Sawyer was a local. Not a transplanted Canadian, but someone who, if a native were to be asked his origin, the reply would be, "Right here."

Wintering in the village for so many years, his neighbors believed he went to Alberta for work but came right back home during his breaks. But of course, it was his remodeling of his house, the removal of the perimeter fence and hosting the spectacular beach party which sealed his native status. He was a local.

Brian did his drinking at the village's only bar, Mariscos Punta Manzanillo. The same establishment that catered his lavish beach party previously, the event everyone still talked about years later.

It was at the Punta one evening where he overheard his neighbors chatting about several large skiffs seen passing close to shore, in tandem, with two crew each. There had never been boats seen in the vicinity, ever. They spoke of how low the large boats were in the water, implying a heavy cargo. Brian knew instinctively what they were carrying.

ॐ.ॐ.ॐ

Stan's daily life had unfolded to RCMP detectives, totally unbeknown to their suspect. They had obtained a warrant for his phone, which lead to a second court approval for his apartment and vehicle.

His phone conversations and texts were recorded, then digitally transferred to the investigator's twelve-foot

LED screen with its ten integrated speakers so they could read the conversation as it unfolded. Most of his communications were vague with few specifics, but when detectives observed the communications collectively, a pattern emerged. Once they confirmed their hypothesis, they shared it with CHAP, notifying every detachment west of Saskatchewan.

Chapter TWENTY-NINE

Rebecca, Penelope, Elisabeth, Jackson and Jason left the Yacht House and headed to Nordstrom, the women needling the guys a bit about the task before them; neither having purchased new clothes and having lived out of a suitcase for an extended period. Elisabeth was in a similar situation, having been deployed with them since leaving Washington, but she was more astute and brought several suitcases and numerous outfits. However, insight wasn't going to prevent her from utilizing every dollar Sorento was allowing.

They pulled into Paseo Nuevo Shopping Center's parking lot, parked and all five headed to Rebecca and Penelope's favorite shop, suggesting the guys check out the men's section. They declined, opting instead to try two shops they read about, styles they would like, leaving the women as soon as they entered the mall.

Jason and Jackson walked in, meandered around then out of each store, disappointed with the selection. Standing outside the last store, Jason turned to Jackson who nodded and they both took off at a fast pace to Nordstrom, stopping at the main door to text Elisabeth with, "Where are you? We need help shopping."

The women were in the shorts department scoffing at a pair of cut-offs, raggedy and bleached for ninety-dollars, so short their butt cheeks would have shown, when Elisabeth's personal phone vibrated. Reading the screen, she bent over laughing, then handing the phone to Penelope who put her hand over her mouth giggling, passed the phone to Rebecca who said, shaking her head and smiling, "Why do men always think they know clothes better than women?" and handed the phone back to Elisabeth who replied, "Exactly," then texted them their location.

Moments later the two men arrived, looking sheepish with Jason going down on one knee, smiling, his hands in a praying manner saying, "Please help us. This mall is a maze and we are untrained."

Rebecca responded by handing Jackson the pair of shorts they had been perusing and said, "Here, try these on for starters."

Jason went along with the gag and placed the shorts up to his waist and said, "Too long for me," which busted everyone up. Elisabeth started walking, turned and waved the men, instructing, "Follow me," with the other women behind her.

Although Elisabeth had never been to this store before, her instincts lead her to a massive men's section. She turned to Jason, patted him on the shoulder and said, "Good luck. Text if you need us," then turned, put an arm around Rebecca and Penelope and headed back to the women's section, leaving Jason and Jackson somewhat bewildered but delighted to have them arrive unscathed in the men's section.

The women, having had their laugh at the teen shorts, meandered over to what they shivered to consider, the Mature Women's section and found some very stylish and dressy shorts.

Rebecca and Penelope held back, allowing Elisabeth to enjoy, both having shopped Denver Nordstrom not too long ago. Elisabeth was eager and found a pair of NYDJ stretch linen blend Bermuda shorts in feather, an off white or cream color. As she was heading to the dressing room, Penelope offered, "I have a pair of these. This style feels snug at first but can stretch out as much as two sizes, so you might want to take a smaller pair as well."

Elisabeth did and while she was gone Penelope took an identical pair and went to the shoe department while Rebecca stayed with Elisabeth. Shortly, Pen returned with a pair of open-toe, tan Sannibell platform wedge sandals with double, two-inch leather straps across the instep, an ankle strap and tightly braided jute, highlighting the two and a half-inch heel.

Elisabeth was already out of the dressing room evaluating the shorts and fit when Pen handed her the sandals. Trying them on immediately, she was impressed and bought the shorts and sandals.

Meanwhile the men were overwhelmed with the massive selection and were leaning against a pillar trying to choose a starting point when a smartly dressed male approached and asked, "Gentlemen, you look lost. My name is Gregory. I am a Nordstrom style expert. How can I help you today?" he offered, extending his hand.

Jason and Jackson shook Gregory's hand and replied, "Nice to meet you Gregory and yes, you probably can," and they explained their predicament.

Gregory had them follow him to the personal shopper section where they sat and shared their needs. At one point, Jason looked to Jackson for guidance. His approval prompted Jason to say, "Gregory, we are Secret Service agents and we need our suit jackets and blazers to be fitted for our sidearm." He produced his identification and added, "We were told recently that we were easily identifiable as law enforcement and needed a look to dispel that."

The agents were expecting a different response than, "Certainly gentlemen, or should I say, agents, let's get started," replied Gregory, seemingly unfazed by the fact that the men sitting in front of him were armed.

They began with several pairs of shorts, dress slacks and paired each with striking shirts. Jason chose several pair of nine-inch, stretch breaker shorts in pink, bluebell and sea urchin, a dark periwinkle. Jackson's choice was a more relaxed look with a pair of jogger shorts by The Rail in blue omphalodes, a light, washed blue.

Gregory encouraged them to choose classic relaxed fit, pleated, cotton pants with comfort waist, a system of elastic which allows the pants to move with the body rather than restrict it. Khaki, navy, chocolate and heather for both men. For their wild side, Jason chose a pair of yellow, while Jackson honed-in on mint, which raised Gregory's eyebrows slightly, but he took it all in stride.

Gregory called one of the tailors, advising his colleague of the status of their customers to avoid an awkward interaction. The tailor fitted each with three stunning, two button classic fit, linen & cotton blend blazers with enough room for their firearms. Jason chose one in natural, navy blue and rust, while Jackson's choice was black, charcoal and chocolate brown.

Satisfied with their selections, they headed to the shoe department and purchased three pairs of loafers; dark blue, black and brown.

Accessories, bathing suits, wide brim hats, sandals and underwear were quick and easy to choose, and they were completely outfitted and found their way back to their colleagues within three hours, Gregory promising to have their suits and blazers ready for them the following day.

Greeting the women as they approached by holding up their numerous packages, Rebecca said, "Welcome back gentlemen. We see you did alright."

Jackson replied, "I think we are good to go for a while, how are you guys making out?"

Penelope stood to one side and swept her arm in an arc, revealing a massive stack of bags, boxes and garment bags reflecting the shop till you drop exercise, adding, "Voilà."

Packages in tow, they headed out to the parking lot, jammed as many in the cargo area as possible and kept the others on Jackson and Jason's lap in the back seat.

As Rebecca was leaving the area, she quipped, "Does anyone want to cook dinner?" as she glanced at Pen with a grin.

No answers.

"How about Mexican?"

A resounding applause from the back seat, prompted Pen to google Mexican restaurants, picked one, called, and ordered chorizo and chickpea tacos, spicy cilantro rice and a chopped salad with a lime vinaigrette.

Twenty minutes for the order to be ready, so Rebecca took her former colleagues on a mini tour down Castillo St., Cabrillo Blvd. and on to Stearns Wharf, while providing a brief history of the area down to the end of the dock, turning and slowly heading for their dinner, reminding everyone of the tremendous history they can absorb while working the area.

At the restaurant, Jackson placed all his packages on Elisabeth's lap, ran for the food, paid, and ran back, jumped in and said, "On Ms. James. Drive us home."

Rebecca put the SUV in gear, shook her head, glanced at Penelope and shared a grin, then headed home.

ℑℬℑ

Tom had packed his bag after Kopas briefed him on the operation and Karen had added to her go bag, somewhat, the night before, planning to complete the job in the morning.

Tom was showered, shaved, dressed, bag at the front door, sipping a cup of instant coffee when Karen came out of the guest bathroom wearing a robe.

"What the hell?" How can you be ready, already?"

Tom's reply was a grin, shoulder shrug and a sip.

Shaking her head as she jogged back to the bedroom saying to herself, *I don't fucking believe this guy. I think he hurries just to piss me off.*

Quickly. Underwear, then slipped into a periwinkle, short-sleeve, ankle length, Alex Evenings A-line dress with rosette lace. Last were a pair of Steve Madden's three-inch, open toe, chunky, platform sandals with wide leather straps and wooden upper sole. Ran her fingers through her hair, shrugged into her shoulder holster and navy-blue Veronica Beard blazer, grabbed her suitcase and walked casually into the living room saying with a grin, "What took you so long?"

Tom smiled, kissed her quickly as he opened the door, grabbed his bag, let Karen pass, closed and locked the door and jogged to the elevator, the doors of which Karen was holding open.

Taxi. Pearson International. Jog to the Air Canada kiosk. Karen was preparing to present her tickets when the reservations staffer looked up from her computer and said, "Good morning Sheriff Winthrop. Welcome back. We have everything ready for your flight. Please follow me through security and to Air Canada's Signature Suite," she said, exiting the kiosk and leading the way down the concourse.

Tom tapped Karen on the shoulder and mouthed, *Sheriff Winthrop?* with a huge grin.

Feeling mischievous, Karen simple shrugged her shoulders as they skirted security, thereby saving considerable time with bureaucratic paperwork and walked directly into the VIP suite.

The staffer brought them lattes and croissants, ensured they were comfortable then said she would be back when first class boarding was announced.

Tom took a sip of his vanilla latte then asked Karen with raised eyebrows, "First class? Sheriff Winthrop?"

Karen put her latte down and replied, "I know. It is crazy. They did this to and from Washington. I asked them not to, but a supervisor insisted. She said that if there was any blow-back, Air Canada would handle it.

218

You know I flew with them all over North America for
several years, hence the sheriff moniker. They said they
just wanted to show their appreciation. I don't know if I
am supposed to say something to David or keep quiet."

"Are you asking me for input?"

"Yes. Of course. What do you think?"

"I think you have a pretty good thing going here
which I would enjoy. When the operation is complete,
mention it to David in passing so he is aware, then drop
it. It appears they are going to give you the royal
treatment for the foreseeable future, so enjoy. David may
have some thoughts for when you are traveling on
business. If he gives you the go ahead, will you take me
with you?" he said with a grin.

"Good. That is what I thought as well. As far as
joining me? Personal? By all means. Government?
Depends on whether you think your skills can match
mine," as she lifted her drink and toasted him.

Chapter THIRTY

Arriving at the ranch, Rebecca drove through one of the four garage doors, parked, cancelled the security system, remotely closed the garage door, then helped carry the food and parcels into the house.

While the men unpacked dinner and sought out plates and cutlery, Rebecca uncorked several bottles of chardonnay, Elisabeth found wine glasses and Penelope discovered several carrying trays and helped move the food to the patio outside the kitchen.

Once everyone was plated and wine glasses full the conversation stopped, while the five enjoyed their meal, savoring the delightfully strong spices, quieted by the salad.

Finishing his first taco, Jason opened a conversation with, "This is the first time we have all been together, sans Jessica, since Rowley and we have a great deal in common. I don't mean to be maudlin here but have any of you evaluated your love life and relationships, or lack thereof?"

Elisabeth let out a groan, replying, "Sure I do Jason, all the time. I can't remember the last time I was on a date or got laid. I remember we were talking about this with Jessica at Rowley and we have had almost identical experiences. We get asked out. Dine at a nice restaurant and chat, trying to get to know each other and the minute I am truthful, the date ends. Sometimes not immediately, but I have never had dessert on a first date and since joining the Secret Service, have never been on a second. Jessica as well."

"Do you ever feel lonely?" asked Penelope.

"Never. And I mean, never. I love my job so much, I seldom think of interpersonal relationships, dating or male companionship."

"What about sex?" asked Rebecca putting down her taco, wiping her mouth and sipping chardonnay.

"You mean you and me?" laughed Elisabeth, then added, "Sorry, I couldn't resist. Sure, I think of it now and then, but I have a great video collection and with my prize dildo, I relieve those fleeting emotions delightfully and I never have to ask him to leave or wonder if he will call me for a second date."

"I've never had that experience, obviously," offered Jackson, "but I too seldom have second dates. I recall once going home with a woman I met at a Washington party and I just assumed she knew what I did for a living. I removed my jacket once inside her apartment and she freaked out and asked me to leave."

Jason said, "Kind of what I thought. We all seem to be in the same place and time regarding a love life. The only exception for me was when I was undercover with the Christians for a Better America grad students at their Colorado retreat. I was sound asleep and one of the students let herself into my room and banged my brains out.

She was one of the leader's daughters and wanted to hook up when we flew back to Denver. Thankfully I received the 911 call from Jackson to head to LAX regarding the Mahalo plane that went down, or I would have had to weasel my way out of that.

"But then she didn't know what I really did for a living. Some dates are cop groupies, while others shun me like the plague. Many male LEOs seem to have similar experiences.

"You didn't know you saved me in Colorado did you Jackson?"

"Always ready and willing to help a fellow agent get out of sexually embarrassing incidents," scoffed Jackson. But I agree about the groupies which is why I refuse to patronize cop bars.

"I guess any negative relationships you two had are ancient history," nodding to Rebecca and Pen.

Rebecca glanced at Pen, then took up the query with, "I am sure we have both had our share of unpleasant relationships and experiences but there would be no point in visiting them. I can't believe we found each other and that I never knew I was gay. But the years I dated guys, they wanted to be the shining knight, saving the weak female and they found out within the first fifteen minutes that a damsel was not sitting across from them.

"Every male with whom I trained, except my partner in the sheriff's department, assumed I couldn't hold my own. When that image was quickly shattered, they retaliated, calling me despicable names and refusing to patrol with me."

Feeling the need to change the subject, and quickly, Penelope jumped in with, "We are what is termed, 'late-to-life' lesbians moving from the straight world to lesbian life and culture, but I don't really think about a label. We don't conduct our daily lives thinking lesbianism, just our authentic and individual selves."

"Most of us just want a normal lifestyle that allows us to marry, work, raise children, take care of the people we love, enjoy our lives…not in fear."
Mary Malia

Chapter THIRTY-ONE

Jessica rose early, dressed in light-weight sweats, completed her stretching routine, strapped on a fanny-pack holding her Sig, then went for a leisurely jog through the San Marcos Foothills Preserve which bordered the Inn.

The Preserve is home to various birds of prey species, coyotes, bobcats and the infamous roadrunner with which Jessica had so much fun mimicking their running antics.

After an uneventful forty-five minutes, she was back in her room, showered, dressed in her power pantsuit, hair moussed and heading to the dining room. There were few diners so early in the morning, so she was able to snag another window table. Service wasn't as formal as last night but her server, Gloria was excellent. In chatting, she discovered Gloria had two teenage girls and the morning shift allowed her to be there when they got home from school. Jessica enjoyed the personal touch to eating out, which enhanced her pannekoek, a Dutch crepe with seared Granny Smith apples, Gouda cheese, and scrambled eggs.

Breakfast arrived quickly given so few patrons. She relaxed with her meal and coffee while watching the ocean and beach come alive with the morning light. Her pannekoek was superb; the tart apples blending smoothly with the light crepe. Scrambled eggs, were, well, scrambled eggs.

Gloria removed her plate and topped her coffee while Jessica checked herself out in the window's reflection. She glanced down at her Jimmy Choo's, pleased with her physical presentation, then thinking, *I better nail this interview, or I am screwed and so is the operation.*

Leaving a twenty-dollar tip, she headed back to her room, brushed her teeth, checked her hair, applied a light-colored blush lipstick, grabbed her leather attaché and was out the door again, to her rental and heading for the eight o'clock meeting.

Katrina Barbados' office was in a trendy, State Street office building, just east of the freeway with ample parking. The forth floor, which seemed to be the maximum and norm for the city, had a spectacular ocean view. The elevator opened to a waiting room adorned with light oak paneling which was complimented by feminine portraits and prints of gardens in soft pastels, a Gesture Feminine by Liz Jardine and others. Highlighting the room were two large portraits of Sandra Day O'Connor and Beverley McLachlin, America's and Canada's first female supreme court judges.

Nice touch thought Jessica as she introduced herself to the receptionist who sat in an alcove, behind a massive walnut desk, the niche fronted by what appeared to be bullet proof glass with several narrow communication slots. Jessica introduced herself then apparently the staffer touched a hidden notification button because seconds later, Ms. Barbados approached her, holding out her hand and saying, "Welcome to Santa Barbara, Ms. Fukishura. Please, join me for refreshments."

Barbados appeared to be in her late forties or early fifties sporting a grey, pixie cut hairdo and, just as Jessica suspected, a classic power suit; an Ann Taylor two button jacket with flared pants in a vibrant lemon yellow paired with two-inch matching pumps. The attorney carried her slim, toned figure with poise and determination, which, combined with the outfit, spoke power, confidence, success and style.

Jessica accepted the handshake and followed Barbados down the short hall and into a corner office with a panoramic view of the ocean, *obviously the view of success in this city*, she thought, as Barbados motioned for her to take a seat on a chocolate brown, leather couch with deep cushions, round arms highlighted with antique brass-finished nail head trim and joined her.

Once seated, Jessica scanned her surroundings and appreciated the décor, a duplicate of the waiting room. She opened her attaché to retrieve her documents but was immediately stopped by Barbados with her raised hand, commenting, "There is no need for supporting documents Ms. Fukishura, I have perused those from Mr. Weber Sr. and my chat with him as well as that of the Dean at Cal, and I am impressed. More than impressed, I'm fascinated. Learning the law as a paralegal, then moving across the country to attend UC Berkeley Law, graduating at the top of your class and presenting yourself in such a professional manner today, very impressed, I must say. What brings you to Santa Barbara?"

"Thank you, Ms. Barbados. I appreciate the compliments. Choosing Berkeley was more a matter of getting as far away from my former husband as it was for their academics and Santa Barbara has always appealed to me for not only the weather but its proximity to Los Angeles, which some feel is the quintessential of jurisprudence. Small city practice with megalopolis clients would be a challenge at which I would thrive."

Barbados replied, "I love it here too and try to enjoy the gorgeous weather and beaches as often as I can. I certainly can relate to distancing oneself from an ex as I did likewise and can empathize. But it is your obvious drive and self-dedication that mystifies me to the point that I want to consider you for my team, small as it is, but there is a minor point which needs clarity and full disclosure."

Jessica sat back slightly on the couch, crossed her legs and prepared for whatever was coming.

"We are a criminal defense firm as you know and from time to time we have had disgruntled clients. It is not my style to dial 911 when I have a problem. I would rather solve the matter myself in dealing with potentially violent clients. And let's be frank, many of them are, otherwise why would they have been arrested?

Specifically, what precipitated our policy was one client who was facing a twenty-five-year sentence for armed robbery. He was caught coming out of the bank, mask and all, carrying a plastic bag of cash so my job was to obtain the least amount of jail time.

He didn't like the twelve years sentence and threatened me, showing his pistol in the process. Since then our staff are armed. You noticed Debbie, our receptionist is behind a bullet-proof partition. Debbie is the daughter of one of Santa Barbara's police detectives and had no problem accepting the firm's paradigm. Will this be a problem for you?"

Jessica couldn't believe what she just heard and quickly formulated a response that would be plausible but also a deal maker. She replied, "I fully understand Ms. Barbados and no, I do not have a problem with firearms. I separated from my abusive husband the first time he hit me. I hit him back, called the police and had him removed from the apartment. He was angry and swore revenge. It was then that I stared carrying this," as she stood up and opened her jacket to reveal her nine-millimeter pistol.

This was Barbados's first experience with an armed applicant, but it took her only a nano-second to respond asking, "Do you have a California carry permit?"

"Yes ma'am, I do. When I presented proof of my ex-husband's threats to the Metropolitan Police Department's chief, a woman incidentally, I had no difficulty obtaining a permit and her letter of approval was accepted by the state of California."

"Well, Jessica, I must say," she responded with a slight smirk, which Jessica wasn't sure how to interpret, "I have never had an armed candidate before and I am delighted," as her face broke into a full smile, so here is my offer." She removed a sheet of paper from a manila folder on the glass coffee table and handed it to Jessica.

Accepting the paper, Jessica exhaled and regained her composure then took a moment to read the contract which offered her a permanent position with a starting salary of three hundred thousand. She anticipated the offer would be high, but never this amount, about two-hundred plus more than she was making for the government. *Maybe it was time for a career change,* she thought.

"Thank you very much for the generous offer Ms. Barbados. I appreciate your confidence and yes, I would be delighted to join your team."

"Perfect. Now, to details. I will show you to your office momentarily, but for now I want to discuss our client base."

For the next thirty minutes, Barbados discussed billable hours, the city's social culture, the number of clients the firm represented and who lived in Santa Barbara and commuted to Los Angeles, many by helicopter.

Once she had completed her summary, Barbados said, "Many of our clients and the movers and shakers are attending a party at a home in the foothills hosted by two women from Wyoming who operate R&P Investigations. I would like you to join me and together we can chat and find out if they are a firm with whom we can work. What do you say? California casual. Will that be a problem?"

"Not at all Ms. Barbados. I can't think of a more enjoyable introduction to your clients. I have the perfect outfit. Thank you for the invitation."

"Very good. It should be fun. The firm needs an investigative team and it is Katrina and the people we will be meeting are our clients, not mine," she offered with a smile. "I'll text you the address later, but for now, let's get you situated in your office so you can have the rest of the day to orient yourself to the city. Could you use a couple of days to find a place to say?"

S.B.S

Brian Sawyer had been brooding since overhearing the local fishermen discuss the unknown boats travelling just beyond the breakwater. They began as periodic sightings but had increased to several times weekly.

He thought he had left that life behind. He had chosen that of the small fishing village and yet he couldn't control the adrenaline rush knowing what was being transported.

Chapter THIRTY-TWO

Winthrop and Hortonn received Air Canada's
VIP treatment from boarding and through business class
service. Tom took it all in stride as they were seated,
offered strong, aromatic Columbian coffee before take-
off, then once they leveled off, they were treated to lox
and bagels, fresh strawberries hors d'oeuvres, then
breakfast burritos with spicy hash browns, scrambled
eggs, green onion and salsa. And more coffee. And real
cutlery.

At one point during the meal Tom said, "I could
get used to this treatment sheriff. Maybe I could become
your official deputy."

Karen didn't miss a beat, put down her fork and
turned to him with, "I don't know Mr. Hortonn, do you
think you could keep up with me?"

Tom learned some time ago that Karen was far
too witty for him to match quips, so he simply nodded,
smiled and toasted her with his coffee mug.

The five-hour direct flight landed them in San
José where they were met by an Air Canada staffer as
they exited the tube, who escorted them through Costa
Rican customs.

Two DIS, state intelligence service, agents were
waiting in an office just off the concourse. They were
friendly, albeit skeptical of any foreign agents operating
in their country even though they had been notified by
David Kopas of their impending arrival and mission.

The operation was discussed briefly and when
Karen advised the DIS agents that they had no intention
of arresting Sawyer but if that became a requirement,

they would do so within the confines of Costa Rican laws and in conjunction with DIS.

Satisfied, the agents gave them preprogrammed cell phones with a direct line to DIS headquarters. As they left the office, the male Air Canada staffer was waiting with their luggage and escorted them to a currency exchange kiosk, explaining they would have a far more favorable reception by locals if they used the Colón.

Using their government credit card, they purchased five-hundred dollars each, thanked the staffer for his advice and then followed him to a silver, Mitsubishi Montero rental. He placed their luggage in the cargo hold, gave Karen the keys, commenting, "Sheriff Winthrop, here is my card. If there is anything you need while in Costa Rica, please give me a call, personally." He bowed slightly, turned and disappeared into the airport.

Karen turned to thank the staffer, but he was already out of ear shot, so she tossed the keys in the air a couple of times, walked to the driver's side and looking over the SUV said, "Are you ready to ride Mr. Hortonn?"

"Yes, Sheriff Winthrop, I am," he replied, sliding into the passenger seat.

And they did, making the three-hour drive to Limón in four, stopping numerous times for photo ops, then for lime and salsa fish tacos in Barrio, making it to Limón in the early evening. Coming into the city, they passed the construction of Moîn, a multi-million-dollar terminal, completion of which was expected in two-thousand and nineteen. * They booked a room overnight at the Hotel de Terraza de Limón.

Their room was more elegant than either had expected with its cream, stucco walls, buff tile floor throughout and an exceptionally modern bathroom, featuring double sinks, hair dryers and a ten by six-foot shower with three rain shower heads. The headboard, nightstands and two cushioned occasional chairs were natural wicker. The individual terrace was accessible through French Doors with privacy provided by numerous Bromeliads, Orchids and Lobster-claws, all in bloom.

Their accommodations were so welcoming, they chose to shower, Karen first while Tom checked in with Kopas. Dressed in the white, fluffy robes the hotel provided, they ordered room service, first bruschetta with prosciutto and then penne with arugula pesto, cherry tomatoes and a bottle of Chilean red.

The service was superb, and their meal presented on the terrace was exceptional. Having researched local wages, they left a thirteen-thousand colón, thirty Canadian, gratuity for their server.

Tom placed their dishes on the serving tray and placed them in the hall. When he returned to the bedroom, he found Karen already in bed…asleep.

Karen woke early, prepared a cup of coffee and sat on the terrace, ruminating about the plan of action and was confident they could succeed without Sawyer, presuming they locate him, becoming suspicious.

It wasn't long before she heard the French Doors open and Tom emerged holding two mugs. Handing one to Karen, he said, "Good morning sleepy head. You obviously needed the rest. How are you feeling this morning?"

"Good morning to you too," she replied, standing and giving him a kiss, putting both her arms around him, one holding her black. "I didn't realize I had conked out so quickly. Sorry about that. I had hoped to mess around with you," she added, sitting back down. "Too bad it is so late in the morning we have to get going or we could have a quickie," smiling up at him, running her tongue around her lips.

With that comment and seductive look, Tom gently reached down, kissed her and opened her robe and off her shoulders, exposing her breasts. Getting on his knees, he took her right nipple between his lips, encircling it with his tongue while gently massaging her left breast.

Karen threw her head back, moaning while grabbing his head, holding it to her chest. Within a few minutes, Karen opened her robe fully, spread her legs and forced Tom's head down. She slid her butt forward slightly to improve the angle bringing instant pleasure. As her orgasm gained momentum, she jumped up, pulled Tom to his feet, turned him to sit as she straddled him, allowing him to engulf her. She was in total control with her hands on his shoulders as she pushed up with her toes and let her body fall. She had been so close to climaxing when she made the switch, her emotions skyrockets quickly, sending her into total bliss, her entire body shaking as she buried her head into Tom's neck groaning in delight.

Hearing Karen's climax, Tom's body responded, climaxing as Karen's subsided, wrapping his arms around her, pulling her tight to his chest.

They stayed like that for several minutes, Karen gently rocking back and forth, her heart rate slowing as she raised her head, tilted it back and said, "That is one hell of a way to start a morning Tom. God, you are so incredibly good for me. Thank you."

Tom looked up at her and smiled, words not available to express that he was feeling likewise.

Feeling Tom slip out of her, Karen swung a leg, dismounted, retied her robe, stepped back, reached down and took Tom's hand, gracefully guiding him to the shower where she spent several minutes lathering, stroking and enjoying the hardness of his body.

Seeing that her actions were raising Tom's awareness and hearing his moans, she stopped, handed him a wash cloth and proceeded to shower, knowing they needed to be at the Limón Airport when it opened.

They dried off, kissing numerous times, then dressed, packed and headed to the hotel's buffet breakfast of scrambled eggs, Casado, pinto beans and rice. And more coffee.

Although they were delighted with their perfect morning, they had to scale it back before arriving at Aeropuerto Internacional de Limón, switching to a solemn mood, a couple seeking information about her missing brother.

Furnished with the information the Idaho State Troopers had provided, they parked and entered the small office and enquired with the only person around,

"Excuse me," asked Karen, "With whom might we speak about buying an airplane?"

"Not here, that is for sure lady. Just in and out is all we provide although we are considered an international airport. There is only one airplane broker in Limón and that is Agrios Citricos, or Citrus Planes. The owner is a transplanted retired Brit, William Davies, who doesn't care if he sells a plane or not, but he is fair, honest and quite a character. You can't miss his place. It is just south of us on highway thirty-six, about 10 kilometers."

"Thanks for the help," replied Karen and the two turned and left.

Driving south from Limón, the highway was close to the ocean but with few homes, which was to be expected given the poor economy, but even so, it was a shock to see economic opportunities not being realized. They knew the area was depressed but that wasn't what was keeping investors and retirees away, it was crime. The province was well known throughout the country for gang activities and as they drove, they discussed whether Sawyer didn't retire here but simply shifted his operation.

The ten kilometers took less than fifteen minutes. Considering their previous discussion of local economy, the Agrios Citricos Airplanes facility spoke of success, not austerity. The property hosted a spacious main office building attached to a rather large hanger, the doors of which opened to a paved runway extending along the beach well above high tide.

They parked and entered the office to find it vacant. Tom moved toward a counter and found a note, *In the hanger. Willie*

Around to the hanger they went and found the only person there was in grey overalls, standing on a platform, wrench in hand, head buried in an engine of an older model twin-engine Piper Aztec.

Making their presence known with the person's head under an engine hood would not be a good introduction, so they moved away from the plane, found two folding chairs and sat quietly beside the mobile tool bench.

They waited. Looked around. Airplane hangar. Airplanes. Equipment. Yawn for cops.

After about ten minutes, overalls pulled its head out from the engine cover, stepped down from the ladder, turned and yelled, "Holy crap. You just scared the hell out of me. You could have coughed or something."

"Sorry sir. We didn't want to say anything, and have you jump and hit your head, it is so quiet here," offered Karen as she approached the man extending her hand.

"Sir, we are Karen and Tom Hortonn," her heart skipping a beat at the sound of those words, "and we are looking for my brother, Brian Sawyer."

The man shook her hand, then Tom's and replied, "Nice to meet you. I'm William Davies, or Willie as folks call me here abouts. Well, I can guarantee he isn't here," the man said with a very strong British accent.

"Come on over here by the work bench and I'll grab us a couple of cold ones and start again," he offered, gesturing with a wave as he rounded the nose of the plane and headed to a seating area beside an elaborate and well- organized work-bench. He grabbed three bottles of a local craft brewery, Treintaycinco's Pelona, an India pale ale, handed one to each of his guests, motioned for them to sit, then grabbed a chair for himself.

Clinking bottle necks, he said, "Okay, now that we are civilized, who are you seeking again?"

"Brian Sawyer. He is my brother from Alberta. I normally hear from him every few months with a text or email but not for over six months now. He normally holidays in Limón, but he hasn't returned home. He flew his own plane here months ago and we are wondering if you might know him, might have seen his plane, or know something about him. We have information about his plane if that helps. This is a very small community and we are hoping."

"Hope no longer Ms. Hortonn, I know Brian. As a matter of fact, I bought his plane. He moved here, lock, stock and barrel, so to speak, some time ago. And the bloody sod didn't tell his sister? Bloody odd that is."

"He is okay, that is great news. Do you have any idea where he settled or what he is doing for a living?" asked Karen.

"Doing for living, I haven't a clue. For all I know the lad is sitting on a beach somewhere getting bloody wasted, no offense love".

"None taken Willie," Karen replied with a smile, feeling comfortable they were making progress. "So, you figure he is somewhere on this side?" referring to the Caribbean Ocean in contrast to the Pacific.

"No doubt love, he holidayed here for years, learned the language. He speaks it like a native and by now he looks like me, lost the pasty white skin of northerners," obviously referring to Willie's very dark skin tone.

"Any suggestions on how we can locate him Willie? We have a photo. Any point in showing it around?" asked Tom.

"I'd keep that as a plan B, Mr. Tom. My advice is to just go from village to village and ask for him. When you hit the right village, he will be well known. I wish I could help more but when he was here last, he had purchased a used car and said he planned to meander."

"Thanks Willie. We appreciate the help. We will head south and see if we can locate him. Knowing he is here somewhere is a great relief and I will contact our family right away to allay their concerns," replied Karen.

Back at the SUV, Karen handed Tom the keys and said, "How about you drive, and I will write the notes, upload them to David and he can notify CHAP?"

Accepting the keys and rounding the vehicle to the driver's side, Tom said, "Sounds good to me."

Back on the narrow highway, Karen pulled her laptop from the back seat, created a file and began keyboarding Willie's conversation.

Fifteen later she saved the file, read it to Tom for his input and approval, then asked him to pull over at the first wide-spot in the road so she could send it.

Momentarily, Tom pulled to a wide dirt spot overlooking the ocean. Tom shut the engine off, stepped out and took up a position behind the SUV with his pistol in hand, down by his right thigh. Karen stepped out of the vehicle and took the encrypted laptop, which contained the transmitting terminal and their satphone, found a somewhat flat rock, connected the two devices, waited until Canada's geostationary orbiting satellite made connection thirty-eight thousand kilometers above her, hit send, waited a few minutes for confirmation, then disconnected the equipment and returned to the vehicle.

Tom waited until she was secure, then holstered his firearm, reentered the vehicle and pulled out on to the highway, heading south again.

Karen had shared with Tom, Chapman's suggestion that they rely on the written narrative rather than trusting Costa Rican communications systems. The Canadians disagreed, but kept their decision to use CISI's satellite system to themselves since they didn't have Kopas' approval.

*Once the port is complete, it will quadruple capacity reducing processing time from fifty hours to thirteen per vessel. Eighty percent of the construction labor is local and when completed, will generate over one-thousand employees.

Unless the country can control crime in the area, the new facility will not only be host to cocaine arrivals and shipments, but the workers could become customers.

Although real estate investors are poised to develop in the area, they remain reluctant given the underlying criminal element.

Criminals work around tourists, not wanting to raise the ire of foreign governments and preferring to allow local dealers freedom to service travelers unencumbered by law enforcement.

Chapter THIRTY-THREE

While the evening wore down, Rebecca outlined the house's particulars to Jason, Elisabeth and Jackson. Ensuring there would be no misunderstanding or midnight alarms, she had them written out on three by five cards.

The first item was the security system's intricacies including the imbedded ground sensors, exterior cameras and flood-lights. Next, she informed them of the six, professional house-keepers' schedule and reminded them that they would strip and change their beds, bath towels etc. They would also do personal laundry…each room had a clothes hamper.

Mentioning the pistol range brought raised eyebrows from all three agents but none were so rude as to comment. Simply advising them of its location and that ammunition was available in the safe for which she provided the combination. The pool was serviced once a week, but she couldn't recall which day. Suffice it to say, that team was also professional and avoiding chatting with them would be appreciated.

She didn't mention the gym, figuring they would find it on their own.

Last was the caterers. She advised that the concept was Jessica's and that they arrive at six am daily with three meals, snacks and appetizers. The warm meals would be stored in the ovens set on warm, while everything else would be in the refrigerator. Dishes and cutlery were our responsibility.

She asked if there were any questions and hearing none, she changed the conversation to tomorrow's dinner party, reminding them of the time. She was going to remind the men about the dress code but thought better of it, thinking they might consider it demeaning.

As a final comment, she said that she and Pen would be up early doing a short trail run behind the property, then some gym and shooting time before breakfast. She invited everyone to join any or part of their morning ritual and got tentative nods from all three.

As they were cleaning up the patio, Rebecca responded to a chime from the main monitoring camera. Nordstrom delivery had arrived with the guy's altered blazers.

Removing the dishes, they headed back into the house, placed everything in the dishwasher with Jason taking the initiative to locate the soap and start the machine. Seeing this, Penelope caught Rebecca's attention grinned and flipped her eyebrows several times.

Elisabeth took time to hang her new clothes, arrange an outfit for tomorrow night and lay out gym attire. The men closed their doors, stripped and climbed into bed, leaving any further domestic involvement for another day.

❦

Karen and Tom spent the rest of the day stopping at every village and vendor asking about Sawyer without success. At the junction of highways thirty-six and two hundred and fifty-six, they veered to the latter, which continued to follow the coast, knowing the former was only forty-five minutes from the Panamanian border.

They remained on that highway through several more villages culminating at the highway's end, bordering the Gandoca Manzanillo Wildlife Refuge, the jungle home to howler monkeys, sloths, poisonous frogs and exotic vegetation. Checking into a small B&B, the Cabaña del Caribe, they left their bags in the room, then followed their hosts' dinner recommendation for the Mariscos Punta Manzanillo, the local pub.

ॐॐॐ

Investigators at the Edmonton RCMP detachment were receiving copies of Stan's texts with increasing frequency. It was common knowledge with the public that the Alberta oil sands' communities were a drug dealer's financial boon due to the very high incomes and lack of entertainment opportunities, particularly during the long winters of minus twenty degrees Fahrenheit.

This is the community from which Brian Sawyer departed during an economic downturn, but had reversed itself, increasing the sale of cocaine. This was the content of Stan's texts. Although they were vague, the inferences were sufficient for Mounties to feel positive that the source could be extinguished.

Chapter THIRTY-FOUR

Surprisingly, everyone was up at probably the same time as Rebecca and Penelope, given that they found all three guests attired in their workout gear, sitting at the kitchen table drinking coffee. Jason had been the first to arrive, scrounged for coffee mixings and had a pot ready when everyone else entered.

Pen grabbed two white mugs from the cupboard, poured black, took them to the table, went back and returned with the carafe and refilled everyone's mugs, then sat next to Rebecca.

They thanked her for the refill, then Rebecca said, "It is great seeing you guys up and about so early."

Jackson raised his mug in salute replying, "I think the last operation has ingrained limited sleep for us all…we couldn't sleep past five. Heading to downtown LA for an early meeting with the drug enforcement team. Jessica texted us all overnight having arranged everything with the LAPD.

"An update for her. She was hired yesterday by Katrina Barbados' law firm and is attending the party tonight."

Rebecca and Penelope's faces went blank in surprise, Elisabeth and Jason remained deadpan having received the same text. Regaining their composure, Rebecca commented, "Incredible. I find her resourcefulness and fabrication talents uncanny. Tonight. She is coming to the party…tonight?" shaking her head in disbelief.

"We know," replied Elisabeth. "We were blown away as well. She just arrived in town from DC the other day and has already established a cover, made the arrangements for our meeting today and the one this afternoon with the SBPD. The woman is non-stop energy."

"Here, here," said Jason and Jackson, lifting their mugs in a salute to their boss. The others joined in, then Jackson offered, "We would love to do a few gym circuits and maybe lay a few rounds in your range, but we have to scoot and get to LA and hopefully miss some of the traffic. What do you say we do a run first, so we can head out and you guys can continue on?"

Pen turned to Rebecca who responded for the two of them, "Sounds good to us. We are meeting with Alane about office space in his building and the party, our accountants, the women's center, then the SPCA for a bundle of kittens, so be thinking of some names."

"You guys have a hectic day ahead as well," said Elisabeth with a huge grin. "Sure, we will come up with some names. Don't forget the litter boxes, one for each kitten, kitten food, not adult and some toys. I want to get them some toys too and maybe a few sleeping pads. Oh, this is going to be fun."

Rebecca and Penelope shared a laugh, never having considered the agents would be interested in kittens.

The five agents completed a short thirty-minute run, fifteen up into the hills behind the property and fifteen back with their return coinciding with the caterer's arrival.

Penelope let them in, shut off the security system, then lead the staffers into the kitchen. Lunch was placed in the ovens on warm while breakfast was placed on the counter. As the caterers left, the team advanced on the morning's cuisine; cheese frittata, homemade hash browns and sliced fruit. Elisabeth retrieved plates and cutlery, Jason and Jackson plated the food while Rebecca refilled coffee mugs.

With plenty of salsa, the meal was delicious. No one spoke during their collective enjoyment but when they were done, they agreed it was a delightful beginning to an exciting day for everyone.

Post breakfast, Penelope and Rebecca cleaned up while the others headed to the showers, dressed and met at the SUV. Although the men were dressed for a scene in Miami Vice with Don Johnson and Philip Michael Thomas, Elisabeth kept her opinion and grin to herself since they did look sharp and their firearms were concealed.

Jackson wore tan slacks, a white button-down dress shirt, with a navy-blue blazer with a blue and white pocket square and navy-blue loafers. Jason had chosen the yellow slacks paired with a Tommy Bahama Parrot Oasis long sleeve yellow patterned shirt, the rust blazer with a yellow rust pocket square and sandals.

Elisabeth met her colleagues dressed in an Eliza J. chiffon, mid-calf, maxi dress with pleated skirt with vibrant white flowers over a navy-blue background. She paired the outfit with a white blazer and the Sannibell wedge sandals.

There wasn't a discussion regarding who would drive. In southern California, Elisabeth took the wheel given her more aggressive driving style, which guaranteed their early arrival. Jason hopped in the front, keyed the LAPD address on First Street into the GPS while Jackson took the back seat.

Traffic was light by local standards and although there was a steady stream, they made it downtown within just under an hour and a half during which time Jackson researched their host, Captain Ortega, head of the narcotics division, a thirty-five-year veteran, former commanding officer of the North Hollywood division with a Bachelor of Science degree in Criminology.

Badging their way through security, they arrived quickly at Ortega's office with about fifteen to spare. An assistant showed them to the conference room, coffee, croissants and donuts. The room was prepared for their delivery with seating for thirty participants. Jason poured them black while Elisabeth arranged her laptop off to the side of the oblong table, connected the cables to the television system, checked her reception then logged into CHAP and waited.

Officers sauntered into the conference room ten before the start time and to a person, they looked suspiciously at the three agents, distrust immediate in their persona. Feds. Those who demand without reciprocating.

As the clock stuck the hour, Captain Ortega entered, visibly surprised to see his guests already in place and seemingly embarrassed that he wasn't there first.

Looking smart and professional in his uniform with seven hash tags and duty belt, Ortega marched to the front of the table, gained everyone's attention and asked them to be seated. As the last officer sat, their boss introduced the agents.

"Ladies and gentlemen, our guests are Secret Service Agents Elisabeth Peltowski, Jackson Pennington and former LAPD Officer, Jason Spencer," Ortega offered then waited briefly as a polite applaud died.

"Let me first ally your prejudices against federal officers. These three, along with their supervisor, Jessica Fukishura, took down the Christians for a Better America and prevented further tragedy when the Mahalo Airlines jet hit the Pacific," Ortega explained, then had to wait some time for the loud applause and standing ovation to subside.

Continuing, Ortega said, "Agent Peltowski will introduce their query with agents Spencer and Pennington spotting around the room to answer questions." Before he could continue, a hand appeared from the table. "Yes, detective. You have a question?"

"Yes sir. I must ask Agent Spencer. Were you the officer responsible for the take-down of the automatic weapons operation in the south district a few years ago?"

Jason, smiling, responded, "Yes, I was part of that operation," then swung into his Caribbean accent continuing, "But I must say man, that it was a great team effort, I just lead the suspects to the SWAT team waiting in the warehouse."

Everyone laughed at his use of the accent, which had been his persona during the undercover months where he made a deal to deliver hundreds of fully automatic weapons smuggled in from Eastern Europe.

The scene was set, and Elisabeth segued by introducing CHAP; describing it in detail, reminding everyone that the LAPD was part of the international data system, and that Captain Ortega had access. She paused briefly to light up the three massive screens above her. She had a captivated audience.

Detail by detail, Elisabeth mapped out what they knew for sure and their suspicions. Specifically, the Caribbean bank notes which the Treasury had traced to Los Angeles. Using Power Point, she flashed a chart image on the screens diagraming the currency flow of the new bills from the Federal Reserve to Los Angeles banks which then turned up in the Caribbean. The chart utilized the mapping process of notetaking, showing currency as the main topic with branches extending from currency to each related sub-topic. One such link was seized currency from drug busts. The money was counted, and serial numbers recorded with the data were sent to the Treasury, creating a circle of evidence. A separate branch on the chart linked the cocaine through microscopic traces on the cash.

The next image showed the serial numbers which Elisabeth asked each detective to compare with the money taken from each drug bust.

Within minutes officers were using their laptops verifying that some of the numbers matched the money confiscated during their operations.

Elisabeth gestured to Ortega who took over the presentation with, "I want all of your information to me immediately. I will arrange a meeting with the assistant district attorneys involved in each of your cases but before then I want a brief bio on each of the defense attorneys involved. I understand three are local and two are from Santa Barbara?"

Receiving affirmative nods from the detectives. he continued, "I also want each of you to consider releasing your suspects without charges being laid, we can file later. Your suspects will be followed by SIS, Special Investigation Services. Agent Peltowski?"

"Thank you, Captain. That plan will work well, and we will have our supplier. We know that every one of the recent arrests dealt with the same cocaine. Your crime lab proved that it comes from Columbia and is rampant across the country. We also believe there is a direct connection between this Columbian supplier, the currency, the Christians for a Better America and federal politicians running for reelection."

A hand shot up from one of the officers, "Agent Peltowski, are you saying that the CFBA was not defused?"

"That is exactly what I am saying detective. The senator was the lead character but not the producer or director. We have traced donations of hundreds of thousands to Orange County, Chicago, New York and Washington, DC, and those are just an iota of the support the group has.

"We believe the drug money leaves here somehow and ends up in the Caribbean. Water, air, tourists? We need that information. Millions are transferred from the Caribbean to legitimate, but unverifiable, American checking accounts. Checks are then written to political candidates, parties or super PACs.

"Reiterating what the Captain said, if you would scour your databases and make the connection with the dealers' confiscated currency, we will have that evidence and coupled with what SIS discovers, we can find the drug distribution location and trace it back. The quantity

251

that is disbursed is massive because we have seen the same cocaine appear in New York and Chicago. We will keep each other current through Captain Ortega and CHAP. Time is of the essence since we suspect another shipment will be arriving soon given the rising street cost vis-à-vis supply."

With her closing comments, she turned the meeting over to the Captain and joined Jason and Jackson as they mingled with the officers answering questions.

Two female officers, Jenny Wong and Teresa Vasquez, were from the Pacific Department on Culver Blvd. just east of Marina Del Rey. They were part of the team which rushed the top story hotel room where the CFBA operative was launching his attack. It was their preemptive assault which prompted him to detonate prematurely before the Democrat representatives from across the country arrived at the convention center.

They knew Pennington and Spencer and wanted to get to know them better.

Not waiting for the men to get around to noticing them, Wong and Vasquez elbowed their way through the crowd of fellow officers and slid in front of the three agents, starting the conversation by extending their hands and Wong saying, "Agents Pennington and Spencer, nice to see you again."

"Hey, how are you guys doing? Didn't recognize you in the sea of faces. How have you been?" offered Jason.

"We are very well Jason and by the looks of the both of you, you are more than very well," as Vasquez eyed both men up and down emitting a warm and seductive smile in the process.

Elisabeth smiled to herself thinking, *what is it with these two. They draw women like they are in heat. Look at them, they are practically drooling.* Stifling a cute comment, she remained professional and said, "Hi. I'm Elisabeth, I don't think we've met."

"Oh. Excuse my rudeness," Jason said, not taking his eyes off the other two women. "Jenny, Teresa, this is Elisabeth, our colleague and resident hacker who found the CFBA operative in the Marina hotel."

The LAPD detectives turned slightly to acknowledge Elisabeth, "Great to meet you. So, how long have you been working with these two delicious specimens?"

Elisabeth was not taken aback by their brashness as she had become used to women coming on to her colleagues for years. She thought of several cute comments but chose not to embarrass the guys by replying, "Quite a few years actually and their magnetism never seems to run out of energy, like the energizer bunny times two." *Whoops, there goes the professionalism*, she thought, waiting for a response.

Wong replied with a sarcastic smile and slight head shake as if to say, *I am ready and just waiting for you to finish your bullshit because you don't know what is going to happen to you in the next five seconds.*

Her words however responded differently, "We met these hunks on the job, and it was days before we stopped fantasizing. How about it boys, are you up for a little off-duty time?"

The men exchanged glances, acknowledging that it had been so long since they experienced female companionship, they wondered if they remembered how to participate. Although wanting to say yes...badly, Jason politely asked for a raincheck as they had to get back to Santa Barbara by noon for another meeting.

Not to be put off, Vasquez said, "I think we can manage that, can't we Jenny?" with a flirtatious head tilt, finger through a hair curl and tongue across her lips. "We are going to hold you to it boys," then each of the detectives kissed the agents on the cheek, slipped their business cards into their blazer pockets, turned and left the conference room, glancing over their shoulder, almost simultaneously with a little finger wave.

Vasquez and Jenn's departure seemed to signal others to wrap it up and officers began leaving. The "J" Team followed the group out, made their last goodbyes and as they headed to their SUV, Jason said, "Guys, we have an hour to spare, how about letting me show you around Los Angeles' epicenter, Olvera Street. It is five minutes from here?"

"Sure," said Elisabeth. "I'm game. Jackson?"

"Count me in," offered Jackson.

"Terrific," replied Jason as Elisabeth tossed him the keys and they all climbed in.

As Jason was driving to Olvera Street, Elisabeth used the short time to needle her colleagues, starting with, "What is it with you two that aggressive women are so bold?"

Jason looked at Jackson through the rear-view mirror, grinned, then said with a straight face, "We don't have a clue and we are offended by their flirtatious behavior."

Jackson tried his best to stifle his laugh and in doing so it came out more like a cough or sneeze, then moved over behind the driver's seat so Elisabeth couldn't see him.

"You guys are incorrigible," she said, shaking her head.

Parking was easy with tourism being low this time of year and as they meandered through the narrow passages, Jason provided a narrative.

"Although Olvera Street is thought by many to be the birth place of Los Angeles, it actually opened in nineteen-thirty. If we are lucky, we will run into a mariachi band and we can stop at any of these stores and browse. If it is the same as when I was a kid, all merchandise is authentic, nothing from Asia."

They stopped at the front door of the Tortilla Factory, a store with warm tortillas being processed right in front of visitors. Jason stepped forward and purchased twelve hot ones, walked over to an adjoining kiosk and prepared each tortilla with grated jack cheese, guacamole and salsa, rolled them and handed three on a plate to his colleagues.

"Oh, my God Jason, this is delicious. I have never had a tortilla with such flavor," said Elisabeth as she bit into the first one.

"Thanks. I used to come here as a kid with friends. We'd hop on the bus and spend a Saturday morning just roaming around and eating these. What do you think Jackson?"

"Outstanding Jason, absolutely outstanding. I love the combination of the mild cheese, guacamole and salsa. It is the simplicity that makes it so delicious I think."

"Anyone who's a chef, who loves food, ultimately knows that all that matters are: 'Does it give pleasure?'"
Anthony Bourdain

They spent the rest of their free time enjoying the various shops with Elisabeth purchasing a large over the shoulder yellow wool handbag while the men bought straw, wide-brim hats.

They gave themselves extra driving time given the late morning traffic heading to the ocean but still arrived ahead of Rebecca and Penelope.

Chapter THIRTY-FIVE

"We are the waistline of the Americas, we are between the producers and consumers and we can't do a thing."
Former Costa Rican President Oscar Arias

Arias was referring to the uncontrollable flow of cocaine into Costa Rica. In the first six months of two-thousand and seventeen, authorities seized twenty-five tons. Former president Laura Chinchilla commented to the Wall Street Journal that Costa Ricans were, "Prisoners of our geography," referring to the country's location between the Columbian producers, the powerful Mexican drug lords and the voracious American appetite for the product.

Their limited coast guard patrols the Pacific, confiscating tons of cocaine, cash and speed boats, while hundreds of tons make their way into warehouses where Mexican couriers load the product into a variety of vehicles to be transported north.

Law enforcement presence is limited as is their training to deal with the sophisticated transportation systems.

Corruption also plays a role in the escalating violence and drug trade. Last year the former head of the Costa Rican Public Force was arrested while moving two-hundred kilos of cocaine in a false-bottom truck.

The country relies on the Canadian and American Navies to assist, but the oceans are so vast and the quantity so great that their presence doesn't seem to make a dent in the industry. One such joint venture known as Operation Caribbe saw the combined forces confiscate four-hundred and eighty tons of cocaine hidden in a false deck of a fishing boat.

What neither of these countries knew is that the Columbian drug cartels use Costa Rica and all the various distribution techniques as a diversion and a write-off. The bulk of their product and financial boon is the submarines for the North American trade with shipping containers and private yachts transporting to the European market.

Brian Sawyer was unaware of this unique business model when he sat next to a group of mariners at the Cuir Ó dhoras, Gaelic for pub, in Limón, owned and operated by an Irish ex-pat, overhearing them share the rumors that abound throughout Costa Rica about the drug trade.

The more the mariners drank, the more vociferous they became, bragging, trying to outdo each other regarding tales of drug smuggling successes and failures.

Brian was known as a Ticos, a local male, and none of his neighboring drinkers paid attention as he listened, drank and nibbled a bowl of chifrijos; chicharrones (pork rinds), rice, beans, pork and guacamole.

As the evening wore on and his beer consumption increased, Sawyer found himself reminiscing about his years in the drug business, the massive retirement income it produced, albeit hidden in his house, not invested, and wondered how he became involved in the local cocaine business.

Chapter THIRTY-SIX

Rebecca and Penelope spent their morning during the "J" Team's time with the LAPD, meeting with Alane, accepting his offer to use a segment of his first-floor office space for their business location and arranging a meeting with his interior decorator. Next was the telephone company for a business line which would be forwarded to their cells, business cards, then visiting Rebecca's accountant whom she had not seen for many years, even though she handled her finances.

Business cared for, they headed to the women's shelter and introduced themselves to the staff. Rebecca presented her credentials, explained Penelope's internship and offered R&P Investigations services for free.

They explained to the overwhelmed team what their overall objective was with a recovery center for homeless teenagers, primarily girls, enlisting suggestions from staff regarding what they perceive as needs, how they foresee them being delivered and any pitfalls they could foretell.

The center's director agreed to meet again in a couple of days at which time R&P would present various location options, noting the concept of converting an existing motel or hotel.

As Penelope and Rebecca prepared to leave, they presented the director with checks of ten-thousand dollars each, wished her and the team a good day and left feeling excited about the future for Santa Barbara's homeless.

The director thanked their new benefactors and saw them out, returned to her office and as she was preparing to process the donations, she glanced at the amounts.

She was stunned. Alejandro had spoken to her about R&P, their background and that they wanted to support the center. He hadn't mentioned their generosity or their plans for homeless teens. She needed more information. A short conversation with her SBPD contact, Elise Pelfini, brought enlightenment and a personal inner warmth that the center and women might be on a new path.

The last stop was to the SPCA where they took quite a bit of time sitting on the floor with a bevy of kittens, all climbing over and around them. The women offered both Alane and Alejandro as personal references which they were sure a staffer called while they were engaged with the kittens. The staffer asked them a slew of questions regarding their lifestyle, whether the kittens would be left for long periods of time and if they would be indoor, outdoor or both.

Rebecca and Penelope had already considered the question and decided they would be strictly indoor family members given the possibility of encountering coyotes from the hills as well as prowling eagles and owls.

Satisfied the felines would receive a good home, the staff had the women sign an agreement to have the kittens spayed at three months of age. Rebecca and Penelope borrowed a cardboard carrying case and left with six female kittens, headed for the pet store.

They arrived at the ranch shortly after the "J" Team and having texted ahead of time, the three were waiting in the driveway for their arrival.

Jessica would have enjoyed watching her hardened, seasoned agents' warm and soft side emerge at the sight of the six newest members of the team.

Jackson and Jason took the five litter boxes into the laundry room and set them side-by-side with three-inches of litter while Elisabeth carried the kennel into the living room, sat it on the floor, opened the door, then sat as the kittens emerged gingerly, one paw at a time, sniffing the floor and mewing.

The guys joined her just as Rebecca and Penelope arrived with a tray of chilled chardonnay and lunch from the oven. Although the chili burger bottom bun was a little soft, the fact that they didn't have to cook, made the soggy bun irrelevant. The patty was topped with bourbon chili, sharp cheddar cheese, sautéed onions with the bun top on the side. The French fries were unaffected by the six hours in the oven.

The five spent ninety minutes enjoying their lunch while simultaneously keeping the kittens from their food and petting them.

Lunch over, Jason and Jackson removed the dishes, placing them in the covered plastic carrying cases ready for the caterers in the morning. The women carried the kittens, two each, into the laundry room, placed each in a litter box and sat on the floor while the felines explored the boxes, did their deed, climbed out and on to the women's laps.

Penelope and Rebecca became so caught up in adoption they forgot about their afternoon meeting and leaving the kittens alone. They brought the problem to the group back in the kitchen as the kittens followed them in, mewing all the way.

What to do with their new family members for the next couple of hours? They brainstormed the problem and chose Jackson's idea; shut the music off in every room but the kitchen and laundry room, place the kitten's beds near the food and water at the end of the island in the kitchen. The theory was the human element would be confined to the kitchen with the hope they would be so tired, sleep would consume them for two hours.

The next question; where can they be during the party? They agreed that the laundry room was big enough and sufficiently disengaged from the entertainment area, they would not be disturbed with the door closed. Beds, food and water included of course.

The major decisions performed, they headed to their meeting, everyone anxious to see Jessica after so long and curious about the overall operational plan.

꒰ℬ꒱

Brian found the mariners' conversation so fascinating, drawing him emotionally back to the drug trade, that he lost track of time. When the bartender announced last call, Brian was surprised and embarrassed that he had difficulty walking. He paid his tab with a generous gratuity, then stumbled across the street to the Sloth Motel*, to sleep off his surprised bender, not trusting himself to drive the sixty-minutes home in the dark and possibly careening off into the ocean.

He was unprepared for what awaited upon his return home.

*The sloth is a native of Costa Rica.

Chapter THIRTY-SEVEN

Penelope and Rebecca led the quintet down the short hall to the chief's office at the Santa Barbara Police station, following the civilian receptionist who knocked, opened the door, then stepped aside, inviting the group into the room.

Jessica sat on the couch beaming with delight at being united with the "J" Team in person and immediately jumped up and embraced them all. She introduced Elisabeth, Jason and Jackson to Chief O'Connor and Detective Pelfini, then said, "Please, grab a seat and I will fill you in."

She began by explaining her position with Katrina Barbados, then elaborated on how she sees the operation developing. "Chief and Detective Pelfini, Elisabeth, Jason and Jackson delivered a seminar to the LAPD Narcotics detectives this morning, so I will ask Elisabeth to provide an overview. Elisabeth?"

"Thank you Jessica," she replied, as she rose and began pacing the room offering, "We began by explaining CHAP, the details of which I will elaborate momentarily," She outlined the Caribbean banks' involvement, the undercover Treasury agent there, the currency serial numbers which the LAPD detectives were tracing and the "J" Team's deduction of the CFBA's involvement.

"How do we fit in?" asked Pelfini.

"I was just about to get into that detective, so thank you for the segue. The cocaine confiscated in Los Angeles is identical to that found in Seattle, San

Francisco and just about every major city west of the Mississippi. LAPD's crime lab confirms it is Columbian.

"The Secret Service chose Santa Barbara for a variety of reasons, the principle one being Rebecca's years of residency, albeit intermittent, the proximity to Los Angeles and community demographics. The population is close to one-hundred thousand, the bulk of which is highly educated with fifty-five percent having a university degree. The community hosts a higher than the nation's average number of attorneys and accountants who do business throughout southern California several of which are being investigated by LAPD.

"LAPD detectives do not believe the cocaine is entering through their ports, and Border Security assure us that the quantity being distributed could not come across the border by land or air. The area between Los Angeles and the Mexican border is far too populated for a drug activity to operate without detection. The Coast Guard continually disrupts fishing boats in the Pacific carrying drugs but what is confiscated is minuscule compared to what we are discussing."

"I know I haven't answered your question detective so here it is," as she explained CHAP, brought it up on her laptop and shared it with the two officers, then continued.

"You will be able to follow the investigation via CHAP and offer your own input. I have equipment performing at Rebecca's residence which is observing every email and text in and out of Santa Barbara. The NSA is monitoring every key stroke from the Los Angeles area. We wanted to split the task of covering

Southern California so with Rebecca here in Santa Barbara with intelligence on the area, that left Los Angeles to the NSA.

"Just a quick update on the federal agency. Most law enforcement agencies and the public have no idea the massiveness of the NSA, National Security Agency, surveillance of emails, texts, and phone calls that have been in place for years, with data housed in the ever-expanding Utah facility, code-named *Bumblehive*, in Bluffdale.

Every computer stroke, text and phone call made in the world is recorded and stored in a system with yottabytes with the *Bumblehive* being the only known location of this capacity. Google's former CEO, Eric Schmidt, estimated that the total of all human knowledge created, "From the dawn of man to the present, if digitalized, would total five exabytes," which is considerably less than a yottabyte.

Probably more information than they wanted, Elisabeth thought, *but I don't know how else to explain the magnitude of NSA's power.* She continued, "This is a joint operation between the SBPD, the LAPD and the Secret Service. Our involvement stems from our belief that the CFBA remains a direct threat to candidates vying for a Congressional seat, primarily liberals, and hence the presidency. Although their presidential nominee was successful, they need to ensure that their conservative candidates win re-election in the mid-terms to prevent the Democrats from taking over the House. But our primary involvement is the currency. Technically we are not part of the Treasury, but in this case, we were sequestered to the department under the direction of supervising agent Sorento, because of our work against CFBA.

"Any information *Bumblehive* acquires from my paradigm will be forwarded to me and I will post on CHAP. LAPD detectives will be posting their findings shortly and we believe they will stir the hornet's nest, so to speak, and we will see a fury of texts which we will capture.

"Any questions?"

There were a few that either Elisabeth or Jessica answered clarifying minor points, then Jessica announced, "I heard there is a party at your place tonight Rebecca. I'd like to be cute and ask if I can attend but apparently, I am already a guest, a plus one."

Everyone laughed and clapped their hands in response to the coincidence, a factor of human interaction in which none believed. Rebecca said, "This is going to be very weird. In all the time we spent in StoneHead, we never crossed paths, none of us," as she swept her arms across the room, "and now all five will be together - but not? This is going to take some work on my part, but I'm good, I'm up to it."

Rebecca took a few minutes to lay out the party's original purpose and format, noting Alane's and Alejandro's organizing role, the meet and greet concept for R&P, sharing their contribution to the women's center and housing homeless teens. "We have no idea who is attending other than those we have mentioned, all of us and of course Jessica and her new boss but Alane and Alejandro have invited the movers and shakers, some of whom may be on the LAPD suspects list.

Between the seven of us here, we should be able to get an overview."

"I think this is a perfect cover with Rebecca and Penelope working the guests for R&P," added Jessica. "Elisabeth, after we meet the guests, might you check with Captain Ortega and see if any are on his list?"

"Will do," replied Elisabeth. "We've all found that facial expressions and body movements are crucial to identifying suspicious behavior. But sometimes it is difficult to translate those impressions to colleagues, so I will be wearing a costume jewelry necklace with a mini-camera. Post party, I will upload the video to CHAP for analysis and input."

"Perfect," said Jessica. "The rest of us can utilize our smartphone recorders if we have concrete details to accumulate. Any questions?"

Hearing none, she set the adjournment by rising from the couch, giving each of her team a hug then saying, "See you guys tonight. Let's see if we can put a cap on this operation," then walked out of the office, followed five minutes later by her team.

§‧β§

Gutierrez took the morning off from her legal operations, leathered up and headed north to a Hermanos breakfast meeting an hour's bike ride north to the beach front Viper Diner in Grover City. The eatery was renown for its catering to classic bikers, some of which were weekend riders with their contemporary machines resplendent with all the accoutrements intended to distinguish them from their big brothers' choppers.

She arrived ahead of the others, entered through the main door, observing a sign announcing, *Closed for a private function. Reopening at noon. We apologize for any inconvenience* and then enjoyed a thirty-minute leisurely cup of black coffee on the fog enshrouded deck waiting for her colleagues.

Gutierrez loved these spontaneous meetings which freed her from the often mundane, yet stimulating, day-to-day manipulation of the illegal affairs of her drug clients.

Being the attorney of choice for many of her well-heeled clients who were constantly being arrested for a variety of drug related charges, brought the additional scrutiny, much of which was generated by anger at her ability to have charges dropped or sentences reduced to time served or probation.

She smiled as she enjoyed the last of her coffee, then turned at the scuffling of boots on the worn diner wooded planks.

Placing her mug on a table, she rose to greet a stream of colleagues, embracing each as they gathered around to relax, enjoy the echo of waves crashing into the diner's substructure, glance at the dense morning fog and gather their thoughts for what was forthcoming.

Cell phones and smartphones were left in their offices, location function disengaged, and no one brought either pen, or paper. All information was committed to memory and never recorded in any manner.

The Hermanos were free souls, placing most of their business empire in the hands of others, often to their detriment, given the vastness of the federation.

Today, each would present a brief synopsis of their assigned domain culminating in significant decisions affecting their future.

Center of discussion was Joseph Scarbodini, a GOP candidate in a Democratic electoral district.

Chapter THIRTY-EIGHT

Karen and Tom enjoyed a quiet evening at the Mariscos Punta Manzanillo over a dinner of beef tamales wrapped in banana leaves, black beans and several bottles of Cerveza Imperial, Costa Rica's most popular beer.

Their host was friendly and as had been their finding in all the beach communities, they introduced themselves as Canadians, but didn't ask about Sawyer.

The restaurateur was polite, commenting affectionately about Canadians in general and how many he sees as tourists but didn't mention Sawyer or any other countrymen or women who may have relocated there.

The owner didn't think of Sawyer as Canadian, he was a Ticos, a local whose heritage was never questioned. Nobody cared. He was simply, "Brian" a friend, a philanthropist, a man ready and willing to help anyone in need.

Not making the connection and not wanting to betray their presence if Sawyer was here, the last village before the Panamanian border, they had paid their tab and spent a restful night at the Cabaña del Caribe.

Rising early the next morning, they were consumed with the perplexity of their investigation and chatted quietly in their room over Britt dark roast coffee, a locally grown favorite. Their conundrum unresolved, they sent a satellite text to Kopas, outlining the situation and asking for input.

His reply was immediate, responding with a call to their encrypted satellite phone. Karen took the communiqué, asking Kopas to hold while they walked to the beach a few meters away for privacy.

Sitting in the sand, both in bathrobes and a 9mm in their pocket, they put the phone on speaker and brainstormed the situation.

Kopas began by confirming their decision to use the CSIS satellite and that he had already posted their progress to CHAP without reverberations from Sorento.

High speed internet was available in their locale, to which they could attest, given the number of dinner patrons using their smartphones last night. So, it was possible Sawyer has a phone but Kopas noted that NSA hasn't picked up any chatter other than locals texting and a few tourists doing likewise to North America and Europe.

Tom suggested, "David, if Sawyer is here, we will make contact in the next couple of days and clone his phone, then send that data to you via satellite. In the meantime, we will circulate and play tourist."

"That should work. Get back to me in the next couple of days and please keep a low profile, keep them hidden."

Karen shrugged her shoulders and spread her arms as though to say, *What, do you think we are newbies?*

Dead line.

Tom placed the phone in his pocket, turned to Karen and said, "What do you think? Doable?"

"Sure, provided you continue to give me those puppy dog, soulful eye glances, hold my hand in public and kiss me frequently," Karen retorted with a grin.

"Doable," replied Tom as he leaned toward her, kissed her while sliding his hand up her bare leg, caressing the inside of her thigh.

"Let's go inside before I embarrass us both by screwing your brains out right here in the sand," as she rose, took his hand and lead him back to their room, closed and locked the door, removed her robe and did as promised.

Showered and physically drained, Karen dressed in a Naomi satin maxi dress in burnt orange with blue and rose flowers, flat ankle strapped sandals, her hair moussed, blush lipstick with a necklace matching the burnt orange dress background. Although the practice was contrary to her nature, she carried her 9mm in a cross the shoulder straw handbag the pattern of which matched her floppy straw sun hat.

Tom chose a pair of Topman kaki knee length shorts and a black T over which he wore his shoulder holster hidden by a black and tan oversized, short-sleeve shirt worn untucked. A western style straw hat offered the final touch to his tourist look.

They walked to the Lime Tree Café a short distance from their B&B needing to be out and about looking for Sawyer. Neither agent felt their bodies could handle more beans, a local breakfast staple, so they opted for scrambled eggs topped with homemade salsa and cheese with fresh fruit side and of course, coffee.

They dawdled with their meal, neither engaging in small talk while they maxed out their peripheral vision, hoping to spot Sawyer. Forty-five minutes later, they paid their tab with Tom's personal credit card then began wandering the streets, hand-in-hand exemplifying their role as tourists.

They stopped for helado, local ice cream, then a taco lunch at a beach food stand and hiked the beach for the afternoon, constantly scanning groups of people. They turned around at the Refugio Nacional and headed back to the village as the afternoon waned.

The most efficient process of course was to ask people, but this being the last village before the Panamanian border, they were counting on him being here and had no desire to spook him.

Exhausted from the long day of trudging through the village they decided to call it quits with an early dinner and hit the sheets, hoping for more success tomorrow.

They entered Mariscos Punta Manzanillo with their only thoughts being on a good drink and meal. As they took one of the only two tops, they glanced toward the bar and spotted Sawyer.

Chapter THIRTY-NINE

Edmonton RCMP detectives were following several threads on CHAP; Jessica and the "J" Team, Karen and Tom as well as their current primary cocaine smuggler, Stan.

The officers wanted to maintain a proactive investigation, which, under normal circumstances would be limited given their lack of solid evidence of Stan's illegal movements, but after uncovering Brian Sawyer's activities, primarily his drug operation and subsequent facilitating the cesium, they were given considerable latitude by senior management.

All detachment commanders were accessing CHAP as were the Canadian Border Services Agency, CBSA and CSIS. The Edmonton detectives were receiving daily and often hourly reports from CBSA agents' data on drug confiscations and contraband such as firearms and explosives.

Canada and the United States share an undefended border of almost nine-thousand kilometers, much of it passing through uninhabited wilderness. In as few as twenty years ago, hunters and hikers from each country would meet in these remote locations to exchange equipment, firearms and ammunition totally undetected and unregulated by either country.

Such is no longer the case with the entire length being monitored by either CCVTs or drones, the images being fed to border agents who immediately post their suspicions to CHAP.

All law enforcement agencies west of Saskatchewan increased their physical and electronic surveillance of known drug dealers, watching for any change in behavior. They were also checking each cocaine seizure for similarities in product and comparing the results with what the LAPD had confiscated, all through CHAP.

The area not covered by surveillance is the Gulf Islands and Juan de Fuca Straight where both countries attempt to regulate surface vessels as accurately as possible. However, many private boats can slip by, usually in the dead of night, and deposit their cargo on remote islands, or inlets, later to be retrieved by the next segment of the transportation system.

Vancouver Island, just west of the city itself, is four hundred and sixty kilometers long, one-hundred kilometers wide with an area of twelve-thousand square kilometers. The largest island on the West Coast of North America boasts a population of eight-hundred thousand but even with this density, there are hundreds of kilometers of unpopulated coves and coast line where any form of illicit activity could go undetected.

Law enforcement for the rugged west coast is shared by Canada's Coast Guard, their Navy and the RCMP's West Coast Marine Services, the latter of which takes the primary lead in enforcement and patrolling the six-hundred nautical miles from the Washington State border to Alaska.

The vastness of the coast line and ocean make it welcome territory for drug smugglers, many of whom drop their payload overboard from fishing boats, allowing the packages to be submersed just below the water level, each with a GPS locator attached.

Once the cargo is retrieved at sea, it must be brought to shore for distribution, which is where law abiding citizens and Mounties are engaged, catching couriers before they hit the main highway east.

To assist in the land enforcement are the small RCMP detachments in Tofino, midway of the island, and Ucluelet, forty-kilometers south. North and south of these communities are hundreds of fiords and inlets, some with indigenous villages but most as uninhabited as they were hundreds of years ago.

One such fiord is the Barkley Sound which leads from the Pacific Ocean to the small mill town of Port Alberni connecting with a major highway leading over the Island Mountain Ranges to the populated east coast.

In addition to monitoring all known drug dealers, the Edmonton RCMP's forensic team was analysing all dealers' and runners' cell phones, laptops and tablets using a unique Canadian software program.

The system first came to light after the Quebec City's mosque shooting where investigators extracted information about the suspect. The software provides access to zip files, RAM memory, directories, social media chat data, P2P file sharing, web mail, videos on YouTube, photos, USB keys, how the user shares information, and the internet browsing history, even if any of the above had been deleted.

In the Quebec case, forensics detected over thirty-one thousand web links, forty-seven hundred Google searches, thirty-three hundred Facebook links and sixty-thousand photos. The software scans all sources and provides a detail analysis which previously took several officers hours to compile.

Corporations and attorneys are using the software to analyse company owned equipment to ensure employee honesty and to thwart industrial spying.

ℨ.ℬℨ

Gutierrez was concluding their breakfast meeting after discussing the various Christians for a Better America mid-term candidates who needed an infusion of cash, a quarterly financial update, an ETA for the next Columbian shipment and the proposed logistics for the Canadian delivery and distribution.

Several members shared their concern regarding the increased number of Los Angeles dealers being arrested and encouraged Gutierrez to put forth a greater effort to insulate their distribution captains.

Chapter FORTY

Jessica stopped off at Nordstrom to figure out the evening's dress code, *California Casual*. Not having a great deal of time, she headed straight for the women's section rather than browsing, which was her normal shopping operating system.

Nordstrom had a wide variety of summer dresses available and after a short search she found a Band of Gypsies, Floral Maxi Dress in a cheery blossoms pattern of softly crinkled rayon with fluttering sleeves and a flattering, wrap-style silhouette. Ankle length in the back and mid-calf in front, the short ruffled sleeved piece had a back-tie closure and surplice V-neck.

Delighted with her selection, she took the dress to the shoe department where a pair of Kayoko sandals jumped out at her. The all leather number with ankle strap and three-inch heel matched perfectly with the white in the gypsy dress. They went with her to the service desk and after a few minutes she was on her way back to the hotel to dress for what she hoped would be an informative and rewarding dinner party.

Rebecca, Penelope and the "J" Team pulled into the ranch's driveway and spotted an unknown SUV parked by the pool house. Alane's lime green Mini Cooper was parked in the main driveway along with the Island Caterer's van.

"Whose car is that?" asked Jackson as Rebecca pulled her Civic beside the Mini and everyone bailed out.

"I don't recognize it. Do you Pen?" replied Rebecca, knowing full well whose vehicle it was. "Let's head inside and see how Alane and Alejandro are doing, then one of us can check out the car," she continued as she moved toward the house, winking at Penelope as she went by.

Entering through the front door, the clatter of dishes and murmur of voices echoed from the kitchen and dining room met them immediately.

Leading the way, Penelope and Rebecca stepped into the living room, then stood aside allowing the others to enter first with Penelope exclaiming with outstretched arms, "Ta da!"

Alane and Alejandro turned from their efforts with the table bouquets with huge grins and simultaneously, with outstretched arms said, "Ta da" pointing to a man arranging the buffet table dressed in black slacks, white double-breasted chef's jacket with black pipping across the bottom, stand-up collar and cuffs.

With the second exclamation the man turned, and he too replied with outstretched arms and, "Ta da."

The new arrivals all moved toward Marc Stucki, former President Bakus' head chef with laughter and delight and enveloped him in hugs. Jackson was the last in line and Rebecca stood aside and introduced them formally. Although they knew each other, Jackson was undercover at StoneHead High and their paths never crossed. Penelope knew Marc from the retirement party he had prepared for Rebecca's retirement, at which Jessica had a difficult time accepting the departure of such an accomplished agent.

Jason asked, "When did you get here Marc, and do you have a place to stay?"

"I got here yesterday and met with the caterers with whom I had been in contact for a while. I stayed in a motel last light and am here now."

"You are staying here? At the ranch? replied Jackson.

Marc bowed slightly saying, "I am the new pool house tenant, thanks to the generous invitation of Penelope and Rebecca. Just until I get settled."

"You are moving here? To Santa Barbara?" exclaimed Jason with uplifted voice as though not totally understanding the course of the conversation.

"Maybe Rebecca and Penelope can answer that better than I, or maybe Alane."

"May I Rebecca?" offered Alane.

"Certainly, please be my guest. You can explain the situation more eloquently and accurately than I."

"As all of you know Marc was President Bakus' personal chef for many years, both at the White House and StoneHead Ranch. When President Bakus lost the election, Marc, and everyone else in the White House was out of a job. His former boss gave him a substantial severance pay and rather than look for work in StoneHead or Washington, we made him an offer he couldn't refuse.

"During the next few weeks and months Marc will be researching a prime location for his restaurant and all the accoutrements it will require. The three of us, plus Rebecca's accountant are behind him so all he has to do is concentrate on making it the best of the best."

"Thanks Alane, I couldn't explain it any better myself. So, Jackson, you are going to have the pleasure of Marc's cuisine which the rest of us have enjoyed on numerous occasions, Jessica for months on end…a little envy from me…but he is here now and that is what counts.

"Marc is everything going okay? Is there anything you need from us besides getting out of your way?"

"Thanks Rebecca, we are on schedule and will have everything ready by the time your guests arrive. And thanks for the introduction Alane, I sincerely appreciate the opportunity."

"My pleasure Marc," replied Alane giving him a little bow.

Rebecca chimed in with, "Since Marc is set and the caterers will be here shortly, I am off to change. Marc is going to be here for the evening, mingling and spreading the word about his upcoming culinary debut," then she moved past the tables and headed out.

Penelope and Elisabeth welcomed Marc again, then followed Rebecca out, anxious to be ready for their guests on time.

Jackson and Jason hung around chatting briefly with Alane, Alejandro and Marc, getting to know the three men better figuring that with almost thirty people arriving shortly, they wouldn't have much of a chance.

Finally, Jason offered, "Guys, it looks like we are going to be around here for a while so let's get together soon, maybe a nice place where you hang out, you can show us around? Whadaya say?"

"Sounds good to me," replied Alejandro.

"Me too," said Alane reaching into his jacket's inside pocket for a couple of business cards and offering them to Jason, Jackson and Marc. "Give me a call after the party and we will have dinner. I figured you guys are going to be too busy during the day for a lunch," offering a wry grin.

"Will do," said Jackson and Jason simultaneously as they headed out of the dining room, shaking Marc's hand as they passed him.

Alejandro returned to arranging the white hydrangea bouquets for the massive oak dining table.

Most would have considered the table gargantuan, but Alejandro had prepared hundreds of such tables for his Beverly Hills clients and knowing the guests, this setting would be the norm.

He had created the ambiance with a lace trimmed burgundy table cloth that extended discreetly one-foot over the table's edge, followed by place settings of Spanish Lace from Wallace. Shaking his head as he laid each piece, thinking that Rebecca probably had no idea that the discontinued pattern is valued at five-thousand for eight place settings and she has enough for thirty-two.

Taking a fork over to Alane, he shared his concern for Rebecca not knowing the value of the sterling. Alane accepted the fork replying with a generous smile, "You are right Alejandro, she doesn't. I don't believe she knows the value of her property or the furnishings, which is why her accountant, Susan Gomez, had an insurance underwriter evaluate the entire house and property after you performed your rescue mission on the gardens. Susan has a limited power of attorney as do

I for her portfolio. One of these days she, Susan and I are going to have a chat and bring her current." Handing the silver back to Alejandro, he concluded with, "It is truly gorgeous isn't it?"

"It is. The table will look stunning when I am finished."

᪥᪥᪥

The CSIS agents were unfazed spotting Sawyer and calmly went about their rehearsed performance with Tom removing his hat to create a calmer demeaner, then ordering drinks and dinner from the passing server.

Chapter FORTY-ONE

Alane hired daughters of several of his clients, high school and university students. They arrived early to set up the parking kiosk…car keys and identification tags and program the front gates to stay open.

The three were ready when the first guests arrived. They looked professionally stunning in white, mid-thigh length Bermuda shorts, black Peplum Tee by Caslon with crewneck and cap sleeves which dropped to just below their waists, paired with black Nike runners.

As the first vehicle came to a stop in front of the ranch's stained, carved oak front door, the valets swung into action simultaneously, opening the driver's and passenger's doors, greeting Rodrigo O'Conner and Elise Pelfini. The third valet lead the way to Alane and Alejandro waiting by the open front door.

O'Conner was dressed in a deep sky-blue double-breasted blazer over an open neck, button-down Cooper's Town white linen shirt, black slacks and laced black wing-tips. He stepped to one side, allowing Pelfini to proceed him in her Charles Henry belted Cami Maxi dress of vibrant purple and several shades of pink vertical stripes. The stunning dress with a surplice neckline with adjustable spaghetti straps was floor length and paired with Sam Edelman Ariella ankle strap pink sandals.

Their hosts greeted Elise with a hug, a cheek to cheek, shaking the police chief's hand, then escorted them through the expansive vestibule and into the living room where two bartenders were set up in the far corner by the furthest French Doors. Alane accompanied their first guests to the bar while Alejandro returned to the entry to greet the next arrivals.

Elise and Rodrigo thanked their escorts, turned to the bar and Elise ordered a Negroni, one part each of Campari, a bitter, spicy, sweet liqueur, sweet red Vermouth and Gin in an old fashion glass. One ice cube. While the bartender, another university student looking sharp in black pants and an open-neck pointed collar white shirt with a name tag that read, Frank, mixed the detective's drink, Roderigo watched in fascination, not knowing what his officer was drinking.

As Frank handed Elise her cocktail, he said to him, "That looks delicious Elise. Please make mine the same Frank. Thanks."

Receiving his drink, Rodrigo and Elise, being the first to arrive, meandered around the living room admiring the ambiance Rebecca had created just as their hostesses entered the room.

Rebecca looked striking in a Bardot Botanica ivory lace dress from Australian designer Carol Skoufit. The cocktail outfit offered lattice trim below the knee with an illusion skirt, a V-neck and adjustable straps. She paired the outfit with ivory Topshop Belle Strappy sandals with a three-inch heel. The look blended smoothly with her crop blonde hairstyle, which was very similar to Penelope's pixie but slightly longer.

They entered together and as Elise spotted the pair, she raved about their outfits. Elise admired Rebecca's, then turned to Penelope who wore a Gordon Merchant Billabong print maxi-dress with a periwinkle background adorned with white gardenias. The floor length was ideal for the shirttail hem, drawstring waist and V-neck. The dress was stunning, highlighting her blonde pixie hairdo, short on the back and sides and slightly longer on the top. Finishing the look, Pen had chosen periwinkle Ziginy Blaker sandals with a crisscross instep and ankle straps.

While Rebecca and Penelope showed Elise and Rodrigo around, Jackson and Jason stood in the upper hallway waiting for Elisabeth. Neither agent had ever attended such an event and were approaching the evening with some trepidation. They were hoping Elisabeth's presence would somehow take the edge off their anxiety.

As they paced back and forth in front of her bedroom door, they checked their phones and reviewed the directions Jessica had texted them earlier in the day. Elisabeth said that cocktail parties usually saw guests coming and going all evening, so they had to gather intel at the earliest possible moment, which this operation would see Jason and Jackson use their uniquely designed federal agency phones created with an algorithm to duplicate each guest's phone's SIM card and store the data until Elisabeth downloaded it to her system. The agency units' storage capacity exceeded 900 GB with a download speed greater than anything available to consumers.

Just as the men replaced their phones inside their jacket pockets, Elisabeth appeared, somewhat startled to find her colleagues standing outside her door. She said quizzically, "What are you guys doing here? Why aren't you down stairs?"

Jason attempted a solemn face and answered, "We just thought it would be more appropriate to enter the fray in your company."

"Oh, yeah, you expect me to believe that? You guys are scared aren't you? Oh, my God, you are afraid to go down there by yourselves," she said with a lift in her voice of incredulity.

Jackson was first to give up the charade with, "Okay, we are. But we are also trying to be gentlemen and not leave you to enter by yourself. We will escort you together."

Elisabeth started laughing, saying, "Jackson you are so full of shit, but I admire your honesty. So let's go already, but first, what do you think of my outfit?"

As Elisabeth gave a little twirl the men were able to appreciate her Milan tie front jumpsuit, in pink with white polka dots. The long, wide-leg design was enhanced by adjustable spaghetti straps and side pockets. Lexie ankle sandals by Stuart Weitzman with a three-inch heel completed the look.

"Very nice. Stunning actually," noted Jason as Elisabeth finished her presentation with a muted curtsy.

"I agree," offered Jackson. Do we meet with your approval?"

Elisabeth noted he was wearing one of his Nordstrom outfits; the two button, natural colored blazer, a blue & white striped button-down, long-sleeve shirt, navy slacks and dark-blue tasseled loafers.

"Very nice. Very nice indeed," she said, nodding several times. "The blazer is fitted perfectly to cover your weapon and a sharp combination," as she pointed to the blazer's shape.

Comment [JM]:

She turned her attention to Jason, who was sporting a chocolate blazer with a similar cut, a tan, pointed collar long-sleeve shirt, open at the neck, khaki pants and brown loafers.

Offering her colleagues an approval spread of her arms and a generous smile she said, "You guys look fabulous and your apprehension is unnecessary. Treat these people like any other group of suspects and you will do fine. Besides you are armed, and we hope they are not," she concluded with a smirk.

"Now, let's get this party going, as she placed herself between them, hooked their arms and headed for the stairs.

Chapter FORTY-TWO

As they descended the stairs into the vestibule, they could hear the chattering of guests interacting. Enjoying. Elisabeth squeezed each of her colleague's arms saying, "Let's do this," then stepped in front of them, entering the living room as the vertices of the human triangle.

She took a moment to scan the room, orienting herself to the environment so changed since earlier in the day. Making her way through the elegantly attired crowd, she spotted Rebecca and Penelope holding court with several people. Closing the distance, she heard Penelope outlining R&P's plans and objectives, summarizing their combined expertise. As Elisabeth slowed, Pen had just mentioned Rebecca's accredited Secret Service career and Elisabeth noted the wide-eyed reaction from the guests.

Elisabeth waited a few seconds, allowing the threesome to absorb the comment, then slid next to Rebecca, touching her arm slightly.

"Elisabeth, you look ravishing, absolutely beautiful. I want you to meet our guests," she offered with her right arm around Elisabeth's waist, unintentionally brushing her abdominal holster band that held her twenty-five caliber Seecamp pistol and agency phone. Giving her side a slight squeeze of acknowledgement, she continued, gracefully extending her arm to each guest, "Marianna Gutierrez is the principal partner in her law firm, and these are her managing partners, Erin Ainsworth, Jacob Petrovic and

Joseph Popovic," extending her left arm in the direction of the three.

Elisabeth shook the hands of each, starting with Gutierrez. As she gripped her hand, she felt her phone's slight vibration as it acknowledged successful cloning.

Elisabeth acknowledged the other attorneys while Rebecca offered her guests a brief bio of her former university classmate, "Elisabeth is a junior high teacher in Omaha. We met at the University of Montana and have kept in touch. She is here for a few weeks of California sun and cuisine, so we are going to have to introduce her to some of our finest restaurants."

Her last comment opened the discussion to which cuisine Elisabeth should enjoy first with all six sharing their experiences. As their discussion was ensuing, Jackson and Jason picked up a glass of Atascadero's premium beer which celebrated the craft brewery's matriarch founder Iona Atascadero. They were circulating, introducing themselves as Rebecca's cousins, Jason portraying the role of an American military diplomat for Algeria, which raised several eyebrows and began numerous conversations.

As the catering staff circulated with canapés, the agents stopped to engage UC Santa Barbara's police chief and chancellor with each commenting on the appetizers; Sicilian arancini, or rice balls stuffed with pork ragu, taleggio cheese and a spicy tomato sauce and an aged balsamic lamb meatball with a harissa red pepper sauce, mint pistou, feta, lemon gremolata and cilantro.

Jackson's background slipped right into the conversation as he shared his work as a high school teacher from StoneHead. He was able to carry on numerous conversations about education and changing careers with considerable expertise. His only fabrication was his career prior to teaching. Not wanting to raise their suspects' red flags, he shared that he had been a carpenter before teaching. Again, not complete fiction as he had done construction before Delta.

Interacting with O'Connor and Pelfini wasn't difficult as they had just met, they were law enforcement and part of the operation. It was Katrina Barbados and Jessica whom the agents approached with considerable trepidation. Both had been undercover, Jackson most recently as a high school teacher and Jason as a graduate student at a Christian university, but during those times, they never interacted with someone they knew, let alone their supervisor.

They were on a collision course with the attorneys when Alane swung in beside them carrying two glasses of Hillside Winery's Merlot, one of the local vineyards' top sellers. The agents looked at him rather perplexed but quickly figured out his ploy, set their empty beer glasses on a nearby end table, to be retrieved by the catering staff, accepted the wine, as Alane welcomed Barbados to the R&P function, then introduced himself to Jessica, Jackson and Jason.

The agents breathed a sigh of relief and easily joined the conversation lead by Alane, whom they would later tease about whether he had a previous life as a diplomat or negotiator.

Several times during the conversation, one or the other had to turn away from Jessica who would ask personal questions, the answers of which she already knew, but Alane had placed himself shielding the agents from her direct view, forcing the conversation source to originate from Barbados.

After a few minutes, the duo moved on, Barbados desiring to introduce her new associate to as many colleagues and business associates as possible.

An hour into the meet and greet, and prearranged with Marc, Alane removed his loafers and stood on an occasional chair by the bar while Marc used a fork to clang the side of a glass, gaining everyone's attention.

"Back here folks. Thank you all for accepting the invitation for this meet and greet put on by our new entrepreneurial team, R&P Investigators, Dr. Penelope Barker and Rebecca Simpson. No jokes about Dr. Watson please," he began and offered a slight pause for the laughter to diminish, then continued, "Penelope as she prefers to be called, is a retired Wyoming veterinarian who brings considerable research and analytical skills to the company while Rebecca is a retired Secret Service agent with over twenty years of undercover assignments to her credit."

Jason and Jackson nudged each other with delight as they watched the astonished looks on the guests. Their body language spoke to the presence of law enforcement royalty, which would raise the level of service to attorneys and accountants to new heights.

Alane continued, "Their office is next to mine," he said taking a slight bow, "Their expertise will be in intensive background checks for financial investors, missing persons, insurance investigations and everything in between...except divorce," the last comment receiving a few chuckles from the guests.

As he completed his remarks, he noticed Rebecca and Penelope slide up beside him, so he added, "Thank you again for joining us. Chef Marc Stucki whom Rebecca will introduce shortly, is giving me a nod that dinner will be served momentarily, but in the meantime, here are your hosts," as he stepped down from the chair smiling as the women already had their heels off and were stepping on to the chair.

Rebecca put her arm around Pen and began, "Thank you very much for joining us tonight. As some of you know I have been a Santa Barbara resident for some ten years now, albeit off and on physically and I apologize to everyone for not revealing my background all during all that time. I was undercover with the federal government for my entire career.

As she finished that last sentence a round of applause went up from the guests generating smiles and raised arms from most. Two guests were not as thrilled with her revelation and their reaction was not missed by Rebecca as she continued, "That is very kind. Thank you for your support and thank you Alane for all that you have done for me creating all of this," she paused to spread her arms out to indicate the house and property, "and for you and Alejandro arranging this lovely evening.

"I know Marc is anxious to have you enjoy his creations so very quickly I want to mention that R&P will be investing in renovating a local building, yet to be acquired, for a site for homeless girls and young women. Specifics will be available as the project gains momentum and although we are not formally inviting your financial assistance, my friends advised me that many of you would be disappointed if you are not invited to participate, so Alane will work out the details as the project moves forward.

"Lastly, Marc Stucki. He was President Bakus' personal chef for his entire presidency and we asked him to Santa Barbara not only to prepare tonight's feast but to establish himself as our newest fine dining establishment," she paused again to hear a round of applause from the crowd.

"In the coming weeks Marc will be out and about searching for the ideal location and arranging renovations and promoting his adventure. We don't know what he intends calling his creation but I for one would like to see it named, *Marc Stucki's*. With his credentials, why not flaunt them?

"So, with that, I give you Marc Stucki to introduce his cuisine.

"Thank you Rebecca, and welcome everyone to this lovely ranch setting. I sincerely appreciate Penelope and Rebecca inviting me to offer you this evening's cuisine.

"If you haven't tasted the canapés, please raise your hand and one of the servers will bring a platter to you. You must try the Sicilian arancini which are rice balls stuffed with pork ragu, taleggio cheese and a spicy tomato sauce," he said with a wide grin. "Then you can take your canapé to bar and they will pair it with a delicious local wine."

"Please make your way to the table which Alane and Alejandro have set with the beautiful Spanish Lace sterling flatware and the exquisite bouquets from Alejandro's garden. The servers will bring the first course, which is local heirloom tomatoes in a delightful salad with burrata cheese, pumpkin seed pesto, arugula and balsamic reduction."

With a sweep of his arm, he invited the guests to the dining table as he stepped back and returned to the kitchen to supervise the serving.

Rebecca and Penelope asked Alane not to assign table settings, preferring to observe who sat by whom knowing the conversations were going to generate intelligence. None of the guests were aware they were being recorded.

Rebecca sat next to Katrina Barbados who had Jessica to her other side and Rebecca's accountant, Sophia Gomez next to her. Penelope was able to slide in next to Detective Pelfini with Marianna Gutierrez on the other.

As the rest of the dinner party found a seat, the bartenders arrived with wine bottles, filling their glasses with chardonnay just as the servers arrived with the first course.

Marc observed the guests as they progressed through his first course, chatting about local and national politics and raving about the salad. As the diners finished, Marc signaled the servers in the wings and they moved as one down each side removing plates.

As the last server left the dining room Marc appeared at the head of the table and introduced his second course which was served while he spoke, "Ladies and gentlemen, I offer you your second course of smoked chicken ravioli with mascarpone, an Italian cream cheese, and spinach. This is paired with chanterelle mushrooms and pancetta crisp, preserved lemon, pea purée with a white wine beurre blanc. Bon Appétit," he concluded and stepped back into the shadows of the alcove.

Twenty-minutes later, amid jocular conversation and exclamations about the outstanding dinner, the servers reappeared, removed the dishes with Marc reappearing at the head of the table offering, "I trust your appetites are truly primed and ready for short rib wellington, my take on braised beef short-ribs, wild mushroom pâté, serrano ham, roasted Santa Barbara carrots, Roquefort cheese pomme purée with a Napa Valley Merlot reduction. Enjoy."

Marc bowed slightly and stepped back into the recesses of the alcove, waited about ten minutes, then reappeared and slowly made his way around the table, stopping to chat with diners who expressed an interest in conversing. As he approached Alane, his new mentor touched his arm slightly, looked up with a broad smile and mouthed, *outstanding, you are on your way.*

That almost covert approval meant a great deal to Marc coming from Santa Barbara's quintessential connoisseur. Marc responded with a broad smile in appreciation, mouthing in reply, *thank you.*

The dining scene was played out one last time. Marc stepped to the head of the table as servers removed the last of the plates saying, "To conclude your dining experience, I offer you a dessert duo. Meyer lemon white chocolate tart, which is Meyer lemon curd, meringue tarragon with white chocolate ice cream, local raspberries and a chocolate and banana brownie, caramelized bananas, peanut butter anglaise, banana gelato and almond Rocha."

As Marc concluded his introduction, servers appeared with the dessert plates, placing one in front of each diner, then returning to the kitchen to await Marc's direction. Surprisingly that occurred sooner than anyone expected as the guests devoured the presentation quickly with several looking around for a server with more.

Marc quickly obliged, signaling servers to deliver additional sweets to most of the smiling guests.

As the last dessert fork hit a plate, the bartenders appeared with cognac snifters replete with Courvoisier XO Cognac, a connoisseur's pairing choice with chocolate, to the delight and astonishment of all.

Having spared no expense for the evening enthralled Penelope and Rebecca's guests, but serving Courvoisier, the choice of most in attendance, put them over the top and immediately on to their list of Santa Barbara's influential couples.

Most diners took their cognac into the living room to sit and chat, most of the conversation involving Marc, his menu and how they could be involved in the launching of his restaurant.

Elisabeth would smile later as she downloaded the video thinking that the evening produced far more than the needed intelligence.

Chapter FORTY-THREE

Karen and Tom's dinner arrived as they continued to observe Sawyer enjoying his evening drinking with his friends. They chatted intimately, creating a plan of action.

Dinner finished, Karen slid her hand across the table and Tom placed his on top, to a casual observer, a couple sharing an intimate moment. Karen removed her hand allowing Tom to palm what she had left, which he held in his right hand between his baby finger and palm, then rose and walked to the bar and purchased three beers.

Sawyer was playing pool in the corner of the tavern with another Tico as Tom walked up, place the beer bottles on the pool table's edge, took out a Colon, the local currency, and placed the purple bill along with the beers indicating he was next in line to play the winner and that person was to take the equivalent of ten American dollars.

Sawyer and the other player nodded to Tom as he chose a spot on a bar stool next to the pool table to watch the match. Hortonn had observed Sawyer win every game so far with competitors choosing not to play him, giving Tom his opening.

As the eight ball entered the end pocket ending the game, Tom rose, walked over to the beer bottles and money, gave one to the loser with a nod and the other to Sawyer holding it in his right hand by the bottle's neck then releasing his baby finger held the other in his left for himself and gestured his bottle forward to Sawyer who did likewise and clinked bottles.

The game was on.
Tom lost.
Then lost again.
And again.
Each loss required him to purchase the beer.

Imperial has an alcohol content of ten percent compared to its North American counterpart of four, but Sawyer was a Tico and undoubtedly used to ten percent. Tom wasn't, which was why as Sawyer concentrated on a shot, Tom emptied his bottle behind his back in the soil of a ficus elastica, a rubber tree, sitting to the side of the bar stools.

Familiar with the local beer or not, Sawyer was showing obvious signs of inebriation to the point that Tom conceded defeat and as Sawyer staggered to the rack to return his cue, Tom spoke with the bartender offering to help Sawyer home.

Tom and Karen had made themselves sufficiently visible that the owner had no reason to doubt their intentions, thanked them profusely for helping his customer home and directed them to his residence down the street on the beach.

Karen paid their tab and followed the two as Tom supported Sawyer with his arm around his waist heading for the beach.

By the time they reached the beach house, the GHB, gamma hydroxybutyric, also known as a date rape drug which Tom had slipped into Sawyer's beer had done its job. Sawyer had passed out.

Tom plopped him on his bed, closed the door and joined Karen in the kitchen searching for coffee.

They took turns sleeping on the couch with the other at the kitchen table, staring at Sawyer's bedroom door with their handgun on their lap.

It had been midnight when they put their suspect to bed so adding normal sleep pattern plus a hangover option, he exited his bedroom at nine in the morning. He looked scraggly with a heavy beard, messed hair and the same clothes he had on yesterday.

Anticipating his rousing about this time, Karen had brewed a pot of coffee, found a bottle of headache tablets and had both ready with a glass of water when Sawyer staggered into the kitchen.

"What the fuck! What the hell are you doing in my house. Get the fuck out of here," he yelled as he ran to the kitchen counter and grabbed a butcher knife and turned to face Karen.

"Good morning Brian, you'll want to put the knife back," she said, raising her pistol, pointing it at his midsection, ten-ten feet away.

Brian's reaction was as expected; he turned so pale Karen was sure he was going to faint. Sawyer wasn't a hardened criminal but a guy who thought growing marijuana was a victimless crime. He put his hands in the air and backed up to the wall with a thud and dropped the knife.

While Karen was stifling a laugh, Tom appeared to her left, unseen by Brian and said, "Brian," as he too level a semi-automatic handgun at him.

"Oh, my God, what the fuck is going on? Are you going to kill me? What do you want? I don't have anything of value."

Karen replied, still pointing her firearm at him, "Well, now Brian, that is not entirely true is it? You have, what, a couple of million dollars hidden in this house?"

Brian went pale again and thought, *Who are these two and how do they know about my money. Oh, fuck, they are going to torture me and take everything I have.* Before he could reply, Karen continued, "No, Brian, we are not going to rob you. We are agents of the Canadian Security Intelligence Service," as she tossed her credential folder across the table. "Take a look, then have a seat."

Brian did as he was told, took a seat at the table and looking at the credentials and shield, slapping his forehead as he felt his world collapse. Tom slipped up beside him, grabbed a chair, pulled it behind Brian, sat down with his pistol on his lap.

Brian sat with his head between his hands, almost sobbing. He looked up and asked, "What do you want?"

Karen replied, "That is a good start Brian. We do want something, but we are willing to reciprocate. Just to be clear so you know we are being straight with you, we could arrest you now, right now and take you back to Canada. We made the arrangements with the Costa Rican government and even though you are a Costa Rican citizen, they are prepared to rescind your citizenship and wave extradition. We can be on a plane to Toronto today."

Brian replied, "What are you talking about? Arrest me for what?"

"Now Brian, surely you gest. You ran a drug operation in southern Alberta for years, shipped the product across the border to Idaho and that weed was sold to finance the Citizens for a Better America's operation to take down a Mahalo Airline."

"That is bullshit. I had nothing to do with that plane landing in the ocean. I was still in Alberta then, how can I be responsible for that?"

Karen continued, "Brian, you are not listening. The marijuana you grew, cultivated and shipped was sold and that money financed a domestic terrorist organization. That is just one charge against you. That container you received from three men in a white van? That was cesium. You put that on the train, and it made its way to Minneapolis, then on to the flight for LAX. The cesium was exposed as the airliner made its descent, disabling the plane's electronics.

"There were no casualties or injuries thanks to the expertise and heroism of the crew but it all started with you Brian. There is an outstanding terrorism Interpol arrest warrant with your name on it."

Sawyer was sweating now, flailing his arms, running his hands through his hair. He tried to get up but was shouted down by Tom's scream.

Sitting down, he offered, "Look, I had no idea what was in that container. What the hell is cesium anyway and why am I being blamed for it? I was told not to look at it and to ship it on CP Rail immediately. Where did it come from? Why am I being labeled a terrorist? I was a simple pot grower."

Karen answered with, "Cesium is a radioactive material which was stolen from a Manitoba mine. There are only two places on earth where it is mined. The cesium was stolen by three petty thieves from Denver.

Two are dead, having been shot by a Mountie. The third chose a deal which would see him out of prison in twenty years. We think you can see that your participation is viewed as equally culpable. But it is not our responsibility Brian. We are tasked with bringing you back. Unless…"

Sawyer saw his life slipping away and had no doubt these CSIS agents would take him back to Canada today if he didn't think quickly. *So much booze last night. Fuck, I can't think straight,* he thought. Karen poured him a cup of coffee and slid it across the table with her left hand, maintaining her pistol leveled at his midsection. Waiting.

Seeing that he had reached his limit, she offered, "So what's it going to be Brian? Are you heading back to Canada in handcuffs to stand trial for terrorism or would you like to hear our offer?"

Sawyer put his head on the table for a moment then looked up and replied, "Sure, why not? It can't be any worse than prison."

Karen began her offer, "Good choice Brian. This is what we are offering. It is a non-negotiable, one-time proposition. Cocaine is being smuggled from Columbia into Costa Rica and sent to America through Mexico. Some of it is getting to Canada. We need to know their distribution system. That is where you come in."

Sawyer sat complacent with his head on the table, held between his hands, waiting for the other shoe to drop.

Karen ignored his posture and continued, "You have an impressive friends' network which you will expand and report directly to us," as she slid a satellite phone across the table.

You will call every other day with this phone. We are preprogrammed number one. Just hit it once and wait for the connection. We will give you the charger.

"Are you familiar with the country's OIJ police force?"

"Huh? What?" he replied with his head still face down.

"Do you know what the OIJ police force is and their task?" *

Sawyer lifted his head and stared bleary eyed at Karen with a pathetic, defeated expression and replied, "Not really. I have heard it mentioned. What of it?"

"The Organismo de Investigacion Junicial, or OIJ is attached to the Supreme Court of Costa Rica and investigates all crimes. They have agents undercover throughout the country with several right here. There was one at the pub last night," she lied, "and they will be your contact and guide you through your task. They will be communicating with us as well, so not cooperating or lying is not in your best interest. Neither is losing the phone, dropping it in the ocean or trying to skip. The phone has a GPS locator, so we will know your whereabouts 24/7.

*The United States is heavily invested in Costa Rica both economically and politically. The U.S. Strategy for Central America governs all seven Central American countries; Belize, Costa Rica, El Salvador, Guatemala, Honduras, Nicaragua and Panama. The US has supported regimes in every country with funds and often CIA involvement. The US has Peace Corp. volunteers in education, youth programs and economic development promoting American interests and attempting to stem the tide of illegal narcotics, primarily cocaine from entering the US via the countries to their north and Mexico. There are one-hundred and twenty-thousand Americans living in Costa Rica, many of them retired military and some submariners.

Chapter FORTY-FOUR

Around midnight the guests began to group, preparing to leave. None had shown signs of inebriation, so Rodrigo and Elise were not concerned any would be driving while impaired.

Penelope, Rebecca, Alane, Marc and Alejandro spread out around the front door, slightly to the side of the scurrying valets and thanked their guests for joining them for the evening. Many handed Marc their business card, commenting, "We will be in touch," or "Let me know how I can help set you up," amid similar words of support and welcoming.

Others made related remarks to Penelope and Rebecca regarding R&P with several attorneys asking for their card as they had a pressing need for their expertise. Sophie Gomez's partner mentioned to Rebecca that he needed her assistance with a financial matter and didn't feel that her association with Sophie would be considered a conflict of interest. Rebecca said she would be in touch in the morning.

As the last of the company saw their way out, Elisabeth, Jackson and Jason headed upstairs to her bedroom while the caterers packed their equipment and cleaned the kitchen. Jason was the last to hit the stairs when he stopped, handed his phone to Jackson, then mentioned that he would be right up. He walked directly to the laundry room.

Elisabeth entered first, sat at her equipment as Jackson placed his and Jason's phones beside hers, Rebecca's and Jessica's who had palmed them to Elisabeth, covertly earlier. Plugging them all into her computer, she set up files for each phone, initiated her algorithm to separate the files to each owner, then set the system to download all data. She would extract the contact lists, phone calls, texts and internet activity from each owner in the morning.

Moving over to another computer and screen she uploaded the house video for the last eight hours, separating the content per room to watch in the morning. She suspected Jessica would be unavailable to peruse the data and although she hadn't been told Rebecca and Penelope had Secret Service clearance, she would presume so until told otherwise and everyone could evaluate the information after breakfast.

Jackson watched her manipulate the computer systems and software, fascinated by her skill, knowing it was actions like this that found the Marina del Rey bomber, allowing LAPD officers to enter the suspect's hotel room, surprising him, forcing the launch of the explosive drone early, thereby limiting the number of casualties and property destruction just as the bomber jumped to his death.

Waving goodbye to the last guest, the hosts thanked the valets, with Alane giving each three-hundred- dollars, thanking them for a tremendous job, then giving them his card inviting a reference for future business.

Alejandro gave each of his co-hosts a hug and said, "Me despido de mis amigos, I bid you good evening," as he bowed, thanked everyone for a fabulous event, turned and headed home.

Rebecca and Penelope shouted after him, "Thank you Alejandro for a beautiful evening. We will do it again soon."

With that they headed into the house, Marc and Alane to check on the caterers and Rebecca and Penelope to look in on the kittens.

The catering team had done such an amazing job with the dinner, serving and cleaning up, Alane gave each a hundred dollars and would pay management in the morning. After they said goodbye to the group, Alane took a moment to welcome Marc again as they arranged to meet the next day to formulate plans for Marc to join the Santa Barbara culinary scene. Thanking him profusely, Marc saw Alane out, locked the door and headed to the pool house, almost bouncing, overwhelmed with the evening's success.

As Penelope and Rebecca approached the laundry- room they heard the distinct muffled sound of kittens mewing. They tip-toed close to the door, not wanting to frighten their new family members, opened it slightly, then acting in unisons, they clasped a hand over their mouths stifling a laughter. Lying stretched out on the floor was Jason, blazer laid across the dryer, tie askew, with six kittens crawling on his chest, legs and face.

The women entered and closed the door quietly and quickly, then leaned against it smiling down at Jason who responded, "What?"

Jason wasn't attempting to extricate himself from his feline captures, so Rebecca and Penelope slid down with their backs to the door and watched. Momentarily a curious kitten meandered over to Penelope and shortly all six were scrambling back and forth between their three parents.

The kittens were quick to run out of steam and make their way to their communal bed. Jason was the first to be feline free, raised himself, brushed his pants, then cleaned the litter boxes. By the time he was finished, all the kittens were asleep, prompting Penelope and Rebecca to get up and all three left quietly.

As they headed up the stairs, Penelope said, "We have to come with some names. How about brainstorming at breakfast tomorrow?"

"Sounds good to me," replied Rebecca as she leaned in to her, planting a kiss on her cheek and pulling her close for a hug.

"Me too," offered Jason. "Considering they were crawling all over my slacks, how about Pants for one name?"

"Pants it is," said Rebecca as they stepped off the stairs on to the second floor and headed to their bedrooms, Jason having completely forgotten his contribution to Elisabeth's task.

S.B.S

Marianna Gutierrez mused the evening as she drove home wondering how, if at all, the entry of Simpson and Barker to Santa Barbara law enforcement would affect her clandestine business. The LAPD was always examining defense attorneys' involvement in their clients' criminal activities but for her, there were sufficient layers between her clients and her drug operation to isolate her. However, the more she thought about Simpson, the more troubled she became, wondering of what she was capable.

She was completely unaware of Jessica Fukishura's involvement and her team's tracking the millions she generated.

S.B.S.

Adrian Achterberg had worked with the submarine captain to modify the Chica de Oro's air capacity, extending the submersible's under water cruise distance before having to snorkel. Modifications were also made to the disposal of human waste system and water purification using reverse desalinization of sea water enabling the mariners to extend their covert expedition for months rather than days.

Achterberg coordinated his interior adjustments with the cartel enabling the cocaine producer to arrive the day after the Chica de Oro was ready for departure.

Chapter FORTY-FIVE

LAPD's Captain Ortega was chairing a meeting in the conference room with his narcotics detectives and two assistant district attorneys. Included in the meeting were Detectives Jenny Wong and Teresa Vasquez who were invited to participate considering their history with Jason Spencer and Jackson Pennington.

Ortega called the meeting to order with, "Okay people, tell me what we have."

When Ortega assumed command of the unit, staff were in constant battle with the other departments and the district attorney's office. Over time, he had convinced his detectives and the district attorneys that criminals were their collective antagonists, not each other and not departments. He developed the collegiality to work together for justice and removing criminals from the streets.

In writing, it may read idealistic, but for the LAPD, which had suffered numerous scandals over the years, it was mandatory, and Ortega was pulling it off.

Each detective introduced their detainees on paper, the charges, investigation and arrest specifics with the appropriate ADA chiming in with their contribution.

Ortega was pleased with the progress in such a short period of time and complimented his team on streamlining the process. "Great job people. Let me make sure I have this correct; the suspects are currently in jail, and they will be convinced by their attorneys that we do not have sufficient evidence to charge them. We can always do that later. They will be released and followed by SIS, Special Investigation Services.

"We still don't know the details about the defense attorneys other than, two are from here and two from Santa Barbara. Agent Peltowski will have specifics on the latter two soon and we will add her information to the operation. For now, we follow the suspects, record their every movement and see where they lead us. From what you've shared, the street supply is dwindling so the dealers will be making a move soon.

Vasquez and Wong, I want you to coordinate with Peltowski and the other agents," he said, bringing a smirk from the women. "Okay, I get it Vasquez and Wong, but let's keep it professional, shall we?" he quipped. "Everybody good to go?" Not seeing any questions, he continued, "Let's put this in motion and report back here at 0800 hours tomorrow."

Chapter FORTY-SIX

The post-dinner party morning saw Penelope and Rebecca the first up with a shooting lesson, gym and run completed before the team scrambled out of bed.

The caterers had let themselves in and arranged the day's meals in the refrigerator and oven while Rebecca and Penelope were training. They were leaving as Elisabeth pounded on Jason and Jackson's bedroom doors and bounded down the stairs, arriving simultaneously with Rebecca and Penelope.

Morning greetings and hugs, then Pen arranged pastries and coffee on the patio behind the kitchen, including enough for the men, knowing Elisabeth had given them their wake-up notice.

The women had just sat down at the wrought iron glass table when Jason and Jackson appeared at the French doors, dressed in shorts and Ts looking somewhat hung-over.

"Good morning gentlemen," offered Elisabeth, "You are just in time for coffee and rolls. We presume you are going to skip this morning's workout."

The men walked around the table, then pulled their chairs out and around so they sat with their backs to the door, as did the women. An observer would find it odd to see none sitting on the other side of the table.

Jason reached for the coffee Pen had poured, took a roll, then said, "Aargh," as he flipped his dreads over his head and off his face and took a sip of coffee. "I ate too much of Marc's exquisite cuisine. My body isn't used to that quality, but I can assure you it will learn," he laughed and raised his mug in salute to Santa Barbara's soon to be culinary king.

Jackson raised his mug as well and said, "Here, here," then started eating and enjoying the coffee while Elisabeth began a mini meeting.

"Just to give you an update, I uploaded all the cell phone data from last night. We can imagine the quantity for the software to sort out," she began, then gave a run-down of how her algorithm works.

"Once the information is categorized per guest, it will list all texts, emails and phone contacts. It will automatically send that data to *Bumblehive,* which you know is monitoring all Southern California.

"I am going to skip a workout and after breakfast check on the system. If it is complete, I will call Captain Ortega and upload the data from their suspects' phones, and we should get a match of all communication between them and their suppliers. I will also find out who Ortega suspects here in Santa Barbara.

Elisabeth's motivation for work prompted everyone else to follow her into the kitchen and arrange breakfast. Elisabeth removed the warm quiche from the oven while Rebecca placed plates and flatware on the kitchen table, Pen cut up fresh fruit and the men cleaned off the patio table, putting their dishes in the dishwasher.

Having cut a piece of bacon and mushroom quiche and piled fruit on her plate, Elisabeth was in a rush to check her computer and ate accordingly. She was finished, dishes in the dishwasher and headed to her bedroom, full coffee mug in hand before the rest were half finished. Waving goodbye, she said, "Give me an hour or so and I should have something to report," and disappeared.

Rebecca and Penelope headed upstairs to ready for their day; interviewing Sophia Gomez's partner and the attorney who wanted their input.

Jason and Jackson each took another slice of quiche and fruit and prepared a plate for Marc and headed out the door and for the pool.

Marc had just gotten up when the agents arrived at the pool house front door. Jackson banged on it with his foot, his hands being occupied with quiche.

Walking to the door, Marc broke into a huge smile as he saw the agents bearing edible gifts. Wearing red board shorts, he opened the door and said, "Hey guys. This is terrific. Thanks for thinking of me. Last night was powerful, wasn't it? Let's go sit in the sun," as he took the plate from Jackson and mug of coffee from Jason.

The three chatted by the pool about Marc's challenges to find a restaurant location and procuring the equipment, designing the entire project, creating the menu then interviewing prospective staff. He didn't tell the agents about his financing which was still impossible for him to understand. Rebecca had invited him to Santa Barbara as the chef for the party, a holiday, then introduced him to Alane, who, unbeknownst to Marc, had set the wheels in motion.

Marc was finishing his quiche when Jason received a text. Looking down at his phone, he said, "Gotta go. You too Jackson. Elisabeth calleth," as they shook Marc's hand again and commented that they would hook up later in the day.

"Oh, I forgot to tell you that the caterers deliver a days' meals for all of us around six in the morning, so if you get tied up in town, everything is either in the fridge or oven," finalized Jason as the men headed back inside.

After the agents left, Marc sat relishing in the ocean breeze. Warmed by the morning sun, he reflected on the financial terms, which were basically none. He was given a blank check and was told to send all invoices and receipts to Alane. Had it not been Rebecca who orchestrated the meeting, he would have exited quickly, knowing it was someone's idea of a cruel joke.

But it wasn't. Rebecca had the idea from the first time she tasted his exquisite cuisine, had collaborated with Alane and he with several of his wealthy friends. Marc would create and Alane and company would handle the financial challenges.

He smiled to himself, remembering when he returned to the ranch, met Rebecca and Penelope, trying to thank them for their outstanding generosity but unable to come up with words to express his feelings.

The women took comfort in his sincerity, gave him a hug and said, "You are part of the family now Marc. There isn't a loan. We all invested in you and we are delighted to do so. And you can stay here. Consider the pool house yours for as long as you want."

Marc had never felt part of a larger family or group as an adult. Working at the White House was phenomenal with considerable respect for the president's chef, but it was business. What he found with Rebecca and Penelope was, as they said, family. People who cared about him, his dreams and goals, wanting nothing in return.

The feeling was compounded that afternoon siting by the pool when Alejandro arrived, totally unexpected, with a tray bearing a pitcher of red sangria; merlot, lime, orange, lemon and Diplomatico rum from Venezuela.

He arrived with his usual exuberance, placed the tray on the glass cocktail table and passed around his appetizer creation of jalapeño chicken wraps; jalapeños, stuffed with chicken, then wrapped in bacon and grilled.

This was Marc's introduction to his future benefactor and Rebecca held nothing back in the introduction, mentioning Alejandro's background and his contribution to the landscaping, embracing Marc while doing so with a sweeping arm, "Alejandro. Family."

The rest of the afternoon was a pleasant mixture of sharing backgrounds and Marc elaborating on his vision for the restaurant, quipping about his family's penchant for sangria.

ℑ·ℬℑ

Jessica arrived at seven for her first full day as Santa Barbara's newest associate attorney, expecting to be one of the first in. She was the last. The entire staff was functioning as though they had been there for some time. They had, most having arrived around six.

Jessica made a mental note to arrive at five-thirty tomorrow. She had to be first.

Although she was last to arrive, her power outfit said she was number one; black stretch knit, high rise trousers by NYDJ, a Magenta Dover blazer by J. Crew and black, two-inch Sam Edelman pumps.

Quickly dropping her briefcase on her desk, she headed for her boss' office, knocked on Barbados' door and asked, "Good morning, Katrina. What would you like me to work on today?"

"Good morning, Jessica. Perfect timing. A colleague here in town just called and her client, being held by the LAPD, insists she represent his partner in a drug arrest which she cannot do as there may be a conflict of interest, depending on what the clients have revealed to detectives. She wants us to take the other client. I agreed and took the liberty of copying the documents for you," she offered, handing the papers to Jessica.

"Give the attorney a call, then take it from there. If you must drive, don't. We have an account with Island Taxi, just give them your card and they will bill us. Oh, and here are your business cards," passing a small box across her desk.

"Any questions?"

"No. I don't think so. I'm on it," Jessica replied as she turned and headed back to her office.

Once at her desk she placed a call to Marianna Gutierrez, remembering her from the party. Nothing exceptional. No gut reaction. No red flags. Seemed like a likable person. Head of her own firm. Mid-fifties. Soignée in a cream Pissarro Nights, short sleeve, beaded, tulle cocktail dress. Her immediate reaction was that she was overdressed for California Casual designation, but then thought her reaction might just be her cattiness emerging.

Gutierrez answered curtly, "Yes," which immediately pissed off Jessica, but she quickly regrouped and slid into her role with, "Good morning Ms. Gutierrez. This is Jessica Fukishura with Katrina Barbados. She assigned me to team with your firm on the Los Angeles clients."

"Yes, yes. Most certainly. I have been waiting to hear from Katrina. Welcome aboard. Get to the airport now and I will fill you in on the flight," she replied, then hung up.

Jessica stared at the phone momentarily, trying to grasp what had just occurred. *Who the hell was this woman to whom she was being forced to be civil?* she thought. *Airport? Flying from Santa Barbara to LAX, then what?*

She hung up the phone, stuffed Katrina's papers into her briefcase, called a cab and headed out of the office.

In route to the airport, she received a text from Elisabeth.

Chapter FORTY-SEVEN

Elisabeth had received the LAPD suspects' flip-phone particulars from Captain Ortega, who powered the devices, allowing Elisabeth to copy all the texts, phone numbers and contacts. Her software provided a list of everyone in California the suspects called or texted during the last sixty days. Ortega emailed her the voice recordings of all suspects gained during their interrogations. Elisabeth's software would compare that data with the voices of everyone at the party and with each suspect's conversations on the confiscated smartphones.

The quantity of data was massive, but her algorithm isolated it to Southern California with remarkable results.

The computer screens revealed a connection between the three suspects, which was to be expected but it also uncovered connections with Los Angeles individuals who were not on Ortega's person of interest list.

They were now.

Ortega categorized the investigation as a high priority which brought in the SIS detectives to shadow all the suspects contacted. The SIS detectives quickly eliminated the individuals obviously not involved, such as the suspects' children's' teachers, honest neighbors and friends, leaving a small group they would follow twenty-four seven.

Elisabeth had just communicated her findings to Ortega and Jessica when Jackson and Jason knocked on her door. Removing herself from the screens, she opened the door, allowing the men to enter bearing a fresh, warm bear claw and a large cup of black.

"You guys are the greatest," offered Elisabeth with a huge grin. She was so emotionally involved with the technology she developed and executed, she tended to drain energy quickly and relished the coffee break.

"Come. Sit, and I will share what I have discovered," she said with excitement.

They gathered around a comfortable seating area by the window with the ocean view. After sitting, taking a bite of the claw and a sip of black, Elisabeth explained what she had found.

Jessica heard her encrypted phone vibrate in her briefcase as her cab pulled into the airport parking lot. Stopping in front of the main terminal, Jessica asked the cab driver to give her five minutes with the meter running. He agreed. She opened her briefcase and retrieved her phone, entered her code, waited five seconds for the connection and read the text from Elisabeth.

What the fuck, she thought to herself. She quickly entered her instructions, clicked off, signed the hand-held billing device for the driver and gave him a twenty for his patience. He was delighted since a tip was already included in the charge to Katrina's firm.

Quickly exiting the cab, Jessica headed into the terminal looking for Gutierrez. She didn't have far to look as Mariana emerged from the shadows of the massive columns to her right saying, "Oh. You're Fukishura. Right, right, from the party the other night.

Good, good. Let's go. The chopper is waiting," then took off at a fast pace with Jessica following quickly behind her, not having an opportunity to reply a greeting.

Directly outside the terminal was an Airbus H155 from Channel Helicopters with its blades rotating and a man holding a door open. Gutierrez entered first, slid to the far side allowing Jessica access. Fortunately, her slacks provided a graceful entry. The door was shut and clasped in place.

The pilot took a moment to radio the tower, receive her take-off instructions, then lifted slowly, checking visual flight rules for other helicopters or obstructions. Clearing the terminal, she increased her elevation, received authorization for five-thousand feet, leveled off and headed south-east for the Los Angeles courthouse.

They landed on the roof of the Los Angeles Court house forty-five minutes later and ten after that were waiting for their clients to appear from the holding cells in a nearby jail.

Chapter FORTY-EIGHT

Elisabeth had just finished explaining her discoveries to Jason and Jackson when her service cell chimed. Excusing herself to her colleagues, she entered her code and read the message. A long one.

Without commenting she handed the phone to Jason, who read it then passed it to Jackson, looking at Elisabeth with raised eyebrows, saying, "Well, there goes our pool time today," with a grin, acknowledging his need to see some action, the adrenaline junkie that he was.

Combining the information Elisabeth shared and the text just now, the agents knew the investigation was moving fast, maybe too fast and if they didn't match its pace, incrementing evidence could be lost or compromised. Without saying a word to Elisabeth, the men headed out of her bedroom to quickly shower, dress and get on the road following Jessica's orders.

Elisabeth felt the adrenaline rush as well and although she was not front and center as the others, she was the pivotal point for all future events. She felt the rush as she returned to her computer screens and began viewing and listening to conversations recorded at the party.

Penelope and Rebecca readied for the day in record time then checked on the kittens, cleaned the litter boxes, filled the water and food dishes, played with them until the felines exhausted themselves and returned to their beds. The women left the door open, wrote a note for the men and headed into town.

Jason was the first of the duo to arrive in the kitchen wearing tan slacks, brown tassel loafers and a short-sleeve, yellow button-down shirt. He grabbed another bear claw and a mug of black, sat at the patio table enjoying the morning, reading Rebecca's note, taking delight that Jessica included R&P in this investigation.

Ten later, Jackson arrived wearing a pair of old white shorts, an oversized blue t-shirt and sandals. No hat. Jason looked at him, checked himself out and realized he was overdressed for their task and said, "Grab a claw and coffee and give me five," and ran out of the kitchen to change.

In Jason's absence, Jackson read the note with the identical reaction as Jason. He had finished both the claw and black when Jason reappeared wearing a pair of worn khaki shorts and a Tony Bahama Costa Breeze Camp shirt in Ocean blue from his old wardrobe, large enough to cover his firearm but still stylish, and sandals.

They flipped a coin to see who would drive Rebecca's new SUV, then headed through the house to the garage and to their reconnaissance assignments, setting the property alarm as they drove out to protect Elisabeth while she concentrated on her IT assignment.

Chapter FORTY-NINE

Anthony Henderson was a successful accountant with an elaborate, upscale office on Mason, a few blocks from the beach. Jason couldn't remember him from Rebecca and Penelope's party, but Elisabeth assured him he was there, socializing with Sophia Gomez and several other accountants. She also pointed out in her encrypted texts to Jason as he sat in Rebecca's Civic, parked on Burton's Circle, the dash cam directly facing Henderson's office, that the party video showed the suspect circulating, chatting with seemingly everyone…but it was Gutierrez whom it appeared to be purposely avoiding.

Meanwhile, Jackson was sitting across and several houses down from Henderson's home on Foothills Road in the rental car in which he, Jason and Elisabeth had arrived. It was a relatively busy thoroughfare, allowing him to park with the vehicle's dash cam facing the house which sat back from the road about fifty meters, hidden behind a grove of evergreens.

The agents utilized their encrypted phones like walkie talkies, speaking or listening with the push of a button on a secure system. Their instructions were to develop a visual on the business and house, record all traffic, which Elisabeth would process through a federal facial recognition program and vehicles through the California DMV.

Elisabeth had confirmed the business and residence were owned by their suspect and tapped all the phone lines coming into each location. Her approval for this intrusive surveillance was the result of the roving wiretap provision of the Patriot Act, as well as the lone wolf provision allowing the government to surveil someone engaged in international terrorism.

The "J" Team's involvement in the cocaine issue was loosely connected to the international money laundering and the financing of the Christians for a Better America.

Every forty-five minutes the men would switch, passing physically halfway between the two locations to minimize the time from their surveillance.

Jessica spent two hours with her client, Julio Fernández, a UCLA business graduate with an advanced degree in social science management. Fernández did not fit the profile of a drug dealer, even sitting across from her, chained to the table, attired in the blue jail uniform. With his smirk of contempt for her and the law, he could easily have been bemoaning California politics in the cocktail lounge of one of LA's finest hotels, dressed in a three-piece, pin-striped suit as he showed no concern for his incarceration or the possible fate awaiting him.

Fernández was a mid-level manager who coordinated the operation of second-level street dealers, those just above the service providers, who accepted the street staff's cash and transported it up the chain.

His arrest was, as he put it, "unfortunate". All his mid-level dealers had a key to a West Los Angeles storage locker with twenty-four seven access. The LAPD had circumvented the camera feed for the floor where his twenty-five square foot unit was located, rerouting it to a surveillance team in a one-hundred square foot first floor unit.

The drug squad wasn't interested in the service providers and street dealers and allowed them to maintain their freedom, anticipating arrests further up the chain. Their tenacity paid off when Fernández appeared in a pair of pressed jeans, white button-down long-sleeve shirt, a blue blazer by Zara and navy-blue oxford lace-ups.

Jessica's client didn't retrieve the cash following a regular schedule, but rather chose different days and hours, not setting a pattern which law enforcement could anticipate. Locating the storage locker was simply a case of following the street dealers who made their drops on either the last day of the month, or the first of the next when the storage facility was the busiest with customers moving in and out to new homes.

Fernández's precautions combined with not spotting a police surveillance was why the appearance of the officers rushing in his direction from both ends of the aisle was a surprise. And more shocking was when they threw him against the bulkhead, cuffed his wrists behind his back, grabbed the key from his hand and opened the unit.

When questioned by detectives, he was given his right to an attorney and mirandized.

He replied, "Lawyer," then refused to respond to any questions.

Jessica had a copy of the police arrest report in front of her as she asked Fernández questions for clarification.

Jessica was functioning with mixed emotions. She had spent years putting guys like Fernández in jail and now she would be facilitating his release. What moved the former thoughts to the recesses of her mind was sympathy, knowing the officers had made mistakes, errors they committed purposely to expedite the sting and would now be embarrassed by the prosecutor. She empathized with their walk of shame since she had experienced a similar criticism during an incident early in her career, putting two colleagues in the hospital from a defensive training incident.

She could hear the castigation of the officers, being shamed for forgetting such an elementary detail as a search warrant for the storage locker before opening it. She foreshadowed Gutierrez lambasting them as well for dragging her client into the fray based on a banal text.

The officers' task was to express indignation surrounding the accusations, testing their thespian skills, offsetting any suspicions Gutierrez might generate.

Jessica asked the uniformed officer guarding the door to obtain an assistant district attorney immediately as her client wished to offer a plea. The guard opened the door, allowing Jessica to leave her smiling client chained to the table while she waited in an adjoining room.

She was not surprised to see Gutierrez sitting on a couch reading her emails and texts. Her recently acquired colleague looked up, smiled, nodded and returned to her task.

Marianna had discovered that her client was not present at the storage locker when Fernández was arrested and that the only connection detectives had with Fernández was an innocuous text between the two clients. She was unaware of the sting organized by Elisabeth and Jessica, in conjunction with the LAPD drug squad, assuming, falsely, that the arresting officers had reached beyond their purview, as they had previously in their enthusiasm to put her client out of business.

Jason and Jackson were not disenchanted with their extended and boring surveillance. Experience had taught them the success of slow and easy case building and today fit that analysis perfectly. Around noon, Jason called Cocina Mexicana for four chicken burritos and two soft drinks, which he had delivered to an address a block away from the suspect's home. Seeing the delivery vehicle with the logo emblazoned on the side-panels, he had the money plus a fifteen-dollar tip ready when the teenager pulled in front of the house. After receiving and paying for the food, he called Jackson, who made the location switch, stopping side-by-side long enough to receive his lunch, then moved on. They would use the empty drink bottles as their urine receptors.

While the men slogged away observing and recording their suspect's locales, Elisabeth viewed all the party video, using her algorithm to match guests' voices with those on the confiscated LAPD suspects' phones and recorded interrogations as well as cross-referencing the guest's phones with the suspects. Gutierrez and Henderson's comparisons were prominent, the software's identification one-hundred percent accurate.

She had recovered from the surprise of Jessica working with Gutierrez and was anxious to hear the details of her day in Los Angeles, to blend their findings.

Elisabeth missed the morning runs while undercover in StoneHead and took the opportunity alone for a little exercise. She changed into a Billabong one-piece blue and white striped bathing suit, hung an oversized bath towel around her neck and walked through the garage, carrying a bottle of sauvignon blanc and a Caesar salad to the pool to do a few laps and regenerate in the afternoon sun.

Chapter FIFTY

Marc had left immediately after Jason and Jackson to meet with Alane and the other investors regarding branding *Marc Stucki's,* its location and the refitting. The discussion centered around a former steak house which had sat idle for three years, the owners unable to negotiate a new contract with the chain.

The building was part of a major downtown revitalization with a train station located in the massive complex, housing one-hundred and fifty condos. Being six blocks from the beach, the wharf, the harbor and museum, the unique train motif would be an added tourist attraction as well as catering to the adult condo clientele.

Also attending the meeting was the general contractor who would be hired, pending Marc's approval, to do the renovations for the railroad concept and Alane's attorney. Also in attendance was a lawyer the financiers hired to represent Marc's interest and finally Sophie Gomez, representing Rebecca and Penelope.

The financial concept or structure was simple in its complexity. Marc would have one-hundred percent control and financial interest in the restaurant's management while maintaining a fifty-percent interest in the building, estimated to be worth eighteen-million before the renovations.

The investors would, on paper, anticipate an eight percent return over a twenty-year amortization. But they were Democrats, patriots, supporting Rebecca in appreciation for her participation in taking down the

Christians for a Better America and preventing the death of over two hundred delegates meeting in the Marina Del Rey Conference Center which the terrorists had bombed.

SBS

Winthrop and Hortonn didn't have difficulty convincing Sawyer that it was in his best interest to cooperate. His alternative was to be returned to Alberta to stand trial for terrorism.

Once reality set in and he realized that his early retirement was drastically modified, he rationalized that he could maintain his current lifestyle unabated by sharing whatever information he could glean from locals regarding the movement of drugs in and out of the country…that is if the cartel didn't kill him.

Tom had remained quiet throughout Karen's interrogation, sitting backwards on a kitchen chair while holding his semi-automatic pointed at Sawyer's back. When he knew the conversation had run its course and Sawyer was convinced, he rose quietly and left the house by a back door, reappearing ten later, observing Karen and Brian in the same position, neither speaking.

He placed a large plastic bag on the chair he had previously vacated, nodded to Karen, then said, "Okay Brian, time for you and me to have a private discussion. Stand up and put your hands behind your back."

Sawyer complied, rather dejectedly, struggling to maintain some semblance of dignity. Tom slipped plastic handcuffs around his wrists, then guided him out the back door for a beach stroll.

Karen quickly removed the items from the bag and proceeded to install the closed-circuit cameras in strategic locations around the house with one each at the front and back doors facing out. The micro units were impossible to detect as she slipped them into dried flower arrangements, door frames and household decorations. The batteries would be replaced by the Costa Rican agents tasked with monitoring Sawyer and transmitting data to CSIS.

Karen had just finished the installation and checking their operation on her encrypted phone when Tom walked Brian back into the house, removed the plastic cuffs, gave him one last word of confidence then joined Karen at the front door to return to their B&B for breakfast.

Later that day they would present themselves to the Canadian Embassy in San José where they would lunch with and brief RCMP and CSIS officers, provide them with the camera monitoring links, a full dossier on Sawyer and the operations perimeters designed by David Kopas.

They stayed at the embassy that night, in separate bedrooms, and were on the first plane to Toronto the next morning for reassignment.

Chapter FIFTY-ONE

Jessica and Marianna sat several feet away from each other waiting for the prosecutors. Jessica attempted to interact with her colleague but received a curt, slight head shake declining the invitation, indicating to Jessica that the LAPD had the room bugged.

After what seemed like an hour to an impatient Jessica, but, was fifteen, two assistant district attorneys entered the room each carrying a thin file folder.

Gutierrez jumped up immediately, curtly introduced Jessica as Barbados' associate, then quickly asked who was prosecuting whom. Hearing which ADA was handling her client's case, she grabbed her valise and said, "Let's get this over with. My client has business to attend to this afternoon," then exited the room, followed by an embarrassed and confused prosecutor.

Jessica had seen this ploy used in the reverse with her being the instigator. It worked most of the time, creating an unsettled climate which put her advisory off guard having to rush to catch up mentally and strategically.

The remaining prosecutor sensed the maneuver being used against him and responded aggressively with a notable hint of arrogance. He didn't know Jessica and was attempting to intimidate her as he had other attorneys.

Fukishura was unlike other attorneys.

"Let's go to a client interview room and hash this case out," he offered as he headed to the door.

Jessica responded by sitting down, crossing her legs and laying the case file on her lap saying, "I don't think so, Murray is it? Have a seat Murray and I will tell you how this is going to proceed in a way that will save you embarrassment and humiliation."

"You are not running the show here miss, whatever your name is. I am. Let's go."

"Sit the fuck down now Murray or I will walk out of this building straight to the LA Times and you will be an asshole on national television before the day's end," she yelled.

The middle-aged assistant DA was so taken aback by the loud, abrupt comment from a person who should be intimidated by him, he sat, staring at Jessica with contempt.

"I am going to tell you how this is going to work. First of all I am not going to sweep this room for recording devices. We both know it would be a waste of time considering your office has been charged with client attorney confidentiality violations by recording conversations.

"I don't know why you think this case has any merit. You are either a very stupid man, ignorant or both. Mr. Fernández's storage unit was searched, the contents confiscated, and he was arrested. The LAPD detectives did not have a search warrant and the last time I looked, there wasn't a law against where a citizen could save his money.

"Here is Mr. Fernández's Writ of Habeas Corpus demanding his immediate release, which I am prepared to present to a presiding judge, immediately, if my client is not released now," she offered, passing the document to her adversary.

After delivering her aggressive ultimatum, Jessica rose from the couch, shoved the case file into her valise and walked to the door, turning briefly to say, "Murray, you have one hour to deliver Mr. Fernández to the reception center and release the contents of the storage locker or I guarantee today will go down in your history as the worse fucking day of your life."

As the door closed behind her she smiled and thought, *Not bad Fukishura, not bad at all for the first time. Maybe I should practice law.*

She arrived at the inmate reception center after a circuitous route and found Marianna sitting in a hardback chair, valise on her lap, legs crossed, checking emails and voice messages. Seeing Jessica, she tilted her head inviting Jessica to sit in the empty seat beside her.

The waiting room was filled to capacity with other attorneys and family members waiting for their clients or loved ones to be released. As Jessica took the seat, Gutierrez, knowing there was only one reason Jessica was there said, "Nice job Jessica. Very well done. How long have you been practicing?"

"Thank you, Marianna. I just graduated. This is my first case."

"Bullshit. I don't believe it," she replied rather forcefully. "This is your first case and you are out," checking her watch, "in what, ten minutes. What did you do to poor Murray? He usually takes an hour to lay out his case and intimidate defense attorneys."

"He tried but I succeeded in explaining that his course of action was fraught with pitfalls and offered him an alternative."

"You must have been very persuasive, given Murray's reputation. I usually spend the first hour sparing with him before he will listen to reason."

"He began with that in mind, but wavered when it was apparent he hadn't read the police report. No warrant for the storage locker. I expect we will be seeing our client's smirk very soon."

"I am beyond impressed Jessica. If today is an expression of your career success, we need to work together more often and maybe, just maybe, you would consider joining my firm."

"Thank you, Marianna. I appreciate the compliment," Jessica replied just as her eye caught her client exiting from the detention center.

"Speaking of our client. Here he is now," continued Jessica as Fernández strutted toward them.

"Ms. Fukishura. My sincere appreciation for an excellent job," said Fernández, extending his hand.

Jessica accepted the gesture, shook his hand, then said, "Did they give you a property receipt for your storage locker contents?"

"Right here," replied Fernández, holding up a slip of paper. "Speaking of which, I must head over to property to do just that," he finished as he turned and headed out the main entry.

"Speaking of clients, here is mine right now," interjected Marianna. "Give me a moment to clear some things with him and we can be off. Since it is late in the day, may I buy you dinner? I really want to get to know you better. I am truly shocked and mystified by your abilities."

"I would be delighted. I will call Katrina enroute to bring her current and will be good for the day."

"Terrific!" replied Gutierrez as she walked quickly over to the lone male exiting the restricted area.

Their clients left the building separately and hailed cabs. They began texting immediately, once inside their cabs, assuming wrongly that a flip-phone could not be traced. Captain Ortega directed the Field Investigation Unit to install GPS devices in each of the suspects' belts, which they relinquished during jail processing, as a back-up locator in case they disposed of their phones. The unit's officers also installed surveillance cameras in each of the suspects' apartments posing as cable technicians and picking the door locks, a highly prized department skill.

This aspect of the operation was detailed in Elisabeth's earlier presentation to Ortega's detectives, the approval of which stemmed from her initiating the Patriot Act.

Elisabeth, still in her bathing suit with a towel wrapped around her waist, began tracking and recording their digital exchange upon the suspects' release and would have a printout available for the "J" Team debriefing later that evening. She knew SIS were duplicating her efforts with physical surveillance.

SBS

Penelope and Rebecca spent the better part of the day with accountant Henri Gagnon, Sophia Gomez's partner, a graduate of Cal Poly's College of Business in San Luis Obispo, California with a degree in accounting and financial management. Originally from Montréal, Québec, as a high school business graduate, Henri yearned for sun and surf, qualified for a student visa, which he segued into a green card then citizenship after accepting a job in San Luis Obispo.

He and Sophia met at a CPA symposium, found they had much in common and within a few years became partners in Santa Barbara.

Chapter FIFTY-TWO

LAPD SIS detectives were tailing the suspects immediately upon their release, with four different nondescript vehicles and four officers changing clothes frequently. The officers' presence was undetectable.

Once the suspects had settled in for the night, the four detectives split into two teams, each covering the front and back of a residence. The teams were relieved every eight hours creating twelve monitoring detectives over a twenty-four-hour period.

It was a costly operation given the number of personnel, but Ortega had been assured, in writing, by Elisabeth, that the Secret Service would pick up the surveillance tab and much of the related costs.

When Rebecca and Penelope arrived back at the ranch, they parked in the garage and found the alarm disengaged and were immediately in Code Orange. Pen wasn't carrying yet, so she stayed several paces behind Rebecca who drew her nine, entered the house and quietly made her way to the kitchen where the garage alarm panel noted the patio door was open.

As she entered with her firearm in a modified Weaver stance; elbow tucked into her side, sights in line with her left eye, Marc and Alejandro turned abruptly from their preparation at the island with instant fear. All they could see was the firearm pointed at them, not the person holding it.

"Everything okay here?" asked Rebecca in a tone neither men had ever heard previously. "Marc, if everything is okay here, tell me what you prepared for my retirement dinner."

"Hm…give me a minute," he replied, running his hands over his face. "I served beef tenderloin wrapped in prosciutto and gorgonzola pome puree, Italian blue cheese and pureed apple," he offered, his hands shaking, not sure what the hell was going on and scared to see a deadly weapon pointed at him.

Alejandro had no other feeling than fear. He too had never had a firearm pointed at him and the only response he could think of was to stand perfectly still.

Rebecca turned slightly and said, "We're good Penelope," then replied to Marc. "Sorry for the scare guys. The security panel noted a side door was open and the system was off. What are you guys doing?"

Alejandro was the first to respond, blowing out a breath of relief. "Me? I am going home and change my shorts. I almost crapped myself. That is an intense side of you I have never seen Rebecca. Yikes! But in hindsight, I should have known when we first met, and I saw your holstered firearm."

"I am truly sorry guys," she replied holstering her weapon, walking over to them, giving each a much-deserved hug.

Marc shook his head in disbelieve saying, "Fuck! I wouldn't want to be a bad guy facing you. He may as well pack his bags and dig his grave. Your stance and voice alone is enough to scare the crap out of anyone. No offense Alejandro," laughing nervously.

Pen approached from behind Rebecca, breaking the tension with, "How about a glass of chilled dry

Riesling?" as she stepped around Rebecca and retrieved a bottle from the wine cooler.

"My apologies again guys. I didn't mean to scare you, but with what's going on, we can't be too careful."

"We fully understand Rebecca and we will be more diligent in the future about alarming the system," said Alejandro.

"That would be great. Thank you. So, what are you guys making?"

Regaining their composure, Marc offered, "When I got home from the investment meetings, which were fabulous and mind-blowing simultaneously, I checked on dinner and it was inedible. While I was considering the options, Alejandro popped in with a tray of his signature jalapeños stuffed with goat cheese and chopped Kalamata olives. They are in the fridge waiting for our enjoyment.

"So, two heads being better than one, we came up with dinner which is a roast beet salad with greens from Alejandro's garden, followed by a slow baked chicken breast with a garlic and thyme glaze, carrots with a carrot puree, also from notre ami," nodding to Alejandro. "For dessert, well, we haven't figured that out yet."

"That sounds delicious guys. Thank you for taking control. Dinner had dried out I presume? Maybe not such a good idea keeping it warm for so long in the oven?"

"It didn't really have a chance Rebecca. How about this? You are being very kind in having me stay with you, how about I contact the caterer and work out some dishes that they assemble, and I cook? That way dinner is fresh?"

Penelope didn't hesitate and jumped in with "Deal," clapping her hands in delight.

Rebecca chimed in with, "I second the motion. Deal passed. What can we do to help?"

"We were just at a break point, so how about the appetizers and the Riesling on the patio?" offered Marc, the tension of the armed encounter seemingly history.

"Elisabeth, Jason and Jackson are upstairs. I think they just got started. I will text them and see if they want to join us?" said Marc.

"How about we introduce them to the intercom?' said Rebecca with a lightness in her voice, as she walked over to the panel by the dining room entry. She showed Marc its functions and he pushed a couple of buttons and said, "Kitchen to Elisabeth. Come in Elisabeth."

Within seconds the panel erupted in laughter. "If we were asleep, we aren't any more." More laughter. "What's up Marc?"

"You guys have time for a break? Rebecca and Penelope are home, we have dinner cooking and Alejandro has appetizers and Riesling?"

"On our way down."

Within seconds they heard the pounding of feet on the stairs as three obviously fatigued and hungry agents ran down and into the kitchen.

High fives all around as everyone grabbed the food, plates and two additional bottles of Isla Winery Riesling and headed to the patio.

Elisabeth was the last to sit down and opened the conversation with, "So, what exciting things has everyone been up to today?"

Alejandro glanced at Marc and the two started laughing, their first sips of Riesling squirting out their noses. Wiping his nose and face, Marc responded, "Besides forgetting to set the alarm, having a heart attack from the repercussions, working with the investment group for the restaurant, not much. How about you guys?"

Marc knew the three agents were not here on a vacation and his years working at the White House educated him on protocol, so he rephrased his question, "Besides business I mean?"

Elisabeth responded with, "We presume the details of this encounter will be shared in detail later?"

Marc, still laughing, nodded and Alejandro waved his hand in agreement.

The agents knew Marc had a top-secret presidential proximity clearance, which was a food clearance, meaning he didn't have a Secret Service agent watching him and his staff in the kitchen. They also knew that Marc had turned down many offers which could have left him financially well off over the eight years at the White House. Last year there were over one-hundred new restaurants which opened in DC and Marc could easily have commanded a three-hundred-thousand-dollar figure but chose to stay with President Bakus.

Marc received the considerable respect he deserved from the agents, but he did not have a Q or L Clearance, referring to access to Top Secret, Secret or Confidential information. They could not discuss their operation with him as the subject, Christians for a Better America, was a terrorist organization which could have ties with either the Russians, who were reputedly involved in the election which President Bakus lost, or any number of international terrorist organizations.

Elisabeth tried again to start a conversation. "I watched videos and listened to recordings all day, then took a swim and drank half a bottle of wine. What about you guys?" she asked turning to Penelope and Rebecca.

Rebecca responded, "We met with Henri Gagnon, Sophia Gomez's partner. They were both at the party." "Henri," she pronounced in labored French, "it seems has a client who has a skimmer and Henri asked us to investigate. We don't have a computer expert yet so..." she glanced back at Elisabeth who smiled and responded.

"I would love to help you out. Just check with Jessica and make sure she is okay with it, then let me know what you need."

"Thanks Elisabeth. Maybe in the next couple of days you could help us find someone we can work with on a regular basis. We think cybercrime will be a large part of our business."

Elisabeth raised her glass and toasted R&P then said, "I know what you guys did for the day," referring to Jackson and Jason, "but the rest haven't a clue. Without violating protocol, can you share?"

"Sure," offered Jackson. "We spent the day surveilling a person of interest and had very tasty chicken burritos. Not as good as yours Marc, but good for a take-out."

"Marc. How about you?" asked Elisabeth, opening another bottle of Riesling, pouring and topping everyone's glass.

"Well, as I mentioned earlier, I am still adjusting to what is being offered. I didn't want to commit myself to a large loan to start my own business. I have been debt free for a long time and have enjoyed the freedom, so I attended the meeting this morning with trepidation, wondering what Alejandro and his friends had in mind."

Alejandro didn't attend the meeting as he had a previous obligation, but he was in sync with the other investors. Marc continued, "I can't share the details, but I will not have a loan. I am now fifty-percent owner of a Santa Barbara building a few blocks from the beach, have total control of the restaurant which is next to the train station and will be refitted with a railroad theme.

Montana Angus beef will be linked to the railroad motif. Coupled with that will be Dungeness crab, presented live in a twenty-five-thousand-gallon tank displayed at the entry. One of the investors has a friend with a crab boat and license who will deliver the crab fresh daily.

I have a rent free three-bedroom condo in the restaurant's neighborhood into which I can move in a week after I pick out furniture from Portofino Furnishings.

So much is being given to me, showered actually, I am confused and am asking why and is there a catch?"

"Let me offer you an explanation Marc," offered Alejandro who had the undivided attention of the group. "I invested in you because it is time, at my age, to give back to the community which has been so good to me.

And I wanted to be part of something bigger than me, namely R&P Investigations and you.

The others have similar motivations and yet slightly different. Each of the investors is a Democrat. The terrorist group Rebecca and other law enforcement officers took down were planning to blow up the Marina del Rey Convention Center with over two-hundred Democrat delegates inside. They succeeded in destroying the building but because of the actions of Rebecca et al, the delegates were not injured."

Alejandro was unaware of Jason and Jackson's role in the operation or that Jason was involved in saving the downed Mahalo Airline from sinking.

He continued, "Each investor is a patriot and believe investing in you is part of the pay back to which I referred, and their opportunity to support you for your eight-year sacrifice working at the White House. We all know you could have had any number of mid-six figure salary jobs in DC," he concluded.

"Wow, I am speechless and overwhelmed Alejandro. I didn't know people felt that way about me. I am humbled and dumbfounded, and thanks doesn't seem to come close to expressing my appreciation."

"You just did Marc. Maybe you could use some of my produce at *Marc Stucki's* periodically," he added with a laugh as he raised his wine glass, stood and offered a toast. "To Marc and to years of success personally and professionally."

The agents stood and shared his toast, clinking glasses with Marc and each other.

As they sat down, Rebecca said, "I have one request."

"Sure. Anything Rebecca. What?"

"Penelope and I want to help you decorate and furnish your condo," she said with a smile and another toast."

Marc laughed and replied, "For sure. I know zip about decorating an apartment. How about you helping with the refitting too?"

"Done and done," said Penelope as she held up her glass to seal the deal.

The remainder of the pre-dinner time was spent chatting about Marc's plan to cook dinners and naming the rest of the kittens; Mr. Big Pants, Fluffy, Lovie, Star and Pinkie.

Once the decisions had been made, they went to check on them and found the six in Penelope and Rebecca's bedroom, curled up on the occasional chair facing the window, in the sun, oblivious to their admirers at the door.

Chapter FIFTY-THREE

Weeks went by with twelve LAPD SIS detectives surveilling Fernández and his colleague, twenty-four seven while Captain Ortega's drug squad street officers continued to arrest and process as many street dealers as possible. The officers noticed a steady decline in the quantity of seized product which experience told them, supply was running low and prices were escalating.

What all law enforcers were thankful for was that Los Angeles dealers didn't lace their cocaine with fentanyl. The synthetic opioid can be five thousand times more powerful than heroin or morphine according to the Centers for Disease Control in Canada and the US. Dealers in other parts of North America sell the laced cocaine to a different market, customers who want a *speedball* effect, the rush of a stimulant, the cocaine, plus a depressant, fentanyl. However, many of these buyers are unaware of the danger combining the drugs poses, hence the thousands of deaths.

Massachusetts saw almost two thousand overdose deaths last year alone. One state.

Earlier this year, two hundred federal, state and local authorities smashed a drug ring operating in West Virginia, Michigan and Ohio, arresting ninety people, who police believe were responsible for forty-two thousand deaths in the three states since two thousand and sixteen.

Los Angeles dealers were making sufficient profit not to have the LAPD, or the Los Angeles Sheriffs expand their purview to include dealers responsible for deaths. They were quite happy the way their business was operating and intended to keep it running smoothly.

When the Chica de Oro returned to its home base, Adrian Achterberg was instructed by the cartel to reconfigure the sub for a longer journey and additional cargo. Given the success of the five thousand kilo delivery to California, the cartel was prepared to step up their operation but first wanted to test run the retrofitting before engaging on the lengthy journey further north.

His modifications to the air and power supply systems involved reconfiguring the computer software which controlled all aspects of the Golden Girl.

The work on the twenty-meter vessel was scrutinized by neither the military nor law enforcement since both were sequestered to the country's eastern border to control the hundreds of thousands of Venezuelans fleeing from their country's economic collapse.

Refugees were in medical distress, hungry and carrying their meager belongings on their backs, fleeing economic mismanagement, political corruption and low oil prices.

Former president Chavez nationalized the oil industry, agriculture, transportation, hydro, telecommunications, steel production and banks.

Under socialist rule, the country went from the wealthiest in South America to an economy which shrank eighteen percent in two thousand and seventeen, has an unemployment rate of twenty-five percent and a two-thousand percent inflation rate. The result has been the collapse of the third least free economy in the world behind Cuba and North Korea.

The second shipment was already at the shipyard, guarded by cartel security and within forty-eight hours the sub was loaded and set sail to follow the same course it took to California, continuing north for fourteen days at an average speed of twenty nautical miles, submerged.

A second crew of retired American submariners replaced the maiden voyage operators who received their million-dollar deposits into a Caribbean account as a trust with a limit of ten thousand dollars monthly withdrawals. Without interest, their earnings would last six years at which time they were expected to return to Columbia for another voyage.

The cartel's American accounting firm had created a false identity and social security number for each crew member as well as companies for which each would be employed, on paper and for income tax purposes.

Their nautical employer could easily have killed them all and saved millions, but they were counting on them returning in six years and felt that was the wiser decision and a sound investment.

Chapter FIFTY-FOUR

Gutierrez and Fukishura didn't discuss their cases on the short flight from the Los Angeles courthouse because of the noise and lack of privacy. Once landed, they hailed a cab to the Chumash Longhouse for dinner.

The Chumash people originally numbered in the tens of thousands scattered along the coast from Malibu to Paso Robles. They called themselves The First People and lived in homes called an Ap, shaped like a massive dome constructed of willow poles.

They were boat builders and traded up and down the California coast until the arrival of the Spanish in the seventeen hundreds when their population was decimated by European diseases and indentured into the Catholic Jesuit mission system.

Spain extended its need to dominate the area and control coastal trade from the British and Russian Empire by backing the missions with troops.

By eighteen-twenty, the mission system extended from Mexico to San Francisco and the area became populated by Europeans via the gold rush. California was ceded to America under the terms of the Treaty of Guadalupe Hidalgo in eighteen-forty-eight.

Few Chumash remained in the area, but those who survived were proud of their heritage and exhibited that joy in individual artistry and culinary skills.

The Longhouse was owned and operated by Chef Miguel Yazzie, the joyous result of the marriage between his Chumash father and Spanish mother. Miguel was a graduate of the Culinary Institute of American in

Napa, California where he combined his inherited love of seafood and the joy of quality Napa Valley wines.

Such were the Longhouse's specialties and what Marianna was excited to share with Santa Barbara's newest legal barracuda, a moniker Gutierrez coined for herself and other women of her ilk who had the fangs of the predatory fish and the reputation to rip their legal opponents apart. Jessica showed her style in the courthouse today and Marianna wanted to know her better, a great deal more.

The taxi dropped them off at the entrance to the cedar constructed Longhouse sitting lengthwise facing the Santa Barbara Wharf. The exterior was emblazoned with Chumash designs, carved into the walls, each different design highlighted by a hidden lamination system.

The grounds were the creation of local horticulturalists who transformed the otherwise barren, sandy coastal soil to a breathtaking sea of color. Diners often wandered the gardens, waiting for their table, enjoying a glass of Napa Valley's finest, taking in the beauty of such native shrubs as the pink flowered Buckeye, Manzanita bushes and White Lanterns.

The attorneys were greeted at the door by a seasoned maître d' who welcomed them warmly and escorted his dining guests to a window table. As they negotiated the short distance, Jessica marveled at the native carvings, baskets and paintings, a number of which she recognized as those of Vancouver Island artist, Roy Vickers.

Jessica noted several of Vickers' originals; *Balance*, depicting a woman in a yoga position on a rock overlooking the ocean, *A Lot of Bull*, three walruses sunning on a large rock in the bay and *Celebration*, a giant blue whale breaching a sapphire ocean.

The duo settled into their chairs and were admiring the stunning sunset as it dropped over the rocking vessels, safe in the harbor, when their server arrived. Marianna, unapologetic for her presumptuousness, ordered two California Martinis; vodka, red wine, dark rum and orange bitters, specifying her choice of Grey Goose for the vodka.

Enjoying the quiet ambiance and mesmerizing view, Jessica, trying to avoid talking about herself, asked her colleague about her relationship with the community.

She was momentarily successful as Marianna shared that she had lived and worked in Santa Barbara since law school graduation, opened her own practice fifteen years ago and limited her business to defending those whom she feels are being thwarted by police.

Their server arrived with their martinis and menus, giving Marianna a natural break in her biography and a segue to Jessica. They toasted their joint accomplishments, took a sip as Marianna asked, "I was quite taken aback today by your incredible court house performance Jessica. In all my years of practice, I have never seen a new attorney outshine a prosecutor with one of her first cases. I was expecting you to clarify the charges and agree on a court date as a stall tactic. I never thought you would get the case dropped. You did just graduate. Do I have that correct?"

Jessica smiled, took a sip of her California and replied, "Yes, I did Marianna, but I really didn't have a chance to razzle dazzle Murray with my legal prowess, I simply reacted to his bullying tactics.

"I graduated in the top of my class at Berkeley and will demonstrate my skills in other cases. This one pushed my emotional buttons created by an abusive partner. First it was verbal, bordering on harassment. I was a paralegal with a Washington firm and, as we all know, there are often long days. He was constantly accusing me of cheating, dating my colleagues behind his back. I argued, trying to convince him I had not demonstrated any behavior to generate his jealousy. The verbal fights were daily and eroded our relationship.

"The verbal jousting escalated one evening, after a long, negative day at work. He hit me. I hit him back, knocking him down. He had seen me fight before and knew he needed to stay down.

"I gave him the option of leaving immediately or I would call the police and report him for assault. He was an attorney and saw the headlines if I followed through.

"He left. I had the locks changed, filed for divorce, which he didn't contest, applied to Berkeley and was surprised by their quick acceptance.

"The rest is history, I guess. Murray reminded me immediately of my bullying ex-husband and I reacted."

Marianna was smiling broadly as Jessica concluded her cover story and said, "A toast to my new kick-ass colleague, may we have many more successful encounters with Los Angeles' finest and counter their incompetent investigations with the release of our clients."

Jessica was delighted that her thespian skills convinced Marianna, now she had to figure out how her new colleague was involved in Elisabeth's discovery.

They were perusing the menu when their server returned with two cocktails and asked if they were ready to order. They were.

Jessica chose the Dungeness crab cakes from the Monterey Crabbery in Northern California. They were served pan-seared with roasted red bell pepper aioli and a Caesar salad, sans croutons. Marianna had the Catalina Swordfish served with guacamole, salsa and a garden salad with a raspberry vinaigrette.

Marianna educated Jessica on the inner workings of Santa Barbara attorneys' social structure, and explained the LAPD pecking order, the latter of which aided Jessica in the development of her cover and explaining Elisabeth's findings.

Their dinner arrived with a third California and discussion subsided while each enjoyed their entrées. The evening was proceeding pleasantly albeit nagging queries hovering her frontal lobe; *where does Marianna fit in the puzzle of drug currency leaving Southern California to end up in the Caribbean, then back to the US in the form of political donations? Are the Christians for a Better America recipients of the drug money, how and where is the cocaine entering California and who are the kingpins behind the massive operation?*

Jessica was musing these and other questions as Marianna placed her fork across her plate, sat back, finished her California and offered, "Jessica, this has been the most pleasant time I have had in a very long time. Your company and intellect are a delightfully refreshing experience. Thank you."

"It has for me as well Marianna. A delicious and enjoyable first day on the job. I don't know how I can duplicate today."

"Well, for starters, first thing tomorrow I am calling Katrina and will glow about your performance today and sell her on the concept of she and I sharing other cases, with you at the pivotal point. Will that work for you?"

"I am embarrassed by your glowing comments Marianna. I didn't receive too many as a paralegal, none from my ex-husband that I recall and of course none from Berkeley professors. But yes, I would be pleased to be Katrina's point for the two of you."

"Good. Then it is settled. Let's have a cognac to seal the deal," she concluded as she caught their server's attention and ordered two Remy Martin 1738 Accord Royal.

Their nightcaps arrived momentarily, and they continued their business chat for another thirty, then Mariana signaled for the check. Jessica reached into her inside pocket just as Marianna said, "No. This is on me. Please. You have given my practice and me a rejuvenation I didn't realize was needed. By the way, you don't carry a handbag. Do you mind my asking why?"

"Just force of habit from school. All the other girls wore a handbag as a form of status, a badge of entry into womanhood and I couldn't take the bullshit, excuse my vulgarity, so it has always been a thin billfold for currency, identification, a credit card and a couple of business cards. No offense."

"None taken. You have a very good point. Besides those of us who do use them carry useless bullshit which tilts our bodies like a pinball machine."

She paid the bill with the portable debit machine, gave the server a twenty-percent gratuity, they bid goodnight to the nightfall over the marina, then made their way to the parking lot, stopping to bring up a taxi app.

The valet parking attendant had left for the evening and they were the only ones in the parking lot when Jessica noticed a lone male approaching from the darkness near the building's corner.

Six-foot, black sweat pants, worn runners, laces hanging from each shoe, long dark duster coat, collar up and over his ears, the coat extended below his knees and a black wool beanie with an array of white fuzzy particles clinging in desperation for a wash. Both hands were in his jacket's pockets.

Jessica was immediately in Code Orange, ready to move when he said, "It's been a hard day for me ladies. Can you spare some change?"

Before Jessica could reply, Marianna said, "Sorry buddy. No can do. Go get a job and stop being a fucking bum."

Beanie was apparently offended by Marianna's directness and decided to up his approach as he pulled a well-worn butcher knife from his pocket aggressively shouting, "You wealthy bitches all think you are better than the rest of us. Right now you fuckin' give me your wallets or I am going to cut you good."

As the word "good" was emitted, Jessica responded by shoving Marianna with her left hand, so forcefully her new colleague staggered backwards as Jessica simultaneously slid her right hand under her jacket and pulled her nine just as Beanie lunged at her.

Rather than shoot, she stepped to her left, lifted the nine up quickly and down on his wrist, breaking it instantly. As he dropped the knife, she shuffled up beside him, struck him in the right shoulder blade and as he went down, she front kicked his right knee, dislocating it painfully.

Seeing that their potential attacker was disabled, she put her nine back in its holster, turned to Marianna and said, "I think that is our taxi heading our way. Let's walk that way and meet it."

Marianna was still in a state of shock and Jessica's heart rate hadn't risen above sixty-five when Marianna stuttered and said, "Ah, yeah, sure. I guess. Sure. Are we just going to leave the guy there?"

"No, I'll text 911 when we get in the cab. They cannot trace my phone. We don't need the hassle of discussing this with law enforcement."

Marianna walked beside Jessica in a daze, unable to comprehend what just happened. *Just out of law school, cracks her first case without breaking a sweat and now beats down an attacker with the movement fluidity of a seasoned fighter and with a firearm no less. Who is this woman,* she thought as their taxi pulled up, Jessica opened the door and motioned for Marianna to enter first.

Once in the cab, Jessica gave the driver directions then turned to see Marianna's shocked facial expression and offered, "May I explain some other time? He will receive adequate medical attention, no jail time but the experience may help him seek other means of income. Are you okay with that?"

"Yeah. Sure. Whatever. I have never seen anything like that before and it is both scary and gratifying."

Feeling a little less light headed, she continued, quipping, "Maybe I should hire you for my protection detail."

Jessica smiled, replying, "Maybe," as she texted minimum details of their encounter; location and ambulance needed.

Returning her phone to her inside pocket, she looked at Marianna, casually saying, "Thank you for a memorable day Marianna and a delicious meal."

Marianna sat stupefied, shook her head and said rather loudly, "Memorable my ass. This is the best fucking day of my entire life. The gods of jurisprudence have descended upon Santa Barbara in the form of Ms. Jessica Fucking Fukishura and the world will be a better place," then reached across and kissed Jessica on the cheek.

ᔑᗷᔑ

After Tom and Karen landed at Toronto's Pearson International Airport, they grabbed lunch at a food kiosk in the airport, then parted company, each to their condos to sleep, unpack, wash clothes then meet for breakfast.

They were exhausted but pleased and excited to have made such inroads in the movement of cocaine from Costa Rica to Canada and were looking forward to interacting with the Costa Rican agents shadowing Sawyer.

They were unaware that Kopas and the Edmonton RCMP detachment commander had other plans for them.

Chapter FIFTY-FIVE

Elisabeth was in the initial stages of researching Henri Gagnon's client when her surveillance system set off an alarm, indicating conflicting system overload.

Dropping her enquiry immediately, she slid her chair over to an adjoining screen and observed that her software had isolated a text from area code fifty-seven, Columbia. Tapping her keyboard, she discovered that the communication was received by four of the tapped numbers.

The adrenaline rush she relished was more than any form of exercise could deliver. Smiling to herself, she performed a few additional strokes sending the information to Captain Ortega, Jessica, Jason and Jackson. Her boss would decide if and when the data would be shared on CHAP.

Once she saved the data on her hard-drive and flash-drive, she jumped from her chair, punching her fists upwards and yelled, "Fuckin' A". You assholes think you can outsmart Peltowski? Guess again."

Captain Ortega received Elisabeth's transmission and stared at it momentarily not totally comprehending its significance. The fact that it originated from Columbia was compelling, but that knowledge didn't send shockwaves through his body as Elisabeth had intended. *What was he missing?* he thought. The laconic text read, *Having a wonderful time on the beach. Margaritas are delicious.*

Elisabeth had spent several years sequestered to Britain's MI-6, their international spy agency, interrupting and deciphering terrorist organization's covert codes. In two-thousand and seventeen, the Taliban, ISIS and Al-Qaeda carried out eight deadly attacks, killing fifteen-hundred civilians in Syria, Libya, Afghanistan, Egypt and Somalia.

All the murderous acts may have been prevented had the British foreign Intelligence Service been privy to America's *Bumblehive* and the Secret Service's software developed by Elisabeth. MI6 had the ability to adopt CHAP but the fact that the system was not formally introduced to either the Chief of the Secret Intelligence Service or his political superior, the Foreign Secretary, CHAP was placed on hold until a bureaucrat was motivated to request the Americans to formalize their offering.

Elisabeth often failed to include her colleagues in her discoveries, believing everyone should understand something so transparent. This shortcoming often brought her into conflict with her superiors at MI6 to the point when Jessica transferred stateside for the "J" Team, Elisabeth was delighted to leave the British to their own incompetency.

There was nothing further that Elisabeth could do until she heard back from Jessica. The "J" Team emphasized team work and communication. The success of the operation against the Christians for a Better America was successful because of the agents' skills with Jessica manipulating activities from the White House situation room in StoneHead, Wyoming.

Waiting for Jessica's orders was paramount and crucial, a requirement Elisabeth had emphasized to Captain Ortega and his drug squad. Cognizant of the "J" Team's success, the LAPD detectives didn't question

Jessica's leadership or her operational skills as they too waited, none knowing that Jessica dined with one of the recipients of the Columbian text.

Ꙅ.ℬꙄ

CSIS agents Karen Winthrop and Tom Hortonn were well rested from the previous day's flight from Costa Rica with Karen spending her free time cleaning her condo and washing clothes. Tom, never having a domestic interest, had a housekeeping service, so his place was immaculate, and his travel clothes went to the cleaners. He golfed in the morning, lunched with former TPS colleagues and had an afternoon massage.

They were breakfasting at the Arthropod, a trendy corner nook on College which offered contemporary ambience with thought provoking morning cuisine. They were enjoying the Scrambled Everything with feta, spinach and chorizo when their encrypted phones chirped simultaneously, the read-out; *report to CSIS headquarters in Vancouver in seven days to discuss continuing operation with division head and RCMP counter terrorism liaison.*

Tom and Karen accepted the week off from Kopas with gratitude but with a certain degree of skepticism, considering his track record of holidays interrupted.

As they finished breakfast, they reviewed their options. Neither wanted to spend any of their seven days traveling so they decided to holiday in Ontario.

Their first choice was an evening at Toronto's Royal Alexander Theatre for the musical, *Come From Away* from playwrights Irene Sankoff and David Hein.

They were anxious to see how the authors had portrayed Gander, Newfoundland, a community of twelve thousand Good Samaritans, which housed and fed seven-thousand stranded travelers after September 11.

They dined at the Calgary Steakhouse and touched base with their university friend Craig "Soul-Train" Stevenson, then enjoyed the musical. They purposely didn't read the reviews before and felt prouder of Gander than they thought possible post presentation.

They spent their week exploring the Ontario neither had previously seen; Niagara Falls, the CN Tower, Algonquin Provincial Park and the Parliament buildings in Ottawa.

At week's end they packed and readied their apartments for an extended absence and flew out Saturday for Vancouver and the mysterious next assignment.

Chapter FIFTY-SIX

Brian Sawyer laid on the beach nursing a bruised ego for the remainder of the day, drinking far too many Imperial pints while darkening his complexion even more.

He felt sanguine about his future in Costa Rica in spite of all that transpired during the past twelve hours with the CSIS agents. He had many things going for him, namely his longevity in the village and the friendships he had cemented over the years. He also had the millions in American currency hidden within the walls of his house.

As he lay in the sand, he mused that he could pull this off if he simply continued living as he had, but with more of an ear to gossip than skulking. That seemed like all the agents were demanding. It wasn't as though they wanted him to start asking questions and putting himself in harm's way. Or was it?

He wasn't about to change his drinking routine because of the agent's interference, so when he figured he had thought his predicament through as thoroughly as possible, he headed back to his house where he showered, dressed in khaki cargo shorts, an old yellow flower-patterned shirt and drove the short distance to the Cuir Ó dhoras.

The Costa Rican agents, cognizant of his lifestyle pattern, were monitoring the hidden camera images and observed Sawyer leave his house dressed to socialize and sent agents to the pub.

Approximately one-thousand kilometers south of Sawyer several of the cartels were shipping small quantities of cocaine, all under one-hundred kilos, worth approximately eight-million American dollars on the streets of Los Angeles, as diversion tactics.

Fishing boats left the ports of Turbo, Necocli and Capurganá, Columbia with the product hidden in ten kilo packages under floor boards, cosmetic navigational equipment and food products in the galleys.

Additional shipments went overland through the famed Darien swamps on the border between Panama and Columbia hidden in spare tires of the modified Jeeps. The all-wheel-drive vehicles had six-foot carriage clearance with severe, fifty-four-inch tires which allowed the most efficient assault on the terrain. This treacherous route was a brutal challenge to foot traffic and motorized travel was never recommended since few, if any vehicles were successful.

The fishing boats and overland cargos were staggered several days apart creating a web of decoys over a two-week period. All the transporters were paid sufficiently to feed their families for several years, whether they were successful or not.

Some of the couriers were sacrificed to the Panamanian authorities as bait, with the drug barons providing the GPS coordinates for the fishing boats and the ETA of the Jeeps to law enforcement so the attention would be given to them and not the Chica de Oro.

Against all odds, many of the Darien Jeep cargo couriers arrived in Yaviza, Panama, just north of the Columbian border, having successfully navigated the treacherous terrain and missed the scrutiny of the Panamanian authorities. The spare tires were transferred to other vehicles which continued north on the Pan-American Highway, six thousand kilometers to San

Diego,   uninterrupted
where the product was cut and sold.

From the various Columbian ports, Costa Rica's south Caribbean coast was less than a day's sailing. The designated recipient community was Playa Gandoca where the flat, wide beach could be accessed by the fishing boat's dingy quickly, dropping the cargo at the base of an avocado grove, unseen.

The cartels found considerable success with frequent deliveries to this location. Locals retrieved the product and hid it in pineapple shipments from the Port of Limón. The odor of the fruit was so overpowering as it sat for several days in the ship's hold, that the cocaine went undetected by the European Union drug enforcement dogs.

Brian arrived in time for happy hour at the Cuir Ó dhoras, then enjoyed a leisurely dinner with friends watching international football on the pub's numerous wide-screen televisions. Early into the evening, his friends chatted about one of their cousins coming down with the flu and unable to work as a courier.

"That is a good job Julio has, can any of you guys take his place for a few days so he doesn't get fired?" offered one drinker.

"Hey, man," replied another, sweeping his arms around the table, "We all have full time jobs at the port. We can't take on something that big. Besides, if we got caught, we would lose this sweet deal."

"What about you Brian?" replied the first drinker. "Do you want to make some easy money? Just driving a couple of times a week?"

Brian looked at each of the men quickly trying to assess their offer; was it genuine, friend to friend, or was he getting sucked into something he would regret.

This wasn't the sort of exchange one could say, let me think about it. It was either yes, or no. He had hung with these guys, drinking, bragging and exchanging male bravado for several years and enjoyed their company. He wondered if taking this job, temporary or not, would jeopardize that relationship.

On the other hand, he had grown restless with early retirement. The Alberta operation was exciting and rewarding; financially, emotionally and even intellectually with his having to manipulate and influence systems and people while eluding law enforcement.

Within seconds, which seemed like an eternity with his friends starring at him, he said, "I'd be happy to help out. When and where?" purposely not asking how much the job paid, wanting his friends to be assured that he was accepting out of group solidarity.

For the next twenty minutes he was given the information, shown the pick-up and drop-off locations on Google Maps, and repeatedly assured that there was no danger, that the Costa Rican government was so inept as to make the movement of drugs a simple financial transaction.

As the evening wore on, the conversation turned to Costa Rica football and their national team, Selección de fútbol de Costa Rica on the wide-screen televisions while they traded off buying rounds of Imperial beer.

Brian's enthusiasm for returning to the drug trade was not hampered by his agreement with the CSIS agents. He figured he could simply tell them there was no information regarding the movement of drugs on the Caribbean Coast and they would be satisfied.

Brian was oblivious to the two DIS intelligence agents sitting at the nearby table nursing their Imperial and cheering as Costa Rica played against Serbia in the
FIFA World Cup in Russia.

They, as most other patrons, were following other games on their phones. The only difference was the DIS agents were also recording the conversation at the table next to them. Brian's.

Chapter FIFTY-SEVEN

While the LAPD SIS detectives shadowed the two drug lieutenants, Jason and Jackson continued their surveillance of Anthony Henderson, taking turns following him at night, establishing his daily pattern as Elisabeth monitored all his communications waiting for either a change in his routine or a message alerting Henderson to an anticipated activity.

Penelope applied for and received her Interim Private Investigator's license as Rebecca's protégé. They spent the weekend in Palm Springs as Penelope successfully completed the required fourteen-hour course in the carrying and use of firearms as well as an eight-hour training in the responsibilities and ethics of citizen arrests, relationships with police, search and seizures and civic responsibilities.

Upon completion of the two courses and with Rodrigo O'Connor's letter of support and her PI license, Penelope was given a temporary firearm's license while her permanent one was being processed in Sacramento.

Rebecca picked her up from the pistol range afterwards and they stopped by a beachwear boutique where they each bought a Maaji, Crystal Porto Sporty two piece, Rebecca's in black and Penelope's in baby blue. They returned to their hotel, the Coachella Inn and Spa where Rebecca had preordered dinner for pool-side.

As they were changing into their suits, Penelope reviewed what she learned from the grueling courses, quipping, "The San Bernardino deputy teaching the course seemed to frown upon shooting a guy for being a turd." She was laughing at her own humor with such vigor she missed stepping into her bikini bottom and fell on the bed naked.

Rebecca was enjoying listening to the recap but having difficulty keeping her mind on the conversation as Penelope stood naked. When Pen tripped, ending up on the bed, Rebecca pulled the remainder of her clothes off, falling on top of Pen running her hands down the sides of her body while letting her tongue slide around Pen's instantly rigid nipples. Hearing Pen's groan of pleasure, Rebecca continued her tonguing, slowly making her way between Pen's legs where she concentrated on moving her tongue circularly, then up and down, stopping at her clit to twirl it numerous times with her tongue and lipping it.

Penelope's body responded with the first nipple bite and increased steadily accompanied with joyous moans while griping Rebecca's hair with both hands. The third time around her clitoris and Pen was over the edge, feeling the climax work its way from her toes, through her vulva and to her finger tips, her body vibrating continuously until she was exhausted.

Feeling Pen's body relax, Rebecca slid up beside her and snuggled into her body, feeling the warmth and sweetness of her body's moisture.

Opening her eyes, Pen smiled, kissed Rebecca, turned her body and kissed her way down Rebecca's torso until her head was nestled between her legs and proceeded to reciprocate the joy she had just experienced.

Rebecca was glowing in the mini-climaxes as they laid under the queen duvet with Penelope hugging her each time Rebecca's body vibrated when the phone rang.

Scrambling over Rebecca to reach the phone, Pen answered to, "Good evening Ma'am, we have your dinner ready and Marco should be knocking momentarily."

"Thank you very much," was all Pen could get out as she hung up, jumped out of bed, ran into the bathroom to use a washcloth quickly, then back to the living room to get into her bathing suit.

Rebecca was right behind her, donning her suit just as the door vibrated from the knock.

Still perspiring, Rebecca opened the door and ushered the delivery server in with Penelope directing him to the patio outside the sliding glass doors, next to the Olympic size pool.

Signing for the bill and a twenty-five percent gratuity, Rebecca saw the staffer to the door, thanked him for his service, locked and secured the door, then joined Pen on the patio.

Rebecca smiled to herself as she pulled the sliding door open to see Penelope lifting the lids of the various Thai dishes, then pouring them each a glass of a Yucca Valley winery's Gewürztraminer.

"What's to eat?" Rebecca asked with a slight smirk, knowing that she had ordered dinner while Pen was passing her courses.

Penelope stepped over, put her arms around Rebecca, snuggled into her neck and replied, "Thai aphrodisiac cuisine," then stepped away knowing what reaction she would get.

Not disappointed, Rebecca laughed so hard she had to wipe tears from her eyes before she could respond with, "I didn't know we needed a sex drive stimulant."

Pen didn't respond to the rhetorical comment but smiled, bent forward to kiss Rebecca then handed her a glass of wine, a plate, fork and napkin.

They spooned portions of the various dishes on to their plates and sat at the round, glass topped wrought iron table. Their dinner consisted of curry crab, stir-fried crab meat in a yellow curry sauce on a bed of fried cabbage, eggplant in a spicy sauce with scallops, green beans and miniature red potatoes and finally sautéed sole with ginger, onion and mushrooms.

Between bites, Penelope nosed her Gewürztraminer, admiring the hint of cinnamon and ginger before offering, "Do you think Elisabeth will have any difficulty getting Jessica's approval to monitor our client's IT system?"

"I doubt it. She will probably give us her time as a business warming gift," Rebecca quipped. "Between Elisabeth, Alejandro, Alane and Elise, we should be able to find someone qualified to be our computer savant. I have to remember that what Elisabeth does is incredibly illegal.

"My problem is she has worked her computer wizardry of which I have taken advantage for years never having to justify how I obtained the incriminating evidence. I have to work on my legal do overs, so we stay on the right side of the law."

"The legality of our business was hammered into us this weekend, so much so, that we might want to consider having an attorney as an ally, a phone call away, possibly on retainer, or speed dial," Penelope replied, smiling at the last part of her comment.

"We can deal with that when we get home. Let's enjoy tonight while we can," Rebecca said as she lifted her glass and toasted Pen's success.

Chapter FIFTY-EIGHT

Jessica spent the few days after her Los Angeles court house appearance completing the necessary paper work related to Marianna's client as well as fending off the numerous accolades from Katrina.

She hoped that her recent success wouldn't generate her boss' inquisitiveness to check Jessica's credentials more thoroughly. Although the Secret Service had completed an intensive background, it would take but one comment from someone from her hypothetical Berkeley graduating class to not recognize her name for the ruse to splatter across their operation.

Pushing that limited possibility from her mind, she immersed herself in the various cases Katrina had assigned while simultaneously texting Elisabeth frequently on her encrypted smartphone for updates on the numerous surveillances.

She was working on a divorce issue handled by another firm where the husband emptied their joint bank account after being served with a cease and desist court order. He had been arrested and Jessica was charged with representing him without getting the firm entangled in the divorce. If she could convince her client that his relationship with his spouse was over, that he was going to be compelled to share everything fifty-fifty, and in doing so graciously he wouldn't risk losing his children's respect, and his local reputation would be assured, the case would be put to rest quickly.

She had a strong persuasive propensity honed by hours of interrogating suspects. She just had to modify the technique somewhat to avoid a disgruntled client.

While working on an affidavit for him, she received an exhilarating text from Elisabeth, "Dinner at the Ranch. Tonight. 6 pm. Italian. Santa Barbara's newest restaurant owner will be there. Marc Stucki's," with a smiley face.

She and Elisabeth had worked together for so long that any further data would be superfluous. She knew instinctively what the evening would reveal, and the thought brought a calmness she only experienced prior to an operation going ballistic.

Jessica took a few minutes to text Sorento and Kopas an operation update, then replied to Elisabeth accepting her invitation and returned to her legal tasks.

𝕾𝓑𝕾

Marc's meager belongings arrived from StoneHead, Wyoming and he, Penelope and Rebecca hauled them to his new three-bedroom apartment in the upscale housing complex next to *Marc Stucki's*. The rest of his personal belongings would be shipped from the White House.

The three-bedroom, two-bath affair was delightfully furnished in neutral colors, but not very masculine, so the three created a teal blue accent wall behind the bar, which created a bright ambiance and blended well with the dark brown laminate floors.

They purchased three, leather covered bar stools, an octagon cream and burgundy rug for under the glossy black coffee table with glass top, several large reproduction paintings of British Columbia's Cariboo

(Marc's origin) depicting moose, black bear and the Cariboo Mountains and numerous big leaf plants.

The apartment lacked linens and bath towels, so they picked up several sets of both in dark blues for one bathroom and yellows and oranges for the guest facility and numerous sheet sets and a duvet for each queen bed.

The bedroom colors were appealing and needed nothing added other than several photos of the local coastline with seals, grey whales and a pod of Orca whales.

The process took two days of considerable camaraderie. Rebecca and Penelope had planned on making the decorating renos a housewarming gift, but Marc insisted he pay as he felt his friends had done far too much for him. The women compromised by purchasing a wormwood wine rack with pull-out drawers for thirty bottles which they insisted Marc choose before taking their purchase to his new place.

The restaurant was equally simple to ready for the grand opening. Marc decided to maintain the former establishment's dark paneling, mahogany tables and chairs while adding recessed lighting to create a more family atmosphere while maintaining a sophisticated ambiance.

He liked the twenty-foot slate wall with a centered gas fireplace, so he kept that but added a massive television screen showing feed from numerous beach web cams situated from Sycamore Creek to the south, and Santa Barbara Point to the north.

They created the railroad theme by positioning period train pieces throughout which coupled well with staff attired in period white jackets, black slacks and black bowties.

The menu would feature Wyoming beef from former president Bakus' ranch where Marc had been the executive chef. In addition, he would have a massive salt-water tank in the entry, featuring Dungeness Crab caught each morning by the retired crab fisherman friend of Alejandro's.

Marc had invited a friend from their days in culinary school and their first apprentice positions in British Columbia, Dereck Johnson. The fusion of their experiences from Canada's finest restaurants coast to coast with their personal friendship, he was positive would be a winning combination.

The kitchen equipment was slightly old but all functioning and spotless. It took two weeks from start to finish, including the county's food inspection and fire department approval, for opening day.

Chapter FIFTY-NINE

Jessica left her office at five-thirty and headed back to the hotel to shower and change. She chose a pair of distressed faded blue jeans, an emerald green Lilysilk, silk blouse and taupe ankle booties by Trolley.

She left the hotel, choosing the backroads to avoid the rush hour freeway traffic. Moments into the fifteen-minute drive she picked up a tail, quite noticeable even in the non-descript, tan, four-door sedan.

Even though the sun was setting, she spotted the male driver easily two and sometimes three cars behind her. Same car. Same driver with no attempt to disguise his appearance and no other vehicle to replace him.

Pulling into a gas station, she quickly memorized his license plate number as she pulled up beside a pump. Before getting out, she texted the number to Sorento with a request.

S.B.S

Sitting at their pool-side patio table, Rebecca and Penelope had just finished the last of their Thai cuisine when Rebecca excused herself, walked through their suite's living room, returning momentarily with a large gift-wrapped box and handed it to Penelope, bending down to kiss her with, "Congratulations on passing all your tests Private Detective Barker."

Pen jumped up with excitement, hugged Rebecca, kissing her once before ripping the wrapping off and opening the box. Inside was a Smith and Wesson M&P Compact pistol and a Galco shoulder holster.

Prior to the crash of the Mahalo Airline in the Pacific Ocean west of LAX, Stan, who had recruited Brian Sawyer, was asked by the CFBA Denver contact to arrange the secure transfer of the stolen cesium from a Manitoba mine. Stan had directed Brian to line one of the Canadian Pacific undercarriage containers with lead, receive the delivery of a package and send it south to the Nez Perce First Nations contacts in Idaho.

This was the treasonous incident for which Winthrop and Hortonn threatened to charge Sawyer.

The success of the operation which downed the Mahalo Airliner, brought Stan in direct contact with Senator Khawaja Aadhean's CFBA replacement at a neutral and public Dallas-Fort Worth International Airport, one of the country's busiest and one where their anonymity would be guaranteed.

The RCMP didn't have Stan on their radar during this time so he was free to move about internationally without scrutiny. It was in this environment that Caleb Attwood recruited the Albertan drug mogul to initiate the expansion of the CFBA cocaine business, starting in Canada's west and expanding nationwide within ten years.

After their brief business meeting, Attwood left, advising Stan to remain at the table for his next connection. Momentarily Marianna Gutierrez appeared and made him an offer he couldn't refuse.

Chapter SIXTY

Jessica left the gas station and continued her previous route. Within minutes the nondescript vehicle was two cars behind. Smiling to herself she thought, *let's see if I still have it*, as she passed a self-serve car wash, circled around, with the tail in place, and pulled into the car wash. Getting out of her car she noticed the tail had stopped a short distance up the road and parked.

I can't believe it is this easy, she thought. Getting back into her car, she reversed quickly, sped up to and directly behind the nondescript, stopping bumper to bumper. Immediately exiting her vehicle, she pulled her nine and approached the driver's side of the front vehicle, pointing her pistol at him.

Her tail had assumed his target would be awhile washing her car and took the time to play a game on his phone. Head down, he missed the quick vehicle approach but as his sixth sense kicked in, he looked up casually to his left, detecting movement.

Jessica had stopped her advancement waiting for what she knew by experience was his inevitable reaction. And he didn't disappoint.

Jessica doubted her tail noticed her gender but reacted to the nine itself as he whipped his head forward, started the vehicle, hit the accelerator and blasted down the street as Jessica holstered her pistol, smiling at the predictability of some criminals.

Returning to her car, she made a U-turn and headed to the Ranch as dusk settled over Santa Barbara.

Elisabeth had asked Marc, who was swamped with last minute opening day chores, to join them. He was delighted to get away for a few hours and headed there early to pick up a mixed case of red and white wines for the occasion.

He had been in the middle of hiring staff and instead of facing an uphill challenge of finding staff because of the competition, he was swamped with a line of applicants extending out the front door and down to the train station. It seemed every server and kitchen staffer wanted to work with the White House Chef.

Seeing the impossible task, he quickly rearranged his interviewing location to include two tables beside the work alcove where the cutlery etc….were located. After he perused an applicant's resumé, he had them set a table and marked their paperwork accordingly. His early years in the industry taught him that few applicants were truthful about their experience and this task revealed all he needed to know. Sous-chef de cuisine was another challenge.

Elisabeth had arranged with the caterer for an Italian meal and was looking forward to what they prepared without Marc's input.

She had ensconced herself in her bedroom/surveillance office continuing her analysis, while the cleaners did their weekly full house routine, leaving the home impeccably clean and inviting for her boss. When they were done, she performed a quick dusting and vacuuming of the situation room, then showered and dressed in an open back midi summer dress by Top Shop which boasted a waist tie in the back and a knee to ankle slit in its blue, white and rose angled strips. She paired her outfit with Steve Madden's Irenee robin's egg blue, angle strap sandals.

Fluffing her damp pixie as she left the bedroom, she met Penelope and Rebecca who had hit the pool for a few laps after arriving from Palm Springs around noon and had just emerged from their bedroom after dressing for dinner.

What was immediately noticeable to Elisabeth was both women were wearing shoulder holsters. She quickly moved to Pen and gave her a warm hug, cheek peck and said, "Congratulations Detective Barker!"

Pen responded with a broad smile, curtsied and said, "Thanks Elisabeth. I appreciate you noticing. It will take a while for me to be the bad ass you girls are, but I'll make it soon," as the three women high-fived each other, then headed down stairs.

The catering staff were putting the finishing touches on dinner...so the trio slowed their pace to peek, the Italian aroma overpowering their senses.

Quickening their stride, they rounded the corner and entered the living room to find Elise, Rodrigo, Jason, Jackson, Marc, Alejandro, Alane and Jessica enjoying appetizers and white wine.

Hugs all around with Elise raving over Pen's new status, perusing her shoulder holster closely, then comparing Pen's to what she wore...almost identical, except Elise's was black.

Alane prepared each of the late comers a plate of baba ganoush...a Mediterranean dip with crushed zucchini, olive oil, mashed egg-plant and herbed Greek yogurt...with a glass of Pinot Grigio or as some know it, Pinot Gris.

The dinner party arranged themselves in the lush living room around the seating group by the French doors, bringing everyone current on their recent activities. Neither Alane, nor Alejandro were made privy to the addition of Jessica although they remembered being introduced to her at the dinner party.

Detecting their inquisitiveness, Jessica offered, "I appreciate the invitation tonight. I have been swamped landing on my feet running since joining Katrina's firm. My first case was helping Mariana Gutierrez's client in LA, afterwards assisting a man to stay out of jail for violating a court order.

"Other than that, just your ordinary rookie attorney and her first two cases. What about you guys?"

Alane and Alejandro were aware of Jason and Jackson's law enforcement status, but not the specifics. It was obvious to them that, although very much welcomed here tonight, the rest shared something the topic of was unknown.

The agents were aware of the inquisitiveness of Alane and Alejandro and how Jason, Jackson and Elisabeth's presence at the Ranch would foster their curiosity, but they could see no alternative but to stay with Rebecca and Pen. Their presence in town would have been far too obvious and more detrimental to their function than what they were currently experiencing.

Avoiding a possible awkward social moment regarding the agents' activities, Alane made it a point of continuing the previous retirement discussion, offering the various options available to all the agents and encouraging them to visit him in town for a comprehensive analysis and financial breakdown of their opportunities.

During Alane's mini-seminar, Alejandro and Rebecca offered themselves as a paradigm to his expertise as recipients of Alane's financial genius. Listening to the details, Jessica couldn't help but let her mind wander to the concept of early retirement. Glancing at her colleagues, she concluded they too were musing their options.

Alane concluded with all agents enthusiastically saying they would make an appointment and were looking forward to what he could do for them. They all had federal government pensions, but they looked around at what Alane had created for Rebecca and they wanted more than what their pension would provide.

About thirty after they sat, the caterer announced that dinner was served. The staff were in the hallway, plates in hand, and as the diners sat, they approached with Sicilian chicken breast; almonds, cannellini bean puree, cabbage, sweet and sour compote and chickpea fries. The servers returned with a roasted heirloom carrot and beet salad; caraway goat cheese mouse with a carrot tarragon vinaigrette.

Before eating, Marc stood and poured each a wine glass of white Sangria from one of several pitchers, then, raising his glass, said, "Thank you for inviting me to dinner. Thank you, Rebecca and Penelope for your hospitality, having me as your pool-house guest. Thank you Alane, Alejandro, Penelope and Rebecca for orchestrating the unbelievable opportunity with the restaurant and apartment. And lastly, welcome Jessica to

Santa Barbara. You and I being the newbies, may just have a special bond."

With the last statement Jessica almost choked on her drink as did everyone but Alane and Alejandro. The agents knew Marc had a great sense of humor, but none had suspected it could be so covert as to slip such a comment into the conversation, a toast, the humor of which only the "J" Team could appreciate.

Marc tried unsuccessfully to stifle a smile but managed to sit and begin his dinner without his quip being acknowledged. What he did notice was that none of his friends would raise their heads.

During dinner, Marc broached the subject of front- end managers and asked the group if they either knew those that he interviewed or had a person they could suggest.

Alane, Santa Barbara's quintessential culinary expert, asked Marc whom he had interviewed. He knew all six applicants and suggested two women, both of whom were in their mid-forties, had a decade of front-end experience in two of the community's five-star restaurants and knew they would be perfect for the position.

Alejandro, who also considered himself a connoisseur of fine dining, concurred and offered a toast to Marc and Alane for their collaboration.

Dinner conversation left the realm of business and segued to politics with everyone having an opinion about the acerbic and as Penelope said, ethically challenged. The struggling NAFTA agreement was discussed as was the proposed wall between the US and Mexico. No one had anything to offer, supportive or critical of the American-China tariff squabble but everyone wanted Marc to elaborate on his menu.

Before Marc could respond, Rebecca said, "Marc, I wouldn't tell these guys anything," laughing and nudging Penelope with her elbow.

Pen followed with, "I agree Marc. Everyone, what Marc has created is one of a kind in Santa Barbara. That is not just our opinion but that of the scores of applicants who expressed amazement at the theme, décor and the opportunity of working with the White House Chef. But Marc, we encourage you to keep your creation a surprise and that way when they see it on opening night, it will knock their socks off."

Marc grinned, nodded and responded with, "Okay. Good idea. Thanks for the suggestion. I am so overwhelmed with appreciation for what you have all done for me, I wanted to share. But I agree. Let's keep it a surprise until opening night, which, by the way, is very soon. I'm putting the final touches on the menu and we will be good to go.

As the last of the group finished dinner, the servers arrived to remove the plates, then present a pumpkin-gingersnap tiramisu; layers of pumpkin-mascarpone custard and gingersnaps brushed with calvados syrup, then frozen.

They diners stopped chatting, taking bites, almost simultaneously. Immediate lip smacking and aahs and oohs with zero conversation.

The servers arrived with pots of herbal tea, filled each diner's cup, then departed.

Elisabeth was delighted with the evening's outcome. She had originally thought of a simple salad and entrée but what the caterer produced was beyond her expectations.

After dessert, the evening slowly concluded with everyone moving to the living room, sipping a dessert wine Marc had brought; Inniskillin ice wine from British Columbia, a dessert presentation produced from grapes that have frozen on the vine.

Half an hour later Alane rose saying, "Gentlemen, I believe it is time for we three to bid adieu and allow our esteemed law enforcers to get down to business. Rebecca, Penelope and Elisabeth, our sincere appreciation for a lovely evening. The meal was only surpassed by your gracious hospitality," concluding with a graceful bow.

Alejandro and Marc followed suit, tipping their slightly bowed heads, walked over to give each of their hostesses a hug, then headed for the front door, Rebecca following so she could see them out, lock the door and set the alarm.

After giving her guests a hug, Penelope left for the kitchen to ensure the caterers had departed, checked the door, waited until she saw Rebecca activate the alarm system, then returned to the living room where Jessica was beginning her update.

"Thank you for coming tonight on such short notice and my appreciation to Elisabeth for her organizing dinner. Oh, and before I forget, congratulations again Penelope on attaining private detective status and your firearms license. Kudos to your trainer too," she added with a smile toward Rebecca.

"A little wrinkle in the operation occurred tonight on my way over here. I was tailed, and I wonder Elise and Rodrigo, if you have a couple of detectives to spare and shadow this guy? My gut tells me he works for Gutierrez, but I'll get to that momentarily.

"What? Wait a minute. What does Marianna have to do with this? You're thinking she hired someone to follow you? We know she has questionable morals defending society low-life but tailing you? Why? asked Rodrigo.

"I'm sorry Rodrigo, Elise, I got ahead of myself. Elisabeth, will you fill everyone in on what you sent me the other day just as I was arriving at the airport?"

"Sure. Glad to," replied Elisabeth as she got up and faced the group. "I apologize for not posting this on CHAP. For now, we didn't want other agencies involved, particularly the DEA, which is the reason for this private meeting."

She brought everyone up to date, with a few questions from Elise and Rodrigo who didn't seem to take offense at being out of the loop temporarily.

Elise offered, "We understand about the DEA, or at least we try. Every local agency has the same problem with them in that they want to be involved in all drug issues from coast to coast."

Nods of agreement from all officers.

"So, just to recap for us, the two lieutenants the LAPD has been tracking sent a text to numerous people, two of which are here in Santa Barbara; Gutierrez and the accountant Jason and Jackson have been watching? And how are you able to have access to the suspects' phones at all and how without a warrant? Are we going to be in the middle of a federal and state shit storm?" asked Elise.

"First to the suspects. LAPD SIS detectives believe they are preparing for a delivery. They have been tracking their movement and the drug squad noted that the street price has risen sharply. Historically because of the lack of supply," replied Elisabeth.

She continued, "How Gutierrez and the other locals fit the puzzle we don't know yet. But when Jessica set the bait with her client at the LAPD court house, Gutierrez was overjoyed and wanted to hire her immediately. The fact that Marianna saw Jessica armed, then observed her take out the guy in the parking lot after dinner, Marianna is sure to think Jessica is connected to some criminal element.

"As to the phones themselves, we have been given a federal warrant for any and all persons, buildings, activities and anything, anyone, remotely connected to our money laundering operation and by extension, the drug smuggling.

"When we met with LAPD detectives at the beginning of this operation", continued Elisabeth, "they decided to arrest the two lieutenants and violate their rights by not having a warrant, so the LAPD technicians could gain access to their phones, plant GPS trackers in both and give me that information, plus the phone numbers. I have been tracking their movements physically and through their phones for weeks."

"Jessica, that was you that put the guy we found in the parking lot in the hospital?" asked Rodrigo, as though he wasn't following the conversation. "He refused to talk, not even his name. If it wasn't for his prints in the system, we wouldn't know his identity," replied Rodrigo.

"Let me get this right. You were asked by Katrina, who is not involved, to help Mariana in LA. You are on your way to the airport to catch a helicopter when Elisabeth texted you about the phone call to Gutierrez? You then set up her client, the one the LAPD arrested illegally. Am I accurate?" concluded Rodrigo.

"Son of a bitch. You guys are good, really good. What would it take for the "J" Team to move to Santa Barbara?" he offered throwing both hands in the air with a nervous laugh. "I was with the Treasury for over twenty-two years and never saw an operation so complex and so smoothly run as this."

All five agents exchanged glances wondering if the other interpreted the comment as rhetorical.

"Thanks for the compliment Rodrigo. That might be something worth considering. Are you hiring?" Elisabeth quipped.

Before Rodrigo could respond, hoping her comment wasn't rhetorical, Jessica said, "We appreciate the confidence Rodrigo, but let's not get ahead of ourselves. This operation could hit the fan and we find ourselves with a handful of squat."

We still need a team to watch Gutierrez. Might the SBPD be able to spare a couple of detectives?"

"We'd like to help out Jessica, but we are swamped with the increase in homelessness. It has gotten out of control. Our patrol officers can't keep up with the number of complaints and I've assigned detectives to determine the drawing factor, other than weather of course."

"Totally understandable Rodrigo. You may find the very drugs we are tracking are here drawing junkies.

Let us know if we can help." Jessica replied, hesitated a moment looking pensive, then said, "She needs tailing. R& P Investigations, would you like a full-time gig for the remainder of the operation? I know Sorento will pay your fee without question."

Penelope and Rebecca exchanged glances and Pen replied, "We're in. We can use one of our SUVs and the old pick-up," looking at Rebecca and adding, "If it can still run. How long had it been sitting there?"

"Too long. But I took the battery out when I parked it the first time and it has been on a trickle charger for months, so other than needing an oil change and lube, it should be good to go. I will bring out my torn and worn Tony Lama boots, dirty hat and jeans and be back in action, Penelope and I rotating surveillance. This will be challenging and perfect training for our newest detective," Rebecca added, looking at Penelope. "I haven't done this in a long time. Thanks Jessica."

"So, we're good to go? Elise and Rodrigo, here is a confidential code," Elisabeth said, reaching into her pocket and handing them a slip of paper. "After you enter your normal password into CHAP, hover your cursor over your password. After giving it a second, hit enter and then the code I just gave you. That will take you to a separate chat room to which only we seven and Captain Ortega have access."

"LAPD won't follow their suspects to drug distribution location as I will do that here and will communicate their positions. They will remain two minutes behind. Elise and Rodrigo, if the distribution point is here in Santa Barbara, can your SWAT team assist? And what about bringing in the county law?

"Our SWAT team will be at your disposal Elisabeth and I would forget about county. We have been squabbling for years over jurisdiction and I gave up trying to compromise. If the operation takes us into their territory, we will assist regardless, assuming of course that the federal government has asked invited us formally," he concluded with a grin.

"Consider your entire department federal deputies," offered Jessica with a smile, "We are not going to become embroiled in a jurisdiction dispute. Besides, we will have the LAPD SIS detectives in the take-downs too, so it shouldn't be a problem."

"Sounds good. It will be interesting to see if our transient problem is fueled by drugs and if so, if the drugs are the cocaine from this operation," concluded Rodrigo.

With Rodrigo's remark, the group rose as one, goodbyes all around and Jason, Jackson and Elisabeth headed to their rooms while Rebecca and Penelope saw Elise and Rodrigo to the front door, locked it and set the alarm.

The two walked through the living room arm in arm with Rebecca saying, "So, Detective Barker, what do you think of our first client?"

Penelope gave Rebecca's arm a squeeze, "I can't believe this is all happening to me, to us. If you had asked me two years ago where I would be this time in my life, I would never have dreamed this…with you, with this new career and me with a firearm," she replied.

"I know," Rebecca said, as they headed up the stairs, "In the short time we have been here, we have been introduced to Santa Barbara culture, businesses, have two clients, one of which may involve long hours. Let's ask Elisabeth in the morning if she can help with our accounting client. We must get on Gutierrez first thing. Hopefully Elisabeth can discover either a transgression or misstep and it isn't a prosecutable offense. My experience tells me the "J" Team's operation is going down very soon. I am very thankful you took the active shooter training in Palm Springs as well as the qualifying courses."

As they closed their bedroom door, they stripped, letting their outfits fall to the floor, crawled into bed, lights out and fell asleep in each other's arms, content with their lives and the friends they had made.

Chapter SIXTY-ONE

The Golden Girl surfaced two-hundred and twenty-five nautical miles west of San Diego, just outside of the American Coast Guard jurisdiction and in International waters. As its conning tower broke the surface, its already extended antenna executed a two second burst of energy on the National Information radio band of two-hundred and fifty GHz. The cocaine barons chose that frequency because the citizen band's heavy traffic made it impossible to detect their short burst.

Once the signal was delivered, the Golden Girl submerged and continued her journey to Point Concepcion undetected...except by Peltowski.

Marianna Gutierrez was enjoying a margarita on her secluded patio the afternoon after Jessica was tailed. A pitcher and additional glass sat on a side table, next to a second cushioned, black wicker chair. Snuggled into a I. Am. Gia Blaster track suit in bold red, black and yellow with a stand-up collar, matching pants and thick yellow socks, she was warm against the chill of the late afternoon fog.

With her feet up on a round, glass topped, wrought iron cocktail table, she nibbled on pita wedges with a spicy dip of ground chicken, cream cheese, sour cream, garlic, cumin and jalapenos.

Marianna was into her second drink when the alley door rattled slightly, followed by the entrance of an average looking, forty-something, dark haired Latino male, attired in jeans, open toed sandals and a navy-blue stand-up collar sweatshirt.

Gutierrez acknowledged him by smiling and pointing to the pitcher with her half-filled glass.

Tailer poured himself a margarita, placed several pita wedges and a scoop of dip on a plate and sat beside his boss.

Allowing him a few moments to enjoy the refreshments, Marianna broke the silence with, "Did it go as expected?"

"Yes Ma'am, exactly as you predicted. I made myself visible and she spotted me immediately. Her attempt to evade was professional and pulling her weapon, I believe, confirmed your suspicions or anticipations."

"Excellent! Well done. There is no information on her whatsoever. Nada. Nothing other than what she told Barbados and I think that may be bogus.

"She knows her way around weapons, is a martial artist and knows the law in greater depth than a recent graduate.

"Now that I have confirmed her skill level, I will get her on our team, but before that, I must dig deeper for the truth. She would be a perfect law enforcement sleight of hand to infiltrate our ranks. I have been stretching my limits and she should be perfect to give me some relief. But not now.

"Fukishura will have traced your license plate number by now, which of course will lead her nowhere. But just as a precaution, leave the non-descript garaged for the next few days.

Our immediate concern is to concentrate on the shipment. They signaled from west of San Diego and should be here within the next twenty-four hours. I'll leave the rest up to you.

She raised her glass and offered a toast to another successful and profitable delivery.

Tailer clinked glasses, refilled their drinks, then sat back to enjoy the short respite with the person who had made him very wealthy in a short period of time.

Elisabeth verified the license plate number Jessica provided and the accompanying name and address. In cross referencing them with the city's current residents' list, she found they didn't match.

Sharing that information with R&P, Penelope suggested she visit the address pretending to be looking for a girlfriend who last lived at that address?

She did, and in speaking with an elderly couple, discovered that they had lived there for ten years and didn't know anyone who fit the description of Tailer. Penelope asked about the nondescript car. Same response.

Pen met up with Rebecca in a grocery store parking lot and shared the information. They texted the data to Elisabeth who decrypted it before reading.

Not expecting this response, Elisabeth called R&P and Jessica creating a conference call on encrypted phones. She communicated the findings with the others who were equally perplexed. Jessica commented, "You know, I thought at the time that Tailer was either incompetent or a low-level minion, but the motive escapes me. Other than those at the dinner party, the only people who know me are Katrina and Marianna and nobody knows my federal connection. What do you guys think?"

"We may all be thinking the same thing Jessica," offered Rebecca. "We suspect Gutierrez is involved somehow in both the money laundering and cocaine smuggling. We don't know with whom, or if she is connected with others. Is it possible she had you tailed to see if you spotted the nondescript to either confirm or rule out your skill set?

Although Penelope had little or no investigative experience, she was highly intelligent and a fast learner, so her opinion was acknowledged as she commented, "I can see that. Since Gutierrez observed your skills, inadvertently as it happened, she could be looking to add someone either to her operation or her office whom she can trust."

"I tend to agree," chimed Elisabeth. "This incident may have nothing to do with our case, but center totally around you Jessica. What if you played it that way, allowing her to believe you have a nefarious psyche and would welcome the opportunity to exhibit that aspect of your character?"

"That may work in our favor," entered Rebecca. "Jessica, if you allowed this relationship to take its natural course, you could be on the inside of a major operation, the scope of which could be massive. What do you think?"

"I think you guys have something. I agree it isn't connected to us. Sure, let's put it aside for now and I will maintain my cover with Katrina and see where Marianna takes this. We all agree?"

Affirmative from everyone, with Elisabeth adding, "R&P, you guys are still on Gutierrez. SIS are following the lieutenants. Gutierrez and the accountant all received the signal from the submarine. We need to know if and how she is directly involved. Right after these suspects received the two second signal, Anthony Henderson used his prepaid flip-phone to text several numbers just north and south of San Francisco.

"All I have been able to discern so far is the recipients are male. I traced each phone's location with all of them domiciled in residential communities, with the exception of one. That text was received by a burner located at Central California Road Maintenance Co. I will have more soon. The content of the text was one word, "Soon."

"Excellent Elisabeth. Let's see where this takes us. Thanks for your tenacity everyone. I must get back to work before Katrina starts questioning my whereabouts."

Penelope and Rebecca took up surveillance of Gutierrez with one at her residence and the other at her place of business. They followed the same operational protocol as Jason and Jackson, rotating every three hours, changing clothing, hats, locations and switching vehicles.

Jackson and Jason stayed on Henderson while Elisabeth worked on obtaining additional information on those Henderson had texted.

S.B.S

Edmonton RCMP detectives tracking Stan's communications revealed a relationship between him and an unknown suspect in Denver and something or someone in Dallas. At the time the Mounties couldn't make any connection between any of them and were at a standstill. They maintained eyes and ears on Stan twenty-four seven, but their surveillance revealed nothing suspicious. They were hoping to have another agency provide a link through their monitoring notes on CHAP.

Edmonton detectives' efforts were not totally empty as their digital surveillance exposed communications with one of Vancouver's high-profile law firms, the connection to Stan sought by the RCMP's anti-terrorism squad and the CSIS Vancouver unit.

Chapter SIXTY-TWO

After weeks of mind-numbing surveillance, LAPD SIS detectives notified Captain Ortega that the suspects were on the move, both following Highway Five heading north. Ortega texted Elisabeth who activated the CHAP chat room, so all participants could be connected in real time. She notified the rest of the team, then ran downstairs, grabbed the coffee pot and grounds and hustled back to her room and prepared for a long night.

Elisabeth kept the SIS detectives comprised of their suspects' positions as they left the Five and joined the One-o-One heading west towards Ventura.

While one screen provided the suspects' direction, another revealed the identity of the road maintenance company managing staff, one of whom received the text from Henderson, while another screen followed the RCMP's investigation in Edmonton.

Jessica was unable to observe the investigation for fear she'd raise questions and relied completely on Elisabeth to orchestrate the operation.

Rodrigo activated SWAT and had them head north accompanied by Elise, while Elisabeth notified Rebecca, Penelope, Jackson and Jason. Rebecca returned to the Ranch to obtain five HK433 Assault Rifles with two thirty-round clips each from her gun safe. Penelope maintained surveillance on Gutierrez while Jason and Jackson continued tracking Henderson.

The agents' adrenaline was rising with Elisabeth's running commentary on CHAP kicking their anticipation into overdrive.

They planned to meet under the overpass of Calle Real and El Sueno Road leading to an onramp to the One-o-One heading north and connect with SWAT when directed by Elisabeth then wait for her signal, *GO*.

CHAP was chiming every few minutes as Elisabeth provided the twelve LAPD SIS agents with an on-going whereabouts of the suspects, currently approaching Ventura, on their north-westerly route.

Brian Sawyer left the pub after last call, unaware of the repercussions of the evening's events. The Costa Rican agents remained at the Cuir Ó dhoras, casually finishing their drinks, then left with the rest of the closers. They waited until they were about five kilometers from the pub before pulling over and emailing the recorded conversation to their headquarters. There wasn't a need to follow Sawyer as his house was under twenty-four seven surveillance.

For his part, Brian felt confident he could help a friend during this brief period without the CSIS agents becoming aware of this actions. His motive for risking his freedom wasn't financial, for he had more than enough money to last a lifetime, rather it was the thrill and the adrenaline rush of avoiding capture.

His remote Alberta marijuana operation had become more of an intricate part of his lifestyle than he previously acknowledged. He created the business from the quarter section purchased by Stan through his Australian dual citizenship. He owned a ski condo three hours from Melbourne with the property manager paying the yearly property taxes on the Alberta acreage.

The underground production exhausted into an adjoining, shallow grotto or small cave with an entrance covered by brush. The diesel-powered generator which powered the grow lamps was housed in the same cave, the location guaranteeing a muffled exhaust.

The daily cultivating, nurturing and harvesting became a labor of joy highlighted by his transporting the crop to the Canadian Pacific Railroad railcars to which he had attached anonymous steel containers under the car carriages.

Working in the oil fields as a welder, he was law-abiding, albeit a few drinking skirmishes at bars. It wasn't until he was asked to engage in the drug trade that he realized that he had a felonious streak to his character, an aspect of his persona with which he felt comfortable.

His first pick-up was two o'clock the next morning and the anticipated thrill created an anxiety which crept into his psyche and kept him awake until almost midnight.

Jason and Jackson reported that Henderson was leaving his home and had just joined the One-o-One heading north. Elisabeth couldn't track Henderson, so she instructed agents to leap-frog him and report any destination changes.

Penelope texted that Gutierrez had not moved since arriving home from her office and appeared to be in for the evening, having observed her crossing in front of her bay window in her pajamas. Elisabeth instructed her to meet Rebecca at the underpass with the SBPD SWAT team.

Penelope arrived simultaneously with the LAPD SIS detectives. The SWAT commander outfitted all officers with neck com units utilizing a channel controlled by Elisabeth and flack vests with ceramic inserts.

The operation was fluid as the SIS detectives approached the overpass and joined the assault team. They too were outfitted with com devices and vests, then sat in their vehicles waiting for Elisabeth's 'go'. Jackson texted that they were approaching the team's underpass location tracking Henderson.

All team members were engrossed in their own thoughts; their immortality and desire to survive the confrontation. Their greatest danger being, not the suspects, but team members who had not trained or worked together. Their faith in the SWAT commander and their skills were all they had to keep them alive as they took down the drug dealers and suppliers.

The Golden Girl had passed Santa Barbara, the Channel Islands and was homing in on Port Concepción.

Elisabeth called off the surveillance of Henderson with Jason and Jackson joining the assault team under the overpass. She didn't need to assure the SWAT commander of her colleagues' capabilities as Elise had accomplished that task, educating the commander on Jason's North Africa successes and Jackson's assault on the Christians for a Better America Idaho compound.

Minutes passed in what seemed like hours for the anxious agents with several having exited their vehicles to walk around, do knee bends and push-ups to keep limber and their bodies primed.

In reality, it was only fifteen minutes before they received the 'go' from Elisabeth with instructions to head north on the One-o-One to Las Cruses, then take Highway One and be prepared to veer to the west on a dirt road.

Coupling the drug lieutenants' movements with the team's presumption that the shipment was arriving by water, she deduced that the only conceivable exchange would be Cojo Bay and Point Concepción, the forestry road to which the lieutenants were fast approaching.

Elisabeth advised the team that the suspects' vehicles had left the One and were proceeding slowly west. After giving them the coordinates, she passed the operation to the SWAT commander but remained in the voice loop to hear their progress.

The mini-sub surfaced, repeating its previous trip's landing procedure, gaining maximum speed, then veering west allowing the Chica de Oro sufficient momentum for its bow to ground on the beach. Moments later the cargo hatch broke seal and several crew members appeared on deck.

They were greeted by the previous, armed welcoming committee, anxious to get the valuable cargo unloaded and them off the high visibility beach.

The assault team had cut their vehicle lights, made their way down the forestry road to within five hundred meters of the beach, aided by Elisabeth's satellite navigational directions. Two snipers advanced to either side of the bay, passing within fifty meters of the waiting trucks and crew. Their night vision goggles aided their covert approach, then became superfluous when they crested the cliff and saw the lighted beach with the drugs being conveyed from the sub to the waiting vehicles.

The other team members had parked their vehicles well off the road so as not to be seen by the suspects as they made their way to the main highway, then located themselves on both sides of the road at angles to avoid cross fire.

The snipers provided a running commentary of the suspects' actions with Elisabeth instructing the team to allow the suspects to leave with the cargo and follow them to the distribution site.

She was unsure how to proceed regarding the sub and its crew. If she had the snipers eliminate the visible sailors, were there others capable of powering the vessel to escape? Then the question remained of how to accomplish that action while allowing the trucked cargo to leave without the dealers knowing the sub had been taken.

Making her decision, Elisabeth ordered the snipers to propel two tracking devices at the submarine once the crew had sealed the hatch and were preparing to disembark. The three-inch/eight-centimeter canister devices, used by law enforcement in thirty-five American states and several Canadian provinces including British Columbia, were fitted into the front grill of a cruiser, laser aimed and launched remotely by the driver. The GPS unit attached to a fleeing vehicle and tracked, allowing officers to break off a vehicle chase, reducing danger to the public.

Jessica had the units modified to use a twelve-gauge shotgun, like the propulsion of the Taser X12 shotgun, which launched their Electronic Control Devices, ECDs or Taser projectiles; two electrodes attached to wires joined at the housing. At discharge, they were embedded in a suspect's body, incapacitating him or her.

The GPS cannister was placed in the shotgun barrel where pulling the trigger would break open compressed gas launching the cannister toward the Golden Girl.

Elisabeth was willing to gamble. If she was right, the sub would leave unhindered, to return to its home base, be located and monitored by special forces, country of origin to be determined. When the sub's final destination was determined, a cellular signal to the units would cut the battery power, allowing them to drop in the ocean.

The sub undoubtedly would be making other trips and with its location identified, a covert team would attach an undetectable, permanent GPS unit which the Canadian and American Coast Guards would track.

Millions had been spent attempting to destroy the South American cocaine industry with every country failing. The American and Canadian governments' plan was to veer away from the producers and work to eliminate as many king-pins as possible. With the multinational coast guards monitoring the Golden Girl on North America's Westcoast, chances of success were good, but much depended upon international law enforcement cooperation. Jessica's objective was to keep the FBI and the DEA out of the loop for as long as possible.

Chapter SIXTY-THREE

Timing was imperative, so as Elisabeth took over the operation briefly, she listened to the snipers relate the suspects' actions. Once the trucks had left the cliff loading area, the snipers deployed the GPS units, waited to confirm their attachment, then slowly backed away from the cliff, observing the trucks moving slowly up the forestry road towards the highway.

Elisabeth had taken the loading time to run to the kitchen, make a quick peanut butter and jelly sandwich and return with time to spare. She savored the childhood delicacy and her fifth mug of black with her feet propped against the bed's footboard as she eyed the stationary dot on her GPS screen.

Just as she finished her PB&J and black, the dot began to move, prompting her to drop her feet and slide to the screens, don her headset and notify the waiting assault team that the suspects had hit the main highway and were proceeding north.

The responding agents, with vehicles lights off, made their way up the dirt road to the highway, turned their headlights on and followed several miles behind the cargo.

Henderson wasn't being tracked, but it was presumed he was part of the cargo caravan which had left Highway One for Two-Forty-Six and was now approaching Santa Ynez.

Elisabeth's satellite imagery provided intricate terrain details enabling her to observe numerous wineries situated several miles off the main highway. The suspects slowed, turned left into a driveway, then slowly made their way toward what appeared to be a long barn-like structure surrounded by vineyards. She adjusted the angle allowing her to see there were vehicle doors at both ends of the structure, large enough to house several dozen vehicles.

Elisabeth provided details of the suspects' location, then returned operational control to the SWAT commander . She refrained from communicating any aspect of their activities to Jessica since she didn't know the specifics of her location or in whose company she might be.

The Santa Barbara officers were required by California law to wear body cameras, which Elisabeth used to her advantage, following Jessica's legal advice. This being a federal investigation, it would be highly scrutinized by numerous government agencies and those favoring a lighter hand on drug enforcement. Prosecutors would be challenged to steer the charges away from simply drug dealing and direct attention to terrorism financing, money laundering and illegal campaign contributions.

The agents left their vehicles blocking the driveway as Elisabeth assured them there were no other exits. All were equipped with night vision goggles, exterior, bullet-proof vests with ceramic inserts capable of stopping a 30.06 caliber rifle bullet, a caliber with greater velocity than the Keckler and Koch MP5 automatic ammunition each agent carried.

The law enforcers communicated with throat microphones, which enhanced their covert approach. The assault was performed by splitting the team into four segments; two agents on each side of the structure to block possible escape routes while one group entered through the west end doors and the last team through the east opening.

There would be no escape.

The laryngophone or throat mic, enabled the agents to assault the interior simultaneously with all officers pointing their weapons west to prevent crossfire.

Immediately upon entering, the SWAT commander shouted, "Federal agents. Down, down, down. Hands behind your heads. Do not move or you will be shot," while other agents tossed concussion grenades forcing the suspects to the ground, attempting to escape the horrendous one hundred and seventy decibels. One hundred and fifty decibels can burst an eardrum while one hundred and eighty can kill. Dropping to the ground and covering their ears was a natural response to the explosions.

The agents' night goggles, ear protectors, balaclavas and automatic rifles were intimidating enough but as each agent pulled hands from ears and used plastic handcuffs to disable suspects' feet and hands, no agents spoke, adding to the confusion.

Henderson and the two lieutenants were immediately separated from the distributors by the LAPD SIS detectives and transported to the LAPD anti-terrorism unit while the rest of the assault team counted the quantity of cocaine and the cash collected from the buyers.

Elise teamed with Jackson, Jason, Rebecca and Penelope in cataloging the drugs and money while the other team members kept their weapons trained on the prone suspects. Two cameras were directed at the cash and drug counting process while agents' body cameras continued to record.

The anticipated task was monumental. They had just started the currency count when the SWAT commander received an encrypted text that the unit's Bearcat was in the driveway needing to get through the road block.

The commander sent one of the team members to move a vehicle, allow the Bearcat through, then return the blocking vehicle in its former place.

Elise was first to hear the rumble from her counting position by the east vehicle door. The 7-liter diesel engine moved the Ballistic Engineered Armored Response Counter Attack Truck BEAR, slowly towards the activity with its two-inch steel armor, encasing a blast-resistant floor, gunports and run-flat tires.

With the enormous number of confiscated vehicles present, there wasn't room for the Bearcat, so it turned and backed in, allowing access to its loading doors, creating a deafening rumbling that made verbal communication impossible. Momentarily, the driver cut the engine bringing quiet once again to the unique scene.

Several flat-bed LAPD tow trucks were enroute to remove the vehicles to a compound where they would be stripped to their chassis to ensure they were drug and currency free. A prisoner bus was in the vehicle caravan and expected within two hours. Accompanying the bus were six correctional officers from the FAT, Fugitive Apprehension Team. These heavily armed and elite trained officers worked with the US Marshall's Service to apprehend high level offenders and would ensure the prisoners arrived at an isolated prison wing as planned.

As Elisabeth recorded body camera video and those isolated on the countering agents, she mused how this operation would severely cripple the Los Angeles drug trade which in the past decade had grown to be a massive industry, one where consumerism is in vogue. Researching Cocaine Bars online results in numerous recommendations with addresses and patrons' evaluations, similar to consumer services for restaurants.

In two-thousand and fourteen California voters passed Proposition forty-seven which reduced the use of cocaine from a felony to a misdemeanor offense. However, for trafficking, an offender could receive twenty-five years for possessing the quantities confiscated in this operation.

She wondered where the millions currently being tallied would be directed. Had Sorento opened the operation to the numerous interested agencies, it would be a feeding frenzy for the four-hundred and twenty million in confiscated currency. She was serene in the appreciation of her absence, agency in-fighting yet had hopes that the operation's secrecy would allow the division between the LAPD and the Santa Barbara Police Department. The likelihood of that occurring was left entirely to the LAPD's ability to keep the media ignorant.

Currently the details were confined to the assault team but once the prisoners arrived in LA, guards would start asking questions, tow truck drivers would talk, and the lid would blow off the operation before the day was over.

Elisabeth, Jessica, O'Connor and the LAPD would pass the buck to Sorento to explain the multi-agency exclusion and the funds allocation. What concerned the "J" Team most was how to interrogate the lieutenants and Henderson without attorneys present.

Chapter SIXTY-FOUR

Vertical gold and cream stripped wall paper, cranberry couch with occasional chair in a cranberry and gold pattern, square, red oak end tables, topped with intricate wrought iron lamps and warm cream shades. Numerous French Impressionist art pieces blended with four off-white sconces and the ubiquitous large screen television atop a six-foot dresser paired with the end tables.

Off the sitting room was an ample bedroom with a queen bed, the décor of which was an extension of the drawing room.

This was home for Karen and Tom for the foreseeable future, the L'océan, French for 'The Ocean' on W. Waterfront Road in Vancouver, British Columbia.

They were once again operating covertly as a vacationing Toronto couple, scrutinizing Vancouver as a possible future home. Their morning runs, daily hotel gym routines coupled with dining habits unique to health-conscious Vancouverites, made blending in transparent.

They had already engaged in preliminary meetings with the RCMP's anti-terrorism unit and CSIS agents with the Force agreeing to Winthrop and Hortonn taking the lead on the burgeoning cocaine industry which the RCMP believe was being spearheaded out of Vancouver, directed by Stan whom they've had under surveillance for weeks.

Edmonton RCMP detectives had traced texts from Stan to several Vancouver businesses, the details of which Karen and Tom were tasked to discover.

In searching Henderson and the two drug lieutenants, the SIS detectives confiscated their phones, the contents of which would expand the list of suspects and widen the net for the LAPD and Secret Service.

The suspects were smug in their belief their phones would reveal zero information regarding their nefarious activities, an attitude which would eventually lead to lengthy sentences. The trio were unaware their every move, every key stroke had been captured by Agent Elisabeth Peltowski.

While the rest of the assault team counted the currency and weighed the cocaine, Jason and Jackson searched the property for signs of ownership. The building had long since been abandoned with the vines overgrown suffering from neglect. Hours had been spent scrounging in cupboards, under piles of decomposing lumber and the remains of a burned residence. Nothing.

They transmitted this information to Elisabeth who had already searched the Santa Barbara records to discover the property taxes were paid yearly by bank draft with a return address invalid for years.

Her tenacity and manipulative skills resulted in her discovering the ownership belonging to a Jeremy Addington, an Orange County businessman with a flair for notarizing his conservative political views in the local media. He supported the current Republican legislators with millions in donations thereby perpetuating their radical views of extinguishing any economic, persons or institutions that threaten their beliefs.

Elisabeth immediately traced all his personal and business communications and bank accounts.

By the time the currency had been counted and the cocaine cataloged, it was well into the next morning. The suspects had been arrested, mirandized, ID bracelets attached to their wrists, plastic cuffs replaced with steel, chained two by two with leg irons and had arrived at the LAPD jail facility where their processing was being finalized and they were segregated in a prison section destined for renovations where they would remain until their first court hearing.

Many of the suspects had lengthy criminal records, some with Los Angeles attorneys on retainer. Others had never been arrested and popped up on the investigators' radar for the first time with this operation. All were given the opportunity to call their counsel for their preliminary hearing.

The two lieutenants and Henderson did likewise, and it was no surprise to Captain Ortega and his detectives that they all called Marianna Gutierrez.

The Bearcat was the first to leave with the currency and cocaine, joined by Jackson and Jason in separate vehicles, leading and following as a protection detail. An LAPD helicopter had joined the caravan, being their eyes in the sky at the request of Captain Ortega.

Detective Pelfini returned with the SWAT team, still on the high of taking down the drug lords who had been working in her city for what appeared some time. She was looking forward to the next phase, wondering who would be leading these operations? She found the submarine concept fascinating. It had been tried and failed numerous times, primarily because the vessels were a rag-tag contraption, not the sophisticated craft she had seen.

Rebecca and Penelope drove back to Santa Barbara in one SUV, stopped to pick up the other from where they had left it by the underpass and headed home to regroup. During the drive to Santa Barbara they chatted extensively about Penelope's first operation and her reaction to being in the thick of law enforcement action.

"It really surprised me actually Rebecca," she began. "I didn't know what to expect and was pleasantly surprised. First that Jessica hired R&P with me as part of the package, and second, that I seemed to slide right into the action without doubting my abilities," she concluded as she turned in her seat to look at Rebecca.

"It didn't surprise me at all considering the training you've had and the skills you have demonstrated. I was concerned about your reaction under pressure and working with a team, but I had your back all the time and knew after that experience that I would go with you into a firefight anytime," Rebecca replied, reaching out and touching Penelope's knee, not taking her eyes off the road.

"Thanks, I appreciate the vote of confidence. I feel different somehow, but I can't narrow it down. All the years I devoted to my practice seem to belong to another dimension, or another person, kinda like discovering I was gay," Pen reached over and placed her hand on Rebecca's shoulder, smiling, then said, "Anyway, we have to get on the issue of Henri Gagnon and find out what Elisabeth has revealed, and we have to meet with the women's center director and Alane to move forward with the safe house. Instead of calling it that, how about something like, *Safe Haven,* but in Spanish?"

"I like it. How is it translated?"

Penelope used her smartphone to Google Translate and said, "Refugio Seguro. I like it. I can learn to let those letters roll off my tongue. What do you think?"

"I love it! And I think we can sell it to the others. With the area's Spanish heritage and culture, it is a perfect fit. Let's call Alane after we get some sleep."

Once home and exhausted from an all-nighter, they replaced the weapons in the safe then scrambled a dozen eggs with hot sauce and ate them on the patio with glasses of orange juice.

Not speaking, they enjoyed each other's company, occasionally touching, with Rebecca leaning over once to kiss Pen with her mouth full of egg.

In fifteen they had finished eating, put their plates and forks in the dishwasher, climbed the stairs, set the alarm, dropped their clothes on the floor and crawled under the covers, confident Jason and Jackson would be close behind them, duplicating their actions.

They presumed Elisabeth was already between the sheets, having guided the assault team through a successful operation, the bounty of which would rival several which made international fame.

In two-thousand and seventeen, the Columbian government seized twelve tons of cocaine hidden underground on four banana farms in an area near the Panama border where several drug lords executed their phantom drug shipments to the Costa Rican coast.

Columbia produces close to one-thousand tons of cocaine annually according to the U.S. Drug Enforcement Agency, the bureaucracy which Jessica froze out of the operation.

Several months prior to the Columbian raid, the Ontario Provincial Police seized one-thousand kilos of cocaine encased in cement blocks which was traced to Argentina. Lab analysis tied its origin to the shipments out of Costa Rica with a value of eighty-four million before it would be cut and sold on the street.

Chapter SIXTY-FIVE

Brian Sawyer was delighted to be active again in the drug business. He didn't realize how much he enjoyed the challenge and excitement. He couldn't analyze his motivation for he exhibited none of the classic behaviors of a criminal. Prior to taking the transportation job, he didn't have any larcenous friends, didn't consider himself anti-social having a wide range of friends in Costa Rica, didn't come from a dysfunctional family or have poor self-control given he had shunned the drug business for many years since leaving Alberta, and he didn't use drugs himself.

Brian just knew that the rush when he approached the small grove of trees nestled in the cove at two o'clock in the morning was what he imagined doing a line of cocaine was like but his rush lasted hours not minutes.

He checked the spot every morning and found a package four to five times a week. He quickly discovered the drops were coordinated with the Puerto Limón shipments to the United Kingdom, Hamburg, Antwerp and Rotterdam.

The Costa Rican agents who shadowed him twenty-four seven didn't interfere with the shipments but rather passed the information on to Scotland Yard and Europol, the law enforcement agency of the European Union. Both agencies tracked the drugs as they left the various ports, modeling their investigations after that which had just concluded in Santa Barbara County, thanks to Elisabeth interfacing her CHAP posts at the conclusion of the take-down.

Jason and Jackson guarded the Bearcat into a LAPD compound, separate from the property room used to store evidence until it would be needed in court. Here the cocaine and four-hundred and fifty million dollars in currency were locked in a vault, electronically guarded.

Although the LAPD high valued contents vault wasn't a Fort Knox, it was impregnable by forced entry and by numerous electronic observation systems as to make it impossible for an insider to gain access.

Unfortunately, the cocaine would not be used for America's medical community even though it was one-hundred percent pure, containing zero toxins. The country's fractured health care system was incapable of interfacing with law enforcement to affect its lawful use and it would be destroyed. The confiscated millions would be divided equally between the LAPD, the Secret Service and the Santa Barbara Police department for use in their crime prevention programs.

Once back at the ranch, Jackson and Jason were too hyper to sleep so, knowing their three colleagues were sleeping, they chose a local Bordeaux, two glasses, prepared a couple of sandwiches, changed quietly into swim trunks, then headed to the pool.

A few laps, the sun, the bold, red wine and they were done in an hour, both collapsing on their bed covers, sans bathing suits where they slept until the next morning.

Chapter SIXTY-SIX

Jessica spent about an hour before heading to the office reading Elisabeth's brief on the operation that, although remarkably successful, would open a Pandora's Box of bureaucratic drama in the next few hours and weeks that would result in her evaluating her future with the Secret Service.

Running late, she grabbed a muffin, yogurt and coffee at a bodega on State Street and arrived at the office just before eight, only to find the staff in full work mode, the receptionist advising her that Katrina wanted to see her immediately.

Knocking on Katrina's door, she was received by, "Jessica, come in, come in and have a seat. Big news."

Jessica removed her blush, double breasted Peacoat with tortoiseshell buttons and classic button-tab cuffs, laid it across the back of an antique brown, leather club chair, sat her briefcase on the floor and said, "Shoot. No pun intended."

"Cute," retorted Katrina. This morning, I am not in the office five minutes when I received a panicked call from Gutierrez asking for our help. Apparently, the client you represented for her in LA has been arrested again along with two others in San Ynez. I don't know anything more, other than Marianna had to recuse herself because, get this, she is being investigated by the LAPD and Santa Barbara Police. Hell of a way to start your morning!"

Jessica leaned back in the chair with an astonished facial expression. She knew about the arrests but not about Marianna. That was a new development since Elisabeth's transmission early this morning. She figured Detective Pelfini was behind the local investigation given she participated in the take-down and was privy to all Elisabeth's CHAP postings regarding the suspects phone calls.

Maintaining her shocked expression, she replied, "Is she hiring your firm to defend her in the event she is charged?"

"Exactly, but with a twist. Her firm is defending the three, but she wants us, more specifically, she wants you to be on stand-by to defend her."

"Well, this should be interesting. You're okay with me representing her for the firm? I mean, this could be huge. Marianna is a corner stone in the community and the legal field, defending her would bring a lot of notoriety to you and the firm."

Katrina smiled and replied, "I have no problem with the flash and bang of a high-profile case but are you okay with it? Marianna asked for you, knowing your limited experience, and with that I am okay, actually more than okay with you handling the case. Please make sure you ask for help and resources. Anything you need, just ask."

"Sounds good to me. Thanks Katrina, for the vote of confidence. This may amount to nothing at all. We know law enforcement and prosecutors like to huff and puff with no end result, this may be just that. Either way, I will be ready."

"Terrific. I will call Marianna and let her know you are available whenever needed," as she rose from behind her desk and extended her hand to shake with Jessica.

Accepting the gesture, Jessica headed to her own office, closed the door, hung her jacket, placed her briefcase on the desk, poured a cup of black and plopped herself into the chair.

Sitting back, she thought, *this is extremely interesting and may work to my advantage. I am enjoying practicing law with Katrina. I could retire from the Secret Service and make Santa Barbara my home. No need to tell Katrina the truth about my background and I could stay connected with Rebecca and Penelope through the law firm. Sounds like a plan to me.*

Acknowledgements

This work of fiction was inspired and grew from the encouragement of university journalism instructor Les Wiseman who encouraged me to submit immediately which lead me to a column with the *Vancouver Province* while still his student. A mere thank you doesn't seem a sufficient response for your years of support and inspiration Les.

The cover photograph is a collaborative effort of the Beltowski and Laina families and the photographic expertise of Steve Cattanach of Ventura, California. Thank you all for the beautiful presentation.

Santa Barbara Secrets is dedicated to survivors of sexual and domestic abuse with the hope and prayer that the characters, their motivation and spirit to overcome adversity, fuels a desire in survivors to grasp Jessica, Rebecca and Elisabeth's energy and courage to make the necessary changes in their lives to move toward a new beginning.

The "J" Team Series wouldn't be without the skills of Elise Laina, whose hours of manuscript editing, recipe offerings and fashion expertise produced a better novel than I could have done solo. Thank you, Elise, for the countless texting back and forth to clarify minute points and to broaden a particular outfit's description.

Appreciation goes to CST. Roy Davidson (Ret.) and CST. Rick Drought (Ret.) for their professional input in explaining criminal behavior and law enforcement's precision apprehension. The Mounties portray themselves; Rick in capturing the cesium thieves in *30,000 Secrets* and Roy contributing to the surveillance of Western Canada's drug lord in *Barkley Sound Secrets*.

I am grateful to the Oregon State Corrections and the Oregon State Penitentiary staff for allowing me to interview inmates, the content of which helped create the drug dealers' personas.

My appreciation extends to Portland, Oregon attorneys who shared their experiences with representing the guilty and innocent and explaining the justice system; the good, bad and the ugly.

I will always be grateful to Colonel Rex Applegate, US Army Ret. for sharing his close combat skills and instilling in me the concept of "Kill or be Killed" the topic of his best-selling work which expounds on the concept of attacking your attacker.

Colonel Applegate was part of Wild Bill Donovan's Office of Strategic Services, the precursor to the Central Intelligence Agency, CIA. The Colonel shared many of his life and death experiences as an American agent and shared his shooting skills, encouraging me to carry a Smith and Wesson hammerless .38 revolver, which I did for years.

I extend my gratitude to the many who have suffered from the effects of shootings, assaults and beatings, who shared their experiences aiding in their recovery and the development of the characters.

My appreciation extends to the many female counsellors who reach out to survivors to help them reshape their lives and move forward and who shared their expertise which guided Rebecca and Penelope in their relationship with the women's centers and their clients.

I am indebted to Kasteen Beltowski RN, for her medical expertise, and support through the character development and writing process.

Taser International shared the particulars regarding their shotgun propulsion system which I modified for the tracking devices. My appreciation to Taser and staff for an excellent law enforcement tool.

My martial arts expertise is credited to Ten Degree Black Belt Bradley Steiner of the American Academy of Self Defense in Seattle and the Washington State Director of the American Society of Law Enforcement Trainers who provided the instructional atmosphere for me to teach Seattle Police Department officers and King County Sheriff Deputies defensive tactics.

Although *Santa Barbara Secrets* doesn't involve classroom management scenes per se, Secret Service Agent Elisabeth Peltowski's contribution to the detection, surveillance and apprehension of the drug dealers has its background in a junior high classroom where her teaching acumen was honed by Dr. Barrie Bennett, retired education professor at the University of Toronto from whom I took many classes in Cooperative Learning.

Lt. Col. Dave Grossman, U.S. Army (Ret) is honored in each of my novels for his tremendous support and the impact he has had on my life. I had the pleasure of attending the Colonel's law enforcement seminar, *Sheepdogs*, the content of which is shared often throughout my novels.

My continuing and deepest appreciation to my spouse for her editing skills and patience during the months of writing, ignoring my waking at one am to write having dreamed the scene I needed.

52378305R00235

Made in the USA
Columbia, SC
06 March 2019